Sue Gedge is a retired drama teacher with a passion for the gothic. She enjoys writing in a secluded corner of the basement of the London Library where the dim light and spooky noises from the overhead pipes have proved inspirational. Her short stories have appeared in various publications, including *Loves Me, Loves Me Not, The Mechanics' Institute Review, His Red Eyes Again, Supernatural Tales* and *All Hallows*. Her novel, *Mandragora by Moonlight: The Apprenticeship of a Novice Witch*, is available on Kindle.

The Practical Woman's Guide
to
Living with the Undead

Sue Gedge

Grosvenor House
Publishing Limited

This book is published by
Grosvenor House Publishing Ltd
Link House
140 The Broadway, Tolworth, Surrey, KT6 7HT.
www.grosvenorhousepublishing.co.uk

This book is a work of fiction. Any resemblance to
people or events, past or present, is purely coincidental.

A CIP record for this book
is available from the British Library

ISBN 978-1-83975-987-1

For absent friends, both living and undead.

One

Never Speak Ill of the Dead

"You wouldn't, by any chance, know how to perform an exorcism?"

"An exorcism?" The elderly gentleman picked up his absinthe, cradling the lead crystal glass between his liver-spotted hands. "My dear lady, why do you ask?"

"I think I've got a ghost." I took a nervous gulp of my wine. "In my house," I added, perhaps a little unnecessarily.

"A ghost? *In-ter-esting.*"

I was relieved to see that, judging from his sympathetic expression, my new acquaintance was quite unfazed by my confession but now I was feeling distinctly unnerved. What on earth was I doing, confiding in a charming but somewhat eccentric person I'd only just met? And in such gloomy surroundings too. I hadn't even known the Lord Halifax existed until I stumbled upon it this afternoon and now that I'd found the place, I doubted if I'd be recommending it to my friends. It was more like a Victorian funeral parlour than a pub, with all that black crepe festooned across the walls, not to mention the alcoves lined with memorial urns. Georgia, the licensee, I'd been told, collected curios. I didn't know *then* just how she'd acquired the elderly gentleman.

That revelation had yet to come.

*

Less than a quarter of an hour ago, I'd been innocently walking home along the canal path, quite unaware of any imminent danger. Thursday afternoon, a few minutes after four, a peaceful scene, the ducks getting on with their duck-like doings, the water rippling gently. I'd been filled with a sense of relief as I put a safe distance between me and Havelock Ellis High School, enjoying the brief respite from my fraught working life. At last, the chance to clear my aching head, soothe my shattered nerves and I wasn't even going to think about my domestic worries, even though they were...

"Oi! Miss!" A clod of mud flew past my left ear.

Damn! I recognized that voice. It belonged to Brian Belluga, an oversized lad in Year 10 who was in the habit of roaming the school corridors armed with a weapon he'd made in his metal-work class, ready to attack any teacher who got in his way. Now what? Should I confront this young yob, or keep walking and pretend I hadn't heard? I didn't want to be a coward, but on the other hand, as a supply teacher, I wasn't obliged to do overtime.

"Woo-hoo!" A chorus of yells and cat-calls erupted a few yards behind me.

Damn, damn and double damn! So Belluga wasn't alone. But on the other hand, I was, and last week Mr. Sheppard from the Maths department had been ambushed in a lonely bus shelter, stripped of his trousers and tied to a waste bin. *Oh*! I didn't want to think about *that*.

"Oi! Miss! I'm gonna follow you and find out where you live!"

Now this *was* getting serious. No teacher at Havelock Ellis High School ever wanted the pupils to know where they lived, apart, that was, from Mr. Pugh who was currently suspended, pending a police investigation. I had to get out of

here. How about dodging behind this huge, bristling, triffid-like plant on the canal bank? No, this was stupid and …
ouch! The damn thing was fighting back. Ah, what about these steps, half-hidden by the plant, leading up to street level? This could be the perfect means of escape. There was no time to lose. Propelled by an instinct for self-preservation and a considerable degree of pure funk, I fled upwards.

*

Oh, thank goodness! The boys hadn't followed me. But now where was I? I didn't recognize. this street at all, a little, narrow one with a terrace of nineteenth century artisan houses on one side and a row of boarded-up shops on the other. At the end of the road, there was an old pub with blacked-out windows and an array of hanging baskets filled with dark purple flowers. I found myself walking towards it, feeling impelled to investigate.

The building was late Victorian, three storeys high, with a yard at the back, and a door at the side, leading, I assumed, to a residential flat above the pub. The sign was swinging in the slight breeze; a portrait of a Victorian patriarch, all mutton chop whiskers and stiff, winged collar, and under it the name: The Lord Halifax. The pub door was standing ajar. I peered inside.

Good grief what a sombre atmosphere! Such dim lighting, all that heavy, antique furniture and the ornate ceiling, resplendent with ebony cherubs, those wreaths of black roses and that stuffed grizzly bear standing on its hind legs at the bar, looking for all the world as if it was about to order a double scotch. As for the waxwork of an elderly man in evening dress that had been placed in the winged armchair in the corner, that really *was* unnerving.

3

"Welcome, dear lady."

"Oh!" I must have jumped visibly. Not a waxwork then, but an actual, living person.

"I do apologise." He spoke in a seductive purr. "I didn't intend to startle you. But please feel free to enter. The ambience of the Lord Halifax is to die for."

Why did I go in? It's a question I can't answer to this day. Perhaps it was something to do with his eyes; they were such a penetrating, gem-stone blue, quite hypnotic. Or perhaps it was simply that I needed a stiff drink after my day at Havelock Ellis High School. Whatever the reason, I stepped over that threshold, changing the course of my life forever.

*

The elderly gentleman certainly had a distinguished appearance, with his fine-boned features and long, grey-white hair. I couldn't guess his exact age. He might have been anything from an emaciated sixty to a well-preserved ninety-two. He looked like a refugee from a more sophisticated past, a retired actor perhaps, or an aristocrat down on his luck, in those elegant clothes, the well-cut evening suit and that silk waistcoat lavishly embroidered with lilies.

"Forgive me for mentioning it, you appear a little stressed and in need of an alcoholic restorative," he said. "Do you care for absinthe?" He indicated the glass standing on the small round table beside him. "Of course, you can't get really *good* absinthe any more. Dear Georgia does her best, but I prefer the wormwood of old. Absinthe, the drink of the dark, made from any species of Artemisia, but usually wormwood. The name, of course, comes from the Greek, *apsinthion*. Will you indulge?"

"I shouldn't start drinking this early," I said. "And I'm not brave enough for absinthe. But now you mention it, I think I *would* rather like a small glass of white wine."

"In that case, help yourself from the bottle in that ice bucket on the counter. You can put the money in the honesty box. Two pounds a pop."

"That seems very reasonable." I reached in my bag for my purse.

"Georgia, our landlady, is very obliging. You should meet her. Got your drink? Good. Now please come and join me."

"I can't stay long." I sat down opposite him.

"No matter. But allow me to introduce myself." He held out his hand. "I am Ralphie Dunglass de Marney, but my dearest friends used to call me Bobbity."

"I'm Dora. Dora Harker." I shook his hand. Goodness, how icy cold it was! Poor circulation, I supposed.

"Delighted to meet you, Dora Harker," he said. "I sense that you are carrying a burden."

"I *have* had an exhausting day at work," I admitted.

"And where do you work?" he enquired.

"I'm a temporary teacher at Havelock Ellis High School."

"Oh!" He winced. "I've heard of that place. And I cannot imagine the pain of trying to deal with morose, monosyllabic adolescents! But now you've found sanctuary. This is an oasis of sanity."

Was it? I wondered, looking around me, at all the black crepe and the urns. "The décor is certainly impressive," I said. "So many…interesting things."

"Indeed," he agreed. "You see the mezzotint over the fireplace? That's a rare depiction of the funeral of the Duke of Wellington. Georgia found it in a skip outside a house in Highgate. She's an avid collector of relics and you might say that I am one of them." He gave a wry smile.

"So, this is your local?"

"It is. I retired here after a long and rackety life, brushing up against the bizarre and the bohemian in the most curious quarters of the world."

"You must have met some fascinating people," I suggested.

"Oh, indeed I did. I once spent a whole day and night carousing with a defrocked priest who taught me all there is to know about casting out restless spirits and other such troublesome riff-raff."

Riff-raff. There was something charming about his accent, those clipped vowels that reminded me of a pre-war BBC Home Service announcer. And his manner was so reassuring, I felt I could trust him. And now that he'd mentioned the very thing that had been on my mind all day…well, why not, come straight out with it?

"You wouldn't, by any chance, know how to perform an exorcism?" There! I'd said it.

*

"So," Ralphie mused. "Are you quite sure your house has been invaded by a presence?"

"It's beginning to seem that way."

"I see." He nodded. "Tell me, where exactly do you live?"

"Arcadia Square. One of the new town houses on the south side."

"Ah! Arcadia Square. Now that *is* significant."

"It is?" I wondered whether I should be alarmed.

6

"Oh yes. Now, let me try to form a mental image of your dwelling place." He placed his finger-tips over his eyelids. "I see a spacious kitchen with scrubbed pine units and an Italian tiled floor. Upstairs, a bathroom with an ivory bath and a scallop shell soap dish, a plethora of soft towels and scented toiletries. It is a pure house, with pale carpets and white walls, highly polished wooden floors and big fluffy duvets on the Scandinavian beds. Everything is spotless, with the scent of furniture polish in the air, and toilets flushing merrily away with that blue stuff in the cistern. Not a speck of dirt to be seen!" He opened his eyes and beamed at me triumphantly.

"It is a little like that," I said. "But nothing like as pristine. I have two sons. When Seb's home from uni he leaves piles of dirty laundry on the stairs and beer cans all over his room, and my younger son has been known to stuff empty crisp packets down the back of the sofa."

"The joys of motherhood!" His breezy detachment suggested he'd never been a parent. "But I imagine you dislike mess. And now you have discovered a bitter truth. Domestos does not kill all known household demons."

"I don't think it's actually a demon."

"Then what is it? A poltergeist, an elemental, or a malignant wraith?"

I took a deep breath. "I think it's one of my mother-in-laws."

"One of your *mothers*-in-law." He corrected me with schoolmasterly severity. "Just how many mothers-in-law have you had?"

"Three." It felt like a shameful confession. "But only one of them has passed away to my knowledge. Although my first mother- in-law might be gone too, but I haven't seen her for twenty years."

7

"And you certainly don't want her to see her if she's dead." Ralphie gave me a sly wink.

"No." Remembering Gertie's face in all its lean, mean malevolence, I found myself hoping, for all the wrong reasons, that she was still in the land of the living.

"So," Ralphie asked. "Have you seen this entity?"

"No, but I'm very much afraid that my younger son Caspian has. He's eight and he's..." *An alarmingly truthful child.*

"And have there been any disturbances?"

"I think perhaps there have."

"Describe them."

"Well....the television came on by itself, blasting out *EastEnders.* I found Quality Street wrappers all over the rug. And then there were the cushions, they'd all been rearranged on the sofa in a way that reminded me of...*her.* And then Caspian said Nanny had called in. I thought he meant Cynthia, but he said, 'Oh no, Mum. It wasn't Nanny Well-Preserved. It was Nanny Barrel-Hips!'

"My dear lady." Ralphie lifted his hands beseechingly. "You're going just a little too fast for me. All these names and chocolate wrappers and now *cushions.* I need a little elucidation. Who is Nanny Barrel-Hips?"

"She was my second mother-in-law," I explained. "As the boys have different grandmothers, we gave them nicknames only, of course, we never used them to their face. Cynthia, Caspian's grandmother, is Nanny Well-Preserved because of all the Botox, and Seb's grandmother was Nanny Barrel-Hips because..."

"Oh, I think I can work that one out." Ralphie nodded. "So, three mothers-in-law, eh? The obvious conclusion from that is that you've had three marriages."

"Yes. I married for the first time when I was eighteen and it was over very quickly. Then I married Seb's father, and that marriage too came to an end. And now I'm divorced from Peregrine, Caspian's father."

"Ah! Commiserations! What a sad saga of divorce and separation."

"Right now," I told him. "I'm relieved to be single again."

"But how tragic to embrace a solitary state while you are still so young!"

"I'm nearly thirty-eight."

"To someone of my advanced years, that *is* young." Ralphie sighed. "And in my youth, I knew what it was to long for the silken hand of romance to caress my life." He took a sip of his absinthe. "So, tell me, when did Nanny Barrel Hips leave this earthly sphere?"

"It was about a year ago. She was going on a pensioners' cut-price holiday to Tenerife, booked into a hotel where a Tom Jones impersonator was due to be doing cabaret. But on the flight..." I hesitated.

"She met her demise?" Ralphie suggested.

"Yes. But I'd like to think she died happy. I can picture her, surrounded by all her friends, passing round bags of boiled sweets and singing resounding choruses of 'Delilah'. And then..." I bit my lip. Oh dear, I mustn't laugh, it wasn't funny, it really wasn't. "There was a freak accident," I said.

"Oh dear." Ralphie looked grave. "The problem is that people who shuffle off this mortal coil when they haven't had time to prepare themselves can be *extremely* problematic. For one thing, they may not even recognize they're dead, and for another, they usually have a considerable amount of unfinished business." He paused. "Did you get on well with your late mother-in-law?"

9

"I'm afraid not." I saw no point in holding back. "She was a self-indulgent, interfering, judgmental old..."

"Stop!" Ralphie held up his hand. "Don't say any more. Never speak ill of the dead!"

"I suppose I should be more respectful," I admitted. "But my feelings haven't changed just because she died. After all, you can't libel the dead."

"The expression 'Never speak ill of the dead' has nothing to do with the laws of defamation," Ralphie informed me. "It has everything to do with self-preservation. If you speak ill of the dead, there's a very real danger they might return for vengeance."

"That's...not a good thought."

"Indeed, it isn't."

I glanced at my watch. Suddenly, I wanted to extricate myself from all this weirdness. And besides, Becca, my school-run friend, would be bringing Caspian home in a couple of hours.

"Well," I stood up from the table. "It was nice to meet you, but I have to go now."

"I do hope you will come again. It sounds as though you might need my help. Oh, and by the way," he leaned forward with an air of confidentiality. "Remember what I've told you. The dead can be extremely unforgiving. I'd be very polite to your late mother-in-law if you *do* happen to see her."

But I *won't* see her, I told myself, as I made my way home, retracing my route along the canal path, going up the big flight of steps by the bridge and turning left into Arcadia Square. This is all nonsense, Caspian has been playing tricks. Or I must be letting the stress of that job get to me, imagining things. I reached into my handbag for my key.

I loved living in this part of London with its tall, cream stucco houses, its little shops and bistros, only a bus ride from the Heath and close to the park too. Sometimes, at night, I could hear the wolves howling in the zoo. I only wished that the house didn't still belong to Peregrine. But I wouldn't think about that now, I'd just get inside, relax, slip off my shoes, maybe have a quick shower and...*oh, good grief!*

The moment I stepped into the hall, I knew something was wrong. The air was filled with the sickly-sweet scent of cheap face powder, the living room door that I'd closed on my way out that morning was half-open. And there was a deafening blast of sound coming from the TV. *Someone had got in.*

I took a deep breath, edged forward and, bracing myself, pushed open the living room door.

"'Ello!"

I screamed and dropped my bag, scattering the contents across the floor. My legs felt as wobbly as if I'd just caught sight of an impossibly large spider in the bath. Caspian certainly hadn't imagined it. Nanny Barrel Hips *had* returned from beyond the grave. Here she was, dressed in a voluminous white pleated skirt and a purple cardigan, sitting on my sofa with the cushions plumped up around her, looking like a self-congratulatory old hamster ensconced in a gigantic nest.

And after the day I'd had at Havelock Ellis High School too. This just wasn't fair!

Two

Mother-in-law Blues

My initial state of shock quickly gave way to bewilderment, mingled with a sense of injustice. How could a ghost appear so solid? I'd have expected more transparency, a certain ectoplasmic mystery. And what gave her the right to come here uninvited? I'd cherished so much hard-earned money and effort on this room after Peregrine left. I'd ripped up his carpet, the one that looked as though it belonged in a gentleman's dining club, all those fussy little shields against a royal blue background. I'd sanded down the floor boards, stained them in light pine and bought some striped ethnic rugs. I'd repainted the walls in cream and terracotta and I'd put up shelves for my books, photographs and cherished DVD collection of classic European films. I'd bought a new, comfortably squashy, oyster-grey sofa. And as the final touch, I'd hung a print of my favourite Jack Vettriano painting in pride of place, the one of the woman sitting on a draped chair by a window, an image that to me spoke of self-sufficiency and independence. And now Nanny Barrel Hips had completely ruined the effect of the makeover by manifesting herself in the middle of my living room in spectral form. It was just too bad of her!

"What are you doing here?" I found my voice at last.

"I was done out of me holiday," she announced. "So I thought I'd come to yours."

"Well, I'm afraid you can't stay." I seized the remote and turned off the TV.

"And why's that?" She lifted her chin, defiant and querulous.

"Because you shouldn't be here."

"And where should I be?"

This was a difficult question touching, as it did, on complex theological and philosophical issues that I wasn't qualified to discuss.

"The point is, Agatha," I bent down and started picking up the things that had fallen from my bag, pens, mascara, my mobile, coins, a cigarette lighter I'd confiscated. "I'm sorry to have to break it to you but you're..."

I stopped. I just couldn't say it. Not the 'D' word. Not dead, or even deceased. This was worse than the time when I'd wanted to tell her she had a big dollop of gravy on her chin at Sunday lunch in our local Toby Carvery. In any case, there'd be no point explaining it to her. She'd always been unable to take a hint when she was alive and she was likely to be even more obtuse now she was a phantom.

"Anyone would think you weren't pleased to see me." She gave her shoulders a little shake, just as she always did when someone neglected to pass her the box of Terry's *All Gold* at Christmas.

"It isn't convenient," I said. "And I don't think it's fair on Caspian."

"Why shouldn't he see his step-granny?"

"That's just it. Caspian *has* seen you. It's lucky he wasn't frightened out of his wits. Don't you see? You're a..."

"I'm a what?"

"You're a bloody ghost!"

1 3

Nanny Barrel Hips stared at me. Then she shrugged. "No need to be rude."

"I don't mean to be rude." I spoke through clenched teeth.

"You're often rude." She folded her arms under her bosoms as if providing a shelf for melons. "You was rude the last time I saw yer."

"Was I? I don't remember."

"I do. It was when we was watching that rubbish."

Oh. She must be talking about the Christmas before last when she invited herself and then stayed until Twelfth Night. I'd sat down to watch a DVD of one of my favourite films, Bergman's *The Seventh Seal.* But there'd been no peace. Nanny Barrel Hips had plonked herself down beside me on the sofa and started a running commentary: "*It's all in black and white, bit gloomy isn't it, what the hell's going on? Them subtitles get on your nerves. Don't much like this, give me a good game show any day, I think Les Dennis is on the other side.*" In the end, I could stand it no longer. "Shut up! Shut up, you silly old bag!" I'd yelled, and then she'd given me such a look of reproach that I had to apologise profusely and rush out to the late-night corner shop to buy her a tin of Cadbury's Roses. Of course, if I'd *known* she was going to be sucked out of a plane toilet a few months later (for that was the detail I'd felt unable to share with Ralphie), I might have been more forbearing but hindsight is a wonderful thing.

"Anyway, I ain't going nowhere," Nanny Barrel Hips announced. "I've been missing the telly. There weren't one where I was, just a nasty white light."

Nasty white light? Wasn't that what Buddhists called the Divine Ground of Being? I seemed to remember a book by

Aldous Huxley…But there was no point in telling Nanny Barrel Hips about *that*.

"Look," I said, "you *can't* stay here. I'm going upstairs for a relaxing bath and when I come back downstairs, I'd like to find you gone. I'm glad to see that you're all right, that you've recovered from your ordeal, but you *must* go. You must!"

I gazed at her plump, complacent face. Had she finally got the message? No, she hadn't. She simply picked up the remote and turned on the TV again.

"Oh good!" She gazed rapturously at the screen. "It's Bradley Walsh."

"*Oh, good grief!*" Clenching my fists, I hurtled out of the room.

As I pushed open the bathroom door, I was engulfed in a cloud of steam. Oh no, don't say something had gone wrong with the thermostat or someone had left a hot tap running or…

"Hello, Dora-Dinky!" A voice I recognized only too well trilled out the greeting I'd always loathed.

I froze. It didn't seem possible, but my problems had just doubled. Here she was, wearing my bathrobe, having swathed one of my fluffy towels around her head. Peregrine's mother, Cynthia, otherwise known as Nanny Well-Preserved had arrived. *And* she was holding my bottle of perfume, *Desiderata*. My birthday present from Seb. She must have gone down the drawer in my bedside cabinet.

"You might have asked me if you could borrow that," I said.

"Don't be selfish, sweetie." Cynthia pursed her lips. "You must learn to share. And you might say something nicer than that. I've taken a great deal of trouble to get here.

It wasn't at all easy, you know." She sprayed a liberal dose of *Desiderata* down her cleavage.

Cynthia, as she never tires of reminding people, was considered the most beautiful debutante of her day. '*What an angel! Those cheekbones! That Clara Bow mouth!*' Cecil Beaton is alleged to have said, on seeing her descend the staircase at the Ritz. Or was it John Betjeman? I don't remember now. Whoever it was, I can't help feeling they were exaggerating. I've always thought Cynthia's nose too sharp.

"Why didn't you tell me you were coming?" I skidded on the wet floor and grabbed the towel rail for support.

"I wanted it to be a surprise."

My mind was racing. If Cynthia had wanted to spend some time in London, why hadn't she checked into a hotel? And how had she got into the house? Had Peregrine given her a key and if so, how dare he?

"I must say," Cynthia fanned out her fingers and gazed approvingly at her well-manicured nails. "I'm delighted to find dear Agatha Dellow here. She's such amusing company. A real gem."

"You're pleased to see her? But don't you remember that Seb's grandmother is…"

"Deceased?" Cynthia completed my sentence with a little laugh. "Oh yes! I know that. But why should I mind? As the bard so rightly said, '*There are more things in heaven and earth, Horatio*'…" She pressed the nozzle of the perfume bottle and gave her perma-tanned neck a dousing.

"But... but…" Choking with distress, I fled onto the landing where I was assaulted by the sound of the over-amplified TV. *Bring on the chaser! It's the beast!* Aaagh! I took some deep breaths. There was only one beast in my life and he owed me an explanation.

I flung open the door to his home office, grabbed the phone and punched in his number. He answered with startling alacrity.

"Peregrine Deadlake."

He had a reverential way of pronouncing his own name, as if he was a gift to the planet. I pictured him, standing in his tiled lounge, dressed in those little fawn shorts and his blue Hawaiian shirt with its livid-yellow pineapples. Some women find Peregrine's brooding, saturnine appearance sexy. I suppose I must have done once.

"Peregrine?" I tried to speak calmly through my ragged breathing. "It's me, Dora."

"*Oh.*" He invested the monosyllable with so much irritability and hostility that I knew we were in for a particularly vituperative exchange. "What is it? Do you want money for new trainers for Caspian with wheels and flashing lights on them?"

"No, I…"

"A mint of cash for a new, state-of-the art computer?"

"No. Listen …"

"Mega-bucks so he can go on a school trip to the bloody moon?"

"*No.* This isn't about Caspian."

"Then you must have run out of gin!"

I took a deep breath. How I hated this room with its grey walls, row of filing cabinets and massive desk. If only I could claim it for my own, get rid of all this stuff and change the décor but Peregrine was insistent that this was still his space and wasn't to be touched. It was to remain unviolated, unlike the woman with whom he'd had an affair, precipitating our final bust-up.

"It's about your mother," I said. "She's turned up here, out of the blue."

"What nonsense!" Peregrine snorted. "Mother is here, in Minorca, with me."

"She can't be. She's here."

"Look, Dora," Peregrine's voice took on that tone of sarcastic patience that was calculated to wind me up. "I'll say it slowly and clearly. My moth-*er* is he-*are* with *meeeee*. She is stay-*ing* at my vill-*a*. She is not in Lon-*don*."

"She's here, Peregrine." I could feel myself trembling.

"Bloody nonsense," he snapped. "I can actually *see* mother from here. She's out on the terrace, lying on her yoga mat. She's doing some kind of relaxation exercise."

"Relaxation exercise?"

"Yes. She's stretched out on her back, completely still. Arms by her side, palms uppermost. Don't they call that the pose of a corpse?"

"Corpse?" My stomach flipped over. Oh, no! Surely she, too, couldn't be a...

"Peregrine," I swallowed. "I don't want to worry you, but I think you should go and check on her."

"What do you mean, 'check on her'?"

"I mean, I think you should go and see if she's still breathing."

There was a brief silence. Then,

"Of course she's breathing!" Peregrine yelled. "In fact," he added more reflectively, "She seems to be breathing in and out quite deeply. Must be part of the yoga."

"Yoga?" I repeated.

"Naughty!" With a tinkling laugh, Cynthia snatched the phone out of my hand and pressed the red button. "You were *not* supposed to tell Peregrine!"

"I don't understand." I stared at her face, at those cheeks and forehead smeared thickly with my avocado skin cream. "Peregrine says you're lying on a yoga mat in Minorca."

"I am!" She flung her arms out in a sweeping, exuberant gesture.

"Then how can you possibly be here?"

"Because I exist in both places. You see, I've learned the art of astral-travelling!"

"Astral what?"

"Astral-travelling. It's an ancient technique." She began to unwind the towel from her hair. "One relaxes the body, goes into a trance, and ventures forth with one's spiritual essence. I've been having lessons from a dear little shaman I met on the beach. He has taught me the skills. At first, I only transported myself as far as the Palm Tree Court Bar, but then I popped over to Formentera. And now I'm here. This is my furthest outing! So thrilling."

"But if you're in spirit form," I was struggling to make sense of the logistics, "How is it that you can touch things?"

"Oh," Cynthia shrugged, "What do the technicalities matter? Mind you, I did have a little problem. I hadn't intended to come here first. I was aiming for Harrods."

"Perhaps you'd like to go to Harrods now?" I suggested. "I can get you a taxi."

"Why would I need a taxi? I've given up all mundane forms of travel. Besides, I don't want to leave *now*. Not while dear Mrs. Dellow is here. I want to have a really long chat with her, a proper chinwag. I always thought she was *such* good value. We've so much catching up to do."

"Cynthia, I've got to say something." *Be firm, Dora. Firm and frank.* "I don't think Caspian should see you in this…astral-travelling form. Especially since the last time he saw you, you were…"

"More than a little tiddly?" She raised an ironic eyebrow. "Say it, why don't you? You might like to know that I've given up drinking since I've taken up so many new hobbies! But to be honest with you, even though he *is* my grandson, I've never really been able to quite *take* to Caspian. He's nothing like my nephew Gerald's boy. And you indulge him *far* too much. Don't blame me if he grows up a complete delinquent! Bye...eee!" With a fluttery little wave, she shimmied from the room.

I'd been angry with Cynthia on many occasions, but this attack on my younger son, *her* grandson for heaven's sake, really took the biscuit. I was so overcome with fury that I kicked the wall, forgetting that this was a bad idea when barefoot. As I hopped around in agony, clutching my stubbed toes, I decided I must make sure Caspian didn't witness any of this mayhem. I must call Becca, ask her to keep him at her place...oh, no, they'd still be at the after-school chess club... In that case, I might just have time to...Yes, that was what I do!

With my foot still throbbing, I ran downstairs, retrieved my shoes, grabbed my keys and phone and fled, slamming the front door behind me. I was heading straight back to the Lord Halifax.

Three

We Need to Talk about Caspian

What a strange street this was, tucked away up here above the canal. Not only were the old shops boarded up, many of the little terraced houses appeared to be unoccupied too. Perhaps the place was awaiting demolition; there'd been quite a lot of redevelopments lately, and a while ago, just before I'd moved into Arcadia Square with Peregrine, there'd been a huge outcry from conservationists when the old church of St. Sebastian's was bulldozed to the ground. That empty site must be quite near here, in fact, now that I came to look, I could see the developer's billboards in the distance, past the fence that marked the dead-end of the road. And the other end of the road, where did it lead? Perhaps I'd investigate that later, instead of taking the canal path home.

So, here was the pub, the Lord Halifax, with its hanging baskets of purple-black flowers and its sign depicting the bewhiskered man. When I'd been here earlier, the door had been open, now, however, it was closed. *Oh! Damn!* Not just closed, but locked. This was odd. Surely it should be open at this hour? Tentatively, I banged on the door with my knuckles. No response. I tried again, louder this time.

"Belt up! You're knocking fit to wake the dead!"

I spun round. A man was leaning out of an upper window of one of the houses opposite, his face a florid gargoyle of outrage. He was wearing a striped grandad shirt and red braces, and the room behind him, lit by a dim bulb, reminded me of the tableau depicting the kitchen of a notorious serial killer in the Chamber of Horrors that had scared me rigid as a child. John Halliday Reginald Christie. Not a nice man. I didn't much like the look of this person either.

"Sorry," I tried to sound suitably apologetic. "I thought the pub would be open."

"Well, it ain't, is it?"

"Yes, I do see that. Um...you wouldn't happen to know when it will be open, do you?"

"No, I don't. They keep odd hours there. And that's a funny place. Dodgy goings on. I wouldn't go in there if you paid me. Doubt if it's opening tonight. I saw *her* going out about an hour ago. *Her*. Or, as you might say, *him*."

"Her? Him? Who do you mean?"

"Don't you know?" The man gave a hollow chuckle. "I'm talking about the so-called landlady. That Georgia. She was George when she was born. Son of a navvy from Somers Town. Then she had it snipped off. Daft tranny."

"Oh." I didn't think any comments I could make about the right to gender choice would be helpful in this situation, although I suspected that if Becca were here, she'd be slapping this man around the head with her *Guardian*.

"I see her go, thudding down the road with her great flat feet." He laughed loudly, throwing back his head and revealing a mouth filled with a petrified forest of browning stumps.

"I apologise for disturbing you," I said, in as polite a tone as I could manage, while simultaneously thinking *You transphobic, filthy old creep.*

"Huh!" The man snorted. "Knocking fit to wake the dead. You want to watch it, lady. You never know what you might be letting yourself in for." He pulled the window down with a bang.

Now what? Don't panic, Dora. OK, so asking an elderly man you've only just met to carry out an exorcism to rid you of your mothers-in-law doesn't seem to be an option right now, but how about simply relying on the good sense and support of your school-run friend? But how on earth could I possibly talk to sane, rational Becca about ghosts and astral-travellers? She'd think I was going crazy. And who knew, perhaps I was. At that moment, as if on cue, the allegro section of *Eine Kleine Nachtmusik* rang out. My mobile and here was Becca's face smiling up at me from the screen.

"Becca?" I started walking slowly back down the street. "Is everything OK?"

"Absolutely fine. I've just picked up the boys from chess club. Now listen, William's got a new game he wants to show Cas, and I've said he can come back to our place for supper and a sleepover if you agree. What do you think?"

"Yes, fine, in fact that's really helpful. You see, I have a bit of a problem and…"

"And I've had another thought. How would it be if Cas came with us to Norfolk this weekend? William would love it and it would give you a break. Then I could drive the boys down there after school tomorrow, if we go straight there we'll avoid the worst of the Friday night traffic."

"Oh, Becca," I felt flooded with relief. "That would be absolutely wonderful! Thank you so much!"

"Hey, don't go overboard, it's the least I can do. I know how stressed you've been lately. So, if you could just pack a weekend bag for Cas, I could pick it up later and…"

"No, no, don't do that. I'll bring the bag to you tonight."

"But Dora, you'll have to catch the bus."

"That's fine. I don't mind catching the bus. In fact, I like the bus. I need to get out of the house, I need…" I found myself gasping for breath.

"Something's wrong, Dora, I can hear it in your voice."

"No, no, nothing's wrong…at least…no, nothing at all."

"OK, see you later then. Oh, and Cas says don't forget to bring his bat. Dora, are you still there?"

"Yes." *Pack a bag.* So I'd have to go back to Arcadia Square and face Cynthia and Nanny Barrel Hips again. Well, so what! I'd be ready for them this time. And annoying as they were, they couldn't do any *real* harm.

Could they?

"Oh, it's *that* kind of bat!" Becca exclaimed, as she flung open the door. She was wearing a plastic apron emblazoned with the slogan *Nuclear Power? No thanks* and was carrying a ladle from which what appeared to be Bolognese sauce was dripping on to the carpet. "I thought the boys were planning to play *cricket.*"

"No," I said, holding the soft toy aloft. "Cas still refuses to play team sports. But this is Boris. He's a Rodrigues fruit bat from the gift shop at London Zoo and Cas has taken to sleeping with him on his pillow every night."

"How sweet!" Becca looked dubious. "What lovely, leathery wings and such fangs! Anyway, come through to the kitchen, you look exhausted. I've just opened some Rioja."

"Where are Cas and William?" I looked around me.

"On the top floor, playing computer games. Or possibly hacking into the Pentagon." She laughed uproariously. "Don't look at me like that, I'm joking."

I wondered, as I picked my way through the bicycles, wellingtons, trainers, piles of old newspapers, crates of wine, boxes of random stuff and all the other clutter that graced the hallway, including an over-spilling, malodorous cat litter tray, how Becca could joke about a thing like that. It had been three years ago, but I still shuddered when I remembered it. The police sirens, the army disposal unit, the hysterical screams of young children, and then, later, the news reports... *Terrorist hoax at Primary School... the boys, who cannot be named for legal reasons, said to be still in the reception class... astonishing feat for a five-year-old...* It was an April 1st like no other.

When I'd first noticed Becca amongst the gaggle of mothers waiting to pick up their kids from Blasted Oak Primary School, I'm ashamed to say I'd been put off by her braying laugh and the way she used to roar up to the school gates in her SUV. But then Becca, in that time of crisis, proved to be a wonderful ally.

"They're going to expel our boys you know," she said, turning to me as we sat outside the Head Teacher's office, waiting to hear the Governors' decision. "And personally, I think it's for the best. State education is all very well, and ideologically, I'm in all in favour, but one size doesn't fit all. Caspian and William are... unique. They've been very naughty but they've also shown considerable ability way beyond their years. They need a school that will value non-conformity and individuality. Now I know a place, it's called Netherwold, it's a small, private school on Hampstead Heath and if your estranged husband will agree to the fees..."

I dreaded approaching Peregrine about the matter, but as it turned out, he was forced to agree. There might have been several other schools that were prepared to give William a fresh start, but there wasn't a single state primary in the whole of North London that was prepared to touch Caspian with a proverbial barge pole.

"Sit down." Becca dropped the ladle in the sink and tipped the cat off a chair. "Grab a glass! Cheers! God, Dora, I hope you don't mind me saying this, but you look awful. Have you had a rough week?"

"Well, yes, you could say that."

"Has something happened in particular?"

I considered making a full confession. *My home has been invaded by two of my ex- mothers-in-law, both of them in spirit form, one dead, the other astral travelling. But don't worry, I've met an elderly man in a funereal pub who says he can carry out an exorcism.* No, I couldn't say any of that, not unless I wanted to be referred to a therapist or a psychiatrist.

"I'm just very tired," I said. "It's a very difficult school. What they used to call a sink."

"A failing school. I know." She grabbed a handful of herbs and began chopping them up frantically. "I think you should quit."

"I can't. I need the money." I took a gulp of my wine.

"Point taken, but must you do this miserable dogs-body stuff at Havelock Ellis? It sounds absolute pants."

"It *is* pants," I agreed. "And that's why I feel I must stick with it. I don't want to give up. I refuse to be defeated."

"Well, I can understand that," she nodded, "but teaching's not really your thing, is it?"

"No," I admitted. "But since the magazine folded, I haven't been able to get any freelance work commissioned. Of course I'd rather be writing film reviews, but I do get well paid for supply teaching. *And* I don't have to stay for staff meetings."

"I can see that would be a bonus." Becca reached for a bottle of olive oil, "But all the same, you need to get this situation with your ex sorted. He should be giving you more financial help."

"The thing is I don't *want* to live on Peregrine's money. As long he's supporting Cas, and paying his school fees, that's fine."

"But it isn't just about money is it? It's about being a responsible father. When did he ever take Cas on a holiday?" She threw the chopped herbs into a Le Creuset pan, picked up a wooden spoon and began stirring vigorously. "And what about the fact that Peregrine insists that you'll have to move out of Arcadia Square when Caspian grows up? Look, I really would like to give you the name of my solicitor. She'd broker you a good deal. In fact, she'd have Peregrine's guts for garters!"

"I don't want to get into yet another fight with Peregrine."

"But Dora, you have rights!" She sighed and topped up my glass. "Promise me you'll think about this?"

"Okay."

"And another thing. You need to have a little fun, meet people, even meet a new partner…"

"A man?" I flinched. "I don't need one of those."

"Don't you? Look, don't take this the wrong way, but you're only in your thirties, and we all have needs. I know you don't want to get married again, and I get that, I totally get that. I don't either. I'm happy meeting up with Robin at weekends in Norfolk, and having freedom here in London. But I wouldn't want to be *completely* on my own. If you met someone…"

27

"I'm happy as I am," I insisted. "I don't need the silken hand of romance to caress my life."

Becca almost choked on her wine. "The silken hand of romance?" she spluttered. "What an extraordinary expression."

"It's just something someone said to me in a pub."

"Ah! I knew it." She looked triumphant. "You *have* been looking! You've been to one of the speed-dating evenings at The Marquess of Granby!"

"I most certainly haven't."

"You should try it." She smiled. "It might be fun. Well, here's my advice. Indulge in some 'me' time this weekend. Relax, watch TV, soak in the bath, play your favourite music, do whatever you want. Make the most of having the house all to yourself!"

The house to myself. I suppressed a groan. If only!

"Don't worry" I said. "I'm sure I'm going to have an extraordinary weekend."

It isn't right that anyone should feel a sense of impending doom as they step into their own home, but such was the case for me when I got back from Becca's. When I'd returned earlier to get Caspian's overnight bag, I'd heard raucous laughter coming from the living room as Cynthia and Agatha enjoyed their 'chin-wag' and now, as I looked inside, I could see the chaos they'd created. Furniture had been moved around. The sofa was scattered with sweet wrappers and it had been moved to a position under the window. My rugs were hanging on the wall. There were bowls of pot-pourri everywhere, making me sneeze.

I went through to the kitchen. The radio appeared to be tuned into a station dedicated to playing wall-to-wall Tom Jones hits, *The Green, Green Grass of Home* segueing into *A Boy from Nowhere* as I entered.

"Shut up, damn you!" I grabbed the radio and thumped it down on the marble worktop, an act that only intensified its volume and brought on a sudden burst of *It's Not Unusual*.

"*Right! You've asked for it!*" I hurled it into the dishwasher and turned on the water, remembering, too late, that it was the transistor Peregrine claimed to have owned since he was a teenager. No great loss then. And it *had* developed an annoying crackle lately.

Upstairs, I found wet footprints on the landing and all my pots of cocoa butter and body lotion scattered across the bathroom floor with the lids off. My bathrobe and towels were crumpled in a soggy heap in the corner. There was a scummy ring around the rim of the bath.

Disconsolately, thinking of all the clearing up I'd have to do, I went into my bedroom. Thank goodness! My most cherished personal space hadn't been trashed at all. My midnight-blue moon and stars duvet was lying undisturbed on the bed, my aromatherapy candles were still arranged along the top of the chest of drawers, and the book I was reading, a biography of Francois Truffaut, was lying open on the bedside table alongside the latest *Empire* magazine. I drew the hessian curtains, undressed, and slipped under my duvet with a sigh of relief. Nanny Barrel Hips and Cynthia might have left their mark, but it appeared they'd left. The nightmare must be over. *Oh, bliss!*

Four

Queasy Like Friday Morning

There are certain workplaces that fill you with that Monday morning feeling even when it *isn't* Monday morning, and since Havelock Ellis High School was just such an institution, the fact it was Friday was no consolation at all. My heart sank as that ominous pile of nineteenth century London brick loomed up at me through the autumn mist. This section of the school, known as the 'old building', was only the first horror to meet my eye since, huddled along the perimeter fence, there were a number of graffiti-covered shacks known as 'temporary' classrooms, although most were so decrepit they must have been there for years. For someone in my position, these were the most compelling places of fear. Once relegated to that shanty town of educational despair the hapless teacher was adrift, abandoned, forced to do battle with the barbarian hordes alone. *Abandon hope, all ye who enter here.* Or as Mr. Wheel, the Head Teacher (now on indefinite sick leave) had proclaimed on the banner he'd strung up last term above the main entrance: '*Welcome to Havelock Ellis, an Equal Opportunities School'.*

I tried to adopt a confident manner as I walked across the gritty killing fields of the playground, ignoring the chants of 'yer mum' and '*you* shut up!' as the 'cussing' contests, the favourite occupation of the younger kids, gathered in strength. A group of gum-chewing, pelmet-skirted older girls by the bike racks gazed at me with undisguised disdain. A hurled football missed me by a hair's breadth as I went in through the main entrance.

The pupils were supposed to stay outside until the bell rang for registration but this rule was clearly being ignored by the three boys I encountered half-way down the corridor. They were engaged in a spitting contest, standing up on the first landing and taking it in turns to send huge gobs of saliva over the stair rail. I didn't recognize them, a large lad with ginger hair, and two smaller boys, pasty-faced, mousy-haired and generally indistinguishable apart from a slight difference in height. I remembered the advice in *The Practical Guide to Teaching* I'd bought on taking this job: *Be assertive with any bad behaviour you see outside the classroom, even if they're not your students. You may have to teach them at some point and if their first impression of you is one of weakness, there will be trouble later.*

"You! All of you!" I reached into my bag for a notepad and pen. "Stop that! Stand still and give me your names."

Another blob flew through the air, landing an inch from my shoe. It wobbled like a dying jellyfish. The boys treated me to a volley of jeers.

"That's enough!" I yelled.

"Fuck off," the red-headed lad said. "You can't do nuffink. You're only the supply teacher."

I did my best to look stern and disapproving but I knew the boy's jibe was cruelly accurate. My status in this school was only marginally higher than that of the pigeons congregating on the window sills.

"I've had a good look at all three of you," I announced. "And I can soon find out who you are."

This statement was a desperate bluff. In a school with such a large intake wrongdoers frequently got away with all kinds of heinous crimes because of the problem of identifying them. And now, unabashed, the red-headed boy was gathering ammunition for another gobbing, cheeks swelling, mouth pursed...

"Teacher!" The smaller of the two mousy-haired boys pointed to the space behind me.

I spun round, expecting to see one of the school's heavies, perhaps Paul Gogarty, the rugby-playing PE coach, or the fearsome Mr. McTaggart of the English department. However, I'd never seen this man before. He looked far too well dressed to be a member of staff. His suit was stylish and expensive-looking and he was wearing a rather lovely shirt in a soft, Pre-Raphaelite green. He was slim and had floppy, dark hair and rather fine features, an aesthetic appearance that suggested he wasn't equipped for this kind of combat. Nevertheless, something about this newcomer had impressed the boys; all their bravado had evaporated in an instant.

"Craig McMasters, Barry Fadden, Andrew Pooley, report to the detention area now." He issued this instruction with effortless authority.

I watched, awestruck, as the boys slunk away. The man, who had the advantage over me when it came to height, gazed down at me with what I took to be a patronizing expression. I felt impelled to burst his bubble.

"You should have escorted them," I said. "They'll pretend to go, and then they'll bunk off somewhere else."

"I can assure you they won't disobey me."

"Really?" I was determined not to be cowed. "Then you don't know this school."

"Oh, I think I've got the measure of the place."

Must he keep looking at me like that? I was becoming increasingly disturbed by his physical presence. Those deep brown eyes, that interesting mouth. He was a good-looking man, no doubt about that, a fact that only served to fuel my annoyance. I glanced down at the smart, pig-skin briefcase he was carrying. It was embossed with three silver initials: *A.R.L.* What an unnecessary affectation, I thought, with a stab of rage.

"Are you new here?" I asked.

"Yes. This is my first visit."

"Then how did you know the names of those boys?"

"It was a matter of preparation. I studied the photos of each year group and memorized all the names."

"But there are one thousand, six hundred and thirty-three kids on roll here," I objected. "That's impossible."

"Not for me."

Good grief! He was either a liar or an autistic savant like Dustin Hoffman in *Rain Man*. Whatever the truth of the matter, he was certainly far too full of himself. I couldn't stand the way he was raking me with his eyes as though weighing me in the balance and finding me wanting. I felt like seizing his briefcase and smashing him in the kneecaps with it.

"And what about the staff?" I asked. "Did you learn their names too?"

"Yes. But I don't know who *you* are, since your photo wasn't on file."

"Ha! So, nobody's perfect!" I could hardly believe I'd just been so sarcastic but something about this man was bringing out the worst in me. He must be an OFSTED inspector, I concluded, the kind of person who swanned into a school to tell all the embattled staff sweating it out at the chalk face just what they were doing wrong. If that was case, I wasn't going to waste any more time on *him*.

33

"Well, if you *will* just tell me your name," he began, "then I…"

"Sorry! Can't stop!" Determining on defiance, I charged off down the corridor, heading for the stairs that led up to the staffroom. And that, I hoped, was the last I'd see of A.R.L.

The staffroom was subject to rigid social demarcations. The English department dominated the long table by the window, where they would sit marking pupils' work and arguing with evangelical fervour about whether or not it was 'classist' to correct spelling and grammar. Jen Fowler, the Head of the English Department, a tall, flat-chested woman in her late twenties, would firmly express the opinion that it was, while Mr. McTaggart argued that she was talking 'left-wing tosh'. A posse of laddish males from CDT occupied the new chairs in the middle of the room, spending their time guffawing at off-colour jokes and passing round ancient copies of confiscated lads' mags. The maths department played solemn games of chess by the tea urn, while the smokers had been exiled like pariahs to an unpleasant, windowless side room, little more than a cupboard, evidently in an attempt to mortify them for their sins. As a supply teacher, my place was with the other unaffiliated staff in an area known as Oddballs Corner.

This was a dingy hinterland graced by a desiccated Swiss cheese plant and filled with several wooden-framed chairs with vomit-orange cushions. The floor was littered with browning apple cores, empty sandwich wrappers, lost trainers, and abandoned exercise books. Zelda, one of the few members of staff with whom I'd been able to strike up a friendship, was sitting cross-legged on the stained drugget, writing furiously on a paper secured to a clipboard.

"Morning, Zelda." I sat down on a chair opposite her.

"Hi." She didn't look up. "How's you?"

"I'm fine," I said. This wasn't entirely true, as I was still feeling rattled after my encounter with A.R.L.

I liked Zelda, scary though she was. She was six feet tall, skeletal, with staring eyes and frizzy hair dyed a defiant red and she wore jazz shoes, tight leggings and a variety of T-shirts promoting her favourite heavy metal bands. She taught a subject called Expressive Arts which, apparently, was a mixture of dance, music and what she described as 'madly improvising'.

"Actually," I said, "There *is* something I want to ask you."

"Uh-huh." She continued writing.

"I was just wondering…" I hesitated. "Do you believe in ghosts?"

"Uh-huh." I could tell she wasn't listening.

"Or do you think," I continued, "That a person, a perfectly rational person, having been under a lot of stress, could begin to hallucinate…could even start to *imagine* that…"

"Right!" Zelda threw down her pen, ripped the paper off the clipboard and waved it at me with a triumphant air. "That's it! I've made a complete report on Chantelle in 9X. Let's hope this is enough to get that girl permanently excluded, although I'm not holding my breath. You know how soft Angie Hucknall is with her little darlings. I don't know what they were thinking when they made *her* the Year Head."

"She *can* be rather too lenient," I agreed. "But listen, about ghosts. The thing is, some very odd things have happened in my house and…"

"Fuck!" Wide-eyed, Zelda pointed towards the doorway. "What the hell's happened to Josh?"

3 5

I turned my head. For a moment, I was too shocked to move. Josh Majendie, the drama teacher, a stockily-built young man with a shaven head, was usually bouncing around like a human Tigger, full of the joys of introducing physical theatre to Year 11. Now, however, he was unnaturally pale and slumped against the doorway with blood gushing down his left arm. A moment later, as he collapsed on the floor with a crash, I leapt up from my seat.

"Let me through, please." I pushed my way through the crowd that had gathered round him. A stabbing, I thought. I knew it was only a matter of time before one of the thugs attacked a member of staff. But why on earth would they pick on Josh, one of the more popular teachers, whose production of *The Rocky Horror Show* last term had been such a triumph?

"Don't worry, Josh." I knelt down on the floor beside him. "It's not an artery, but we need to stem the bleeding. Can someone fetch the First Aid box, please?" I took off my jacket, rolled it up, and placed it under his head.

"It's all right...I can sit up." He made a brave but ineffectual attempt.

"No, no, stay where you are for a moment." I put my hand on his shoulder.

Someone handed me some paper towels; I pressed them against the wound. *Oh good grief, so much blood!*

"What happened, Josh?" I asked.

"I was attacked outside Chalk Farm Station." He raised himself up on one elbow. "I thought that it wasn't too bad at first, but then as I was coming up the stairs, I realized I was bleeding and..." He gulped and put his hand over his mouth.

"Who the hell did this?" Mr. McTaggart demanded.

"It was an old man." Josh swallowed. "He looked like a rough sleeper, a tramp, he had bleary eyes and he was wearing a tattered raincoat and...this is the really weird thing, you know those lines in *King Lear*, 'Howl, howl, howl, ho...'"

"Typical! Someone's stolen the First Aid box!" Jen Fowler pushed me to one side. She picked up a waste bin and thrust it at Josh. "Are you going to throw up?" she demanded.

"I hope not." The expression on Josh's face as he caught the whiff of decaying sandwiches and mouldy orange peel suggested that if he hadn't been nauseous before, he certainly was now.

"Good!" Jen Fowler put the bin down. "So, this man, I take it he had a knife?"

"No. He bit me."

"*Bit* you!" She repeated, in a tone of disbelief.

"Yes." Josh sounded almost ashamed. "He sunk his teeth into my arm."

"What did he do that for?" Mr. McTaggart sounded outraged.

"I've no idea." Josh sank back in a defeated manner.

There was a stunned silence. Then Jen Fowler took command.

"You need to go to casualty," she announced. "I'll run you up to the Royal Free in my car. And the supply teacher here," she pointed at me, "can take your first lesson."

The supply teacher. I felt furious. I'd covered several classes in her department and she still couldn't be bothered to learn my name. And now she was hauling Josh to his feet with as much care as if he'd been a sack of potatoes. What a bitch. I remembered Zelda's nickname for her; the politically-correct beanpole. I smiled inwardly.

"Which class have you got, Josh?" I asked.

"9X," he said. "In the drama studio. A double period."

My stomach did a back-flip. In the drama studio, alone with 9X. A double period in a room with no chairs, no windows and walls lined with black curtains behind which pupils bunking off from other lessons lurked. Terrible things happened during cover lessons in the drama studio. Enterprising pupils turned off all the lights, plunging the space into a chaos of colliding bodies. Vigorous use was made of fart spray. Doors were locked, cutting off all means of escape. Fights broke out. And it was as far away from the main building as it was possible to be. In the Drama Studio, to adopt a well-known movie tagline, no-one would hear you scream.

"I've got an idea, Miss Fowler," I spoke in what I hoped was a bright, helpful tone. "Why don't *I* take Josh to casualty in a cab, while *you* teach 9X?"

"I'm not a supply teacher!" Jen Fowler snapped. "It's *your* job to cover for absent staff!"

"It's all right, Dora," Josh assured me. "You won't have to *teach* 9X. There's a man from TOSSA coming in."

"Tosser?" I repeated.

"Haven't you heard of TOSSA?" Jen Fowler glared at me. "The Teaching of Social Skills Advisory Service? You'll have to keep up with the acronyms if you want to get anywhere in teaching. Right, Josh, let's get going!"

"Thanks, Dora!" Josh gave me the thumbs up sign.

"Don't mention it." I tried to smile but I was feeling even more depressed than ever.

Five

The Man from TOSSA

Jen Fowler's comments had infuriated me. '*Get anywhere in teaching*'. As if I wanted to get anywhere in teaching! I was only doing this job because I'd failed at the career I wanted and my ex-husband was as stingy as hell.

And there must be easier ways to make a living, I thought, as I began my disconsolate trek across the playground. The agency had assured me that it didn't matter at all that I had so little classroom experience. All I needed was common sense and stamina. After all, most supply teachers left Havelock Ellis on their first day, often as early as the mid-morning break, so anyone who could stick it out would be appreciated. And thus I'd ended up here, armed with nothing more than my *Practical Guide to Teaching* to support me, battling away and doing my best to survive the job from hell.

According to the *Guide*, it was essential for the teacher to arrive for a lesson before the class. However, given the size of the school site and the distances I had to travel, this was often a physical impossibility and so it proved this morning. To my dismay, I saw that 9X were here before me. There they were, half-way up the wire fence by the drama studio. A sixth member of the class, a sandy haired, obese boy,

39

nicknamed the Honey Monster because of his resemblance to a character from a breakfast cereal advert, was making an inept attempt to climb up after them. The class greeted me with a cacophony of grunts, yowls and weird snorts.

"Come down, all of you." I tried to sound calm and authoritative.

None of them moved, apart from the Honey Monster who lost his footing and flumped to the ground, causing the others to screech with pleasure. I glared at these habitual offenders whose names I knew for all the wrong reasons: Nando, Chantelle, Rizwan, Bradley and Desmond O'Leary.

"I said, get down!" I raised my voice against my better judgement.

"Shove off!" Chantelle yelled. She blew a sphere of pink bubble gum, and then sucked it back into her capacious mouth with a resounding smack.

"Please mind your manners, Chantelle."

"I weren't talking to you." She pointed to the Honey Monster who'd just struggled to his feet and was making a second attempt to climb the fence. I couldn't help admiring his spirit; it was a poignant display of bravado given his victim status in the class.

"Why are none of you in correct school uniform?" I demanded, hoping that a change of subject would have some effect.

"I've got me tie on!" Rizwan, a dark-skinned boy with sharp white teeth, indicated the stripy piece of tattered material that was tied, Rambo-fashion, around his forehead.

The pupils at Havelock Ellis, I'd noticed, specialized in subverting the school uniform. Blazers would be tied around the waist by the sleeves, over-sized school shirts would flap outside trousers, skirts would be rolled over at the top until they resembled little more than a belt. Most of 9X had gone further and abandoned the uniform altogether. Chantelle was wearing a denim skirt and a pink hooded top with the words 'Raga Girl' embroidered on the front, Bradley was in a Nike shirt and black jogging bottoms, and Nando's plump legs were encased in stone-washed jeans. All of them, apart from the Honey Monster, were wearing state-of-the-art trainers that were almost certainly the result of successful shop-lifting expeditions. The Honey Monster not only lacked expensive trainers but was wearing the correct shirt, tucked in, baggy school trousers and a school blazer. And very miserable he looked too.

"Hello, Miss." He tugged at my sleeve as if to reassure me that not everyone in 9X was an enemy.

"Hello," I said. It was difficult to know how much kindness to show him in front of the others. Too much obvious sympathy from a teacher might mean he'd be beaten up later.

"We ain't coming down," Chantelle announced.

"Any more defiance and you'll all get incident reports!" I bellowed, and then realized this was an ineffectual threat. 9X loved incident reports, a form on which their misbehaviour was recorded and sent to the Year Head. They saw them as a badge of honour. Twenty-five incident reports were supposed to lead to an hour's detention with the Head Teacher, but this could no longer happen because of Mr. Wheel's absence and their Year Head, Angie Hucknall, was more likely to give them with a sweet.

"How many reports you got, Rizwan?" Chantelle turned to him.

"Nine since last week," Rizwan grinned.

"I've had twenty-*free*," Chantelle boasted, "And there's two detentions what I bunked. I've had a referral to the Ed. Psych. and me mum's got to come in and see Miss Hucknall *and* I got sent out of As-sem-*belly*."

"Assembly, Chantelle," I corrected her. "There's only one 'e' in the word."

"Yeh? So what?"

"Chantelle, I'm not going to accept such rudeness. If you don't come down from there…"

"Listen up, all of you!" A cheerful antipodean voice rang out.

A man with blond hair tied back in a pony-tail had arrived. Dressed in a sweat-shirt, shorts and baseball boots, he was clutching a handful of felt tip pens and had several sheets of sugar paper in various pastel shades tucked under his arm.

"Hi, kiddos, my name's Tel," he announced. "How about you all come down from there? We can go into the drama studio and chill out for a bit. Then I want us all to talk about why we feel like swearing at our teachers."

He didn't need to introduce himself; I guessed who he was at once. This just had to be the man from TOSSA.

Ten minutes later, I was beginning to feel grudgingly impressed. Under Tel's tutelage, 9X had become surprisingly compliant. He'd sat down on the grubby carpet and they'd all sat in a semi-circle round him and listened while he explained the principle of brainstorming ideas. Now they were all working in pairs, scribbling their thoughts down on the sugar paper, apparently utterly absorbed in the task. I had no idea whether they were doing anything educational but at least they weren't tearing the place apart. It was little short of a miracle.

"You don't need to stay." Tel came over to me with a grin. "I can handle this little crew of swabbers. Why don't you go and grab yourself a coffee before the next lesson?"

"That would be nice," I said. "But are you sure?"

"Cripes, yes!" he assured me. "I'm a qualified teacher and I do oodles of these workshops every week all over London. I'm here to give you guys a break, as well as stimulate the brains of these little muckers!"

"Thanks," I said. "Then I will."

Brilliant! The lesson had another hour to run, so I'd got time to go up to the staffroom, have a coffee and summon up the energy to survive the rest of the day.

"Hey, you! The supply teacher!"

Oh, hell. Paul Gogarty was waving to me across the playground. Behind him, a chaotic mass of pushing, shoving, younger pupils were boarding a number of coaches that were lined up outside the gates. I couldn't pretend I hadn't seen him.

"Glad I saw you." He flexed his rugby prop-forward right arm in what I could only assume was supposed to be a winning display of male strength. "I'm just taking Year 8 to the baths for their swimming gala. I need your help. I'm short of a female teacher to supervise the girls' changing rooms. Angie was coming, but she got speared through the leg with a javelin yesterday afternoon when she was supervising the field events."

"Goodness!" I said, "Is she all right?"

"Oh, yes." He laughed with callous disregard for female suffering. "Angie's got well-covered legs, so it didn't penetrate too far. But she's off school today, I just found out. So, are you coming?"

"Of course I'll come," I tried to sound bright and obliging. "Do I need to tell anyone where I'm going?"

"No time, love. The coaches have to leave right now. Hop on board." He gestured towards the first coach.

43

Love. Was that supposed to make me feel better? What an awful prospect: Paul Gogarty's company, the entire Year 8 group in an echoing swimming pool, the cries and splashing of over a hundred kids, the trauma of supervising the girls changing room, where some of them would be trying to do substance abuse with deodorant aerosols. Feeling travel sick on the journey and having a headache by the end of the day. I almost wished I was staying at the school, with 9X and the man from TOSSA.

*   *   *   *

I pulled my hessian curtains over the window and lay down on my bed. Four in the afternoon, and I did, indeed, have a headache after my day at the swimming gala. But I'd be fine after a nap. I was planning to see the screening of *Bicycle Thieves* at the Everyman later in the evening, Caspian was on his way to Norfolk, and I had the weekend all to myself. *All to myself...all to myself...* Drowsy and contented, I drifted off to sleep.

"Wh....yyyyyy are you in bed?" The full force of Cynthia's patrician vowels jerked me awake.

"You can't just barge in here!" I sat up sharply, clutching the duvet to my chest.

"Whad-ja-upter?" Nanny Barrel Hips appeared by the wardrobe.

I just managed not to scream although more with revulsion than terror, startling as the suddenness of her manifestation had been. That garbled sound, *Whad-ja-upter,* had always set my teeth on edge. It was a word that could roughly be translated as *what are you up to*? but had never made any sense, since Nanny Barrel Hips used to say it when it was quite clear what I was doing, chopping carrots, watching TV, reading a book and, most often, relaxing and *not wanting to be disturbed*. Eventually, I realised that *whad-ja-upter* wasn't a question at all and that what it really meant was *stop doing that, and pay attention to my needs. You haven't offered me a cup of tea for at least an hour.* How awful to discover that death could leave a person's irritating little quirks so unscathed.

"Ah!" Cynthia beamed. "Agatha! You know, I think Dora needs our help. Just look at the walls in here. Doesn't she know rag-washing is completely out of fashion?"

"Posh stuff." Nanny Barrel Hips looked around her, disapproval oozing from her plump features. "I like a nice wallpaper, me! I fancy some big, blue cabbage roses on a pink background."

"Excellent!" Cynthia clapped her hands. "Post-modern irony, acknowledging the culture of the nineteen-sixties working class!"

"Can you please both leave me alone?"

"Now, now Dora," Cynthia frowned. "I think you're in such a bad mood because you need to apply a little feng shui to this house. You really should have known better than to place your sofa facing north."

"If I'm in a bad mood, it's not because of the position of my sofa. You've both invaded my private space and I don't understand what either of you want from me. It's clearly nothing to do with wanting to see your grandchildren. Do you realise, Agatha, that since you've been here you haven't mentioned Seb once?"

"Whad-ja..."

"Don't ever say that to me again!" I seized my copy of *Empire* and hurled it in the direction of Nanny Barrel Hips. As it hit the wardrobe, I found I was alone.

Goodness. Was that all you had to do to exorcise unwanted spirits? Throw a copy of *Empire* at them?

Apparently not. After a brief silence, shrieks of laughter erupted from downstairs. So, Cynthia and Agatha had no intention of leaving. Well, just you wait, the pair of you, just you wait! If I can find him, before long Ralphie Dunglass de Marney otherwise known as Bobbity, will be coming here to bell, book and candle you both and send you on your way!

Six

The Trouble with Tenants

Nine o'clock, Saturday morning and now, thank goodness, the door of the Lord Halifax was open. I peered in: an imposing figure, almost six feet tall, was engaged in polishing the furniture. She looked like a hostess from the Bloomsbury set, Lady Ottiline Morrell perhaps, in that long muslin frock, glittery scarf, gold sandals and feathered toque, although Lady Ottiline, of course, would never have done her own housework. I watched as she pulled back one of the black curtains, letting in a shaft of sunlight that somewhat diminished the gothic mystery of the place, revealing a crack in the ceiling plaster and a patch of mange on the left thigh of the stuffed bear.

"Hello," I hesitated in the doorway. "Are you Georgia?"

"I am she." She spoke in a husky voice. "But I'm afraid we're not open yet."

"I'm sorry to disturb you," I said. "But I'm looking for someone I met in here on Thursday afternoon. Ralphie Dunglass de Marney. Do you know where I might find him?"

"Ah!" She smiled broadly. "You must be Dora Harker. He told me about you."

"He did?"

"Yes, he found your conversation quite intriguing, it seems. Do come in. Please close the door behind you."

"Thank you." I stepped inside. "So, do you think he'll be in here later?"

"Certainly he will, but not until much later. He always avoids my Saturday morning clean-up. As you can imagine, this is just what he dislikes, everything upside down, the curtains open, the mirrors uncovered..." She put down her cleaning cloth. "I suppose he told you that he's a resident here, that he lives here as my lodger?"

"No...I don't think he did. Although I did get the impression he was something of a fixture in the bar."

"Oh, he's that all right!" Georgia laughed. "So, do you want me to give him a message, once he surfaces?"

"Yes, please, that would be very helpful."

"No problem. And may I say how glad I am that you've befriended him. He needs company. He's been separated from so many of his old friends and of course, some of them are no longer with us, if you understand what I mean."

"I know life can be lonely for older people." I glanced at the memorial urns in the alcoves. *Surely* they didn't contain actual ashes?

"Particularly for those who once led a full social life," Georgia agreed. "So, your message? What would you like me to tell him?"

"Can you say that the problem in my house that I mentioned to him has doubled? That not only has...the thing I feared happened, something else, or rather someone else...it's difficult to explain. But I think he'll understand. And could you please tell him it's urgent."

"Oh dear, that sounds ominous! Are we talking about an infestation of some kind?"

"That *is* one way of putting it."

"In that case, I'm sure Ralphie can handle it. Does he know where you live?"

"It's number 3, Arcadia Square."

"Ah! Say no more! Well, I'll give Ralphie your message and I'm sure he'll pay you a visit. It will be so good for him to go out; he so rarely does these days. But don't let him take advantage of you. He's a very charming and cultivated man, but there are times when his continuing presence can begin to pall. Still, that's the problem with revenants. When would you like him to call? Would early evening be convenient? Shall we say about six?"

"That would be great. Thank you. I really appreciate it."

"My pleasure."

Thank goodness, I thought, as I left the Lord Halifax. Help was on its way. And Georgia had been very sympathetic, even though I hadn't been fully explicit about the nature of my problem. It was only later that I wished I'd paid closer attention to what she'd been telling me. I suppose when you're distracted by unwelcome visitors in spirit-form, it's easy not to listen carefully and mistake one word for another.

Determined to salvage what I could of my free weekend, especially since the weather was so lovely that day, I went to my favourite café in Delancey Street for a coffee and croissant breakfast, browsed around Camden market, bought a picnic and went to sit up on Primrose Hill with the newspaper. I was just reading about the forthcoming Tarkovsky retrospective at the BFI, and thinking that perhaps it was now time to return to Arcadia Square, when a message popped up on my phone:

Mother in intensive care. Mystery illness, coma. Your fault. P.

My fault? What had I done? And how could Cynthia be ill in Minorca, when she was busy applying feng-shui to my North London living room? (And she'd better not touch my Vettriano print!) Puzzled, I keyed in a reply:

My fault, how? D.

I waited a moment. Then,

You upset her! P.

How had I upset her? She was the one who always upset me, with her alcoholic moments, her lack of interest in Caspian, and now all my irritation completely compounded by the way she'd appeared in my bathroom, using my perfume, astral-travelling and...*oh! Astral-travelling.* Of course! I might have an inkling about what must have happened. The sooner Ralphie arrived to sort things out, the better. I leapt to my feet, and headed off as quickly as I could back to Arcadia Square.

"Sweetie!" Cynthia flung open the living room door. "Where have you been? Come and see what I've done with your books. Don't you think those shelves look better with the spines turned against the wall?"

"Since you mention it, I'd really prefer..." I was interrupted by the first few bars of *Knees up Mother Brown* chiming out from the hallway. "What on earth was that?" I demanded.

"Whad-ja think of that?" Nanny Barrel Hips appeared on the sofa. "New door bell."

"Jolly good fun, isn't it!" Cynthia exclaimed. "I installed it this afternoon. It plays at least twenty other tunes!"

"I preferred the old one."

"Spoil-sport!" Cynthia made a *moue* of reproach with her collagen-swollen lips.

"She was always stuck-up," Nanny Barrel Hips agreed.

"Look," I said. "There's something I need to tell you, Cynthia. I think you're in considerable danger. Peregrine's sent me a message and…"

Knees up Mother Brown chimed out again. Oh, thank goodness! Please let that be Ralphie and not Brian Belluga who'd found out where I lived after all.

"Good evening, dear lady."

Oh! What a relief to find Ralphie, so elegant and civilized, standing on my doorstep. He was carrying a death's head walking stick and there was a blood-red rose in his button hole. His expression was one of calm resolve and authority.

"Georgia gave me your message," he said. "I take it that your ghost has manifested itself in visible form?"

"Yes. And it *is* Agatha, Agatha Dellow, my late second mother-in-law. But someone else is here too; my third mother-in-law, Cynthia. She's in spirit form as well. It seems she's taken up astral-travelling."

"How very ingenious." He smiled. "She must be a very resourceful lady."

"And also very annoying."

"I see." He nodded. "Well, I am confident that I will be able to persuade both of these spirits to leave. But first, you must invite me in. We must observe certain formalities. Not all the stories are true. I don't fear crucifixes or running water, but you *must* invite me in, or I can't help you."

The stress of the past two days must have affected me even more than I'd realized. I was feeling quite dizzy. Perhaps it was the way Ralphie was gazing at me with those blue gem-stone eyes. And I couldn't understand what he was saying. He seemed to be talking weird gibberish.

"Who's this then?" Nanny Barrel Hips appeared in the hallway.

51

"Oh, how delightful!" Cynthia brayed, coming up behind her. "A gentleman caller!"

"Come in, Ralphie," I said hastily. "Do come in at once."

Ralphie stood in the living room, leaning on his death's head walking-stick. Nanny Barrel Hips sank back into her hamster nest of cushions, while Cynthia, apparently anxious to impress, moved around the room, adopting the strange, swimming walk and the faux-seductive expression of Gloria Swanson at the climax of *Sunset Boulevard.*

"Perhaps you would like to sit down?" Ralphie gave her a dazzling smile.

"If you wish!" With a flirtatious giggle, Cynthia perched on the arm of the sofa, arranging her legs to their best advantage.

"I'll come straight to the point." His tone was kindly but firm. "I'm afraid that both of you have outstayed your welcome."

"I wasn't welcomed," Nanny Barrel Hips retorted.

"Nor was I," said Cynthia, with a skittish toss of her head.

"My dear ladies," Ralphie purred. "That is beside the point. In the condition you are both in, that is spirit form, you cannot stay here in perpetuity against the wishes of your hostess. Now, I'm not unsympathetic. I crossed over in 1944 and ever since, I have been aware I must earn my keep. I was fortunate enough to be in London for VE Day, it would have been so *tiresome* to have missed it, I was able to mingle with the crowds and gain sustenance from many. But I would *never* enter someone else's home without an invitation!"

I was delighted to see that Ralphie seemed to be winning them over with his nonsense. Cynthia was gazing at him with the rapt attention that she usually reserved for an Italian waiter brandishing an enormous pepper mill, and even Nanny Barrel Hips looked impressed.

"Now." He turned towards Cynthia. "Forgive me for saying this, but I suspect you are quite a novice when it comes to astral-travelling. You really shouldn't stay out of your body for too long. Flesh needs the support of the spirit. Tell me, where did you leave your earthly body?"

"I was on a sun-bed in Minorca."

"And how long ago was this?" Ralphie asked.

"It was…" Cynthia frowned. I wondered if her memory had been affected by her antics.

"It was Thursday afternoon," I said.

"Oh dear." Ralphie looked reproachful. "Don't you realise that anything could have happened to your body in your absence? Hypothermia, deep-vein thrombosis, an attack by wild animals, sunstroke, murder, assault, abduction, wrinkles…"

"Wrinkles!" Cynthia looked horrified.

"Starvation, dehydration…"

"No, no!" Cynthia protested. "My son was there. He'd have soon put me to bed, or put a blanket over me, or…"

"Actually, Cynthia," I said. "You're in intensive care."

"*What!*" She jumped to her feet, her mouth a perfect scarlet 'O'.

"Peregrine couldn't wake you up," I continued. "He didn't know you were in an astral-travelling trance, he still doesn't know, he thought you were in a coma, but I expect they're looking after you, doing all kinds of tests…"

"No, no!" she sounded anguished. "I know what they do to you in those places! Dash it, I must go back at once."

"Yes, you must," Ralphie said. "Flesh needs the support of the spirit and any further delay could be fatal. But while you're about it, why not take Mrs Dellow with you?" Ralphie suggested. "She deserves a good holiday."

"I do," Nanny Barrel Hips agreed. "Last one I went on was a bit of a let-down. We never even got there."

"The thing is," Cynthia looked confused. "I'm not at all sure I *do* know how to get back. Not without Pablo here."

"Pablo?" Ralphie looked quizzical.

"He's my little shaman."

"Oh, we can manage without Pablo, delightful as he sounds! Now don't concern yourself with the details. I can spirit you both away to Minorca just like that." Ralphie snapped his fingers. "I only need your consent."

"Will there be any pain?" asked Cynthia.

"None at all," Ralphie assured her. "And, let me assure Mrs Dellow that she will find the psychic transportation I can arrange far less hazardous than embarking on a package holiday with certain budget airlines." He turned to me. "Dear lady, I wonder if I could ask you to leave us? These arcane procedures work better without an onlooker and besides, you may find it tedious. I shall have to recite all fifty pages of the *Resurgam Horribilis* of Simon Magus the younger, and you may find the smell of burning feathers somewhat overpowering. I'm sure you don't mind? Good."

I sat in the kitchen, sipping a G. and T. I could hear some of the proceedings through the wall, and they seemed interminable. Odd smells wafted in, not just the burning feathers but a mixture of nutmeg and roses and with the additional unpleasant pungency of blocked drains. Then I heard the Cynthia shriek, there was a burst of Tom Jones singing *Delilah*, and at last, mercifully, there was silence.

"They have departed." Ralphie appeared in the doorway.

"Oh, thank you so much!" I took a gulp of my drink. "I'm really, really grateful to you, Ralphie. I can't tell you what a relief it is to have the house to myself again."

"Indeed. I have never had a mother-in-law, but I can appreciate that they can be very vexing. And to think you've had three."

"I still don't understand why they came."

"Unfinished business, as I said before. But it could be that the unfinished business is yours, not theirs, and that is what has helped to conjure them up."

"I don't understand."

"Don't you?" He frowned. "Tell me," he continued. "That first mother-in-law of yours, what was she like?"

"Oh, she was really evil. And she did something terrible, and I was very young, so I remember writing reams of stuff about her in my diary, I daresay none of it was very polite. But these days, I just want to forget about Gertie Shuttlehanger."

"*Gertie Shuttlehanger?*" Ralphie sounded aghast. "But no-one could be called Gertie Shuttlehanger!"

"My first mother- in-law was. And she was a ghastly, wicked, old harridan who..."

"Hush!" He held up a warning forefinger. "Enough! You could be tempting providence. You're talking about a woman who could be listening to you from beyond the veil."

"Oh, I don't think that's likely!" I laughed. "Anyway, I can't thank you enough for what you've done today. How can I repay you? What can I do for you in return?"

"Now that you mention it, there is one thing." Ralphie treated me to one of his most charming smiles. "You see, I'm looking for a new place to lodge. I'm becoming rather weary of the Lord Halifax. I have no quarrel with dear Georgia, of course, but I need a change of scene. It's all that gloom. The urns, the black drapes, that *terrifying* bear. And the cellar where I sleep is really rather damp."

"You sleep in the cellar?" I was startled by this revelation.

"Indeed I do." He stared at me with his hypnotic eyes.

"Well, that does sound rather uncomfortable, but I'm afraid I…"

"Let me assure you that I will be a quiet, well-behaved guest. I'm sure you must have a spare room in a house this size and I have really taken to your clean, well-lit home. For several months now, I have been *longing* to experience certain modern conveniences and little luxuries. And I will pay rent. So, if you would permit me?"

"I'm sorry," I said, "But I can't…you see, I like my privacy and…"

"But don't you see?" He moved towards me. "You need my protection. I've rid you of those spirits but others could come."

He was standing very close to me, and the whites of his eyes were beginning to turn red. My mind was racing. He slept in Georgia's cellar? He crossed over in 1944? Crossed over in what sense? *Not all the stories are true, I don't fear crucifixes, you must invite me in…* What was that word Georgia had used? Tenant? No! *Revenant.* Yes, that was it! Good grief! Surely he couldn't be a…

"Ralphie," I was babbling now. "I know I invited you in, but I'm afraid it wouldn't be convenient for you to stay. I *am* grateful for what you've done here, but surely there's something else I can do to thank you instead? I could buy you a bottle of absinthe or…"

There was a sudden, loud thump. It seemed to be coming from the roof space.

"Grief!" I jumped. "What was that?

"I suspect you have another visitor." Ralphie looked up towards the ceiling.

"A visitor?" I repeated. "Do you mean a burglar? Well, if someone's got in through the sky-light, there's nothing worth stealing in the loft. All that's up there is Seb's train set, and Caspian's pram, some of my old clothes and my student essays and..."

"And your diaries containing all the rude things you wrote about your first mother-in-law?"

"You surely don't think that…"

A crash. The clatter of the loft ladder being let down onto the landing. The sound of heavy feet stomping down the stairs. A tumultuous banging on the kitchen door.

"Come in!" Ralphie held up his death's head walking stick. "Come in and show yourself, whoever you are!"

The door flew open. A tearing wind cut across the room. A plate hurled itself off the shelf. Two more plates followed and a casserole dish, all of them whirling through the air before falling with a shattering cacophony onto the Italian tiles.

"Ralphie!" I screamed. "What have you done?"

"My dear lady, *I* have done nothing." He spoke with worldly-wise regret. "I'm very much afraid that *you* are the catalyst for this latest manifestation. I did warn you not to speak ill of the dead."

"But I…" I jumped out of the way as a kitchen knife came towards me, then flung itself at the ceiling, embedding its point in the coving.

"Ooops!" Ralphie sounded unperturbed. "I'm afraid she means business."

"She?"

"What was that curious name again? Shuttlehanger? My dear lady, surely you can see that it would be most ungallant of me to leave you alone with such a malevolent spirit. Now you really *will* have to let me stay."

Seven

Living with the Undead

The fine weather had been superseded by grey skies and a chill wind. Litter was careering down the street like tumbleweed. As a sheet of torn newspaper wrapped itself around my ankles and a piece of grit landed in my eye, I wished I'd had the sense to put on my coat. This was nothing like the Sunday morning I'd been envisaging, a lie-in with a book, then a long soak in the bath accompanied by the Archers omnibus, followed by Sunday lunch in my favourite bistro. Instead, here I was fleeing my own home, driven out by flying crockery and yet another mother-in-law, this one manifesting herself as a poltergeist.

A large, grey-white, shaggy mongrel mutt was snuffling and scavenging along the gutter outside the Lord Halifax. I didn't like the look of this animal at all. It wasn't wearing a collar and there'd been a number of reports in the local paper of unprovoked attacks by stray dogs. I wasn't anxious to add to the statistics.

I approached cautiously. The dog lifted its head, staring at me with feral eyes. I froze. What to do now? Try to befriend it, but how? I'm not the kind of person who'd say something brain-numbingly stupid as *nice doggy*.

This wasn't, in any case, a nice doggy. It had the appearance of a ruthless beast, more wolf than lovable woofer. If only I had a biscuit in my pocket. That might appease it. Unless, of course, it was rabid, in which case my situation was hopeless.

Just stare it out and it'll retreat out of sheer embarrassment. I wasn't sure where I'd heard this piece of advice, but for all I knew it was complete nonsense and I was about to get my throat ripped out. But no, it seemed to be working. With a display of canine nonchalance, the dog turned away, trotted over to a wheelie bin, cocked a rear leg and began to pee in a surprisingly copious manner. It was as if a river had burst its banks.

Stepping aside from the flood, I went around to the side door of the pub. There was no response when I pressed the bell. I bent down, and peered through the letter box into a dingy hallway. There was a smell of dead mice and stale beer. A wooden carving of some fiendish Pacific Island deity at the foot of the uncarpeted stairs grinned back at me.

"Georgia?" I called softly. "Are you there? *Georgia!*"

No response. I straightened up and tried the bell again; it emitted a strangulated phuttering as if a mechanical toy was choking to death on its own cogs. A few moments later, much to my relief, I heard the sound of feet clumping down the stairs, and then the door opened a crack. Georgia, clad in black silk pyjamas and black velvet mules with diamante buckles, peered out at me.

"Georgia!" I gasped, the words tumbling out in my anxiety. "Thank goodness! I'm so sorry to call on you so early but I don't know what to do. My house is in uproar, the first two spirits were expelled but now there's a poltergeist, and Ralphie's insisting that he has to move in, and I've only just found out that he's a vamp…"

"Sssh!" Georgia placed a manicured finger on her red-painted lips and shook her head vehemently. "Stop! Not on the doorstep. Come in. For one thing, this damp is playing havoc with my chilblains." Grabbing my wrist, she pulled me into the hall and slammed the door behind us.

"Sorry," she whispered. "Perhaps you didn't realise how loudly you were talking. I was afraid Mr Jakes might hear you."

"Mr Jakes?"

"The man who lives over the road."

"Oh," I winced at the memory of Thursday night's encounter. "Yes. I think I've met him."

"How very unfortunate for you. Then you'll know he's not the kind of person who ought to overhear such things." She pushed open an inner door. "This way. Let's go through to the bar."

"I really am sorry to disturb you," I said, following her. "But it's an emergency."

"So it would seem. You look like you need a drink." She pulled a bottle out from the stuffed bear's crooked arm. It was Scotch, I noticed, Glenfiddich.

"Isn't it too early for spirits?"

"It's never too early for spirits, as no doubt you're beginning to realize," said Georgia. "Oh, I'm sorry, that was really a wicked pun! And this one's on the house. With soda or without?"

"Plenty of soda, please." Suddenly, I felt no shame at all at relenting so easily. "You're right. I do need a drink. My nerves are in shreds."

"Oh, dear." Georgia swished the soda into the glass and handed it to me. "So sorry to hear the exorcism backfired."

"So you do believe in…?"

"Paranormal phenomenon? Of course. I haven't been the landlady of the Lord Halifax all these years for nothing. And this is one of the most haunted areas of London."

"It is?"

"Oh, yes. But don't worry. I'm sure Ralphie will soon sort out your problem."

"Will he? How do I know that *he* didn't summon up this latest spirit? You know, the way a cowboy plumber will fix one leak but create another one when your back is turned?"

"Oh, no." Georgia was vehement. "Ralphie would never do such a thing. He's a perfect gentleman."

"But he's a vamp…"

"Please!" She held up her hand. "Don't use that word. It's no longer in polite use."

"Isn't it? Then what should I say?"

"You could say undead, but even that term's regarded as debased these days. There are other terms. 'Blood Group X' or 'They who have taken the pathway of the dark' or 'Those with a return ticket from the Bourne from which no traveller is said to return'. But the expression they prefer is Night Wanderer."

"I see." I stared at the curtained mirrors, suddenly aware of their significance. "I'm finding it difficult to take this in, to tell the truth. I didn't even know until yesterday that vamp…that Night Wanderers even existed in the real world."

"I assumed you knew about Ralphie." Georgia returned the bottle to the crook of the stuffed bear's arm. "I thought I'd told you."

"I wasn't listening properly. when you said revenant I thought you said…"

"Tenant? Well, that *is* true. He *is* my tenant. But now, it seems, he wants to be yours. I'm not entirely surprised if he wants a change of habitat. He *has* been complaining about the damp in my cellar just lately. Although he's always been grateful for the refuge."

"Refuge?"

"Yes. It came about when the Council bulldozed the old church of St. Sebastian. I salvaged a lot of artefacts from there as you can see. It was a dreadful business. Not just an act of architectural vandalism but also an attempt at undead ethnic cleansing. The inhabitants of the crypt should never have been evicted in such a brutal manner."

"The inhabitants of the crypt? You mean they were vamp...Night Wanderers?"

"Yes, and worst of all, they were my clientele. If you'd come in here while St Sebastian's was still standing, you'd have found the place simply teeming with Ralphie's friends. Elegant, cultured people, all of them, although, as you'd have noticed, very pale. As pale as if they'd just stepped out of their tombs, which, of course, they had." She sighed. "Some of my regulars had been in that crypt since the foundation of the church in 1780. And now... well, as you can see. It's always deathly quiet in here. You were the first outsider to wander in here for months. It's just as well I don't rely on the pub for my income."

"You don't?"

"No, I run a collectables and antique business on e-bay. It's really proving quite lucrative. But I do feel nostalgic for the old days and so, I know, does Ralphie. Of course, only a few people knew the real reason for the destruction of the old church. The official story was that the building was dangerously unstable, that one of London's lost underground rivers was undermining the foundations, turning the graveyard into a quagmire and that the interior was too damaged by bat droppings to be restored. But the real reason was to get rid of the Night Wanderers."

"And were they...I hardly know how to put this.... Were they... killed?"

"Fortunately most escaped. The night before the work was due to start, the panic was appalling. It spread across London, and many other Night Wanderers joined the refugees from St Sebastian's and fled England by Eurostar."

"Why didn't Ralphie go with them?"

"He just couldn't get a cab to St. Pancras," Georgia said. "They were all taken. And besides, as he said, he wasn't too keen to relocate at his age."

"This is all very interesting but..." *Interesting?* What was I saying? This was as appalling as it was unbelievable. "But, all the same, I really can't have Ralphie staying in my house."

"But you need his protection," Georgia insisted. "You see, when the council destroyed St. Sebastian's, they made a grave mistake, if you'll forgive the pun."

"A grave mistake? What do you mean?"

"They didn't understand that Night Wanderers maintain a psychic balance," Georgia explained. "They are the aristocracy of the supernatural sphere. Their very presence can repel troublesome spirits. But now, with only Ralphie left here to act as a vigilante, it seems that the dark portals through which disturbances used to leak are now gaping wide. No wonder a poltergeist has got into your house. And you could be in serious danger. Couldn't she, Ursa Major?" She patted the head of the stuffed bear.

"Serious danger?" My mouth felt dry.

"Arcadia Square has always been a strange place." Georgia informed me. "I think you should be prepared for the worst. The recent visitations you experienced could be just the beginning. But don't despair. It's a great privilege to be offered the protection of a Night Wanderer, especially one as distinguished as Ralphie. I'm afraid you don't have any choice. You really do need him."

"I see." I put down my empty glass. "Well, thank you for the drink. I suppose I'd better go home now and see what's been happening there."

"You mustn't worry." She placed her heavily be-ringed hand over my mine. "Ralphie will give you every assistance. And do call back in any time. I'm always ready for a chat."

"Thank you," I said. I tried to sound grateful, although my brain was reeling. Why on earth was all this happening to me?

*   *   *   *

To my relief, I saw that the dog had gone, but now an old, derelict man in a stained raincoat was rooting through the wheelie bin. His bushy grey hair looked like a joke Hallowe'en wig, and his lips were moving as he muttered to himself. He glanced up at me. There was something vaguely familiar and disturbing about those eyes. They hardly looked human at all. *Goodness,* I thought, suddenly remembering the attack on Josh outside Chalk Farm Station, what if this was the assailant? Oh, poor Josh, I'd hardly given him a thought, I'd been too distracted by my problems. I hoped he'd be back at school by Monday. In the meantime, I'd better ring Becca. I took my mobile out of my bag.

"Hi, Dora!" She sounded breezy and upbeat. "I was about to ring you. The bloody Range Rover's fucked to buggery."

"Oh, good grief!" My stomach lurched in shock. "Has there been an accident?"

"Oh, no, everyone here is fine. We've up since before dawn. The boys wanted to go mushrooming."

"Mushrooming?" I didn't like the sound of this.

"Yes, it was Caspian's idea."

"Oh. And are you quite sure…"

"Don't worry, they're with Robin and he won't let them pick any death caps. He's a countryman and knows what he's doing. But about the Range Rover. Too complicated to explain, but we might be stranded in Norfolk for another night. The garage can't do anything until Monday. I'll leave a message on the Netherwold answerphone explaining the situation, but I'm afraid Cas might be here with me until Tuesday. I am so sorry."

"Actually…" I hesitated. "That'll be fine. In fact, it's better that Caspian doesn't come home just yet. I've got a bit of a problem."

"A problem? What kind of problem? Not your bloody ex, I hope?"

"No, it's not Peregrine. But…" I took a deep breath. "A rather eccentric acquaintance has arrived and I can't get him to leave."

"He won't leave?"

"No."

"And is this person…. well, *undesirable* in some way?"

"It depends what you mean by undesirable," I said. "He's a very charming and cultured man. But the problem is, he's not exactly alive."

"*What!*"

"I was speaking metaphorically." I was pleased with this hasty improvisation.

"Oh, *I see.*" Becca sounded relieved. "Well, I know what you mean. Some people can be very draining, can't they?"

Draining. An image of an unnaturally pale body, sucked dry of all its blood by a creature with Nosferatu teeth flashed into my mind. I suppressed a whimper of dismay.

"You must be *firm* with this friend," Becca continued. "Just tell him it's not convenient."

"I'm not sure he's open to persuasion."

"Really? Then why not drop a subtle hint? Think of something that would persuade him to leave. Play some of Seb's heavy metal music. There must be something that would repel your unwelcome guest. Does he have any allergies?"

"Allergies?"

"Nothing lethal of course, nothing to cause anaphylactic shock, but something that makes him sneeze. Or serve a meal containing an ingredient he doesn't like." She laughed carelessly. "Anyway, must go. Porridge boiling over!"

"OK. Thanks Becca. And thanks for everything."

"No probs! See you soon, I hope. Bye."

"Bye."

I dropped my phone back into my bag, musing on what Becca had just said. *There must be something that would repel your unwelcome guest. Serve a meal containing an ingredient he doesn't like. Garlic!* Of course! Wasn't that the most obvious thing? It *was* time to put in my on-line grocery order after all. I usually did it on a Sunday. Yes, that was what I'd do. I'd spend the day at the NFT, see a couple of films, and go back to the house in the early evening, and then I'd hang up a string of garlic. Ralphie would be bound to return to the Lord Halifax after that. There's always a simple practical solution to an awkward social situation, no matter how bizarre.

Eight

Home, Sweet Home

I stared, aghast, at my front door. Who on earth had done this, sprayed a huge, red, swirling hieroglyph over the eggshell-white paintwork? There were some obvious suspects, perhaps a member of one of the gangs of teenage boys in hooded tops who hung around the square after dark, doing wheelies on their mountain bikes and trying to run over cats. I just hoped it was a random piece of vandalism and not a coded message from a Havelock Ellis pupil. And I dreaded to think how Peregrine would react if he saw it. Oh, grief! I'd have to repaint the entire door.

There was no sign of my grocery order in the porch, but there *was* a large brown paper parcel on the step addressed to *Lord Ralph Dunglass de Marney 3 Arcadia Square, London, N.W.1.* I picked it up somewhat gingerly. The label was handwritten in faded brown ink and the stamps in the top right-hand corner appeared to be foreign but were too heavily-franked over to be distinguishable. How could this parcel have arrived from abroad so quickly? Well, Ralphie wouldn't be staying long. Not once the garlic arrived.

I unlocked the door and stepped inside. Damn! There appeared to have been a power cut. The house was in complete darkness and nothing happened when I flicked on the light switch in the hall. I groped my way through to the kitchen.

"Surprise!"

There was a violent crackling and then the room was suddenly flooded with brilliant light. Ralphie was standing in front of me, holding two lengths of electric cable, one in each hand. It seemed he'd just touched them to produce this effect, causing no harm to himself whatsoever. And he was wearing a string of garlic round his neck.

"What the…?"

"I do hope I didn't startle you, dear lady," Ralphie purred. "That was not my intention at all."

"Well, you did startle me," I snapped. "I've been out all day, and I didn't expect to come home to find you performing conjuring tricks."

"This is not a conjuring trick." He spoke with pained dignity. "This is all part of the ritual I have undertaken to eject the angry spirit from the house. It—or should I say *she*—has left the building. And I have, as you seen, cleared up the mess."

"That *is* kind of you." I looked around me. I supposed I should be grateful. There wasn't a sign of any broken crockery anywhere. "Erm…. I'm just wondering…the garlic?"

"A very pleasant young man delivered it. I think he said something about a cardi?"

"Ocado."

"Ah! Well, it's certainly come in useful. It has helped to repel the angry spirit, and has also protected me."

"*Protected* you?"

"Oh, I'm not averse to garlic, even if the scent does clash with my *eau de toilette*." He took off the string and threw it into the vegetable basket. "I daresay your Mrs. Shuttlehanger wasn't a fan?"

"No." I could hear her voice right now, *nasty foreign muck*. "But I thought that you…"

"Me?" He smiled. "Ah, I daresay you've been exposed to a lot of myths in your time. There *are* those amongst us who can't abide garlic, just as some people are allergic to peanuts, and others go into anaphylactic shock with a wasp sting, or avoid sugar because of diabetes. I had mild diabetes back in '36, but now, having passed through the void, I am cured of *that*. And what is more, I don't suffer from Van Helsing's Syndrome."

"Van Helsing's Syndrome?"

"The term for the minority of us who are garlic-intolerant," he explained. "Ah! I see you have brought in a parcel."

"Yes, it seems to be for you."

"Good. Then my plasma has arrived!" He beamed, clasping his hands together.

"Plasma?" Hastily, I put the parcel down on kitchen table with distaste. "Are you telling me that this package contains *blood*?"

"Naturally. I have a standing mail-order for it. It's authentic Eastern European plasma. You *can* get South American, but I find that a little rough, and as for Australian, I find that far too light and larrikin! No, I prefer the best Carpathian vintage. I'm something of a traditionalist."

"And what about the people who supply this blood?" I wasn't at all sure I wanted to hear the details, but my curiosity was aroused all the same.

"Oh, they give it willingly," Ralphie assured me, "The process is hygienic and harmless. No-one need give more than a pint or two at a time, and no-one's health is affected."

"So they don't…erm, that is, they don't…"

"Ah! I think I can interpret your delicate hints. No, the people who are kind enough to become donors do *not* pass

7 0

over and become Night Wanderers themselves. So much fiddle-faddle has been spoken about these matters. One bite and you're vamped! It never *did* happen in that way, not even in the old days. To pass on the glorious chalice of immortality, there has to be a mutual exchange of bodily fluids over quite a long period of time. Many fail in the attempt."

"And how did you...?"

"My dear lady!" He lifted up his hands in protest. "I cannot possibly reveal the details of such intimate matters considering our short acquaintance."

"Sorry," I said hastily. "I didn't mean to be intrusive."

"I forgive you. Now, let us turn to practical concerns. I shall need a place to rest while I am here."

"To rest?" An image of an open coffin flashed into my mind. "You mean, during the daytime?"

"I mean, during any period of the day or night," said Ralphie. "Rest is often necessary at my age. I thought that, with your permission, I might move into the room upstairs, the one with all the filing cabinets. It's not a large room and it does seem to have a most *unsympathetic* atmosphere but I can adapt it to my needs."

"There might be a problem," I said. "My ex-husband's left some of his things in there, and he won't be at all pleased if..."

I was interrupted by the cheerful chiming of *Knees up Mother Brown.* That door-bell! I must get it fixed!

"Dora!" Zelda burst past me into the hall, her arms wind-milling wildly. "I've been thinking about this, and now I've decided it can't wait until Monday. I just had to come and warn you. Josh just called me! You're in deep shit."

"I am?"

7 1

"Yes. This afternoon, Josh got home from the hospital, would you believe he was there all weekend? He had some allergic reaction to an injection and...well, never mind that. So he's having a cup of tea, when the phone rings and it's Langford, and what he wants to know is..."

"Langford?" I was having difficulty keeping up with this. "Who's Langford? Zelda, you're going too fast for me. Look you'd better come through and explain."

"Right." Zelda collapsed on the sofa. "It's like this." She took a packet of tobacco and some papers out of the pocket of her jeans and began to roll a cigarette. "Oh, sorry," she waved the tobacco in the air. "I should have asked. Do you mind if I smoke?"

"Go ahead. "I said. "Only I'll just let some air in, if you don't mind." I lifted up the lower section of the sash window. "So, who's Langford?"

"Some kind of educational consultant, a trouble-shooter. He's been sent to sort the place out before the next OFSTED inspection. He was in school on Friday; I'm surprised you didn't run into him. He's a particular type, smart suit, superior attitude, carries a briefcase marked with his initials..."

"Those initials wouldn't be A.R.L, by any chance?"

"Yeh. That's him. Aidan R. Langford."

"Then I've met him. We didn't exactly hit it off."

"That doesn't surprise me, he's an arrogant bastard. Within one school day, he managed to put a number of noses completely out of joint. Anyway, he phoned Josh this afternoon to tell him that last Friday some time before lunch, 9X went missing."

"They went missing? Their poor parents must have been frantic!"

"Well, no, actually." Zelda grinned. "Not those parents. They let their kids run wild most of the time. Nando's on some kind of ASBO, and his father's always anxious for the school to hush up any trouble he might be in. And as for Chantelle…" she rolled her eyes. "Anyway, they're not missing now. They were just off the site for Friday's lessons. Of course, no-one reported it because it was such a relief not to have to teach them. It was only when they were all brought back to school by a police officer an hour after the end of afternoon lessons that the alarm was raised."

"What alarm? If they'd all been found…"

"Yes, but that kid they call the Honey Monster, he wasn't with them, and they all denied knowing anything about his whereabouts. But then, the caretaker found the Honey Monster in the disused toilet block, imprisoned in one of cubicles. There were chains and padlocks across the door and his trousers had been stolen. Apparently the rest of 9X had put him in there before they bunked off. He'd been there for hours."

"Oh, that's awful. He must have been terrified."

"Actually, it could have been a whole lot worse," Zelda said. "Rizwan had lent him his Gameboy, and they'd left him a six pack of Coca-Cola, ten Maxi-packs of crisps, and a jumbo bag of mini Mars bars, so at least he didn't go hungry." She took a drag of her cigarette. "At least not at first," she added, with a wicked grin. "Anyway, Langford wanted to know who was in charge of them during the first lesson on Friday. And so it seems you were the last member of staff to see 9X and Langford knows you left them with the man from TOSSA. So, as I say, you're in deep shit."

"How distressing." Ralphie appeared in the doorway, leaning on his death's head stick. "I couldn't help overhearing some of that. I'm *so* glad that I don't have to deal with today's young people."

"Have we met?" Zelda gawped at him. "You look familiar. You weren't in Downton Abbey, were you?"

"Alas, no." Ralphie held up his hands in a gesture of regret.

"Zelda," I said. "This is Ralphie. Ralphie, this is Zelda."

"Delighted to meet you." He bowed. "I am the new lodger, you know. I hasten to add that I shall be offering my hostess suitable remuneration. I am not...what's that term they use these days? *A sofa surfer.* I shall pay handsomely for the privilege of living in such a delightful house."

"That's nice," Zelda said. "Well, I can't help feeling that's going to be useful. You'll need the income, Dora, if Langford gives you the sack from Havelock Ellis."

"The sack?" I repeated, aghast. "Why should he sack me? And how can he anyway?"

"That's the extraordinary thing. Apparently he's been invested with absolute authority in order to..." She was interrupted by an outburst of manic shrieking coming from the street.

"Effing hell!" She jumped up, scattering her tobacco over the rug. "What's that? It sounds as if someone's being murdered."

"Or perhaps a banshee has terminal toothache," Ralphie purred. He walked over to the open window and pulled up the roller blind. "Interesting," he murmured, turning to me. "It seems your latest visitor has reached the physical stage of her manifestation now. Do come and take a look!"

Nine

A Scare in the Community

"I'd much rather not 'take a look'," I said. "That woman is the last person I want to see."

"I'm afraid I must insist," Ralphie gazed at me with a regretful expression. "If only for the purpose of identification. I'm sure that it must be the person I think it is, but I need you to confirm it, dear lady. Turn off the light and come and stand here, to one side, and then perhaps you will be unobserved."

"Well, if I must…"

I went over to the window and peered out, and then wished I hadn't, since the sight was enough to chill my blood.

There she was, Gertie, my first mother-in-law, pacing up and down in the middle of Arcadia Square. She looked very much as she had done when I'd last seen her, her feet encased in a pair of clumpy zip-up suede boots and her grey hair sticking out in all directions like a Brillo pad that had seen better days. I even recognized her dress. It was the one she used to call 'me frock', a tube-like, knee-length, belted shift, made from a cheap nylon material and printed all over with a hideous design of geometric grey lines against a brown background. It was a garment that gave her the appearance of a caddis fly grub camouflaged with twigs at the bottom of a particularly dirty pond. So death had done nothing for her dress sense.

"Marks and Spencer's!" she shouted to no-one in particular. "You can't find anything you want in Marks and Spencer's!"

"She sounds very confused," Zelda observed.

"There *has* been a little derangement," Ralphie agreed. "It sometimes happens like this. When a spirit returns to this earthly plane through several paranormal dimensions, the mind is jolted. Rather like a diver getting the bends."

"Marks and Spencer's!" Gertie turned on her heel. "Why can't you buy decent underwear in Marks and Spencer's? They've got G-strings, and frillies, and cut-aways, DIS—gusting stuff—utterly, utterly DIS—gusting, fit only for the whorehouse, and they've got French knickers and bikinis with red silk rosebuds on them! What's a woman to do? Where's your ordinary basic knicker gone, eh?"

"Poor thing," Zelda murmured. "They should never have closed the long stay ward at George Gissing Hospital. People turned out of safe institutions, left to fend for themselves, no care in the community…"

"I have every reason to believe," Ralphie purred. "That she has come from an even more infernal place than George Gissing Hospital."

"But the poor woman shouldn't be wandering around the streets unaccompanied," Zelda insisted.

"She shouldn't be wandering them at all," I told her.

"Quite." Zelda nodded. "Not without proper social support."

"That isn't what I meant," I said. "The reason she shouldn't be out in the street is because she's a…"

"British Home Stores!" Gertie shook her fist. "It went downhill when they stopped selling ham and cheese. *Where* did their food counter go? Boo-ti-ful, it used to be, boo-ti—ful. And now the shop's gone altogether. It's a scandal. And there are *foreigners* serving in Selfridges." She turned to face us.

"Oh, good grief!" I dropped on to my knees. "Please. Don't let her come any closer."

Attempting to conceal my panic, I pretended to be preoccupied with picking up the shreds of Zelda's Old Holborn from the rug but I could feel my hands shaking.

"Do not fear, dear lady," Ralphie purred. "She can't get across the threshold. The house is protected. I have painted a Mandala of Raphael on the front door."

"A Mandala of Raphael?" I sat back on my heels. "Do you mean that red squiggle? I was going to paint over it."

"I would strongly advise against that," Ralphie said gravely. "Not unless you want to let a number of particularly malignant spirits back into your home."

"She's not malignant. She just needs help," Zelda said.

"Believe me, she's malignant," I said. "And she was always like this. Every so often she'd take the train into London and start an argument in every shop in Oxford Street. You might say it was her own version of retail therapy."

"You *know* that woman?" Zelda sounded astonished.

"Unfortunately, I do." I got to my feet, dropping some shreds of tobacco into the waste paper basket. "For a very brief time, she was my mother-in-law. My *first* mother-in-law. I haven't seen her for twenty years. And now, thanks to Ralphie, she's back."

"Not guilty, I'm afraid." Ralphie held up his hands. "*I* am not the person who helped her back across the Styx.

My talents, as surely you know by now, veer towards ejecting spirits rather than conjuring them up. But perhaps she has a message for you. Madam," he lifted the window up higher and leaned out. "Can I be of any assistance?"

Gertie took several paces forward.

"If you've got something to say to me, say it," I said, staring back at her. "And then you must leave. I can't think why you're here. Haven't you done enough damage already?"

"Me?" Her eyes glinted. "I never done nothing. *You* were the one who brought shame on me family! *You* abandoned me son. Whore! Adulteress!"

"My marriage to your son was annulled," I said. "*Annulled.* Don't you know what that means?"

"You weren't going to be good enough for him," Gertie spat. "Remember what you did?"

"I remember what *you* did."

"I done me duty! And you'll never be free! Not you! Don't say I never warned you. And the bad times are coming for you, believe me. And you deserve the worst, you stuck up little…"

"How dare you? You of all, people…"

"Stop!" Ralphie laid his hand on my arm. "Slanging matches with spirits are never a good idea. Mrs. Shuttlehanger, we must bid you good night."

Gertie remained where she was, staring straight at me, her face ghastly and pallid in the street light.

"Ah!" Ralphie murmured. "I think a little diplomacy is called for here. Madam," he smiled at Gertie. "From your remarks, I gather you are interested in shopping. Are you aware that there's a very good late-night grocers in Regents Park Road? You may find that they have some excellent bargains on offer. Not to mention the twenty-four-hour Tesco's up by the railway line."

"Twenty-four hours!" Gertie gawped at him.

"I believe so," Ralphie told her. "Perhaps that's an innovation for you, shops staying open all day and night. It must be something that's happened since your…*ahem*… demise? I'm just wondering, have you been to Harrods? I really think you should pay it a visit. Knightsbridge is *so much* more rewarding than Oxford Street these days. So many well-loved department stores have been closed and replaced with noisy dens purveying buckets of American coffee. I wouldn't go in one of those places if I were you. But I *can* recommend a trip to Harrods. If you leave now, you will be the first in the queue for the mid-season sales. You could take a short cut across the park."

Gertie hesitated only for a moment, then, after shooting a look of pure hatred in my direction, she turned and lolloped off, laughing manically as she went.

"An interesting interlude." Ralphie closed the window. "So, she's gone, but I can't guarantee she won't be back."

"She simply mustn't come back." I sank down on the sofa. "I don't think I can stand any more of this."

"Have courage, dear lady!" Ralphie admonished me. "Yes, it would appear your past is coming back to haunt you. And only by confronting it, will you be able to move on. Remember what I said about unfinished business? *Your* unfinished business."

"Ah! I see!" Zelda sat down cross-legged on the floor and began to roll another cigarette. "You're a therapist, Ralphie."

"You might wish to interpret it that way." Ralphie smiled at her. "I do happen to know a considerable amount about the demons that plague human lives."

"You're talking figuratively of course?" Zelda suggested.

"If only I was," Ralphie purred. He turned to me. "My dear lady, I need to know a great deal more about your first

79

marriage if I am to be of any assistance. Do you feel able to give me an account of it?"

"It's a rather weird story," I objected. "And it's getting late. Perhaps some other time."

"No, tell it now!" Zelda reached for a match to light her roll up. "Always do what your therapist tells you."

"Ralphie isn't my…" I broke off, and took a deep breath. "All right then, here it is. That woman, Gertie, put a curse on my life. And you might as well both hear how it all came about."

I was eighteen, at college and I was in the bar after the Film Society's screening of the Greta Garbo/John Gilbert classic *Flesh and the Devil.* I was minding my own business, not looking for company, when a young man with mousy hair and a rather heavy chin sat down next to me and asked what I'd thought of the film. I was about to say something pleasant and non-committal and make my excuse to leave when he launched into a lecture on the cameras they used during the period of silent cinema, droning on and on about the technical details, not allowing me to get a word in. I was desperate to get away but then he just happened to mention that he was reading Kevin Brownlow's *The Parade's Gone By.* Now my interest was aroused. I'd been in the library only that morning looking for the book and I'd been told that it had gone missing.

"You've a copy of *The Parade's Gone By*?" I said. "Could I borrow it, do you think? I need it for an essay I'm writing."

"Of course," he said. "I'm still reading it, but I'll be finished by Sunday. I could give it to you then. Can you meet me outside college at half past one? By the bust of Nelson Mandela?"

"O.K," I said.

"Great!" He stood up, and began putting on his anorak. "See you Sunday, then. I'm Colin, by the way, Colin Shuttlehanger. And I know who you are, you're Dora Harker."

It only occurred to me much later that he might have been stalking me for weeks. But I, in my innocence, hadn't noticed anorak man at all.

Ten

There will always be Shuttlehangers at Slodger's Farm

That Sunday, Colin was waiting for me by the Mandela bust as arranged. He appeared to have made an effort to scrub up well, although not, I'm sorry to say, in a way that appealed to me. His anorak and jeans were gone, and now he had adopted the 'young-fogey' look; cavalry twills, a checked shirt, a tweed jacket, a green spotted bow tie and brown lace up shoes. Even more disconcertingly, he didn't appear to have the book with him.

"Hi!" He grinned. "Shall we go then?"

"Go?" I must have sounded puzzled. "Go where?"

"To get the book," he said. "It's at home."

"Ah, no, wait a minute, I never said that I…"

"I've been looking forward to this afternoon." He looked hurt and disappointed. "You said you'd come."

"I said I'd come *here*," I objected. "I didn't say I'd go to your house."

"I've got a really good collection of movie memorabilia." He took a set of car keys out of his pocket, jingling them under my nose. "And I've got a rare poster of *Casablanca* and a set of stills from *El Cid*. And my mum will be getting tea ready."

"Your mum?" Could this get any worse?

"Yes. She likes me to bring friends home. I don't have many."

Oh dear. This really was rather sad. I told myself to be kind. I was also eager to get my hands on the Brownlow book, so I agreed to go. After all, I thought, no harm could come to me if his mother was going to be there. Just how wrong can you be?

Despite not suspecting the worst, I was, all the same, feeling deeply uncomfortable as we hurtled down the A11 in Colin's rusting Triumph Herald. Eventually, we left the motorway, branching off into the duller, flatter reaches of East Anglia, passing furrowed fields, dikes and slurry pits. At last, Colin drove into a muddy yard and pulled up outside a squat building disfigured by gritty-grey weather-seal walls and a rickety 1950s storm porch. Some semi-featherless chickens were scratching around in the dirt. There were several burnt-out, rusting cars and a sign reading 'Slodger's Farm'.

"Welcome to Shuttlehanger Hall!" Colin switched off the ignition and roared with laughter. This was my first indication that Colin's sense of humour was going to prove self-congratulatory and charmless.

I tried to hide my dismay as he led me into the farm house through a hall lined with gum boots and macs and into a large old-fashioned kitchen. There were shelves lined with ornamental plates, depicting members of the Royal family and views of the Costa del Sol, and the walls were decorated with hand-embroidered samplers and corn dollies. A family gathering appeared to be in progress. A row of faces gawped up at me from a long wooden table laden with plates of sandwiches, sausage rolls, watercress and dishes of trifle. It was a scene that could have come straight out of a production of Arnold Wesker's *Roots*.

"Sit down, gal." An elderly woman in a floral wrap-over apron pointed to an empty seat beside her. "I'm Colin's Auntie Nell."

Reluctantly, I squeezed into the space on the oak settle. Four pairs of male eyes looked across the table at me. All too soon, I would learn their names and peculiar proclivities. Simple cousin Pete, uncle Benny the alcoholic, Barnaby, the middle brother and closet transvestite, and Colin's youngest brother Ezra, he of the spatula fingers and the talent for strangling pigeons.

My mind was racing. What was I to do? An escape plan seemed like an urgent necessity. Perhaps I could pretend I wanted the bathroom, slip outside, squelch my way back across the muddy yard, run down the lane, and then hitch a lift with the first person who came along, even if he was a red faced, beer-bellied lorry driver from Hartlepool. But wouldn't that be dangerous? How far was it to the nearest station? Did I have enough money on me for the fare back to London?

"What size shoes do you take?" Auntie Nell thrust a plate of sandwiches at me.

"Size five and a half," I replied, an automatic response, although I was distinctly puzzled. In an effort to be polite, I took a sandwich, and surreptitiously lifted the upper slice of Wonderloaf to inspect the contents. Tongue, a meat product calculated to make me heave.

"Ha!" The old woman wiped her fingers on her skirt. "Size five and a half. Then your body will be fit for child-bearing." She poured me a cup of turd-brown tea from a huge pot encased in a grey knitted tea-cosy. "If the feet are too small, then the pelvis will be too narrow. Colin, you have chosen well."

Chosen? I nearly choked as I took a sip of the lukewarm tea. It had a harsh, metallic taste. I felt distinctly sick.

I was about to ask where the bathroom was when the door opened.

"Here's mum!" Colin exclaimed, in what seemed an unnecessarily enthusiastic tone.

Thus it was, I saw Gertie for the first time. She was, I remember, wearing a green and yellow full-skirted, cotton shirt-waister dress, the one I later learned she called 'me-Sunday' to distinguish it from her weekday 'me frock'. She was carrying a huge glass bowl.

"Here we are! Me chocolate soufflé! It's cooled nicely in the back larder," she announced.

"My mum's speciality." Colin nudged my elbow. "Soo—oooo delicious! You must have some. It's really yum! It's made from eggs, butter, sugar, cream, rum and…"

"Now then." Gertie set the bowl down on the table, "Don't be giving away all my cull-i-norry secrets! Afternoon, gal." She turned to me. "I'll be offended if you don't tuck into this."

She dolloped a generous portion of the thick, glutinous brown mixture into a willow pattern bowl and plonked it in front of me.

"Don't wait for us, you get stuck in!" She handed me a tarnished apostle spoon. I hesitated. Everyone's eyes were upon me. I picked up the spoon and took a tentative mouthful. To my surprise, I found the soufflé was gorgeous; creamy, smooth, chocolate paradise, nirvana, bliss, heaven. I took another spoonful, then another. Then I looked at Colin again.

Goodness! He was a really nice looking, sweet guy. Sexy even. Why on earth hadn't I seen that before?

In the following weeks, I began walking around in a peculiar daze. It hardly seemed possible, but I believed I'd fallen in love. Colin certainly seemed besotted with me. He followed me around at college all the time. Every day, when I went to the student pigeon holes, I'd find that he'd left me little gifts wrapped in waxed paper; squares of Gertie's date and walnut loaf, squidgy pieces of her chocolate orange brownies, generous portions of her seed cake. I ate all these treats with joy, and each Sunday, when he took me back to Slodger's Farm, I always took a second helping of his mother's chocolate soufflé. And then one spring evening, he got down on one knee, and offered me the heavy Victorian ring that had belonged to his great-great grandmother. We were engaged.

*

"I've got a bad feeling about this wedding, Dora," my Uncle Horace said. "This Colin. He doesn't seem your type. Have you got anything in common with him?"

"We both think *Les Enfants du Paradis* is the best French film ever made," I said.

"But that doesn't mean you have to marry him," Uncle Horace objected. He stared at the catalogue of bridal dresses lying on the kitchen table in front of us. "Dora, you know that Auntie Pam and I will always support you, but I'm not at all sure you're doing the right thing here."

Sweet old Uncle Horace, I thought. He and Auntie Pam had been my guardians ever since I was three and they'd always been very protective. I supposed that was why Uncle Horace was being so critical of my fiancée, but I was sure he'd soon learn to appreciate Colin's encyclopaedic knowledge of New Wave Cinema. And if he knew that Colin was saving himself for our wedding day, thus ensuring I was a virgin bride, then Uncle Horace would be sure to approve.

The wedding dress was ordered, the caterers were hired and all the arrangements were made. And then, about two weeks before the wedding, when I tried on my dress for a final fitting, I found to my consternation that the fabric was stretched tight over my stomach and under my arms. There could be no doubt about it. I had put on weight and if I put on any more, the dress might split. This must be result of eating so much of Gertie's chocolate soufflé. I had to go on a strict, cabbage soup diet at once!

I didn't tell Colin about my diet. I wanted to surprise him with the new, slim-again me. When I found his daily offerings of cake in my pigeon hole, I took them outside and fed them to the birds (those birds, how tame they were, I had them eating out of my hand as if I was St Francis of Assisi!) and at Slodgers, I managed to feed my portion of chocolate soufflé to the cat, putting my bowl under the table when everyone was preoccupied with discussing the complexities of crop rotation. The cat, an aggressive creature that had scratched me in the past, was obviously very grateful, jumping up on my lap, purring and licking me; it was now my most passionate admirer. And then, the night before the wedding, I had a dream in which Colin was shoving his mother's date and walnut loaf into my mouth, choking me with it while yelling "Eat up, eat up!"

I woke up in a cold sweat. The wedding was only a few hours away and here I was, filled with doubt. *Why* had I been spending every Sunday at Slodger's Farm, gorging myself on those family teas, and watching inane games shows on TV, and standing out on the scrubby stretch of grass at the back of the house, joining in with a game of putting? I didn't even *like* putting, and my lack of skill seemed to provide Gertie with grim satisfaction. "She's an educated, clever girl, but not so good at the simple things of life that we loike," I overheard her mutter to Auntie Nell. And then she'd prepare to play another shot, putting her head down and sticking her bony bottom, clad in nylon ski-pants, up into the air, a posture that gave her a striking resemblance to one of the cows grazing in the paddock. If I married Colin, she'd be my mother-in-law. This was all wrong!

But how on earth could I get out of it now? There were all those wedding presents to consider, and all the guests that had been invited, several long-lost cousins, aunts on their way from Birmingham, and even an aged uncle from the Outer Hebrides. Auntie Pam would be mortified if she had to turn them all away. And what about Uncle Horace? He'd parted with a large sum of money, hiring the room and ordering the food for the reception. If the wedding was cancelled at such short notice, he'd never get his deposit back. I couldn't let them both down after all they'd done for me.

I tried to tell myself it was just pre-wedding nerves. Or perhaps I was getting a cold. Maybe it would all seem different in the morning.

Eleven

A Toast to the Gride and Broom

And so it was that Colin and I exchanged our vows in a room graced with sludge green walls and a brown cord carpet. The Registrar, a man with a nose covered in broken veins, mispronounced my name, calling me Deena, but I felt too numb to correct him. As we emerged into the day-light and posed on the steps for the photographer, I was dizzy with disbelief. Was I really Dora Shuttlehanger now? What a ludicrous name! And to think that once the honeymoon was over, I was destined to go and live with Colin in the converted barn at Slodgers, surrounded by flat fields where carrots were grown under a leaden Fenland sky. Surely this couldn't be real?

"Now it's traditional for the gride to kiss the broom." Colin turned to me with a grin. Then he laughed uproariously; how he loved his deliberate Spoonerisms. My spirits sank even lower; I didn't want to kiss 'the broom', especially as I'd just noticed that his face resembled a slice of suet pudding. But with all the relatives lining up behind us, I was forced to comply. And then it was off to the Eel Catcher's Arms for the reception.

It's odd how clearly I remember the details of that wedding breakfast. Chilled vichyssoise, *veau en papiette* with sautéed potatoes and green beans, raspberry compote with *langue de chats*, coffee, After Eights and, of course, a towering wedding cake. I sat at the head of the long table with Colin, trying to smile radiantly at passing well-wishers while feeling like jumping in a lake. Then Colin nudged me.

"Look," he said, "Mum's brought some of her chocolate soufflé. It's over there on the sweet trolley. Let me get you some."

"Why has your mother brought her own food?" I didn't try to disguise my annoyance. "How rude! Uncle Horace has spent a fortune on the catering. And no, I don't want any of your mother's soufflé. The very thought of it makes me feel ill."

Gertie must have heard me, even though she was sitting at the other end of the table, resplendent in 'me two piece', an outfit made from bobbly orange and purple wool-mix material. The glare she shot in my direction was venomous. And then, as Colin and I left the Eel Catcher's Arms and crossed the car park to get into the bridal car, which was, in fact, Colin's Triumph Herald, driven by simple Pete and with a white ribbon on the bonnet, Gertie came towards me. I braced myself, overpowered by the strong whiff of her 4-7-11 Cologne, fearing I was about to receive a Judas kiss, but instead, she grabbed my wrist. "*Why* didn't you have my chocolate soufflé, you stuck-up, silly gal!" she hissed into my ear, "Didn't you see it there? Don't you know what's good for you?"

I wanted to tell her it hadn't been good for me at all, but before I could say anything, cousin Pete revved up the engine, Colin pulled me into the car and we accelerated away in a hail of confetti.

That evening, I was standing in a cold bedroom on the tenth floor of a draughty hotel in Hamburg, contemplating my escape, when Colin informed me that he was going to the bathroom for 'a dump'. Was he always going to be this unromantic, I wondered? I opened my suitcase; I didn't want to unpack but I was getting a headache and thought there might some aspirins in my sponge bag. And that was when I found it, lying between two sheets of ice-white tissue paper under my nightie. The *thing*.

What was this abomination doing in my case, this nasty little wooden figure with its bulbous, feature-less head, grossly distended belly and pendulous, crudely suggestive phallus between its legs? I could hardly bear to touch it, but nevertheless I picked it up, holding it between my thumb and forefinger. Then, suddenly decisive, I threw it on the floor and stamped on it, relishing the crunching, destructive sound. With a feeling of exhilaration, I opened the window and flung the fragments out into the rainy, Hamburg street.

As soon as Colin emerged from the bathroom, I hurtled in there myself, locked the door, and stayed there, ignoring his pleas. I hoped that sooner or later he'd fall asleep, something that seemed likely given the amount he'd had to drink. I'll skip the details about what happened next—or rather what didn't happen—but suffice it to say, the next morning, as we mooched around Hamburg in the rain, I was still a virgin bride.

The city was cold and grey, dominated by the statue of Bismarck on his huge column. We took a trip on the lake, ate frankfurters and saw a street in the red-light district with a metal gate across it. There was a man walking out of the gate who looked vaguely like Uncle Horace. I knew it wasn't Uncle Horace of course, but the sight prompted a stab of guilt. He'd tried to warn me, and now, I knew he'd been right. I'd made a dreadful mistake.

That evening, we sat at a table in a gloomy restaurant, surrounded by wooden panelling overhung with banners of medieval guilds. Colin was hunched over his food in his usual porcine manner. I looked down at my plate, at the indigestible selection of pickles, cold potatoes, slivers of chewy cooked meat and an item that appeared to be a miniature rubber bath mat. I took a sip of beer, and said,

"This isn't right."

"The food's not that bad," Colin looked up at me. I noticed what a long, ugly upper lip he had.

"I don't mean the meal," I said. "I mean us. This isn't working."

"Oh." He looked vaguely ashamed. "If you're talking about last night, then I'll try and make it up to you. Tonight, when we get back to the hotel, I'll do my stuff."

"No! Please!" I realized my voice had risen almost to a shriek. "There's no need for any 'stuff'. There's no nice way of putting this, but I just don't feel the right way about you. I thought I did, but I don't. I shouldn't have agreed to marry you. I'm so sorry."

"Are you saying you don't love me?" He sounded astonished.

"I'm afraid that's exactly what I'm saying."

"But I wanted you to love me!" He stabbed a gherkin with his fork. "Mum said you would." He thrust the gherkin into his mouth and chewed furiously. "She promised me. She said you'd love me. *You were supposed to end up loving me.*"

"What do you mean, *your mother* promised?" I stared at him.

"She said you would if you ate the cakes and the chocolate soufflé."

"The chocolate soufflé?" I was horrified. "Are you saying that your mother put something in it to make me fancy you? Some sort of aphrodisiac?"

"Not exactly." He stuck his fork into another gherkin.

"What do you mean, not exactly? Tell me the truth! Did your mother put something into the food you've been giving me?"

"My mother knows some very old recipes, that's all I'm saying."

My stomach lurched. Suddenly, the whole business had become clear. I remembered that moment when I'd found Colin attractive; the moment I started eating the soufflé. I remembered how the cat had behaved towards me when I fed it my portion, and how my feelings had changed so radically when I was on the cabbage soup diet. But what had Gertie used? A love potion? Surely such a thing didn't exist? But it seemed that it did.

"Oh, good grief!" I flung my napkin down on the table. "Of all the horrible tricks! I'm going back to England. Without you!"

"Oh, no, you're not! You're coming with me. Back to the hotel and…"

"Let go of me!"

"Come on!"

Colin flung open the door of our hotel room, seized my suitcase, and threw it open. It was still half-full of my clothes; I hadn't had the heart to unpack completely. He knelt down and began rummaging through my things, frenziedly hurling items of diaphanous nylon over his shoulder.

"Where is it?" he whimpered. "Where has it gone?"

"Where has what gone?" I demanded.

"Granny's manikin." He threw a pair of honeymoon-style lace knickers across the room. "Mum put it in your bag!"

"Do you mean that ugly, obscene carved wooden doll with the phallus?" I said. "I destroyed it."

"*What?*"

"Yes. I stamped on it and threw the pieces out of the window."

"Aaaaagh!" Colin's hands flew to the sensitive part of his anatomy. "What about my manhood? What am I going to tell Mum? What if one of the others wants to use it?"

"Use it? Use it for what?"

"What do you think? That manikin has been in my family for generations! They say that great-great-great-great-great-great-great-granny had it in her apron pocket as she hid under the floor of the barn when Matthew Hopkins came!"

"Matthew Hopkins." I swallowed. "You mean the Witch-finder General?"

"Yes, of course I mean the Witch-finder General. You've seen the film, haven't you? Directed by the late Michael Reeves and starring Vincent Price in the eponymous role, and the producer was…"

"Never mind the film," I said. "Are you telling me that horrible thing was some kind of fertility totem? Are you saying there have been witches in your family for generations casting the evil eye on their neighbours, creating love spells and talking to toads?"

"I'm saying nothing." Colin looked sulky. "But this is really going to upset my Mum."

I was far too young and angry to feel sorry for Colin. Perhaps it would have been kinder to explain to him that it would be better for him find a girl who liked him for himself, not one who'd been drugged by his mother into compliance. But all I could think of was his aunt's dreadful comment about the child-bearing hips and so, without a backward glance, I took the next flight home and went back to Uncle Horace and Auntie Pam.

Uncle Horace was very decent about it. He never even mentioned the cost of the wedding reception. And he seemed relieved when I told him the marriage hadn't been consummated.

"I could have told you not to marry a man with no balls," he said.

Then he drove me to Slodger's Farm to collect my things. I wanted my collection of *Cahiers du Cinema* and my clothes. As far as I was concerned, Colin was welcome to keep the wedding presents, the sets of saucepans, the three toasters, the Wok and the Japanese tea set.

I was just putting the last box of my belongings into the boot of Uncle Horace's Volvo Estate when Gertie appeared. She was wearing zip-up boots and a green quilted housecoat over 'me frock' and she was holding a dead branch in front of her face. She peered at us through the bare twigs as she walked slowly towards us. It was both menacing and absurd.

"Get into the car, Dora." Uncle Horace leant across from the driver's seat and opened the passenger door.

I leapt inside, but before Uncle Horace could start the engine, Gertie slammed the branch down on the bonnet.

"She won't get away with this!" she yelled. "Insulting my family!"

"There's nothing to be gained by discussing this matter," Uncle Horace spoke to her through the driver's window. "The marriage is going to be annulled."

"An—ulled? An—ulled?" Gertie raised the branch above her head.

"Yes," Uncle Horace said calmly. "Your son has failed to plant his turnips. Now please get out of the way." He revved up the engine but Gertie refused to move. She stood there, still as a stoat, holding up the branch.

"Out of my way, woman!" Uncle Horace bellowed.

It was quite clear she had no intention of moving, but fortunately, there was another way to exit the farmyard, so Uncle Horace put the car into reverse and hurtled towards the back gate. Hens scattered, mud flew up in the air. I gazed at Gertie through the windscreen; her lips were moving rapidly, as if she was repeating some ancient incantation. Then, "Shame on her!" She waved the branch around wildly in the air. "Tell that gal from me, I'll see to it! She'll never marry again and be happy. Never, never!"

And that was the moment when she cursed my life, and brought the biggest tragedy of my life down on me, and for that, I can never forgive her.

Twelve

Annulled, Widowed, Divorced

"But," Zelda was frowning at me. "The curse didn't have any effect, surely? You *did* marry again. Twice, I'm sure you told me that."

"Yes, I did, and Seb and Caspian have different fathers. But the thing is, Gertie said I'd never marry again *and* be happy. And I wasn't, not for long. Both my marriages came to an end. Mind you, getting divorced from Peregrine was a blessed relief."

"Hmm…" Ralphie was standing by the window, a thoughtful expression on his face. "A fascinating story. I shall have to reflect on what I've heard. All I can say at this stage is that it seems remarkable that such a beautiful youth should have felt the need to resort to witchcraft to secure a bride."

"Colin was not a beautiful youth," I said.

"Ah! Then who," he pointed his death's head stick at the silver framed photograph on the bookshelf, "is that?"

"That's my second husband." I swallowed painfully. Even after so much time, that sunlit image, his blonde hair, the carnation in his button hole, his very special smile, had the power to bring a lump into my throat. "Seb's father."

"The son of Nanny Barrel Hips?" Ralphie sounded astonished. "But he's an Adonis."

"Bloody hell!" Zelda gawped at the picture. "*That's* your second husband? He looks just like Dave Dellow of Chappaquiddick!"

"That's because he *was* Dave Dellow of Chappaquiddick." I seized the photograph and held it protectively against my chest.

"But that's amazing!" Zelda's voice rose with excitement. "Why didn't you tell me?"

"I don't like talking about it."

"*Chappaquiddick*?" Ralphie sounded puzzled.

"They were a band," Zelda told him. "Indie, progressive rock. So sad. They were just beginning to be famous when..." She stopped suddenly. "Oh, shit, Dora. I'm sorry."

"You can say it." I placed the photograph back on the shelf. "Dave died. And I was a widow at twenty."

"My dear lady..." Ralphie gazed at the photograph with a sorrowful expression. "How tragic."

"Yes." I said. "But please don't ask me to talk about it. I've done enough reminiscing for one evening. Zelda, do you mind terribly if I turn you out? I really want to go to bed."

"Of course," Zelda nodded. "But tomorrow...let's meet up at lunch time. Kris's Kebab House, like we often do on a Monday? For one thing, I'll want to hear about how you got on with Langford."

"I can honestly say I don't care what happens with him," I said. "But OK, then, Kris's Kebab House it is. But please don't ask me about Chappaquiddick. I think it's better to let go of the past."

"I'm very much afraid, dear lady," Ralphie spoke in a tone of regret, "That, while you might wish to let go of the past, it would appear your past is very unwilling to let go of you. This is only the beginning. We have much more work to do."

I was exhausted but couldn't sleep. With a sigh, I switched on my bedside light and picked up a book at random from the pile on the bedside table, a monograph on German Expressionist Cinema. So much the better; a hearty whack of difficult prose might prove soporific. I began to read: '*The Structuralist exegesis of Dr Mabuse is informed with a perpendicularity of intention that belies the interface of the pre-war fabric of society and the Weimar legacy. In the 'Cabinet of Dr Caligari', we see the Expressionist ethic without being conscious of the influence of Formalism.....*'

Impossible to concentrate, too many troubling thoughts buzzing around my mind like wasps caught in a jar. I'd told Zelda I didn't care about A.R.L, he of the pretentious briefcase, but what if I did lose my job at Havelock Ellis? The agency would send me to another school, but, as the saying went, better the devil you know. Reputedly, there were some even more difficult schools in this area, Krafft-Ebing Senior School for Boys, for example, where all kinds of mayhem took place, chairs hurled into the staff room, the fire alarm constantly being set off and female teachers being sexually harassed. Oh dear, I was wide awake. Best to go downstairs and make myself a mug of camomile tea.

I sat at the kitchen table, sipping my tea, and staring at the cork notice board on the wall. All my usual memos and notes were there, trade cards from plumbers and electricians, holiday postcards from friends, my latest pay slip, a Post-It note reminding me to book a dental appointment, Caspian's term dates, a recipe for aubergine and pimento dip, a cutting from *Time Out* about a new child-friendly restaurant, a drawing that Seb did when he was eight, but now, as I suddenly noticed, there was something new. A faded piece of vellum bearing the handwritten words, *Order more plasma in November.* So Ralphie *was* planning a long stay.

Strangely enough, I was beginning to feel a little reconciled to this prospect. What if Georgia was right when she said that I needed Ralphie's protection? What had he said about my past coming back to haunt me? I *needed* some guidance to deal with that!

I'd always prided myself on my practical skills. I kept my fridge scrupulously clean, wiping it with an anti-bacterial cloth on a daily basis. I never wasted food, always whizzing left-overs through the blender to make stocks, soups and sauces. I folded linen neatly, I kept drawers and cupboards tidy. When Seb was born, I put in a bulk order of embroidered name tapes for his school uniform, enough to last until he was in the sixth form. I grew plants from avocado stones and pips. I was never late paying bills. I kept files of recipes, household tips, and leaflets covering everything from stain removal to serious litigation. But now I was out of my depth, not just with the horrors of Havelock Ellis High School, but with a house full of ghosts. Who, apart from Ralphie, could help me with that? I'd never have thought of painting a mandala of Raphael on the front door. I didn't even know who Raphael was.

The kitchen phone interrupted my thoughts, bursting into life so unexpectedly that I jumped, spilling a drop of hot tea on my hand. *Ouch!* Who the hell was calling me at this hour? I picked up the receiver, fully expecting to hear the ramblings of a drunken, heavy-breathing pervert.

"Dora!" Damn! It was Peregrine, a prospect far worse than the pervert. "Do you mind telling me what you're playing at?" His voice was ragged with rage.

"Sorry?"

"Did you send all these aged plebs here?"

"I don't know what you're talking about. And don't you think it's rather late to call me?"

"If I can't sleep, why should you!"

"I wasn't asleep but...look, what exactly is the matter?"

"Mother's out of hospital, I'm glad to say, she made an astonishing recovery, but now she's brought a whole crowd of old women here, crazy old women in floral print dresses and tennis shoes. They've been drinking Pina Coladas and singing *The Green, Green Grass of Home* out on the patio all night. One of them looks like Agatha Dellow."

"Perhaps it *is* Agatha Dellow," I suggested.

"What are you talking about? Agatha Dellow is dead!"

"I know, but she wouldn't let a little thing like death stand in the way of a good knees-up."

There was silence at the other end of the line. Then,

"Have you gone completely mad, Dora?" Peregrine demanded to know.

"Quite possibly." I was doing my best to stifle my laughter. So not only had Ralphie managed to transport Nanny Barrel Hips and Cynthia back to Minorca, it sounded as though they'd managed to pick up all the other plane crash victims on the way. What a lovely afterlife for them and what a perfect way to wind up Peregrine.

"This isn't funny, Dora." There was a tinge of menace in his voice. "It's a living nightmare."

"Join the club!" I was feeling really lightheaded now. "I've been having rather a difficult time here too."

"I'm not interested in your problems. How would you like to be swamped by a load of vulgar old women? And now...oh God!" He gave an anguished gulp. "They're having a barbecue. They've got prawns and pieces of...Fish! They're cooking fish."

"Yes, you do have issues with seafood, don't you?" I said. "That must make living in Minorca very awkward."

"Yes, it's.... agh! The smell...the smoke...I ...aaaaaaargh!" I heard an elongated, gurgling retch and then the line went dead.

I replaced the receiver with a smile. Schadenfreude can be very consoling in the right circumstances.

When I finally managed to sleep, I was troubled by surreal dreams. Cynthia was dancing on a beach while balancing an enormous pineapple on her head, surrounded by brightly coloured birds that were flitting through luminous green leaves, while Nanny Barrel Hips played the maracas. Then I saw that the birds weren't birds at all, but bats. Multi-coloured bats, a new species, with wings as iridescent as butterflies. But then the bats turned black and the sky was growing dark and a hunched figure with long fingernails and pointed ears was silhouetted against the wall and now he, no, *it* was tapping on the door and...

I reached out for my watch. Six thirty a.m. What a ridiculous dream. But some-one really *was* tapping on my bedroom door.

"Dear lady? Are you awake?"

"Ralphie? What do you want?"

The door creaked open an inch.

"I have taken the liberty of preparing you a breakfast tray," he purred. "May I come in?"

"Um...yes." I must have sounded a little ungracious, groggy and confused as I was.

"I hope this is not an intrusion." Dressed in an exquisite lemon silk dressing gown embroidered with peacocks, he came into the room carrying a vast, silver tray. "Shall I place the repast on your bedside table?"

"Yes, thank you." I sat up blearily. "That's really kind."

I looked down at the tray. It seemed he'd gone to a lot of trouble; tea in a bone china cup, a silver toast rack containing three tiny triangles of lightly tanned bread, two boiled eggs in a double egg cup, a gold-rimmed saucer containing some delicate curls of butter, fresh fruit, and a lead crystal glass filled to the brim with a red liquid...*oh no*. What was it?

"Goodness, this looks wonderful," I said. "What's that, by the way?" I pointed to the glass.

"Home squeezed cranberry juice," Ralphie told me. "With just a *dash* of angostura bitters! *So good* for the kidneys."

"Ah!" I breathed a sigh of relief.

"The eggs are free range. Georgia has them delivered by a man who keeps his own poultry in Cricklewood. Now, let us welcome the day!" He walked over to the window and seized the curtain cord.

"Ralphie, don't!" I shouted at him in a panic. "You mustn't let in the daylight!"

"Ah-hah!" He turned towards me with a smile. "You are labouring under yet another misapprehension, similar to the myth about garlic."

"It's just that I thought...if the sun comes out..."

"Oh, dear me," he purred. "Let me assure you that even in the full blaze of June, nothing too serious would happen to me. We do not burst into flames, or crumble into dust, and I wouldn't dream of making a mess of your understated taupe carpet. The worst outcome would be a rather extreme suntan, and a gradual loss of tissue, which at my age, I agree, is not desirable. But I would need to go out in strong sunshine for *at least* twenty years before there would be any real damage. Of course, I do prefer the night, so much more *glamorous*. And today, in any case, as you will soon see, it's another foggy day in dear old London town."

He pulled open the curtains revealing a dense murk. If a hansom cab had rattled past, transporting Sherlock Holmes and Dr Watson to the scene of a heinous crime, it wouldn't have seemed out of place.

"Curious, don't you think?" Ralphie mused. "All this mist and far from mellow fruitfulness? It seems that this entire area of North London is bathing in dry ice. And yet I understand the sun is shining in Kensington."

"Is it?" I took a sip of the cranberry juice.

"So I've been told. Now about my arrangements. I hope you don't object, but I have borrowed your spare key. I found it on the shelf in the hall."

"You need a key?"

"Naturally. Do you suppose that I can re-enter your house in the form of mist coming under the door or through the keyhole, or that I can come through the window transformed into a bat?"

"I hadn't really thought about it." This wasn't entirely true. The tropes from every vampire film I'd ever seen had been flashing through my mind over the past few days.

"Have you not?" He flapped his hand playfully. "All the same, it is my duty to inform you that such transformations are the invention of some highly imaginative, but entirely inaccurate, authors. And now, before I leave you to finish your breakfast in peace, there's something I would like to mention. The story you told us last night, about your mother-in-law putting a curse on you. Are you quite sure you interpreted the events correctly?"

"What other interpretation could there be?"

"Well, she may have been a rural witch, capable of casting love spells but what if she was incapable of bringing about such a curse? Might her words simply have been a prophecy? You say she was waving a tree branch. Did you happen to see what kind of tree it was from?"

"I can't say that I did. Does it matter? "

"Indeed it does. If it was an elder branch, she might have been waving it to ward off the demon she could see standing behind you."

"A demon? Standing behind me?"

"It's possible, I'm afraid. More people have had their lives dogged by demons than you might suppose."

"I see." I picked up a spoon and tapped the top of my egg. "Well, all I can say is I think I have worse things to worry about than demons right now. In a couple of hours, I've got to return to Havelock Ellis High School and that will be quite hellish enough."

Thirteen

The Hum of Death

Mmmmmmmmmmmmmm...

Once again, I'd drawn the short straw. First lesson, Monday morning, and here I was on the second floor of the old building in a classroom without a door, struggling with 9X. And now, just when I thought the situation couldn't get any worse, they'd decided to treat me to the death hum.

Mmmmmmmmmmmmmm...

I glared at them, determined to regain control. I needed to identify the leader. It seemed to be Chantelle; there she was, leaning back in her chair, her lips pressed together, giving the others sideways glances of command. They were all joining in, Rizwan, intermittently baring his white, sharp teeth, Bradley accompanying the humming with a steady *thump thump* of his fist on his desk, Desmond O'Leary, grinning and flipping a 'bendy' ruler to and fro, Nando, in a cheerful display of versatility, humming and wiggling his hands in the air. Even the normally inoffensive Honey Monster was participating, perhaps in the hope that a display of peer group solidarity would prevent him from suffering another imprisonment in the disused toilets.

"Be quiet all of you!" I raised my voice above the din. "Any more of this and I'll make sure you do an hour's detention. I shall report this to Miss Hucknall. That's enough!"

Mmmmmmmmmmmmm! The death hum gathered in intensity.

Damn! I'd made a classic mistake. The death hum, a continuous, buzz saw sound calculated to send any vulnerable teacher into a breakdown, operates simply but effectively. The moment the teacher speaks, the class begins the hum. If the teacher tells them to stop, the humming gathers in volume. It will only stop if the teacher is silent. An inexperienced teacher might assume at this point that the battle is won, but, alas, the moment he or she speaks again, the humming resumes. Silence is the only possible counter-attack but that, of course, prevents the lesson from being taught. You can't win.

I'd done my best to begin the lesson in a calm, authoritative manner, explaining that Mr Wheel was still away and that I'd be taking their Citizenship lesson in his place. That hadn't been enough for them.

"So where's Mr Wheel, then, Miss?" Chantelle had demanded to know.

I'd considered my answer carefully, having been instructed to be economical with the truth when it came to dealing with questions about the whereabouts of Mr Wheel. No-one must admit that he'd been found huddled under his desk at the end of last term and was unlikely ever to return, not even to teach the two lessons a week on his timetable or take advantage of the free lunches on offer for senior management. If anyone, pupil, parent, representative of the local press or the man in the corner shop asked about Mr Wheel, they were to be told he was engaged in prestigious professional business.

"I believe Mr Wheel is at a conference," I said.

"What's a conference, Miss?" Nando looked at me with an innocent expression.

"A conference is where important teachers go," I said.

The class looked thoughtful. Then Chantelle grinned.

"I bet he ain't really at one of them conferences, Miss. I bet he's in the funny farm."

"Nonsense!" I snapped.

"You ain't allowed to say 'nonsense' to us," Bradley retorted. "That means you fink we're thick."

"Of course I don't think you're…"

"Yes, you do miss! You hate us. Well, we don't like you either."

"Don't be silly. Now, let me tell you about the work you have to do."

"No fanks!"

"That's quite enough rudeness! Now, just listen up…"

Mmmmmmmmmmmmmmmm…

And that was how it started. They'd obviously planned it. Today, the death hum, tomorrow it would probably be water bombs. And now someone had farted, causing Desmond to break off from his humming to protest in the loudest possible terms, glaring at the possible offender (it was almost certainly Rizwan). I walked briskly around the room, slapping a piece of A4 paper down in front of each pupil. Then I picked up a board marker, and, being careful not to turn my back on the class, wrote the words *Name* and *Date* on the whiteboard.

"What we gotta do?" Chantelle demanded.

I said nothing, but pointed to the words on the board. A moment later, the Honey Monster began to write, the tip of his tongue appearing between his teeth as he attempted to carry out the instructions. The rest of them continued to stare at me blankly.

"I ain't got no pen," Bradley announced.

"You know perfectly well that you should always bring a pen...."

Mmmmmmmmmmmm!!

Oh, good grief. Annoyed at having been caught off my guard so easily, I gave Bradley a cold stare. Then I turned back to the board. *'Turn to page 33 of the text book'* I wrote. *'Read the information in the box and then answer the questions. Draw a picture if you finish early. N.B. Anyone without their own pen will be penalised i.e. Bradley 2 debit points.'*

"Miss, I can't read your writing," Chantelle objected. She blew out a large, pink balloon of bubble gum that popped around her mouth, leaving a sticky circle of gunge. "Can you read that out loud to us?"

I shook my head at her and smiled, putting as much evil triumph into my expression as I could muster.

"Cow!" Chantelle muttered.

I wrote her name on the board, and added the note *'1 debit point'* underneath.

"Double cow," Chantelle commented.

2 debit points.

"Triple c..."

"I don't get it, Miss," Desmond twanged his bendy ruler.

"Ain't got a pen," Rizwan whinged.

"*'I don't like Mondays...'.*" sang Nando.

I handed Rizwan a pen and wrote some more observations on the board: *'I don't like Mondays either. Get on with your work and shut up, you little beasts!'*

I sat down at the teacher's desk. Chantelle frowned, her lips moving as she read the words I'd written on the board. Then she gasped with exaggerated indignation.

"I'm going to report that!" she announced, "That's racist what you writ!"

"And sexist!" said Nando.

"Calling us 'nanimals ain't right," said Desmond.

I stared serenely at the class. Eventually, Rizwan and Nando began flicking through their books, apparently in a desultory attempt to find page 33. It occurred to me that this part of the task could take them a considerable time, since neither of them could count past twenty. I looked at my watch. It was now 9.15 a.m. Forty-five minutes to go. Oh, what torture.

"I don't get this work, Miss," Desmond O'Leary said. "I don't see the point of it."

I flipped open the teacher's copy of the *Key Stage 3, Personal and Social Educational Programme Citizenship Module* that was lying on the desk in front of me. On page 33, underneath a photograph of a man of swarthy appearance crouched on the floor of a squalid room while two white police officers manhandled him, was the caption: *How do you think the man in the photograph feels about his situation? What might he be thinking? Write a response to this stimulus.* Well, it seemed that for once, Desmond's judgement was right. I wasn't sure I got the point either. Wouldn't some solid facts about legal aid be more useful?

I stood up, added the words '*Just do your best*' to the instructions on the board and then began walking around the classroom. Bradley picked up his pen and began doodling on his paper. Nando, I saw, was adding a large, erect penis to the photograph of the man. I looked down at the Honey Monster's work. His big, childish handwriting was only too decipherable: *This bloke is probly an ill eagle immingrunt. I hope the pleece gives him a good kicking.*

Hmm. I had the feeling that this wasn't the required response and wondered if I ought to introduce the Honey

Monster to a more liberal train of thought. I supposed he was only echoing the views that he heard expressed at home, probably from his mother, a large woman with tattoos and a tanning-studio suntan who'd attacked Angie Hucknall at parents evening and called her a leftie bitch.

"I'm gonna write a play," Chantelle announced. "I'm starting with what the man on the floor's saying."

"How do you know what he's saying?" Nando demanded. "It's a picture, innit?"

"What I *fink* he's saying, geddit?" She glared at Nando, "And I fink he's saying, 'Yo bruv, don't be disrepectin' me none!'"

"Well, Chantelle." I remembered from the *Practical Guide* that a good teacher should always be offering positive reinforcement. "That's really quite good. You're using colloquial speech in a vivid way and..."

Mmmmmmmmmmmmmm!

"Oh, for crying out loud!" I picked up the white-board rubber and brought it down sharply on my desk. "That's enough!"

Mmmmmmmmmmmmmmmmmmmm

"9X, you can stop this now!"

Mmmmmmmmmmmmmmmmmmmmmmmmm

"It's a silly game and...."

The humming had suddenly stopped. It seemed too good to be true.

I looked at the class with suspicion. Were they planning to launch into something more horrible now, perhaps a physical attack? Or had I really gained control over them at last? For a split second, I congratulated myself on my classroom management. Then I turned, and saw A.R.L standing in the doorway. Damn the man! He'd hijacked my pitiful authority once again.

"Good morning, class." ARL eyed 9X with a glimmering firmness that suggested he'd be taking no prisoners if any disruption began again. "We've met before, haven't we? When that police officer escorted you back to school on Friday. I hope you all remember what I said to you then."

"Yes, sir. Good morning, sir." It was a miracle. 9X had been transformed into a group of Botticelli cherubs. I could almost see their wings.

"Now, as you can see," A.R.L continued, "Mr Wheel isn't here for your lesson but you're lucky to have Miss Harker here to help you. Now, I'd like you to work quietly and sensibly, and do you best. Will you do that for me?"

"Yes, Sir. Safe, sir." Several heads nodded eagerly. The bloody man had them eating out of his hand.

"Good. Then everybody get on with the work, please," he said.

I watched, infuriated, as Nando began scrubbing furiously with a broken piece of rubber at the phallic artwork he'd created only minutes earlier. He wasn't the only one who was suddenly stricken with guilt. I was very much afraid that at any moment the keen eyes of A.R.L. would light upon the words 'little beasts' in my handwriting on the whiteboard. I stood up and positioned myself carefully in an attempt to conceal the damning evidence.

"Can I have a word?" ARL murmured in my ear. "We'll just step outside for a second."

"Oh, but I don't want to leave the class." I backed up against the board.

"We can keep an eye on them from the corridor. If you don't mind..."He gestured towards the doorway.

"OK. "I made a grab for the board cloth and held it behind my back. Then I made a desperate swipe at the board, hoping I'd hit the right spot.

"Is something wrong, Miss Harker?" A.R.L looked bemused.

"Of course not." I swallowed. This was crazy. I must look a complete fool, wriggling around in front of him. "Please lead the way."

"As you wish." He turned on his heel and went out into the corridor.

We stood next to an ancient display of torn and faded anti-smoking posters designed by some Year 7 pupils.

"So," I said, determined not to meet A.R.L's eye, but focusing on a gruesome drawing of a blackened lung instead. "How can I help you?"

"I attempted to introduce myself to you when we met on Friday," he replied. "Perhaps you will allow me to do so now?"

"If you really think that's necessary, although actually I...."

"I am Aidan Langford. I'm here in a consultative capacity and in the absence of the Head Teacher, I am in complete charge of the school."

"Complete charge?"

"Yes. And I can assure you I've been sent here by the highest authority. I need to talk to you on an urgent matter. I can't go into the details now since you need to return to your class. I'll see you in my office at ten o'clock. I understand you will be free then."

"Yes, I am." My heart sank. "But I'm afraid I don't know where your office is."

"It's on the top floor of the new admin. block, far end of the corridor."

"Right." I nodded. I was imagining how satisfying it would be to thump him. Why must he wear that well-cut suit and smell of such enticing cologne and walk around the school having such a calming effect on the most obstreperous of pupils?

"Then I'll see you later then, Miss Harker. Please be punctual. I require your cooperation in this matter." He turned on his heel and walked swiftly away. The bastard! The absolute bastard! 'The highest authority'. What a pompous git.

9X were still scribbling furiously. Some of them had even turned their pieces of paper over and were writing on the second side.

"Good," I said. "I see that you *can* all behave when you choose. So keep it up, please."

"That's because we *like* Mr Langford," said Nando. "We don't like *all* teachers."

"Do you fancy him, Miss?" Chantelle asked. "You went all pink when he came in."

"Miss has got the hots for him!" Bradley grinned.

"Mr Langford is the best-est teacher in the school," the Honey Monster announced.

"Shut it!" Nando threw his ink-rubber at the Honey Monster, hitting him squarely in the middle of his forehead. "Who asked you—loser!"

"*Loser! Loser! Loser*!" Desmond and Rizwan took up the chant, banging on their desks and putting two fingers up.

"That's enough all of you!"

Mmmmmmmmmmmmm.....

Damn. Back to square one. I picked up the marker, and wrote '3 debit points for everyone' on the whiteboard, and sat down again, trying not to give in to the impulse to bury my head in my hands.

There was no doubt about it. This *was* the job from hell.

Fourteen

He Will Rise

Josh was leaning against the wall behind the fire-escape, smoking a large and suspiciously pungent cigarette. I was glad to see he hadn't lost his zest for dangerous living, but nevertheless, I was dismayed by his appearance, so different from his usual, ebullient self. His face was tinged with a greenish pallor, his injured arm was in a sling and his general demeanour was depressed and defeated.

"Oh, *Josh!*" I exclaimed. "You look terrible."

"Thanks." He smiled wanly.

"You know I didn't mean it as a criticism," I said. "What I really meant was, are you sure you should be in school?

"Almost certainly not." He took a puff of his reefer. "I still feel like crap."

"Oh, poor you. I was really worried when Zelda told me they kept you in hospital. Whatever happened?"

"First they couldn't stop the bleeding, then I had a bad reaction to an injection they gave me. I was out of it for hours. Delirious"

"Delirious? What on earth was this injection?"

"I'm not sure. It wasn't an ordinary tetanus jab, I know that. The doctor I saw seemed to think there was a risk that the man who attacked me might have been carrying some disease. Something with a long, Latin name. I've forgotten what. So they gave me this injection, and it was bloody awful, this great long needle, straight into my stomach—oh, sorry, you don't want all the gruesome details."

"It's OK." I winced inwardly. "And what was Jen Fowler doing while all this was happening?"

"Oh, she wasn't there. She'd dumped me at the triage desk and scarpered long before that."

"Typical of her! And what about the police? Have they caught this man?"

"They won't even be looking for him. I haven't reported the incident."

"Why not?"

"What would be the point?" Josh shrugged.

"But he might attack someone else. It sounds as if he was deranged."

"Oh, he was bonkers all right, completely out of his skull. He came out of Chalk Farm Station making this weird sound. Like I said before, I thought of *King Lear*, '*Howl, howl, howl, howl, howl,*' difficult lines for an actor to deliver, but this old guy certainly gave them some welly."

"He was howling?"

"Like a wild beast," he grinned ruefully. "Then he sank his teeth into me."

"Grief! And didn't anyone help you?"

"Not a soul. All these commuters just pushed past me to get into the station. Anyway, it was really foggy, I'm not even sure any-one saw, or if they did, they didn't want to get involved. Like I said, I didn't even realise I was bleeding until I got into school. And then...well, you know what happened. Thanks for the First Aid, Dora, you were brilliant. And now I feel bad about dropping you in it with this Langford man, telling him you were with 9X."

"That's OK. If you hadn't, no doubt Jen Fowler would have done it. But I can't believe he phoned you up at home! Couldn't he have waited until Monday? Did he even *bother* to ask you how you were?"

"Oh, he did say something about filling in an accident report, but when I told him the attack happened off school premises, he lost interest. At least he doesn't know about the other stuff."

"What other stuff?"

"I'll show you. But I'm swearing you to secrecy. The drama department is under enough of a cloud already."

"Kids have broken in here before." Josh unlocked the door of the drama studio. "But usually, all I find are a few empty crisp packets and coke cans. But *this* is something else." He switched on the light.

"*Oh!*" I clapped my hand over my mouth and nose, half-choking on the smell, part butcher's shop, part urinal, part something unspeakable from the sewers. "Good grief!"

"Yes, it is a shocker," Josh agreed.

"That's not a real pig's head, is it?" I glanced up at the hideous thing that was swinging from the ceiling, accompanied by the buzzing of flies.

"It's real, all right," Josh assured me. "But most of the blood's a stage effect. I keep a stock of fake gore for when we do the Scottish play."

"The Scottish play? Do you mean Mac...?"

"Don't say it, Dora." He held up a warning figure. "You must know the superstition. I don't want to tempt fate. Whatever's been going on in here is bad enough."

I gazed at the torn curtains, the graffiti, the improvised altar built from stage blocks, the naked mannequins arranged in various suggestive poses, the black candles, the goat skulls, the upturned crucifix, and the words 'HE WILL RISE' scrawled in red chalk across the carpet. "But surely," I said. "This is just a stage set?"

"I thought that at first," Josh said. "I assumed my Year 11 GCSE group had got carried away. But then it occurred to me that even my Year 11 group would have known that a play that involved peeing all over the carpet, throwing fake blood everywhere and leaving a turd behind the curtains was unlikely to earn them an 'A' grade from the exam board. Besides which, they're doing *An Inspector Calls*. Does this look like the set for *An Inspector Calls* to you?"

"No," I said. "Unless it was a very avant-garde production."

"The Birlings enact a Black Mass after supper?" Josh suggested. "Well, you might get away with that at the National Theatre, but the exam board tends to be rather more conservative." He picked up one of the goat skulls and stared into its hollow eye sockets. "And there's another thing. Apart from the fake blood, none of this stuff is from my props cupboard. And I've seen my Year 11s, the only group who are trusted with a key, and they swear they didn't rehearse in here on Friday afternoon. No, I think all this must have happened over the weekend."

"Look, Josh, I feel really bad about this, I should have stayed with 9X and made sure the room was locked up properly at the end of the lesson."

"Oh, but it was locked. That's why no-one else has seen this today. Anyway, it's not your fault."

"I'm glad of that," I said. "By the way, are you coming to Kris's Kebab House for lunch? I'm meeting Zelda there."

"Hope so, provided I'm finished at the hospital by then."
"The hospital?"

"Yeh. Got to go back, outpatients, at eleven, for another injection. They told me I'd got to have a whole course for a month."

"Oh, *Josh*!"

"Don't worry about me! I'll be fine. See you later then. Good luck and don't let the bastards grind you down!"

The sign on the door read *A. R. Langford, Sentinel Services Ltd.* I took several deep breaths. I'd had to climb four flights of stairs to get here. It seemed strange that ARL had chosen to establish himself in this eyrie, away from all the chaos below, but perhaps it was symbolic of his high and mighty attitude, seeing himself as superior to the common throng.

I peered through the door's glass panel. There he was, sitting at his desk in his shirt sleeves, tapping with furious concentration at a keyboard in front of a large computer screen. And what an austere room it was, all gleaming white walls, and minimalist furnishings, just two moulded plastic chairs in front of the desk, and a complete lack of personal effects, not a photograph, picture, pot plant, collection of mugs or coffee making equipment to be seen. I knocked; he looked up with a frown.

"Come in." There was nothing in the least welcoming about the way he issued this curt instruction. I walked in, trying to appear as bold and unconcerned as possible.

"Please sit, Miss Harker."

"Perhaps if you're about to bollock me, I'd better stand."

I'd tried to make this sound like a light-hearted riposte, but the moment I'd said it, I knew my attempt at humour had misfired.

"There's no need for that kind of language." He continued to frown at me. "Now please take a seat."

"Right." I sat.

"Now." He picked up a pen. "I understand that you were the teacher who was supervising 9X before they disappeared from the school site last Friday. But I also know that weren't on your own with them."

"That's right. There was the man from..." Oh dear, I wasn't going to be able to say it without laughing. "There was a visiting speaker, a kind of workshop leader."

"The man from TOSSA?" His frown deepened.

"Yes." I suppressed a giggle.

"Why are you laughing?"

"I'm not. I'm really not. It's just...*TOSSA*. It sounds so..."

"I'm glad you find this funny." The irony was heavy. "Because I'm afraid you may be guilty of a serious infringement of our duty of care."

"Really?" I was astonished. "But they were working so well with him and..."

"Did you check this man's I.D.? And more importantly, did you stay with the class for the duration of the lesson?"

"Well, no, I..."

"You *didn't* stay with the class?"

"No. The man said he was a qualified teacher, he seemed to know what he was doing and..."

"Describe this man."

"Um...he was quite muscular, about five foot ten, blond hair, pony tail, Australian accent, sun-tanned, in his thirties, he was wearing shorts, he said his name was Tel..."

"I see." He threw down the pen. I noticed that there was a little, bloodied nick on his jawline, where he must have cut himself shaving. Ha! So he wasn't perfect! "So you admit behaving in a manner that was completely irresponsible."

"Irresponsible? But how..."

"Miss Harker, I have to inform you that this morning, the school received a phone call from the Social Skills Advisory Service conveying their apologies on behalf of their representative who had been unable to keep his appointment on Friday. It seems that the man you in left in charge of 9X was an imposter."

"An imposter? Oh dear." How was I going to bluff my way out of this one? Now that I came to think of it, Tel never actually *said* he was the man from TOSSA. "But he seemed very competent."

"Whoever he was, you should have stayed with the class. Any adult entering this school has to undergo certain checks and it's quite clear this man had no authority to be here. And at some point, possibly during this lesson, but certainly after you abandoned them, the class left the school premises while we were legally responsible for them. And Darren Dalston underwent a distressing ordeal."

"Darren Dalston?" I was puzzled for a moment. "Oh, you mean the Honey Monster!"

"The Honey Monster?"

"It's his nickname." I could feel the laughter bubbling up again. ARL's manner was so freighted with righteous indignation that I couldn't help seeing the funny side. "Haven't you seen that old TV ad, it must be on YouTube, where some kids run over a hill, chasing a big furry, lumbering creature? When Darren Dalston tries to run, he looks just like the monster, he's got the same coloured hair and he has that kind of wobble and..."

"Stop right there, Miss Harker!" He held up his hand. "Your attitude is highly unprofessional."

"I'm sorry. It's just that..."

"This isn't a laughing matter. Perhaps you might like to know that I spent a considerable amount of time with

Mrs Dalston over this weekend, doing my best to persuade her not to sue the school."

"Oh dear." I tried to look suitably admonished. "But I heard the rest of the class left the Hon...I mean Darren, plenty of food."

"Junk food on which he gorged himself, making himself quite ill." Aidan Langford's frown was now so deep and rigid it might have been carved out of Easter Island rock. "Did you know he was on a special diet?"

"No, I didn't, but that sounds like a good idea. The poor kid needs to lose weight."

"The diet I'm referring to concerns his allergies, not his need for weight loss."

"Oh." I bit the inside of my cheek in a frantic effort to control myself. I couldn't help it; the more disapproving A.R.L. became, the more I felt like screaming with laughter.

"Can you *please* take this seriously, Miss Harker."

"Yes. Yes, of course." I clenched my fists, driving my nails into the palms of my hands.

"Anything could have happened to that class while they were absent from school premises. They could have been playing chicken on the railway line, one of them could have fallen in the canal or they could have been lured away by a stranger. I was hoping you might share my concern for a group of vulnerable pupils."

"Vulnerable? 9X?" I wasn't going to stand for this. "They're the most evil bunch of kids ever!"

"I can't have you say that."

"Why not?" I wasn't laughing now, I was furious. "Look, I've had enough of this. I'm not happy with the way you're talking to me. You should be glad that *any* supply teacher stays here. I've worked my socks off at this place and now you're treating me like an offender. I'm sorry if I made a mistake, but I wasn't to know. Have you any idea what it's like to be a supply teacher in this school? When I arrived here, no-one told me anything, I was just pitched into the nearest classroom and told to get on with it. No-one helps, no-one supports me and that's because everyone else is at the end of their tether. Since coming here, I've had to stand in for sick teachers, stressed-out teachers, teachers who've been driven to nervous breakdowns, teachers who've abdicated, and, in the case of Mr Pugh, one who was caught flashing at small boys up on the Heath!"

"That's enough!" He slapped the flat of his hand on the desk.

"Don't shout at me," I said.

"I'm not shouting!" he bawled.

"Yes, you are!" I yelled.

Neither of us spoke for a moment. The silence seemed loaded with mutual antagonism.

"And stop frowning at me like that," I added more quietly. "It's not intimidating me in the slightest."

He glared at me. Then he slumped forward and put his head down on the desk.

"I'm not trying to intimidate you." His voice emerged as a mumble. "If I *am* frowning, it's because I've got a splitting headache and the light's hurting my eyes." His shoulders shook. For one dreadful moment, I was afraid he was going to burst into tears.

"Hangover?" I suggested.

"Migraine," he muttered.

Despite myself, I felt a pang of sympathy. Who were Sentinel Services and why had they sent one man all on his own to clean up this terminally dysfunctional cess-pit of a school? It hardly seemed fair.

"Would you like some codeine?" I asked. "I've got some in my bag."

"No, thank you." He opened his desk drawer, took out a pair of Ray-Bans and slipped them on. "Miss Harker, could you just go now, please?"

"You mean, leave the school?" I swallowed.

"No. Just leaving my office will do." He gazed at me from behind his dark glasses, inscrutable and unforgiving. "For now," he added.

Fifteen

Return of The Prodigal

"So, you've had your second punch up with Langford." Zelda dipped her pitta bread into the taramasalata, scooping up a generous portion. "But it sounds like you got the better of him."

"Not sure about that." I gazed at the brightly painted mural of the Acropolis on the wall behind her. "He's probably plotting to get rid of me right now."

"He'd have to be an idiot if he is. I've never known a supply teacher stick it out at Havelock Ellis as long as you have. You deserve a medal."

Kris's Kebab House was a tiny restaurant tucked behind the old engine sheds in Engel's Crescent. It wasn't smart, but the service was quick, the food was cheap, and there was something comforting about the stained tablecloths, the threadbare carpet, and the somewhat limited loop of bazouki music that meant you were likely to hear *White Rose of Athens* and *Never on a Sunday* at least five times in the course of one meal. It was an unassuming place, perfect for grabbing a temporary escape from the chaos of Havelock Ellis.

"I bet you," Zelda continued, "he'll be out on his ear first. The staff won't stand for it. What about Mr Randle? He thought he was about to be made Acting Head, and instead, this man swans in and starts laying down the law. This won't end well, believe me." She bit into an olive. "Ah, here comes Josh. Josh, over here!" she waved enthusiastically. "We've saved you some dips and I've got some amazing news. Dora was married to Dave Dellow of Chappaquiddick. Can you imagine that? *Chappaquiddick!*" She threw her arms up in the air, yelling so loudly that the several people turned to stare.

I put my hands over my face and tried not to groan. This was just the kind of public exposure I'd been dreading for years.

"Awesome," Josh said. "That is really awesome."

"You're looking better than you did earlier this morning, Josh," I said. I was anxious to change the subject but the fact was, he did look better. He'd positively bounced up to our table, a huge grin on his face.

"I *do* feel better," Josh said. "I saw a different doctor at the hospital and he's given me a clean bill of health. No more injections! And now I'll really feel great if I can get some red meat inside me." He clicked his fingers at the waiter. "Costas, plate of lamb kebabs, please!"

"Josh?" Zelda stared at him. "I thought you were a vegetarian?"

"Oh, I've given that up!" He reached across the table, picked up the carafe of water and drank straight from it noisily. "Who wants to live on lentil bake and leaves? Anyway, never mind that, I want to hear about Chappaquiddick. Dora, why didn't you tell us about this before?"

"Josh, I'm sure if you'd asked for a glass..."

"Ooops, sorry, wasn't thinking." He put the carafe down. "But Dora, about the band..."

"I really don't want to talk about it."

"Look Dora," Zelda said. "I do realise this is a painful subject for you, but you *should* talk about it. Suppressed emotion isn't good for you."

"I didn't know either of you would have been interested."

"Really?" Josh's eyes widened. "But I *love* Chappaquiddick. When I was thirteen, I hated my step-father and he couldn't stand me. You know what got me through? The rough, raw music of Chappaquiddick. I had only one weapon against my step-dad. My CD of *Pussy's in the Well*. I locked myself in my bedroom and played it night and day. He hammered on my door but he couldn't get in. And I felt...invincible." He flexed his arm above his head.

"I'm glad it helped," I said. "But I really don't like revisiting this stuff, sorry."

"And I can understand how awful what happened must have been for you," Zelda said. "But sometimes it's better to confront things."

"I don't want to confront anything," I said. "I've put it all behind me. Every so often, someone tracks me down, a music journalist, usually, and they want an interview, and I always refuse. And then, about ten years ago, some people asked me to join them on a candle-lit vigil at the place where it happened. Such ghouls!"

"Were they ghouls or did they just want to pay tribute?" Zelda asked. "Think of it as a legacy, right? Despite the tragedy, the music lives on."

"Music? It wasn't music!" I was losing it, and I knew it, but just couldn't stop myself now. "If you want the truth, in my opinion, Chappaquiddick was the most cacophonous,

127

most excruciating, most ear-drum busting band in the known universe!"

"Oh, Dora, how can you say that?" Josh sounded appalled.

"I say it because for me, it's true. It was Dave I loved, not the band. Oh, I liked the other guys, but I always felt Dave was too good for them. I'd always hoped that one day he'd go solo, or join another group, but he was so loyal, so unambitious. And if he hadn't been in that band, if he hadn't been there that night, then maybe he'd still be...he wouldn't have been..." I bit my lip.

"Oh, *Dora.*" Zelda leant across the table and touched my hand.

"Have you got any of their unreleased material?" In his excitement, Josh seemed to be oblivious of my distress. "Are still in touch with Dingo? Is it true that he told the inquiry into the accident that he saw...?"

"Leave it, Josh!" Zelda sounded a warning note. "Let's not go there!"

"No," I agreed. "Let's not."

"Sorry." Josh looked contrite. "But the thing is," he persisted, "if you do have any memorabilia, I'd love to see it. Oh, great here come my kebabs!" His face lit up as the plate was put in front of him.

I was experiencing a mixture of emotions. Josh's current behaviour was insensitive to say the least, but I'd encountered this kind of thing before on the few occasions I'd run into a Chappaquiddick fan. And that story about his step-father had been rather touching. I remembered the box of tapes, up in my loft space. There didn't seem to be much point hanging on to it. Why not give it to someone who'd appreciate it?

"I think I might have some unreleased material, as a matter of fact," I said. "If I can dig it out, you'd be welcome to it."

"Wow!" Josh pulled a lump of grilled lamb off a skewer with his fingers and thrust it into his mouth. "That would be fantastic." He tore at another piece of meat. "Dora, you rock!"

Then he threw back his head and let out a wild, howling whoop. It was good to see that his hospital treatment seemed to have worked, even if it had made him a little manic.

The theme music from *Buffy the Vampire Slayer* was thumping out from the living room as I returned from school that afternoon.

"Exquisite! Superb!" I heard Ralphie exclaim.

It appeared that he'd discovered satellite TV. There he was, dressed in his lemon silk dressing gown, elegantly stretched out on my sofa with the remote in his hand.

"Ah, forgive me, dear lady." He stood up and bowed. "I should have asked your permission but I am just enjoying a well-earned interlude from my studies. And I did appreciate that!" He turned off the TV with a flick of the remote. "I know so little of popular culture."

"You enjoyed it?" I must have sounded surprised.

"Indeed I did," he assured me. "Although those American high school accents were difficult to understand. And the events were completely inaccurate, of course. All those Night Wanderers dissolving into clouds of dust the moment they were staked. That could never happen."

"Couldn't it?"

"Of course not. Do you know what would actually happen if someone was inconsiderate enough to drive a stake through one's chest?"

"I imagine it would be very painful."

"Indeed it would." Ralphie sat back on the sofa. "The wound would fester for months, possibly years, and the poor Night Wanderer would suffer endless agonies. There would be no instantaneous release. But let me not dwell on morbid matters. I shall certainly watch some more of this drama, if I get the opportunity, if only to feast my eyes on the fair-haired one."

"You mean Buffy? Sarah Michelle Gellar?"

"No, no, no!" He fanned the air in of vehement denial. "Not the *girl*. I am referring to the ravishing man in the red shirt and the superb black leather coat."

"Oh, you mean Spike."

"Yes, Spike!" Ralphie looked wistful. "Such cheekbones! He reminds me of someone I used to know. Poor Klaus. " He took a silk handkerchief from his pocket and dabbed at his eyes. "I do hope you don't let your younger son watch this programme, by the way, it's far too disturbing in places. Where is your son, by the way?"

"Caspian's been staying with a friend," I said, "But he should be home tonight. Oh, hell. What's that?" I bent down and examined the edge of one of the rugs.

"What is what, my dear lady?" Ralphie was still staring into the middle distance, lost, I could only assume in visions of Spike and Klaus.

"Something's been spilt...oh, and it's under the rug too." Lifting it up, I found a pool of green, scummy liquid. It looked thick and glutinous, rather like washing up liquid, except that unlike washing up liquid, it was giving off a semi-phosphorous glow.

"Ah!" Ralphie murmured, looking down.

"Well," I grabbed hold of a sheet of newspaper and laid it over the wet patch. "That should soak it up, whatever it is. I just hope it's not rising damp."

"Something *is* certainly rising," Ralphie observed. "Oozing, in fact, and I'd suggest rising damp is the least serious explanation. The disturbances are widening. Like ripples in a pond. We must keep a careful eye on this situation."

"Must we?" I moved the rug to one side. "Well, I can't worry about it now. I've had another hard day at school, I'm off to unwind."

I lay back in a luxurious froth of cranberry and juniper bubbles, resting my head on the crocodile-shaped bath pillow that Seb gave me for my birthday. I was so hoping that he'd be coming home for the Hallowe'en weekend. He could take Caspian trick or treating, and then later, we'd have a takeaway and watch a few DVDs. Seb wasn't really into European classics, preferring action and car chases, but he was always willing to let me choose the film. Sometimes we'd watch a horror movie; we were probably the only people on the planet who'd laughed all the way through *The Blair Witch Project*.

Oh, how lovely to be able to pamper myself like this. The boys used the top floor shower room, so this was my haven, filled with fluffy white towels, bath oils, perfumes, novelty soaps, tubs of cocoa butter, gels, and defoliating scrubs. Thank goodness it was now Cynthia-free!

The soothing sound of Albinoni, courtesy of Classic FM, was coming from the radio, (a waterproof one shaped like a penguin in a striped bathing suit, one of Seb's presents). Three vanilla-scented aromatherapy candles were flickering on the window sill. I'd recently hung a new mirror above the wash basin. It had a wooden frame decorated with a hand-carved relief of scallop shells and angel fish. Peregrine hadn't seen that mirror yet. He wouldn't like it when he did, but that was just too bad. This was my space now.

I reached for my sponge, a beautiful, real sea-sponge that I'd bought in the market, but it wasn't in its usual place on the edge of the bath. I looked around, and saw that it had fallen down between the basin and the WC. Damn! In a moment, I'd have to step out of this lovely warm water to get it and... *oh!* Now I'd seen something horrible.

There it was by U-bend; a cobweb, and not just an insignificant, wispy cobweb, the kind that could be flicked away in an instant. No, this was a thick, horizontal shelf that must have made by a very large house spider, one that could be lurking right here in my bathroom, waiting to put in an appearance. And here I was, vulnerable and naked.

Shameful as it might seem to others, I have a real problem with spiders. I've been known to go into a clammy sweat at the sight of a relatively small one. I knew that wasn't an old web since I'd cleaned the bathroom thoroughly after Cynthia's departure. So where was it at this moment, the spider that had created it? Lurking behind the U-bend? Hiding under the bath? Or crawling down the tiles on the wall behind me? Grief!

With a frantic splash, I leapt out of the water, grabbed a towel, shook it out vigorously, and then wrapped it around me. Then I made a thorough examination of the bathroom, looking around the rim of the bath, then the wall tiles, and finally, forcing myself to peer round the back of the basin and under the bath. Then it occurred to me that I hadn't looked up at the ceiling. That was where spiders usually chose to position themselves, didn't they, clinging on with their horrid little sucker feet? Once I'd been lying in bed and I'd seen a massive spider, immediately above my head, and I'd screamed and it had dropped and....*no!* That wasn't a memory I wanted to revisit.

Bracing myself, I looked up. No spider. There was, however, a disturbingly complex crack in the plaster. Cynthia, I thought, bitterly. She must have caused it, filling the room with all that steam, turning it into a Turkish bath. But wouldn't it have taken more than a little steam to damage the plaster like that? It wasn't a superficial crack. It looked like a serious structural problem.

Please let it not be subsidence! I remembered the surveyor warning Peregrine about London clay drying out during hot summers and how the south side of Arcadia Square was the most vulnerable, possibly because the post-war developers had cut corners in some way to make a quick profit. If only we'd been able to afford one of the older, period houses on the north side of the square.

I blew out the candles, turned off the radio, put on my bathrobe and slippers and went out on to the landing. Oh no! Here was another long crack, across the wall this time. What on earth was happening? I'd have to ask a qualified builder to come and take a look; perhaps there was the name and address of one in the household file. I pushed open the door of Peregrine's office.

Good grief! What an overpowering scent of *pot pourri*. And what an extraordinary transformation the room had undergone. Green velvet curtains with gold silk tassels were hanging in place of the grey Venetian blinds. Peregrine's desk was covered with an embroidered green silk cloth and the filing cabinets were draped in yellow velvet. Palms, ferns, aspidistras, and several other plants with a dangerous, carnivorous-appearance were standing in big Italian pots around the room; the shelves were laden with blue china cups and plates and vases containing peacock feathers and sunflowers. There were other things too; a stuffed owl, a hookah, an ivory skull, a pewter candlestick, an ormolu

133

clock, and several decorative art nouveau plates. Elegant coats, cloaks and hats were hanging on a bentwood hat stand in the corner. A gentleman's leather travelling case, complete with hair brushes, manicure items, bottles of pomade and fragrances was lying open on a small walnut wash-stand. A Turkish rug and some cushions had been placed on the floor; there was a stuffed armadillo, a winged arm chair covered in a red brocade fabric, an elephant's foot umbrella stand, and a fire-screen covered in lacquered images cut from the Strand magazine.

So Ralphie had made this place his own. I couldn't imagine how he'd managed to move all this stuff in here but I was certain Peregrine would go ballistic if he saw it all. That was a very satisfying thought.

I lifted the yellow cloth, pulled opened the top drawer of the filing cabinet and began searching through the A4, pastel-shaded cardboard files, all labelled in Peregrine's fussy, over-neat handwriting. They were in alphabetical order: 'Council Tax', 'General Household', 'Insurance', and 'Guarantees'. I took out 'General Household', and began leafing through it. Nothing here about suitable builders. I put the folder back, closed the filing cabinet and was about to leave the room when I noticed an ancient-looking tome lying on the floor, held open by an object that resembled the mummified limb of an animal, possibly some kind of ape. Intrigued, I knelt down over the book and began to read:

'Part the fifth: 'A treatise on the Demon Asmodeus, he of the fishy fume.

'And whatte saye ye of Asmodeus, he who depiseth the Assyrian sheat-fish and loveth the newlie wedded bride? I saye that he walketh amongst us and woulde stille have thee powere to maime and kille, the soothsayer answereth. He is

not one but many. He dyeth not, but lusteth after virgins and married women. First he came outte of Persia and he meeteth Kinge Solomone and help builde the Temple, then he boasteth of marring the lives. "I hatch plots against newly-weds. I mar the beauty of virgins, causing their hearts to grow cold," saith Asmodeus. Only the Archangel Raphael, accordinge to the scriptures of the ancients, didde ever succeede in truly routing the demon, when he didde burn the fish liver on an altar in the wilderness, to save the girle Sarah whose bridegrooms the demon had slaine for that he wished to enjoy the girle himself. Ffishe do repell the demon, he aborreth it and cannot abide it, and thus he did flee into Babylon, driven off by the smoke. Asmodeus maye enjoye many women after whom he lusteth, and he is cunning. You will knowe him by his.... My reading was interrupted by the door-bell chiming out the *Dead March in Saul.*

"Ralphie?" I called out to him as I ran down the stairs, "I know I said I didn't want *Knees Up Mother Brown*, but that didn't mean I preferred some dreadful..."

Da, da, da-da, da de...

"All right, I'm coming!"

He stood on the step, a symphony of black. Tight black trousers. A black T-shirt. Black boots. Black gloves, adorned with spiked metal claws. Black, spiky hair, with a lock falling emo-like over one side of his forehead. Black lip gloss and deep, dark eyes, rimmed with kohl. In stark contrast, his face was whiter than death, his expression solemn, detached and unblinking. He was mysterious, unknowable, and alien.

"And who have we here?" Ralphie asked, coming up behind me in the hall.

"Ralphie," I said, my heart stirring with its customary maternal anxiety. "Meet Caspian."

Sixteen

The Beautiful Dead

After twelve years of bringing up Seb, my sunny-natured, uncomplicated, sporty first son, Caspian defied all my maternal expectations. I knew, from the moment of his birth, that he was going to be disturbingly different. I'd never seen such unblinking solemnity, such knowing intensity, in a baby; there were times when I almost doubted if he was a baby at all but rather some kind of changeling or extra-terrestrial visitor.

As he grew older, his predilection for the dark side became increasingly marked and I quickly learned that he had little interest in simple childish things. Before he was born, I'd papered his room with cheerful images from the *Babar the Elephant* books, but at the age of two (and I swear he *was* only two), he informed me he was too old for 'anthropomorphic pachyderms'. His eyes shone as he watched the villains in children's cartoons; his favourite films were *The Nightmare before Christmas* and the *Night on the Bare Mountain* section of *Fantasia*. The death of Bambi's mother left him unmoved. Deer, he remarked, after seeing the film, needed to be culled or they'd cause too much damage to trees. At four, he begged me to take him to the Chamber of Horrors and the London Dungeon.

At fairgrounds, he only ever wanted to ride the ghost train and while other children screamed in terror, he cheered with delight. And now he insisted on dressing as a Goth. And he was still only eight.

"Cas?" I stood on the threshold of his bedroom. "What do you fancy for your tea?"

"Whatever you decide will be acceptable." He continued to tap at the keyboard of his laptop, studious, composed and, as ever, detached and distant.

"How about pizza?" I suggested.

"Home-made?"

"Of course."

I glanced over his shoulder, hoping he wouldn't notice I was checking up on his activities. The image on the computer screen seemed harmless enough, a river, probably the Amazon, flowing through the rain-forest, but ever since that dreadful business at Blasted Oak, I'd felt apprehensive whenever he was surfing the web, this son of mine who, I feared, was capable of circumventing every parental control and firewall in the entire cyber-world.

"Can I have plenty of black olives and anchovies on it?" He clicked on the mouse.

"Yes, I think I can manage that."

I glanced up at the ceiling; oh dear, those hairy plastic spiders hanging from the coving were a bit much, although, I reminded myself, they weren't entirely realistic, since massive South American bird-eaters tend to stay on the ground. He must be in the process of decorating his room for Hallowe'en, although it was always Hallowe'en in Caspian's room. The walls were painted black and the shelves were crowded with black candles, pewter goblets, gargoyles, and Mexican Day of the Dead figurines. A poster of Max Shreck as Nosferatu was blu-tacked to the back of the door and Boris the bat was in his prime position on the bed.

"I've been thinking." Caspian turned to face me. "I'd rather like to keep piranhas. I'm sure you won't object."

"Piranhas?" I repeated. "But surely they're not the kind of fish you can keep at home? Aren't they river fish? Don't they need a huge tank?"

"Not necessarily," he informed me. "And plenty of aquariums supply them. You can get all varieties, red-bellied ones, Caribe piranhas, black piranhas, and there's one particular type called a piraya. That's a very good variety. They're particularly vicious, but fine if you handle them properly."

"Handle them?"

"I don't mean literally." I thought I detected a slight edge of scorn in his voice. "I meant, if you don't stick your fingers in the water."

"Right." I decided it was better not to argue at this stage. "But just how much do you know about looking after piranhas?"

"Plenty. I've done the research."

"I see. Well, I'll have to think about this. And I'm not sure your father would like it."

"But we don't have to do what he says, do we?"

"I'm afraid we do. This is his house."

"It ought to be our house. Why isn't it?"

"It's complicated." I suppressed a sigh. "Right then. Pizza, it is."

I was in the kitchen, mixing the dough, when I noticed another cobweb, a huge one high up in the corner by the window frame. *Oh, hell.* What on earth was happening? If only Seb was here. If there were any live spiders lurking around the house, he'd soon deal with them. One autumn, he trapped a huge hunter with visible fangs in a clean pickle jar and walked all the way to the top of Primrose Hill before releasing it just to ensure it would never darken our home again. Dear, supportive, common sense Seb, my open-faced son who'd never caused me a moment's anxiety. I was seized by the conviction that if Seb came home, all the cracks and the cobwebs and the strange visitations would just disappear and life would return to normal. No ghosts, no astral travellers, and certainly no vamp...

"Ahem!" Ralphie appeared in the doorway. "I hope I didn't startle you, dear lady. You seemed lost in your thoughts."

"I was just....no, no, it's fine." I looked away from the cobweb.

"Allow me to observe how much I have enjoyed conversing with young Caspian. He is a remarkable boy. And his grasp of Latin is impressive. I understand he goes to a private school."

"Yes, Netherwold. It's a school where they encourage individuality."

"A perfect choice for the boy I'd say." He nodded. "Now, I've just come to inform you that I am on my way out. I need to check in on Georgia at the Lord Halifax, and I believe I may have left certain books there that it would be prudent to consult. I don't wish to alarm you, but I fear that something untoward is on the move."

"Something untoward?" Oh good grief, what now?

"I'm afraid so. That green slime in the living room is not a good sign. I hope there will be no further incursions tonight but I strongly advise you to secure all the windows and on *no* account should you attempt to remove the Mandala of Raphael from the front door."

"I can't leave it there forever. My ex-husband will be furious if he sees it."

"I expect he will," Ralphie purred. "That's rather the point."

"I don't understand."

"To put it bluntly, I believe that your ex-husband, Mr Peregrine Deadlake, may have something to do with the disturbances you are experiencing here."

"Peregrine? But why would he want cracks and green slime to appear everywhere?"

"Oh, he wouldn't want it, but it *could* be a side effect."

"A side effect of what?" I reached in the cupboard for a tin of anchovies.

"At this moment, I don't feel at liberty to say. More research is necessary, and, I'm afraid, I will need you to tell me more about the gentleman. Do you know what prompted him to buy this house?"

"He said it was a good investment."

"Did he now? *Hmm.*" Ralphie looked thoughtful. "Well, I must be on my way, but let me assure you, I have everything in hand. I have encountered cases like this before, and although they are complex, they are not insoluble. Good night, dear lady!"

I was lying on a makeshift raft that was being tossed around on a black, oily sea. The sky was livid red with dark thunderclouds racing across the horizon, and now a vast shape was moving towards me. For a moment it seemed to be a ship sailing to my rescue, but then I saw that it was Havelock Ellis High School, floating on the water, and there was Peregrine at one of the windows, gazing down at me with a supercilious expression. *Help*, I shouted, *hel*p, but he simply laughed at my predicament.

"You'll get nothing from me, Dora, you brought this on yourself," he said.

"You bastard," I yelled. "You utter, utter....*aaagh!*"

I opened my eyes with a start. Oh hell, what a ridiculous nightmare. I must be more stressed than I realised and to think I'd come to bed early to try and get some rest. And how *dare* Peregrine invade my subconscious? I felt furious. But what on earth had Ralphie meant when he said that the disturbances in the house might have something to do with...

Wotcha, girl.

Oh! Had I really heard it, that husky whisper, as gentle as the September dew on Hackney marshes? I must be still dreaming. It just wasn't possible. There was no way *he* could be here.

"Wotcha, girl."

"Davey?" I was trembling. If this was a dream, then it was a good one. One I'd wanted for twenty years. I stretched my hand out towards my bedside light.

"Don't do that, girl, I ain't ready." His voice sounded stronger now. "Too much light and I might be gawn."

Gawn. I could hardly breathe. I'd always adored the way he spoke. His accent was of the same provenance as that of Nanny Barrel Hips but while she sounded raucous and aggressive, his dropped h's and glottal stops had always seemed soft and sexy to my ears.

"But I want to see you!" My heart was thumping.

"You'll see me in a minute. But don't get up. You have to stay where you are. We can't touch each other or nothing. Sorry."

"Oh, Davey, where are you?"

"Lift your 'ead and look towards the window. Can you see me now?"

"Yes," I breathed.

I could hardly believe it, but he was there, and it was real. He looked so gorgeous, doused in the orange street lighting leaking through the chink in the curtains, his blond hair fanning out in the slight breeze from the open window. He was standing in his characteristic pose, thumbs hooked into the belt of his denims, shoulders back, his gaze direct and honest. Every detail that I'd cherished, those fabulous, sculpted cheekbones, that generous mouth, the eyes as blue as a swimming-pool, five feet ten inches of staggering physical beauty that might have been chiselled out of Carrara marble by a Renaissance master. Dave Dellow, the boy I met in Dawlish, the boy I married, the boy who was destined to stay twenty-two forever.

"Is it really you?"

"Yer, it's me." He nodded.

I wiped a tear away as surreptitiously as I could. Dave never liked excessive displays of emotion. He was the strong, silent type, an East End lad of the old school, and yet capable of great tenderness. The most considerate lover any woman could have. I didn't know what to say; I had so many questions and yet I hardly knew how to ask them.

"How have you been, Davey?" I said at last.

"Fine," he said. "Apart from being dead, of course. I find that rather a bloody nuisance."

"It's more than a nuisance. It's..."

"Don't upset yourself, girl. It can't be helped. So, how's the kid? Me son?"

"You know about Seb?"

"Course I do."

"He's not a kid any more, Davey. He's at university."

"Cor, fancy that." He sounded surprised. "Don't take after me then. I mean, he must have brains. Doesn't the time go fast? Last time I saw him, he'd just been born."

"You saw him? But you were already…"

"Dead? Yeh. I'm sorry about that. But there it was. I tried to talk to you, but you were spark out. But I managed to into the 'orspital, and I saw you on the bed, and he was beside you, in that little cot on wheels."

"*Oh.*" I felt as though the lump in my throat would choke me.

"But after that," he looked rueful, "I couldn't seem to come back. Not until now, that is. I'm not sure how I've managed it this time, to be 'onest. Some people can do it easily, but it's taken me a while to get the hang of the trick. Sorry about that. I always struggled with stuff."

"You didn't struggle, Davey," I said. "You played the guitar like a genius, and you made love like an angel. And now," I added sadly, "I suppose you are one."

"Not me." He grinned. "Anyway, what would I want with a bleeding 'arp?"

"Oh, *Davey,*" I giggled. "You haven't changed. You could always make me laugh. It's so good to see you again."

"It's all right seeing you too," he said.

Neither of us spoke for a moment. It was one of those comfortable, loving silences that we used to enjoy. So much of our communication had been non-verbal, purely physical in fact, but it had never seemed to matter.

"I expect you think I was daft, getting meself killed like that," he said.

"It wasn't your fault. You weren't driving. But I don't blame Dingo either. Oh, Davey, I've got to ask you this. You see, at the inquest, Dingo said…"

"You mustn't dwell on it, girl. It's water under the bridge. No good crying over spilt milk. What's done is done. You make your bed and you lie on it. No point being a dog in the manger. Worse things happen at sea. A bird in the hand is worth two in the bush. You've got to row, row, row your boat swiftly down the stream. When your cup's half empty, it's really half-full, ignorance is bliss, when you come to the end of a perfect day…"

"Davey, oh, please stop!"

"What's wrong, girl?" He sounded perplexed. "Ain't I making no sense?"

"No, no, it's not that." I saw to my consternation that he was becoming increasingly transparent; the wardrobe door was clearly visible through his chest. "It's just that I have to ask you…"

"I know. I'm talking rubbish." Dave grinned. "It's a funny thing but being dead makes you do that. There's all this stuff floating in your 'ead and you can't get the words out. But it was always like that with me, wasn't it? I was thick and you were clever. All that stuff you'd been studying, all those books you had, about *Battleship Potemkin* and the films of Ingmar Bergman, who wasn't the same person as Ingrid Bergman you said, and you knew about tracking shots and what the gaffer does, and the best boy and even what a focus puller is, and…oh sorry, I've gone off again, haven't I, and I *did* have something important to tell you. Only I can't quite remember what it was, no, wait, it'll come to me in a moment."

Now he was fading like an old photograph that had been over-exposed to sunlight.

"Oh, Davey!" I leaned forward, anxious not to lose sight or sound of him. "Davey, stay here! I've got a question, it's important."

"Sorry girl. I've got to go." I could hardly see him at all now.

"You have to stay. Please, you must try!" All I could see was the vaguest outline. The bedroom seemed to be filling up with mist.

"Listen." His voice was fainter. "What did you go and marry that bloke for? The one who owns this gaff? I didn't want you to live like a nun, after I was gawn, but you could have done better for yourself."

"It was a mistake." I bit my lip. "I didn't need anyone else. There could only ever be you."

"But I'm dead, girl, it's no bleeding good. Here, it's coming back to me, I had a message for you, henbane, you've got to get some henbane..." His voice was echoing as if it was coming from the bottom of a fathomless well. "And that night, I remember now, I said to Dingo....watch out for that tree... henbane....don't forget the...henbane..."

"Davey, never mind the henbane, what about the tree!" I was desperate to keep him with me; he had to explain this.

"Funny way for a tree to behave, I never saw a tree before that could do that."

"The tree? That's it! The tree....Davey! Davey, wait! Tell me what you saw, this is import..."

A car backfired out in the street, and then there was silence. He was gone. And now I was feeling my loss all over again as the memories came flooding back.

Seventeen

Death of a Guitar Hero

"So what have you been doing since I saw you last?" Stacey
Warrington yelled over the roar of Ken the Chin's motorbike
as we bucketed down the Great West Road.

"Not a lot," I shouted back.

This wasn't strictly true. It was, in fact, fewer than ten
days since my acrimonious split from Colin Shuttlehanger
but I didn't feel like going into the details with Stacey, who
knew nothing about my disastrous wedding. For one thing
there was the possibility she'd be miffed that she hadn't
been invited and for another, she might laugh at the whole
sorry tale.

"I've been having a boring time too," Stacey said.
"Working in Woolies is no fun."

I winced at the pressure of her weight. We were squeezed
together in the sidecar, Stacey sitting on my legs and our
luggage on her lap. Not only was the situation uncomfortable,
it was probably against all safety regulations, especially as
Ken the Chin's mate Carlotta was riding pillion with his
rucksack stuffed with illegal substances.

It was odd, being with Stacey after all this time; she'd
phoned me up completely out of the blue, asking me to
come along on this trip. I still wasn't sure why I'd agreed to

it, except that after the disappointments of my so-called honeymoon, I fancied a summer adventure.

I'd been friends with Stacey during our first three years at secondary school and then she'd moved out to Reading with her mother; after that, we'd exchanged Christmas cards and the occasional holiday postcard, but we ceased to be close confidantes. Auntie Pam was relieved; she'd never cared for Stacey, who lived on a Council estate and whose father was banged up for GBH. Stacey had bushy brown hair, smoked, was on the pill from the age of twelve and always copied my English homework. It was Stacey who told me, as we hid in the stock cupboard of the Domestic Science department, illicitly eating the dried fruit and sticking our wet fingers into the jars of sugar, that you should always close your eyes when kissing a boy and make liberal use of your tongue. She also told me that if you saved up ten thousand bus tickets, London Transport would give you a Route-master of your own and that you couldn't get pregnant if you did 'it' standing up. I admired Stacey's fearless approach to life even though she frequently got me into trouble. On the other hand, her friendship was also a strong protection from the bullies who hung around the bike sheds at Brondover Girls School. And now here we were, heading for Devon, with two dangerous-looking leather-jacketed boys I barely knew.

"Do you really think we can trust them?" I'd asked her, suddenly getting cold feet at the last minute.

"What? Ken the Chin and Carlotta?" She rolled her eyes at me, as scornful of my qualms as she had been all those years ago when she'd encouraged me to break into the biology lab to steal two white mice. "Of course we can! They're sweet blokes!"

I didn't share Stacey's confidence. Neither of them looked particularly sweet to me. Ken the Chin, so named because of his Hapsburgian protuberance, was a six foot two, fifteen stone amateur wrestler and brick-layer. Carlotta, whose real name was Carl, was a sinuous, six-foot male who spent most of his time chewing on a matchstick. He rarely spoke and then only in monosyllables. His usual response to any situation was to look at the ground and mutter *'rats!'* He knew, Ken the Chin assured us, where to get 'good grass', and he was great fun when 'rat-arsed.' I had yet to see him 'rat-arsed' but after a couple of pints in the pub, I got the distinct impression that Ken the Chin had unwelcome designs on me.

"Where in Devon d'ya wanna go?" he asked as he strapped on his crash helmet.

"How about Dawlish?" I said, remembering a British Rail poster of a gorgeous amber swathe of beach, a vivid blue sea and cliffs resplendent with semi-tropical vegetation.

Ken the Chin must have wanted to please me in his Cro-Magnon fashion, since he duly set off for the destination I'd suggested. We stopped once on the journey, in order for Ken and Carlotta to relieve themselves in a roadside hedge. When we arrived in Dawlish, we found the place enveloped in a sea-fret. Stacey and I emerged, cramped and bruised, from the confines of the sidecar and checked into a ten pound a night B. and B., while Ken the Chin and Carlotta announced their intention of sleeping on the beach.

An hour or two later, we met them at a pub at a place known as the Warren. The large bar area was crowded with people in their late teens and early twenties; apparently a live band was booked to play there that night. Ken and Carlotta slurped back Newcastle Brown, and Stacey and I sipped Dubonnet with ice and a slice. Stacey had changed into a backless, silver lame dress and a pair of high heeled sandals. I was wearing a Laura Ashley skirt and a white blouse, and had made up my face with care, including the liberal use of lipstick in a shade known as 'Courtesan red'. I felt simultaneously eager to have a good time and determined to repel the advances of Ken the Chin.

"You're a bit of a miserable cow, aren't you?" he said, putting his arm around my shoulders and breathing beer into my face. Perhaps this was his idea of seduction. I attempted to wriggle away from him along the fake leather banquette.

"Rats!" Speaking to no-one in particular, Carlotta spat out his matchstick.

"Gawd, what a tosser!" Stacey pointed to a middle-aged man with a quiff of grey hair who had come up to the microphone on the stage beside the bar. A pair of silver-grey curtains shimmered behind him; there was a mild air of expectation in the room.

"Boys and girls, ladies and gentlemen." The man spoke into the microphone. He was interrupted by a sharp whistling sound as the PA system threatened to malfunction. "This group of lads have just signed a recording contract. They're going places."

"Oh, yeh?" Carlotta was clearly unimpressed.

"You're in for a special treat tonight." The man with the quiff beamed at the audience. "So put your hands together and welcome the band. It's...." There was a drum roll and another whistle from the PA system, "CHAPPAQUIDDICK!"

Someone from behind the curtains shouted "Mind my fucking foot!" as a cymbal crashed. Then the shimmering curtains parted, there was a flash of coloured disco lights and a white-faced youth with dusty brown dreadlocks ran forward and grabbed the mike. He was wearing baggy, slashed jeans and a faded grey T-shirt. He shook his shoulders, and then, jerking spasmodically, he began to sing through a mouthful of uneven teeth:

"Mother Hubbard, Mother Hubbard, why is your cupboard bare?

Open your door, give me more,

Mother Hubbard, you're a whore, whore, whore!"

His movements suggested a person afflicted with some dreadful palsy and his voice, raucous, urgent and anguished, added to the impression of pain. Behind him, a spindly, hunch-shouldered man was playing the drums and nodding his head in time to the beat. On his left, a boy with a shaved head was making sounds using a variety of strange devices; sink plungers and bits of lead piping, one of those children's whirly tubes and a hand-held vacuum cleaner. I didn't know them then, of course, but later I would know exactly who they were. Dingo Potts, Loon Tailor and Mad McArthur.

"Don't see how we're going to bop to that," Stacey wrinkled her nose in disgust.

"*Rats,*" Carlotta agreed.

"Shall we go outside?" Ken the Chin placed his hand on my knee.

I was hardly aware of the intrusion. Everything around me, the tacky stage, the crowd in the bar, Ken the Chin, Stacey and Carlotta, had receded into an irrelevant blur. It was as if I couldn't hear or see any of them. I was too busy staring unashamedly, in an ecstasy of admiration and sheer unadulterated lust at the person who had just come on to the stage. The guitarist.

"I said," Ken the Chin moved in closer. "Shall we go?"

"Excuse me." I thrust him aside, got to my feet and pushed my way to the front of platform. I couldn't wait a moment longer. I had to be there. I had to get *him* to see *me*.

There he stood, blond, beautiful and godlike. And I, for the first and only time in my life, I had fallen in love at first sight.

I stood there, applauding wildly at the end of each number, but, it seemed, to no avail. But then, just as the set ended, he knelt down at the edge of the platform, and looked me straight in the eye.

"Wotcha, girl," he said.

If any other young man had greeted me like that, it might have seemed casual and opportunistic, but it wasn't, not in the way he said it, so soft and intimate. I noticed the tiny, v-shaped scar just under his left eye; it was the sexiest thing in the world. And I felt as though we'd known each other for a long, long time.

"Hi," I said.

"Want to go for a walk on the dunes?" he asked.

"All right," I said. I tried to sound casual, but my heart was racing.

We sat down on the sand. Marram grass tickled my cheek.

"What's your name?" he asked.

"Dora. Dora Harker," I told him. I had reverted to my maiden name. There would be no more 'Shuttlehanger' for me.

"I'm Dave," he said, "Dave Dellow. Cor—if you married me, you'd be Dora Dellow. 'Ow about that?"

It seemed entirely natural that he was talking about marriage. He leaned towards me. Then a coarse, unearthly cry fractured the night.

"What's that!" I jumped.

"It's just an old mad beach donkey." He put his arm round me. "What did you think of the band?"

"I thought *you* were brilliant.Chappaquiddick, though, it's rather an odd name, isn't it?"

"Is it?" he frowned, "We used to be called Nagasaki, then we was Gangrene, then Dingo changed it to Chappaquiddick."

"All in very bad taste," I giggled.

"Why's that then?" He stroked my arm.

"Those names," I said.

"How do you mean?"

"Well, Nagasaki is where they exploded an atom bomb, gangrene's a flesh rotting disease, and Chappaquiddick was where a girl died in an awful accident in the sixties."

"I never knew that. Dingo said it was a place in America."

"It *is* in America. That's where it happened. Senator Edward Kennedy's car went into the water and a girl drowned, Mary Jo Kopechne."

"You know a lot of stuff." he said "First I've heard any of this. I thought Nagaski was food you had with noodles. And gangrene—well, that's the colour of me mum's curtains, you know, like lime green, sea green, gang green…"

"Oh, oh…." I started laughing and then I stopped because he was kissing me.

I'd never known anything like it. It wasn't as though I'd never been kissed before. I'd experienced every form of kissing at silly teenage parties. I'd had dry kisses, wet kisses, tongue wrestling kisses, kisses where teeth unfortunately clash, shy kisses and cursory pecks, sex-mad kisses and kisses that tasted of nicotine and cheese and onion crisps. But Dave's kisses were entirely superior to any of that. I'd just found the world's most expert and wonderful kisser, and as an added bonus, he looked like a Greek god.

There was no point in resisting destiny. The next day, I abandoned my college course, wrote an apologetic letter to Uncle Horace and Auntie Pam and went on the road with Chappaquiddick.

I was in heaven, even though I had to put up with the company of Loon Tailor, Mad McArthur and Dingo Potts.

Sleeping in the van was uncomfortable, and so was going without a shower for days. It wasn't healthy, living off a diet of booze, fags, Coca-Cola and chips. I had to listen to the rambling conversations between Loon and Mad McArthur and endure bitchy comments from the groupie girls that Dingo picked up along the way. They never liked me, those girls, because I had my hands on the best looking and only monogamous guy in the band, and I longed for them all to go away.

Every warm summer night, Dave and I made love, after those gigs where Dingo urged the band into a frenzied climax, shaking his dreadlocked hair and rasping out his twisted nursery rhyme lyrics: *Cut off their tails! Cut off their tails! Cut off their tails with a carving knife!* Dave and I fell upon each other in meadows, on haystacks, in long grass, in parks and on waste land, in forests and down by the river by the reed beds, by gorse bushes and once even on a newly mown cricket pitch. There's nothing like love in the open air, even if you do get bitten by mosquitoes and find squashed spiders on your skin, and run the risk of picking up a tick and getting that awful disease that ticks spread. Except that none of those things ever happened as ours seemed to be a charmed life.

Dingo, I realised, was the driving force behind the band. He'd recruited Loon when they were fourteen and then they'd met Mad McArthur when they were playing at a holiday camp in Pwellhi (a place which Dingo pronounced 'Pure helli', claiming that was an accurate description). McArthur was a semi-alcoholic, Loon Tailor always wore the same pair of jeans and a red T-shirt, and had only two fingers on his left hand, and Dingo's personal hygiene left a lot to be desired. His clothes appeared never to have been washed, and his hair, I was convinced, was lice-ridden, but he wore his dreadlocks and his abnormal pallor with pride. His expertise, if that really is the word, consisted of arranging the lyrics to the so-called 'music'. I say 'arranged' because Dingo never wrote any original material, but simply adapted nursery rhymes, and jokes he'd read on toilet walls:

"He kills cornflakes! He kills cornflakes!
Cereal Killer! Cereal Killer!"

Cereal Killer made the charts at number fifty-four after John Peel played the record very late one night when only insomniacs and truckers too stupefied with cholesterol to take anything in were listening to the airwaves. It was that song that prompted Kumquat records to offer the band the contract for the album, *Who Killed Cock Robin*. And then it seemed everyone was quoting those lyrics:

"I said the sparrow, cos your eyes are too narrow…"

And then Dave asked me to marry him.

"First you marry a man with no balls, and now you've married a man with no brain," Uncle Horace told me over his third glass of fizzy white wine at the wedding reception. "Dora, I despair of you."

He said this with a twinkle in his eye, and I tried not to mind, although I thought he was being unfair. It wasn't Dave's fault he hadn't had much education and I found his simplicity touching. What did it matter if he didn't know the names of any film directors, or even that films *had* directors, if he'd never read a book, apart from the reading primers he'd been given in the Remedial department at school, if he didn't know whether the Tudors came before the Plantagenets or whether it was the other way round? He believed that the sun went around the earth, that God had a long white beard and that Elvis Presley had been the King of America, sitting on a throne with a crown on his head in a palace called Graceland. What did I care? I loved him. He was angelically beautiful and he was good and kind and gentle.

My guitar hero and I found a small flat in the London Borough of Havering over a TV rental business, and next door to what was described as a 'Quality Fishmongers'. The quality fishmonger, Mr Jowls, was in the habit of loping down to a shed at the end of a long narrow garden where he smoked his own haddock and kippers and he had a rubbish tip piled high with fish guts, fish heads and flies. The smell was intolerable, especially in warm weather, but we didn't care. We were too happy. And then, without warning, in the worst possible way, it was all over.

It began just like any other day, except that I woke up feeling queasy and dizzy. The band had a gig that night, somewhere up near Huntingdon, but I couldn't face all that bumping around in the van along country roads, coming back late at night, after three hours in a smoke-filled venue, not when I was feeling so sick. And so Dave set off without me.

I went to bed early. I remember thinking I was glad Mr Jowls was on his annual holiday. The shop was locked up, and he hadn't been around to smoke his herrings and haddock for several days. If I'd had to put up with that fishy stench, it would have been intolerable. I had no idea why I was feeling so ill, unless it was something to do with the kebabs we'd had last night. Eventually, I went to sleep and I dreamt about Gertie, of all things, the way she'd waved that branch at me and muttered her dire predictions: *Never marry again and be happy, never be happy...* Then I heard Dave's voice.

"Sorry to leave you like this, girl," he said. "Especially with you up the duff an' all."

I opened my eyes with a start. Up the duff? Was that it? Was that why I felt so odd?

I picked up the bedside clock. It was ten minutes to midnight and at that exact moment, although I didn't know it, there'd been a collision and the van had landed upside down in a ditch on a lonely fenland road. Dingo had lost his sanity, Loon Tailor had lost his ability to walk, and Dave, my beautiful Dave, had lost his life. With only Mad McArthur left unscathed, for the simple reason he hadn't been in the van at the time, the touring days of Chappaquiddick were over.

Eighteen

The Uses of Henbane

I stood at the sink, slowly sipping a glass of water. Half past three in the morning, a ridiculous time to be up. I'd feel wrecked later, but there was no going back to sleep, not after what had just happened. Not after what I'd just heard.

"Funny way for a tree to behave, I never saw a tree before that could do that."

Oh, good grief, I had to get my head around this. That's what Dave had said and as far as I was concerned, it could only mean one thing and it was mind boggling. Now I knew for certain that Dingo hadn't been lying when he made his statement at the inquiry into the accident. He hadn't been crazy, or hallucinating while on drugs. Some people had even suggested he'd dreamt it, after falling asleep at the wheel. I never thought that; I'd always suspected he'd been telling the truth. And now I knew for certain. Dingo *had* seen what he said he'd seen, moments before the crash. There could be no doubt about it. *Because Dave had seen it too.*

"I sense there has been another visitation?"

"Ralphie!" I spun round, spilling my water. "Please stop doing this! I never even heard you come in."

"Apologies, dear lady. I came in quietly, so as not to disturb anyone. I thought you might be in bed. But here you are."

"Yes. Here I am."

"And you have a pensive air. More than pensive, I think, quite moved. I have the impression that something significant has happened." He peeled off his white evening gloves. "You have seen an apparition. Am I right?"

"Yes. How did you know?"

"Psychic disturbances leave a trace in the ether that those of my kind can pick up immediately. And may I ask who..."

"It was Dave." I felt very bleak, admitting this. I doubted if he'd ever come again and yet I also knew how frustrating it would be if he did. We were never going to touch each other again, we were never going to make love on a beach, or in a hayfield, or anywhere else. '*I'm dead, girl, it's no bleeding good.*'

"Ah!" Ralphie spoke softly, folding his gloves carefully and placing them in the pocket of his overcoat. "I suspected that more of your past would come back. It must have been a very poignant meeting."

"It was."

"And...Forgive me if I'm intruding, but did your late husband give you any special message? Something you could share that will help me combat the demonic forces that are attempting to converge on this house?"

"Demonic forces?"

"Alas yes. I fear the Mandala of Raphael will only protect you for so long. The front door, after all, is only one portal amongst many. Did your Adonis impart any advice?"

"He did. But what he said didn't make much sense."

"Are you sure? I think you should tell me."

"He said I should get some henbane."

"Henbane! Ah!" Ralphie nodded sagely. "On the contrary, it makes perfect sense."

"But I don't even know what henbane is!"

"Henbane is a poisonous plant of the nightshade family, *Hyoscycamus niger,* recognisable by its light green flowers and hairy leaves. As well as having a dangerous effect upon domestic fowl, it is a vital ingredient when fighting evil. Henbane will provide excellent protection. Gather some at once and place it around the house, on window sills, by the doors, around sky-lights and loft openings, everywhere that can be considered a threshold. It will help."

"I see." I considered this. Perhaps I really had been given some practical advice. "And where do I find it?"

Ralphie thought for a moment.

"Don't go to Homebase," he said. "The wild variety is better for repelling demons. It is best gathered by moonlight, but dusk will do. The last time I saw some growing, I was up on the Heath, on a little pathway that leads from Kenwood towards the Spaniards Inn."

"That's near Caspian's school. I could certainly pick some from there. But this seems..."

"Nonsensical? Trust me, it is anything but. Always take great notice of communications from behind the veil. Was anything else said, may I ask?"

"Well, since you mention it, there was one thing....it's to do with what he saw, just before he died. Something that Dingo saw too. But it's a really painful story...I'm not sure I can..."

"You can trust me."

"Yes." I sat down at the kitchen table. "I believe I can. So, Dave was in a band, and the other members were Dingo, Mad McArthur and Loon Tailor. Not long after Dave and I were married, the band had a gig out in East Anglia and on the way back, there was an accident. Except it might not have been an accident. The official story is that the van hit a tree. But at the inquiry Dingo said..."

"What did Dingo say?" Ralphie was looking very solemn.

"I've never forgotten it. Dingo was white and shaking, his arm was in a sling, he was on the verge of a breakdown. But he was so very clear. No, he hadn't fallen asleep at the wheel. No, he hadn't been drinking. He was driving along a straight, narrow road with ditches on either side. The moon was full. He'd been humming to himself, working out the rhythm for a track for their next album. There were willow trees along the side of the road. And then...." I swallowed. "And then, Dingo said, a weeping willow heaved itself up and walked out of the ditch on its muddy roots straight on to the road in front of him. He hadn't hit that tree. The tree had hit them."

"A Rusalka." Ralphie looked thoughtful. "An arboreal demon that attacks on dark, lonely roads. And now you know that Dingo wasn't the only person who saw it."

"Yes. And it confirms what I've always feared. Gertie, with her witchcraft and the curse she placed on my life, was the person who raised it."

"Hmmm." Ralphie looked thoughtful. "Certain parts of East Anglia were once infested by such entities. There was a warlock in the 1850s known as Cunning Mitson who claimed to have power to make trees walk although no eye-witness ever corroborated his claim. I have absolutely no doubt that such phenomena exist. But I find it difficult to believe that such a primitive rural witch as Mrs Shuttlehanger would know how to summon a Rusalka."

"But who else could it be? The band *was* travelling through East Anglia," I said. "And when I looked at the map to see where the accident happened, I realised that Slodger's Farm was only two miles away."

"Then it's a possibility, I suppose." He nodded. "Tell me, what happened to the oddly named Dingo after the accident?"

"He had a breakdown. Now he lives with his mother in Leigh on Sea and he spends most of his time making weird garden statues out of plaster of Paris using a bread knife. I visit sometimes. I've always told him I don't blame him for the accident. That it wasn't his fault. And now, I'm afraid it was mine. If I hadn't insulted Gertie by destroying that manikin..."

"You mustn't think like that. And as I said before, Gertie's words to you that day could have been a prophecy rather than a curse. Now, my researches have led me to certain Biblical sources. Are you familiar with the *Book of Tobit*?"

"I can't say that I am."

"Then I suggest you familiarise yourself with the story of the Archangel Raphael and the demon Asmodeus. And, as well as the henbane, acquire some fish."

"Fish?" I wasn't sure I could take any more. My head was spinning.

"Yes, fish. Freeze it, and then when the time comes, we can burn it on a makeshift altar if the need arises."

"An altar?"

"Yes. In case of the return of Mr Peregrine Deadlake."

"Oh..." My head was spinning. "I'm sorry, I don't think I can any more in tonight. I'm tired...I have to go to work in a few hours...."

"Of course. Good night, dear lady. And rest assured, I am on the case, as they say."

I snuggled down under my duvet. All this was so surreal. Cobwebs, cracks, slime...fill the deep freeze with fish...read an obscure book in the Old Testament...gather henbane.... What on earth was happening here? I couldn't take it all in, but now I came to think about it, the fish wasn't such a bad idea. Peregrine was allergic to fish. If for any reason he came back to the house and found fish here, he'd freak out completely. Ha! Here was my chance to fight back against all the agro he'd subjected me to over the years. Perhaps I'd let Caspian keep those piranhas after all.

Nineteen

A Mission Statement

Zelda was in her usual place in Oddballs Corner, surrounded by the familiar debris of dirty mugs and tattered exercise books, her feet resting on the coffee table as she leafed through the appointments section of the *Times Educational Supplement.*

"Hi, Dora." She looked up as I approached. "I've just seen a brilliant job advertised in here. It's in Papua, New Guinea. Think I might apply." With a cynical laugh, she flung the paper to one side. "Or failing that, I could always get a job in a chip shop. Would you believe I've been here for twenty years? Let that be a warning to you."

"Are you seriously looking for another job?" I sat down on one of the vomit-orange chairs.

"Probably not." Zelda shrugged. "Sometimes I fancy a change and then I realise that it might be just as bad somewhere else. I'm not the kind of person who gets promoted. Anyway, it might be interesting to stick around at Havelock Ellis for a bit and watch the fireworks."

"Fireworks?"

"There are bound to be fireworks now we have our so-called trouble-shooter. Anyway, what are you doing here?

You're a supply teacher; you don't have to stay after hours for the torture of a Havelock Ellis staff meeting."

"I received a memo from A.R.L. saying all teaching staff had to be here, even temporary ones."

"Hah! That's him all over!"

"Quite. On the other hand maybe the meeting will be interesting." I glanced towards the far end of the staffroom, where Angie Hucknall and Jen Fowler were busy re-arranging the chairs into rows, much to the annoyance of those who were being asked to break up the informal groups in which they were settled. Mr Pickering, a geography teacher with a permanently flushed appearance, was standing by the tea urn talking in a loud voice to Mr Randle, the man who, according to Zelda, had expected to be made Acting Head Teacher. McTaggart was also sounding off to anyone who would listen. '*After–school meetings...general cock-up as usual from the Governors... time to call in the union...*' Some plates of biscuits had been placed on the table next to the urn. "*I'm not going to be softened up by a few custard creams!*" I heard a middle-aged woman in a hand-knitted cardigan exclaim as she parked herself at the side of the room and began attacking a pile of marking with irritable efficiency. As more and more staff drifted in, the atmosphere of discontent became increasingly obvious. I overheard fragments of conversation. '*And then he said...Would you believe that! The bastard! Bloody cheek! Obviously overpaid if he can afford a suit like that...*'

"He's only been here three days, and already everyone hates A.R.L.," Zelda said. "Mark my words, the moment he walks through that door, there'll be a massacre. And the arrogant sod deserves it. Anyway, on a different note, have you seen Josh today?"

"No, I can't say I have."

"Neither have I. I hope he's OK. I'm worried about him."

"Are you? I thought he looked fine yesterday when we met him for lunch. Although actually...yes, I know what you mean."

"Quite. He was behaving oddly, very oddly. He's always had plenty of energy, but there was something manic about the way he was bounding about. And he wolfed down that meat, which considering he's supposed to be a vegetarian seemed particularly..."

"Good afternoon, colleagues." Silence fell as A.R.L. otherwise Aidan Langford, entered the room. He was wearing his usual expensive-looking suit, but this time with an azure-blue linen shirt, quite a heavenly shade, I thought before pulling myself up with a jerk, reminding myself that this was the man who'd already annoyed me twice. Staff who'd been walking around chatting to others quickly found chairs but Mr Pickering remained standing by the tea urn.

"Is this going to take long?" he demanded, striking a gladiatorial stance. Mr Pickering had a reputation as a bully and a heavy drinker, and on one infamous occasion he'd hurled a pupil across a classroom, an incident that the union rep. had managed to smooth over with considerable difficulty. Now, he looked eager to crush another opponent.

"An interesting inquiry, Mr Pickering," Langford smiled at him. "The short answer is that the meeting will take much longer if staff attempt to interrupt with irrelevant questions uttered in an aggressive manner. Now, please take a seat."

Mr Pickering breathed heavily. He opened his mouth, as if about to utter a cutting retort, then, having apparently decided to keep his powder dry for the moment, he gave a heavy snort and sat down in the front row, folding his arms and continuing to glare at A.R.L.

"Before I get to the main purpose of this meeting," A.R.L. said, "I should inform you that Mr Wheel has decided to take early retirement. He's been advised by his doctors not to return to the school. There will, of course, be a collection for his leaving present; the envelope is in the school office and there's a card for everyone to sign. I'm sure you will all want to wish him well."

"Will we?" The woman in the hand-knitted cardigan looked up from her marking. "And what gift do you propose we give him for his send-off? The chocolate tea-pot award?"

Angie Hucknall's shocked gasp was followed by an outburst of general laughter, the loudest guffaws coming from the P.E department.

"Well said, Veronica!" Paul Gogarty slapped his thigh.

"And just think of the golden handshake he'll get from the Borough," Mr Randle added. "Thousands of pounds for a man who couldn't organise a piss-up in a brewery."

"Good riddance!" I heard someone yell.

"Stop it!" I shouted. "This is horrible and unkind."

There was more laughter and a wild shriek of derision from Jen Fowler. I felt my cheeks warming; I had no idea why I'd called out like that. I didn't know Mr Wheel, he'd left on sick leave before I arrived, and I had no particular reason to spring to his defence. Everything I'd heard about him suggested that he did, indeed, deserve the chocolate teapot award. And then my stomach flipped over as I realised just who it was I was defending from this horde of jackals. And it wasn't Mr Wheel.

Aidan Langford's face was deathly white but when he spoke, his voice was steady and assured. Controlled anger, then, rather than fear. Yes, he could look after himself.

"Yes, please desist," he said. "There'll be no more of this behaviour. I'm more than a little surprised to find it seems to be the custom here for people to call out in a meeting without raising their hands and being invited to speak. In future, hands will be raised, but only when I've finished speaking and asked for comments, not before. However, I will make one exception to that rule. If you wish to finish your contribution to this meeting, Miss Harker, I will hear you. I see that your hand *is* now raised."

I got to my feet.

"I apologise for calling out," I said. "Let me introduce myself My name's Dora Harker, although most of you, apart from my friends, Zelda and Josh, don't seem to know that and just call me 'the supply teacher'. Which quite frankly, is rather insulting, considering I've been here for weeks." I shot a semi-venomous glance in Jen Fowler's direction. "I just wanted to say that this is a very difficult school and it's no laughing matter if someone becomes ill because they're working in a perfectly awful environment. What if Mr Wheel was doing his best? What if he started out as a young teacher, full of ideals and then it all went wrong for him and then...I'm sorry, I've no idea what I'm talking about, except I'm thinking it might better if people could be more kind."

I sat down, feeling like a complete idiot. Jen Fowler was gazing at me with undisguised contempt.

"Thank you." Aidan Langford said. "Miss Harker has a point. A little kindness goes a long way."

"Teacher's pet," Zelda muttered in my ear. "What's come over you, Dora?"

"I don't know," I muttered back.

"And that," Langford continued, "is the keynote of the approach I intend to initiate in this school. It needs an injection of love."

"Love!" Mr Pickering thrust his clenched fist into the air. "What kind of twaddle is this?"

"Mr Pickering," Langford looked at him coolly. "What part of 'no more interruptions' did you not understand? You don't have the right to ignore my requests."

"Blimey." McTaggart had the sense to keep his voice low.

"To continue," Langford said, "there will be a radical overhaul of all procedures and an end to institutionalised chaos. I will explain what I mean by that. In the course of a normal school day, a bell rings every hour, or so, and one thousand, six hundred and thirty-three pupils get up, leave their desks, and move to another classroom. Often the time-tabling means that extensive distances have to be covered, up and down staircases and along corridors, across the playground, and then, when these pupils finally arrive, someone shouts at them for being late. Could anything be more pointless? We must give these kids a base and some ownership of their environment. I don't deny that some subjects need to be taught in specialist areas, but many core subjects could be taught in form rooms. Moving on from timetable reform, the entire ethos of the school needs to change. There should be more positive reinforcement. Children need praise far more than they need punishing. Yes, there should be sanctions, but this is a school, not a detention centre or a prison. If this school *is* failing, and the last Ofsted Report said that it was, one reason is that the pupils have been alienated by unsympathetic treatment. And they don't see any relevance to their lives in what we have on offer here. We have to change that. We have to provide lunch time activities, chess clubs, music rehearsals, revision clubs, sports and counselling sessions. From tomorrow, pupils will no longer be locked out of the building at lunch time. I have already removed the sign that says pupils are forbidden to knock on the staffroom door."

"*Excuse me!*" Mr Pickering hauled himself to his feet.

"Questions at the end, if you don't mind, Mr Pickering." Aidan spoke patiently but I thought I detected a dangerous glint in his eye.

"*And I'd prefer to speak now*! I want to know what you plan to do to restore discipline in this place! We don't need the kids in the building at lunch-time. We need more detentions, more punishments, more kids being put on report and expelled and someone who can really yell at them and scare the pants off them! As for 'ownership'," Mr Pickering looked on the verge of apoplexy, "and 'lunch time activities', if you think I'm going to give up my lunch hour for those brats, you've got another think coming! We can't have kids in the building all through the lunch hour! They'll be a riot! They'll burn the place down. And even worse, they'll start knocking endlessly on the staff room door. We'll never have a moment's peace! We'll never get any rest from the blighters!"

There was a general murmur of agreement. Aidan Langford gazed at Mr Pickering with a quizzical expression. Then he said,

"You've now ignored my instructions twice, Mr Pickering. One more strike and you're out. But since you've raised the question, I'd like to point out that you're not here to have a rest from the pupils, Mr Pickering. That's what the weekends, the evenings and the holidays are for. And that's all I have to say for now. I think everyone's anxious to get home. The staff meeting is over, although if you or anyone else wants to stay behind for a private chat, I'm available. We can discuss things until midnight, if you wish. Although I'm sorry to say, that however long we talk, my views will remain the same. And if you think of our children as blighters, then I'd venture to suggest that you're in the wrong profession."

169

"Oh really? Well, let me tell you, I don't just think of these kids as 'blighters'," Mr Pickering advanced towards him. "I think of them as scumbags! And you'll soon come to regret swanning in here and trying to take over with your namby-pamby notions, believe me."

"Thank you, Mr Pickering." Aidan spoke calmly and without rancour. "You're sacked."

There was a communal gasp, and then the silence in the room was absolute. I noticed that Jen Fowler was gazing at Aidan with undisguised adoration; she'd never liked Mr Pickering and she was clearly turned on by this display of authority. I didn't know whether to be impressed or horrified. On the one hand, Aidan had refused to be bullied but on the other hand, cynical, foul-mouthed Pickering had a point. Child-centred idealism was all very well as an educational philosophy, but this was Havelock Ellis High School and there were certain uncomfortable realities to be faced.

"Just a minute," Paul Gogarty raised his hand. "May I say something?"

"Yes?"

"I'm the union rep. here and I have to say that you can't just dismiss a member of staff in that manner."

"I think you'll find," Aidan smiled at him with surprising good-humour, "that I just did."

I found the letter lying on the mat when I got home. The envelope was marked with the embossed Netherwold School shield, a wyvern rampant on a sable field, and the words **For the attention of the Parents of Caspian Deadlake** were printed in bold font. Oh, no, *please* don't let Caspian be in any trouble! I couldn't bear a repetition of the horrors of Blasted Oak! I slit the envelope open and unfolded the sheet of cream vellum paper inside:

Dear Mr and Mrs Deadlake,

I would very much appreciate it if one or both of you could call in at the school at your earliest convenience so that we can discuss the progress of your son. Please be assured this is part of our regular assessment programme and there is no cause for alarm. Please telephone the school to make an appointment. I am free to see parents in the afternoon from around 2.00 p.m.

Yours faithfully, Dominic Montague, M.A Cantab

Ah, well that was a relief! *No cause for alarm.* I just hope Mr Montague meant it. I wouldn't bother Peregrine with this; the last thing I wanted was to give him an excuse to turn up in London.

"Ah! You are home, dear lady," Ralphie came down the stairs carrying two large leather-bound books. "Have you collected the henbane yet?"

"I haven't had the opportunity. Although I've just been summoned to Caspian's school, so I could try looking for some in the place you mentioned on the Heath."

"An uncanny coincidence and very opportune, I might say." He nodded. "We need some henbane urgently, I'm afraid. Because, much as I hate to be the bearer of bad news, I'm afraid you must prepare yourself for another unpleasant development."

Twenty

Demonology for Beginners

"Oh, my God!" I clapped my hand over my mouth and nose, almost heaving with disgust. What fresh hell was this?

Ralphie had tried to warn me, but the word 'unpleasant', uttered in such an urbane tone, hadn't prepared me sufficiently for the noxious horror that overpowered my senses as I entered the living room. Oh, that sickening squelching sound as I stepped over the threshold, the glistening, noxious lake of slime covering most of the floor, the floorboards that looked as though they were turning to mush. And worst of all, the appalling smell. It was like a mixture of raw sewage, rotting seaweed and bad eggs.

"Now, as you can see," Ralphie spoke in a calm, business-like manner, "I've packed away all the contents of your lower shelves and moved everything I could to the upstairs landing in boxes. Unfortunately, I was unable to move the sofa, of course, but I have covered it plastic.. As for your rugs, I fear they are ruined. I've rolled them up and put them out the back by the wheelie bins."

"Thank you," I was too distressed to sound fully grateful. "But what's happened? Is it a burst pipe? Are the drains leaking in some way and coming up through the floor? Have you called a plumber?"

"A plumber?" Ralphie raised one eyebrow. "Unless you can find a plumber who is well versed in these books," he tapped them with his forefinger, "Namely *Darnley's Demonology,* and the *Herbal Healings of Hieronymous Capellanus,* I'm afraid a plumber can do nothing here. This is a paranormal disturbance."

"Oh, no, not another one!"

"I would suggest that this is not so much another one but simply a different aspect of the *same* one that has been apparent in this house for some time. But do not panic, dear lady. There are certain steps we can take, including the use of henbane when it is available. In the meantime, I suggest you close up this room, wedge some old rags underneath the door and seal the frame with tape. I'm afraid the living room is out of action for the moment. And then I suggest you come through to the kitchen and tell me about your third husband."

"Peregrine? You want me to tell you about him?"

"I do. He is the last piece of the jigsaw when it comes to understanding your marital history. And your marital history, is, as I have previously intimated, intrinsic to the hauntings and strange phenomena that are taking place here. And I've had my suspicions concerning Mr Deadlake that for some time."

"I don't really feel like talking about Peregrine right now."

"Perhaps not, but this would be a good opportunity, before your son comes home from school. Now, I appreciate that this will be painful for you, but there must be some disclosure if progress is to be made in combatting these dark forces. I've taken the precaution of making a pot of herbal tea. We can share it while you talk."

"All right then," I said. "I might as get it over with."

Seb was a wonderful consolation after Dave died, such a bright, cheerful, fun-loving boy, an easy baby, a happy toddler. By the time he was eleven, we were living in a council flat in a 1960s tower block near the Hackney marshes. I'd been back to college when he was five, supplementing my income with part-time jobs, serving in a rather downbeat, greasy-spoon café in Dalston, helping out at a second-hand book shop in Islington, and then I tried to establish myself as a freelance film reviewer, writing short pieces for a listings magazine. At weekends, I explored London with Seb, taking him to every free treat the capital had to offer, tobogganing on a tray down Primrose Hill in the winter, picnicking on Hampstead Heath in the summer, peering over the fence from Regents Park at the elephants at London Zoo, seeing the Oxford Street lights at Christmas. And then, when he was in Year 6, Seb went on a five-day school journey to the Isle of Wight and I had a phone call from Jay, the editor of a small press listings magazine that I'd written for occasionally.

"I've got a touch of 'flu," she coughed, "Absolutely maddening as I'm supposed to be meeting the screen-writer Paul Jervis for an interview. Can you go in my place? Have you seen *Brotherhood?*"

"Oh, good grief yes! That film about the Pre-Raphaelite painters, part-Ken Russell, part-Peter Greenaway and part-Monty Python."

"That's the one! John Ruskin having surrogate sex with a stuffed walrus, and Lizzie Siddall dancing naked on a roof with Dante Gabriel Rossetti's wombats."

"And then the wombats break into a chorus of 'Only a bird in a gilded cage'? Of course I'll go, I'd love to meet the madman who wrote that. Where do I meet Paul Jervis and how do I recognise him?"

"Meet him at Flumbles, in Camden Lock. He's about thirty-five, dark-haired and handsome in a louche kind of way. You can't miss him. He'd always got a glass of chardonnay in his hand and he undresses women with his eyes. Have a good time!"

Flumbles has closed down now, but it was popular in those days. People went there to eat pasta and drink Aqua Libra, and sit at rough wooden tables while they chattered animatedly about arts and politics. There were candles stuck in old green bottles, and the place overlooked the water. The terrace was particularly nice, with its strings of coloured lights hanging across the railings, and all the bay trees in pots and the view had a certain romantic appeal, a bit like Venice, but with barges and converted warehouses in place of the *palazzi* and the gondolas.

I found Paul Jervis standing at the bar.

"Hi," I said brightly. "You look like the person I'm meeting tonight. Hello, I'm Dora."

"Hello, Dora." He gave me a long, cool stare. "Yes, here I am. Our table's just over there."

His eyes were very dark and he wore a ring on the little finger of his right hand, a plain silver band. There was something about him that was both intimidating and tantalising. It was the set of his mouth, perhaps, that sardonic, knowing look, like a Regency buck.

"Oh," I said. "I didn't know there was going to be a meal. I thought we'd just talk over a drink in the bar."

"Of course we're having a meal," he said. "Don't worry, it's on me. And may I say how gorgeous you look?"

Gorgeous? I was in jeans and a t-shirt and I hadn't put on any make-up. Either I'd really impressed him, or he was a liar. Whatever the truth of the matter, I wasn't going to refuse a free meal at Flumbles.

We sat down at the table. The waitress brought the menu and a bottle of champagne in an ice-bucket. I ordered a tricolori salad starter and a pasta dish for my main; I can't remember what he had, but I think it must have been red meat of some kind.

"So," I said, "Let's talk about *Brotherhood,* shall we?"

"I'm sorry?" He frowned at me. "You look more like the kind of girl who'd want to talk about sisterhood."

"Not at all," I took out my notebook. "I'm a film buff. Anyway, to get back to *Brotherhood*, I think it's a fascinating screen-play. Let's start with the walrus scene, shall we? I assume it was a coded reference to Ruskin's sexuality? Or was it a reference to Lennon and McCartney, 'I am the walrus'? Of course, the Victorians were obsessed with taxidermy, a plundering of nature, which in itself is a form of ecological colonialism. Do you agree?"

"I haven't the faintest idea what you're talking about. But do go on. Some men are afraid of intellectual talk from women, but I find it rather a turn on. However," he paused. "I should like a little more explanation."

"I'm talking about your script, the one you wrote for *Brotherhood*. You are Paul Jervis, aren't you?"

"No," he said. "My name's Peregrine Deadlake. I'm an investment banker."

"*Oh!* Oh, how embarrassing. Oh, I'm so sorry, I shouldn't even be drinking this champagne." I pushed my chair back and grabbed my handbag from under the table. "I'll go, I'll..."

"Stay." He smiled at me. "Please. The truth is, I've been stood up. I was waiting over by the bar for my girlfriend, all ready for a romantic meal, when she dumped me by text.

I was about to leave when you walked in. I'd prefer you to stay. Quite apart from anything else, I'm starving and I don't like eating alone. And you're...well, there's something about you. But perhaps you're married. Perhaps you're not free. I can see that you're wearing a wedding ring."

"I'm a widow," I said. "And I need to get home."

"Do you? Do you really?" He looked crestfallen.

"I have an eleven-year-old son."

"And where is he now?"

"He's on the Isle of Wight," I admitted

"Well then." He refilled my glass. "You don't have to go just yet."

I thought he was absolutely charming that night. We talked about films, about London and about travel, but mainly, I realise now, looking back on it, Peregrine talked mainly about himself. He talked about his flat overlooking the river, and his mother's big house in the country and his successful career. All this might have seemed egotistical, had it not been for the glimpses of vulnerability that he exposed, stories about his loneliness when he was sent away to boarding school at the age of eight, how his father died when he was ten, how he'd overcome crippling shyness in his teens, how sad he'd been when his fiancé broke off their engagement. I now think that some of those stories weren't true, that they were just a play for sympathy. Then he flattered me, telling me how brave I'd been, living as a widow all these years and bringing up my son on my own. The food was good and the champagne was effervescently heady. By the time we were on to our main course, I was feeling quite flirtatious and reckless.

"Try this—it's scrumptious," I held out a forkful of my meal to him across the table.

"Mmm," Peregrine nodded, accepting it, tasting it on his tongue and then swallowing it. "What is it?"

"Penne rigata al'adriatico," I said.

"What a perfect Italian accent you have," he said. "You're a very accomplished, lovely lady."

After the main course, I had a crème brulee, and then we had coffee, brandy and mints. He paid the bill, refused to allow me to contribute the tip, and we went outside. We stood together on the towpath by the canal. The night air was balmy and jazz music was wafting out from a nearby club: *Bewitched, bothered and bewildered.*

"Do you want to come back to my place?" he asked.

"Oh, look, I..." This was going far too fast. I was absolutely certain that there was only one way an evening at his place could end up, and the idea scared me. "No," I said. "I won't come back tonight. It's too soon. I hardly know you."

"I'll call you a cab, then." He took out his mobile. "But I would like to see you again." He moved towards me, as if about to kiss me, and just as I was considering whether to allow this to happen, his expression changed. His forehead looked clammy and he began to swallow furiously.

"What is it?" I said.

"Ah!" He pressed both hands to his stomach.

"Are you all right?" I asked. It was a redundant question, I realised.

"Just a twinge, *aaaaaagh!*" He balled his hands into fists and jammed them into his guts.

Oh, *God!"* He doubled up and then collapsed on to his knees at the edge of the canal.

I knelt down beside him.

"Shall I call an ambulance?" I suggested.

"No! I'll be all right. It must be...something I ate...that food you gave me..." He rocked backwards and forwards, and uttered a nauseous groan.

"What, that mouthful of *penne rigata al'adriatico*? There was nothing wrong with that. I feel fine."

"What was in it?" His forehead was almost touching the ground.

"Um...tomato, garlic, cream, dill, onions, calamari, and some flakes of fish. Salmon, I think."

"*Fish!*" he gurgled.

"Fish?" I stared down into the canal. Had he seen something moving in the water? I knew people sometimes fished here, so there must be some perch, and maybe some dace.

"It must have been the f....." He was unable to finish the word as, with a spectacular, cathartic retch, he was violently sick into the canal, narrowly missing a passing duck.

I looked away, giving him the chance to recover his dignity. The poor man, I thought. All that seductive charm, and here he was, brought low by eating a tiny portion of seafood. And, not only had he been taken ill, it was my fault. I was the person who'd forked the dangerous food into his mouth.

"Sorry." He got to his feet. "How bloody embarrassing."

"Do you feel any better?" I asked solicitously. He didn't look much better. His eyes were streaming.

"Not a lot," he smiled wanly. "My stomach's still doing the rumba. And I don't seem to have a handkerchief." He patted his jacket pocket.

"Have these," I reached into my bag and gave him a handful of tissues.

"Thanks." He blew his nose noisily.

"I'm really sorry about this," I said, "If I'd known you were allergic to fish, I'd never have given you that mouthful of pasta."

"It's just one of those things," he said, "I should have checked. I don't have any other allergies. I just have to avoid..." he gulped, "Sometimes, I feel ill if someone just *says* the word 'f....'"

"I'm really, really sorry," I said.

"It wasn't your fault. And I feel stupid. Here I am, with one of the loveliest ladies I've met in a long while and I behave like this."

"You can't help it," I said. "Shall I go back into Flumbles and get you a glass of water?"

"What I really need is a stiff brandy. Do you like brandy, Dora? Because there just happens to be a bottle of a very fine, fifty-year-old Napoleon brandy in my flat. It's not far from here. I'd be really grateful if you would come back with me. I promise not to throw up again, but I do feel rather fragile. I think I might need some TLC."

And so I went back to his flat, and Peregrine lay on his couch looking pale and interesting, while I loosened his tie and mopped his fevered brow. After a while, he rallied, and we drank brandy, and watched a late night showing of *Miracle in Milan* on his state-of-the-art TV. And then my fate was sealed.

"Now you've done it." Uncle Horace took a swig of his fifth glass of champagne and staggered slightly. "Do you actually love this man, Dora?"

I didn't know what to say. I was Dora Deadlake now and it was too late to analyse the matter. I'd told myself I was doing this so that my unborn child could have a father but, as I stood under the canopy of the marquee on the lawn of

Cynthia's Oxfordshire house, holding a plate of canapés in my hand which, in my queasy, early pregnant state, looked as appetising as pigswill, I was afraid I'd succumbed to the lure of wealth and false charm.

I looked desperately around for Auntie Pam, but she was nowhere to be seen. Over by the buffet, I could see Nanny Barrel Hips. She was dressed in a truly shocking pink two-piece, the back of the skirt riding up over her plump bottom, and she was stuffing forkfuls of peach gateau into her mouth. I had no idea why she was here. I hadn't any memory of having invited her but she seemed to be getting on remarkably well with Cynthia, my new mother-in-law. And there was Peregrine, under the copper beech tree, talking to a beautiful woman with flame-red hair. Why was he paying her so much attention? Shouldn't he standing here with *me?*

"I'm sorry, but I have to be frank with you, Dora." Uncle Horace picked up a vol-au-vent. "I've got grave doubts about this marriage. First you married a man with no balls, then you married a man with no brain, and now you've married a man with no heart! Will you never get it right?"

"Dear, dear." Ralphie shook his head, having listened to my sorry story. "I think I get the picture. It sounds to me as though your third marriage was doomed from the outset."

"I'm afraid it was. And then, after a few years, I discovered Peregrine was having a full-blown affair with Jennifer Sheringham, the woman I'd seen at our wedding. I can't think how I could have been such a fool."

"You are not a fool," Ralphie said gravely. "You have been living under a curse. You are not to blame for the demonic power of Mr Deadlake."

"Demonic power?" I stared at him across the kitchen table.

"Indeed. I have reason to believe your third husband has sold his soul to a demon."

"*Sold his soul?*"

"Yes."

"That sounds extraordinary."

"You think so? By my estimation, there are at least a million people living in Britain today who have harnessed the power of demons for profit, power and gain. Open any newspaper and you will see the faces of those who have mortgaged their souls to these entities; politicians, business people, so-called 'celebrities', members of the legal profession, bankers and journalists, the list is endless. Don't you believe me?"

"I find it rather far-fetched, but what you're saying does seem to explain a lot."

"Indeed it does. And such people are easily identifiable. After a while, they begin to be afflicted by the characteristics of their Masters. A follower of Beelzebub, for example, will attract flies. A devotee of Dagon is likely to get into deep water. And by the same principle, a follower of Asmodeus will be repelled by fish."

"Fish," I repeated. I had a cold feeling in the pit of my stomach. "Oh, good grief, *fish*."

"It's all here in *Darnley's Demonology*," Ralphie opened the book. "The story of Asmodeus and the angel Raphael. '*And what say you...*'. "

"I've read some of that," I said. "I was upstairs and I saw that book."

"Then perhaps you know that the demon Asmodeus appears in many ancient texts such as the Talmud. In the apocryphal *Book of Tobit,* for example, he is described as killing seven bridegrooms of a woman named Sarah until the angel Raphael drives him away with the fumes of burning fish. *Asmodeus of the fishy fume.* The demon of marital unhappiness. The demon that has blighted your life. The demon to whom your third husband, Peregrine Deadlake, has sold his soul."

Twenty-One

Fowler By Name and Foul By Nature

"Josh, you missed a blinder at that staff meeting yesterday," Zelda said. "An absolute blinder. Don't you agree, Dora? Dora, are you even listening?"

"What?" I realised my thoughts had wandered. While Zelda had been eagerly describing the staffroom shenanigans to Josh as we sat together having our mid-morning coffee break in Oddballs Corner, I'd been preoccupied with thoughts of green slime, cracks, cobwebs, and the demon Asmodeus. It was more than a little strange to find that my life had done a complete flip-turn over the past few weeks. I used to look forward to getting back to Arcadia Square after a day spent in this school, kicking off my shoes, pouring myself a large G. and T. and forgetting all about 9X and all the other hooligans. Now, with my home life rapidly disintegrating around me, Havelock Ellis High School was becoming something of an escape. At least the bedlam here took my mind off my personal problems.

"Oh, yes, of course," I said. "That meeting was quite something."

"And the result is that Gogarty and Randle are on the warpath," Zelda continued. "They're calling a union meeting. Gogarty wants to discuss how we're going to respond to the way Pickering was sacked, publicly, high-handedly and without any of the set procedures."

"I couldn't care two hoots about Pickering." Josh took a large bite of his corned beef sandwich. "Horrible man." He chewed noisily, rather too noisily, in fact. That seemed odd, as Josh had never been in the slightest bit uncouth when it came to eating; I could only assume he must be particularly hungry. Perhaps he'd missed breakfast.

"No-one cares about Pickering," Zelda said. "It's rather more a question of who's going to be disposed of next. It could be any one of us; in fact, it probably *will* be one of us. Drama, dance, the arts, they're always the first to go when cutbacks are made. And Langford has already had a go at me about my t-shirt."

"He did what?" Josh stared at her. "What's wrong with your t-shirt? 'Pissing in the Shower' are a great band. You saw them at Glastonbury, so why shouldn't you wear the t-shirt? I'd say he was bang out of order. Neither of us teach subjects that require formal clothes, do we?"

I looked at Zelda's t-shirt. It was quite discreet in its way, the modesty of the nude figure in the shower being protected by a large loofah and the 'i's' in the offending word replaced by asterisks but on the other hand, perhaps the loofah was somewhat phallic and as for 'p*ss*ng...No, I *wasn't* going to agree with A.R.L. on this one. Zelda and Josh were my allies in this school, my only allies and friends, we were the mavericks of Oddballs Corner and we needed to stick together.

"Anyway," Zelda said. "There's this document going around, Langford's proposals. Apparently he wants to dismantle most of the time-table and let the kids choose their own study programmes. He thinks a lot of exams are pointless. He thinks shedloads of impossible stuff. There's definitely a pie-in-the-sky element to most of his ideas."

"Well, maybe if all the traditional methods have failed, it could be time to try something different," I suggested. "At Caspian's school, they give the kids a lot of responsibility for their own learning. It seems to work."

"Yes, but your son goes to a progressive private school with only a small group of exceptionally clever boys on roll," Zelda objected. "This is Havelock Ellis High School, a bog-standard comprehensive full of sociopaths. We can't let the lunatics take over the asylum."

"I think they already have," I said.

"True enough," Josh gulped down the remainder of his sandwich. "Have to say this educational debate is doing my head in." He yawned, stretching his arms above his head.

"You seem tired, Josh," I said.

"I am. I was up at half past four this morning. I couldn't sleep, I was feeling cooped up, so I went up to Highgate Woods and had a run around."

"In Highgate Woods? I didn't know you were keen on jogging." Zelda sounded surprised.

"I am now," Josh assured her. "You know, I've got this yearning to do something different with my life, something *outdoors*."

"Outdoors?" Zelda laughed. "You? You don't even *like* outdoors. You're always going on about that camping trip you hated."

"But this morning, when I was running through the woods, I felt so *free*. I wanted to strip off all my clothes and roll on the ground. Get the dew on my skin."

I stared at Josh. Was he having a laugh? He did look as though he'd been exercising a lot lately. His bare arms in that black sleeveless vest seemed quite sinewy, his calves did too, in those cycle shorts. I hoped Aidan Langford wasn't about to turn on Josh too; he'd almost certainly object to that red baseball cap he'd taken to wearing recently, placed backwards on his head as if he was getting down there with the kids.

"Oh, bad luck, Dora," Zelda nudged me, speaking in a whisper. "The Politically Correct Beanpole's spotted you. She's heading this way."

"There you are." Jen Fowler strode into Oddballs Corner, her spindly legs slicing through the air like scissor blades. "English, next lesson, 9X, Hut Three, Mr. Scunley's class, here are the worksheets." She thrust a pile of papers into my hands.

"Excuse me?" I gazed at her with an innocent expression. I couldn't help thinking that her tight grey sweat shirt, emblazoned with a luminous, be-winged pink pig, looked ridiculous on her.

"Is there a problem?" she demanded.

"I'm not sure I quite understand," I said, a certain devilment catching hold of me. "Are you asking me if I would be kind enough to cover 9X's English lesson? It's just that the way you spoke to me wasn't very…"

"That's your job, isn't it?" Jen Fowler interrupted. "Standing in for absent colleagues? Now, I've given 9X plenty of questions to answer on their English text. They've been reading *Lord of the Flies*. Don't forget to set the homework and don't let any of the trouble makers sit together."

"But they're all trouble-makers," I said.

"Are you being sarcastic, Miss Harker?"

"Not at all," I said. "And thank you for learning my name at long last. I just hope there'll be enough seats if I'm going to separate them all and leave spaces in between."

"I'm sure you'll manage." Jen Fowler's eyes narrowed. "One other thing; I'd be grateful if you'd mark the homework. I won't have time. Tell Darren Dalston to collect it and bring it to you early next week. If you have any problems, you'll have to ask Mr McTaggart. I'm going to be busy." She turned on her heel and strode off, banging the door behind her.

The moment she was gone, Zelda gave vent to a snort of laughter.

"You really don't like her, do you?" she said.

"Do you?"

"No, not at all," Zelda said. "And she was mean to poor old Scunley. She was always going into his lessons and telling him his teaching technique was crap. She called it performance management but really, it was just an excuse to bully him."

"9X and *Lord of the Flies*," Josh reflected. "What an ominous combination."

"Yes, shame you weren't forewarned, Dora," Zelda said. "You could have equipped yourself with a conch."

English Hut Three, a dirty Portakabin with wide windows impressively splattered with pigeon shit, was situated between the disused toilets and the wire perimeter fence. I found the Honey Monster sitting on the wooden steps stuffing crisps into his mouth in a joyless manner. He was wearing a school blazer that appeared to be at least two sizes too small. His solid, sullen figure exuded despair.

"Hello, Darren." I adopted a breezy, cheerful tone of voice. "Where's everyone else?"

"Dunno." He raised his grubby face to me, "They never tell me nuffink. They go off all the time and have fun without me. And they cussed my mum. And they took my pen. And they stamped on my lunch. And I got happy-slapped."

"Happy-slapped?" This was a new one.

"It means hitting someone while you film them on your mobile, Miss."

"Oh dear." I felt quite unequal to dealing with this catalogue of woe. I wondered if the bottomless pit of the Honey Monster's victimhood could ever be filled with consolation. Still, at least he'd had some crisps, and while the rest of 9X were missing, no-one could tease him.

"Let's go into the classroom and get started on the work, shall we?" I said. "Have you brought your English book?"

"No, Miss. It got flushed down the loo."

"You can work on paper then." I went up the steps and pushed open the flimsy door. "In you come, Darren. You can sit wherever you want."

It appeared that English Hut Three hadn't been cleaned for weeks. The floor was awash with chocolate bar wrappers, paper aeroplanes and blobs of chewing gum and the teacher's desk was piled high with books and papers, crushed beer cans and torn up newspapers. There was also an unpleasant smell, as if someone had been sick a long time ago and the odour had been preserved for posterity.

"Where did Mr Scunley keep the copies of *Lord of the Flies*?" I asked.

"There, Miss." The Honey Monster pointed to a yellow plastic crate under the teacher's desk.

"But that's empty," I objected.

"I know, Miss," the Honey Monster said. "On the last lesson we had with Mr Scunley, he sat in his chair, ripping all the books up, then he took them all outside and set fire to them."

"He did?"

"Yeh, Miss. He was crying and all that."

"*Crying?* Poor Mr Scunley!"

"I don't feel sorry for him," the Honey Monster retorted. "I fink he was gay,"

"But, Darren, even if he was," I said, "that is, I don't know if Mr Scunley *was* gay but even if he was, no, I don't mean *even* if he was, I mean *if* he was then that's no reason to…" I was floundering now, and I knew it.

"What, Miss?"

"What I'm trying to explain," I sat down at the teacher's desk, "Is that it isn't nice to be unkind to people. You wouldn't like it, would you?"

I realized, too late, the implications of what I'd just said. The Honey Monster, apparently too obtuse to pick up the irony of my last remark, slumped down at a desk in the front row.

"Miss, the last supply teacher let us play hangman on the board," he informed me.

"We're not going to do that," I said. "You have a worksheet to complete on *Lord of the Flies*."

"But I can't remember nuffink about *Lord of the Flies*."

"Perhaps you'd better do some silent reading then."

"I ain't got a book."

"I see." I searched through the morass of books and papers on the desk in front of me, and finally found a dog-eared copy of *Charlie and the Chocolate Factory*.

"Try this," I said, passing it over to him.

The Honey Monster flipped helplessly through the pages.

"Miss, I can't," he announced dolefully.

"You can't what, Darren?"

"I can't do silent reading. I can't read without making a noise, Miss. I have to say it all out loud. Or I don't get it."

"Darren, that's absolutely fine," I beamed at him. "Just try and keep it to a low mumble, O.K?"

"Yes, Miss."

I picked up a sheet of A4 paper and wrote out a list of the missing members of 9X, ready to make an exact note of their time of arrival for the lesson. Heaven only knew where the little horrors were lurking, but they were definitely on track for a Head of Year's detention for lateness. On the other hand, it would be a merciful release if none of them showed up for the lesson at all. I could do with some peace and quiet.

"I see you've lost your class again, Miss Harker."

I looked up with a start. I'd been sitting there at Mr Scunley's desk, doodling idly on a piece of paper, blocking out the sound of the Honey Monster's 'silent' reading and generally letting my thoughts wander. And now, here was Aidan Langford in the doorway of English Hut Three with the rest of 9X behind him. They looked astonishing, all dressed in perfect uniform and oozing obedience. Why, when they were with this man, did they desist from their normal grunts, farts and animal noises? There was something superhuman about his ability to control these kids.

"Where on earth have you all been?" I said, hoping to sound like a teacher.

"That's a very good question," Langford said. "But for the last twenty minutes, they've been with me." He glanced at his watch. "Now, class, there are only two minutes left, so there's no need to go into the classroom. Just line up and collect the work that you should have done in this lesson from Miss Harker and complete it for homework."

"Darren can bring the exercise books to me next week," I added. "I shall enjoy marking them." This was, of course, a complete lie.

As I stood in the doorway of English Hut Three handing out the work-sheets, I felt unsettled by the proximity of

Aidan Langford. What an annoying man, in his beautifully-cut dark suit and yet another silky-soft shirt, a delicious buttercup yellow this time. It came as a relief when the bell rang and 9X raced off across the playground.

"Do you have time for a quick word?" he asked.

"Of course." My heart sank. What had I done wrong now?

"First of all," he began, "I don't understand why you didn't try to discover the whereabouts of the rest of 9X just now."

"How could I have done that?"

"You could have telephoned the school office on your mobile and reported them missing."

"Oh, I don't think that would have been a good idea," I said. "The office staff don't like to be contacted by the teaching staff. The first week I was here, I phoned them to report an emergency, some old tramp had got into the playground and he was standing at the window, exposing himself to a year 7 class, and Marie, she's the one who wears the weird hairnet, just said, 'Don't shout at me,' and put the phone down."

"That was completely unacceptable." I was pleased to see that Langford looked suitably appalled. "Marie, you say? I shall certainly speak to her about this."

"Oh, no hang on…it was weeks ago…and it didn't matter, because I got the whole class to shout 'Pervert!' in unison and the tramp fled. I wasn't trying to get Marie into trouble."

"Nevertheless…"

"No, please leave it. I know you take pleasure in winding up the staff but…."

"I don't take pleasure in that at all." He looked genuinely startled. "But I do have a job to do, turning this school around and making it a happy place for everyone."

"A happy place? You've got your work cut out there."

"I know."

"Well, since you're here, I think it's only fair to tell you, there's a mutiny brewing. Gogarty and Randle are calling in the union in the hope of getting rid of you."

"Really?" He sounded amused. "After less than a week? That's very flattering. The uprising usually takes at least a month to kick in after I arrive."

"You find it flattering?"

"Perhaps that was the wrong word. But I expect resistance. This place is so full of negative energy, so much anger, so much desolation it's inevitable. Haven't you noticed?"

"Of course I have. And if it wasn't for my friends, Zelda and Josh, I'd never have stayed. Anyway, I think it's a bit mean for everyone to gang up against you quite so soon. After all, there's always the possibility you might turn out to be nicer than you seem."

"Nicer than I seem," he repeated. "You certainly have a facility for back-handed compliments, Miss Harker."

"It wasn't meant to be a compliment. Only I thought the way you handled Pickering was impressive. I almost admired you at that moment."

"Did you, Miss Harker?" He gazed at me with an intent expression.

"The key word in what I just said was 'almost'," I told him.

"I see." He nodded. "Well, I have a proposal for you. How would you like a permanent job here?"

"I'm sorry, but the answer's no."

"That's a pity." He gazed through the window of English hut, his expression suggesting he found the mess inside distasteful. "But if you change your mind, you can always let me know."

"I won't," I said. "But there's just one thing. You are allowed to call me Dora, if you wish. "

"I don't think that's advisable." He drew back. "Formalities are essential on school premises. Good afternoon, Miss Harker." He turned on his heel and walked rapidly away.

Twenty-Two

A Series of Macabre Surprises

"Cheers!" Josh raised his glass. "Here's to a great evening."

"Cheers!" I chinked my glass against his.

"Mud in your eye!" Zelda downed her retsina in one gulp and poured herself another glass from the carafe.

Afternoon school had just ended and they'd persuaded me to join them for a drink and a light snack of bread, olives and dips in Kris's Kebab House. We were the only customers in here; perfect conditions for a gossip, and I wasn't in a hurry to get home as Caspian was staying at Becca's for a sleepover with William.

"What a week!" Josh said. "Who'd have thought Pickering would be arrested by the police on that internet porn charge? That's rather put the kibosh on the union protest, hasn't it?

"It has," Zelda said. "And it's uncanny. Do you suppose Langford tracked him down?"

"Possible, I suppose," I said.

"Anyway," Zelda continued, "It seems there's a real mystery about Langford. No-one seems to know where he's worked before, and this organisation, Sentinel Services, there's no trace of them online, according to Paul Gogarty. The whole thing's weird."

"Weird or not," Josh refilled my glass, "let's stop talking shop. Now, what about the Hallowe'en disco, Dora? You are coming, aren't you? It's next week, in the Drama Studio."

"I'm not sure."

"You must come," Zelda said. "It's fancy dress, I make a bowl of killer punch and it's for staff and their guests only. No Havelock Ellis pupils, of course, we don't want the party to turn into a slasher movie. But you can bring your son. He'd love it."

"You're right, Caspian would," I said. "Only usually Seb comes home for Hallowe'en and takes him trick or treating."

"Come to the disco after that then," Josh said. "It's great, because only the cool members of staff come along. You won't see McTaggart bopping around in a Frankenstein mask or Jen Fowler dressed as Leather-face. Everyone contributes some food and wine, we make brilliant decorations and all the music's themed of course. '*We did the mash...we did the monster mash!*'"

Without warning, he leapt up, bopped around while humming the tune. Then he jumped on to his chair and whipped off his baseball cap. Zelda let out an audible gasp, while I gawped in astonishment. Neither of us could speak for a moment. Then, in a small voice that seemed quite unlike her usual forthright manner, Zelda said,

"Josh. Your hair."

"My hair?" He stepped down. "What about it?"

"You mean you haven't noticed?" I said.

"What?" He put his hand up to his scalp. "Oh, yeh, I decided to grow my hair."

"I can see that, Josh," I said. "But it's grown such a lot."

"And so quickly," Zelda added.

I thought back, trying to remember when I'd last seen him without his cap. It must have been that Friday morning when he'd staggered into the staffroom with blood gushing from his arm. He'd been his usual, shaven-headed self. But now he had all those huge, untidy tufts, sticking up all over his head. How could that have happened in such a short time?

"Did you rub something into your scalp?" Zelda asked him. "Some weird Chinese ointment? I mean, that *is* your hair isn't it?"

"Of course it's my hair!" He gave it a tug. "Look, would you two mind not staring at me like that? I don't know how this happened. I can only think there must have been hormones or steroids or something in that injection they gave me at the hospital. Can we talk about something else? For example, Dora," Josh replaced his baseball cap. "What about those Chappaquidick tapes? Have you found them yet?"

"I'm sorry, I forgot to look." I quickly finished my drink. "But I will, I promise. Give me a couple of days. Anyway, I'm off now. I'm having a quiet evening in. See you later, guys." I wasn't sorry to be making my excuses and leaving. I was suddenly feeling deeply uneasy although I didn't entirely know why.

Oh no, now what? What was a coffin doing on my doorstep?

At least, if it wasn't a coffin, it certainly looked like one, an oblong box with a mitred end, long enough to contain a body. It was covered in stained, green leather and there were metal studs along the edges, and a handle in the shape of a two-headed serpent at the side. If it *was* a coffin, it was clearly an antique, perhaps a casket that had lain for centuries in an ancestral vault, containing the remains of a deceased aristocrat with a dubious reputation. Where had this extraordinary object come from? It didn't look as if it had been delivered by Parcel Force. No, it must have been transported over a treacherous, winding mountain road on a coach driven by a cloaked, hunchbacked retainer and drawn by four, black plumed, madly whinnying stallions who were being whipped into a nostril-flecked frenzy.

Cautiously, I bent over to examine it more closely. There was a scroll tied up with a red ribbon and fastened with a thick seal tucked under the handle. I pulled it out, unrolled it and squinted at the spiky, Gothic script:

'Property of His Excellency, Count Valkhov. Touch it ye not those who are too ignorant to understand. Dabble ye not with the forces of darknesse. If undelivered to the rightful address, return this boxe to Pere Lachaise, otherwise, beare the consequences of thefte and deception.'

I knew Pere Lachaise. That was the cemetery in Paris where they'd buried Oscar Wilde and Jim Morrison and many other celebrities of the bohemian world. So who was Count Valkov? And if this coffin belonged to him, did that mean that Count Valkhov was inside?

Oh! A dreadful image came into my mind of an emaciated corpse with hands like bunches of brown, dried bananas crossed over its chest, a wizened head resting on a pillow edged with lace, and lips that had shrunk back to expose long, yellow teeth, set in a macabre grimace. No! I didn't want anything to do with this box. Best just step over it, open my front door and...*agh!* I'd stumbled against the box, and now, with an ominous creak, the lid was beginning to rise.

I'm proud to say that I didn't scream, although that was only because I felt as though all the air had just been sucked out of my lungs. When I did open my mouth, no sound came out. I held my nose, trying to block out the musty, sickly sweet smell, a mixture of damp old church, rotting apples and dead mice. A moment later, the lid crashed against the front door.

I stepped back, whimpering. I was afraid that, at any moment, a desiccated corpse would swing up in a stiff, ninety degrees, Jack-in-the-box elevation confronting me with centuries-old decay. I approached the box again and steeled myself to look inside. Oh! What a relief.

No corpse, no vampiric presence. Just books, nothing more, ancient, leather-bound tomes, all of them lying amongst sprigs of mistletoe and dried ivy leaves, and stamped with the insignia of the two headed serpent.

I wasn't sure what to do now, but I'd seen enough horror films to know what I *shouldn't* do. I shouldn't, for example, pick up one of these books, open it at random and start reading the text out loud, particularly if it happened to be in Latin, Aramaic, or some forgotten tongue spoken only by Egyptian necromancers in the tenth century BC. Nor should I put my hand on any woodcuts depicting weird, demonic entities, thus accidentally releasing said entity, and allowing it to creep up beside me later while I was innocently reading by candlelight. And if any of these books were grimoires (I only had a vague notion of what a grimoire was, but I knew it was something very dangerous with occult implications) then I really would be in serious trouble. I wasn't at all sure I wanted this 'property of Count Valkhov' in my house.

But, on the other hand, I could hardly leave such valuable contents on the step. I opened the front door and dragged it into the hall.

"Ralphie, are you there?" I called up the stairs. "I think this must be for you.

No answer. I kicked off my shoes and padded through to the kitchen where I sloshed some gin and tonic into a glass.

There was a note on the fridge door, sticking out from under Seb's Mont Blanc fridge magnet.

Gone to The Lord Halifax to collect some pieces of the dear blue china that Oscar gave me. Do meet me there later. I would like to reciprocate your confidences and tell you about myself.

Yours, R.

Blue china. I had to smile. How superbly *fin de siècle*. Of course I'd go to the Lord Halifax. Ralphie's life story was bound to be entertaining.

Twenty-Three

Autobiography of a Revenant

The fog was behaving in an uncanny way, swirling a few feet above the ground, sweeping around the lamp-posts and kissing the bumpers of parked cars with freakish playfulness. I'd never seen anything like it, other than as a special effect in a creaky old horror film. The silence was unnerving too, resembling the unearthly quiet that is said to occur before a natural disaster, when all the small mammals have instinctively scuttled away and the birds have abandoned the trees, leaving humankind to its fate.

This all seemed odd. At this time of the evening, Arcadia Square was usually teeming with people from the entire spectrum of multi-cultural, mixed social class North London, kids from the nearby council estate kicking cans down the road, girls clattering by on their kitten heels *en route* for the pubs and clubs, men with briefcases striding along the pavement with an air of go-getting superiority, cars returning the sons and daughters of the middle class from their after-school sessions of music, Kumon maths, yoga and ballet, homeless men stumbling towards the hostel by the market. But right now, the street was deserted; there wasn't so much as a mangy, feral cat yowling around the dustbins.

As I turned into Kinsey Crescent, I glanced nervously at the privet hedges skirting the gardens. Anyone or anything could be lurking behind them. I walked on, reminding myself to look confident and assured, and took the new route I'd discovered to the Lord Halifax, avoiding the canal, and going across the old housing estate and through the alleyway by the children's playground.

As I stepped into the pub, I was engulfed by the scent of the roses that Georgia was arranging along with some ferns in a black marble vase. She was dressed in a full-length, sparkling sea-green gown, a diamante choker, and a silver tiara with green and purple feathers and was humming an aria from *La Traviata*.

"Hello, Dora." She looked up at me. "Ralphie's down in the cellar. He won't be long. So, how are things in Arcadia Square?"

"Getting increasingly strange."

"Oh dear." She gave the ferns a final tweak and placed the vase on a shelf. "I'm sorry to hear that. Ralphie did suggest that the situation was more complex than he thought at first. Well, he's fetching you a bottle of wine. It's on the house. Now, before he gets in here, I can't wait to show off my latest acquisition. Would you like to see it?"

"Is it in here?" I looked around me at all the spooky relics that made the Lord Halifax such a special place.

"No. It's in my garage."

"You've bought a car?"

"I've bought a vehicle, yes, but it's so much more than just a car. Why not come outside and take a look?"

"Here she is." Georgia lifted up the garage door and turned on the light. "Isn't she beautiful?"

"Amazing," I gazed with genuine admiration at the vintage vehicle with its wide, sweeping running boards, polished wood wheel-spokes, Gothic windows and huge headlamps like the eyes of a malevolent troll. "Is it very old?"

"Yes, she's a 1928 Charrington," Georgia told me. "A cathedral hearse. This is a very rare model. This one did service in Alberta and for the past ten years she's been languishing in a yard in Sevenoaks. But now she's fully restored and she's mine. Here, take a look inside." She opened the hatch door at the back.

"Really, really amazing," I said, peering in at the vaulted roof, the black pillars, and the purple curtains. "It's like a chapel of rest on wheels."

"And that's more or less what it is," Georgia said. "Although I'm not going into the undertaking business. But I *am* going to set up a very special chauffeuring service. I shall take my Charrington through the Euro-tunnel to Paris and Belgium and I shall bring the Night Wanderers of North London back from exile."

"But aren't there certain regulations?" I asked. "Surely you can't just drive through the Euro-tunnel with bodies in coffins?"

"Who said anything about coffins?" She frowned.

"But don't the undead have to...that is..."

"Goodness no!" She shook her head. "You've been watching too many films. The real life of a Night Wanderer is very different. I'd thought you'd have known that. After all, you've got Ralphie staying with you. He hasn't brought a coffin with him, has he?"

"Well, no, but I thought that perhaps some of them..."

"*For the love of God, Montresor!*" Ralphie's voice rang out with all the theatricality of an old- style actor as he appeared before us, holding up a dusty bottle with an air of triumph.

"Ah, you found it then," said Georgia, "The last bottle from my crate of Amontillado."

"Indeed," Ralphie agreed. "*The thousand injuries of Fortunato I had borne as best I could, but when he ventured upon insult I vowed upon revenge*'. I expect you are familiar with the work of Poe? Montresor lures his enemy into a cellar and then entombs him alive. As he is about to apply the mortar to the final brick, Fortunato cries out..."

"*For the love of God, Montresor*!" Georgia repeated.

"Don't." I shuddered. "I saw the film version when I was twelve and had nightmares for weeks."

"A chilling tale indeed," Ralphie agreed. "Now, on to more cheerful topics. Let us go back into the Lord Halifax and open this bottle."

"Perhaps," Ralphie filled our glasses, "Georgia should have taken a leaf out of Montresor's book when the officials from the council came snooping around here, asking intrusive questions about her clientele. Although it *would* have been distasteful to have one of those pompous people permanently walled up in the cellar of the Lord Halifax."

"Quite," Georgia said. "Now let's taste the wine. It's come from the vaults of the Palazzo del Croce in Venice and it's more than two hundred years old."

"Do try it," Ralphie urged me.

I picked up my glass and took a sip. The wine tasted appalling, as if the murky, stinking waters of the Grand Canal had seeped in through the cork during a flood. I opened my eyes wide, trying not to choke.

"What do you think?" Georgia asked.

"It's good," I lied, suddenly seized by a strange, spinning sensation. I had to grab the edge of the table to steady myself.

"A mature, acquired taste." Ralphie drained his glass and poured himself some more wine. "I propose a toast. To absent friends!"

"Absent friends," Georgia repeated solemnly. She raised her glass and took a hearty swig.

I took another sip of the wine. Perhaps it wasn't so bad; it took time to be a proper connoisseur.

"How I miss them all," Georgia sighed. "You know, Dora, there was a time when this place was full. Clarimonde Barnett used to sit there by the urns, and the Varneys always crowded round that table by the bar. Albert Karnstein was so fond of the red plush winged chair and the Mornington Crescent set would fill that alcove. This place was a Mecca for Night Wanderers. And now, where are they all? Scattered across Europe, thanks to the interfering acts of a few bureaucrats. Oh, when I think of the old days, I could weep."

"*Nil desperandum,*" Ralphie said. "Our friends will return."

"Indeed they will," Georgia agreed.

"And now," Ralphie turned to me. "I will explain why I asked you here tonight, dear lady. I am in the mood to reminisce. You have told me so much about your life that I felt I should return the compliment. Georgia, of course, has heard it all before."

"Indeed I have." Georgia put down her glass. "So, if you'll excuse me, I'm off to watch Coronation Street. I'll leave you to it."

"Such a wonderful lady," Ralphie observed, watching her go. Then he turned to me and launched into his life story.

"In the year I was born," he began. "Abraham Lincoln was assassinated, Lord Palmerston died, William Booth founded the Salvation Army and my father was arrested in Piccadilly after an unfortunate incident involving a drayman's cart, a consignment of dry goods from the East Indies, three police officers and a rent boy. I don't think I need to describe the incident in any further detail."

"Really?" I was rather disappointed to hear this.

"Yes. But suffice it to say," Ralphie continued, "as a member of the aristocracy and a close friend of the Marquess of Queensbury, my father was released from custody and no charges were ever brought against him. When I was two, he went to live abroad and I never saw him again. My mother did not pine. She was a devoted traveller, passionate about Italy and the *Risorgimento*, but soon she, too, had left to live with an opera singer in Milan.

"Thus I grew up in my grandfather's house in Shropshire. I had very little interest in ordinary, boyish pursuits. No climbing trees or bird's nesting for me. From an early age, I spent my time reading the erudite tomes in my grandfather's library. He possessed, amongst other delights, a number of remarkable works on the subject of the Neo-Platonists, Simon Magus, Dr John Dee and Paracelcus. So I became well-read in many occult matters, and by the time I went up to Oxford, I fancied myself an expert in the mysterious arts.

"I found few kindred spirits at Balliol at first. All those tiresome devotees of Muscular Christianity, the hearties who spent all their time fencing, rowing and wrestling! I must admit that some of them had delightful physiques but they were so loud and so aggressive at times, and I preferred to be sequestered with a charming little gaggle addicted to poetry and strawberries and fine wine. We read Baudelaire, Walter Pater and Huysman together and we embraced the aesthetic ideal in spiritual form." He took a sip of his wine.

"Then I met Oscar in London. You won't find me mentioned in any of the biographies of Wilde, by the way.

After our quarrel, that arrogant pup, Bosie Douglas, contrived to get me airbrushed out of literary history. But it was when I was with Oscar, that I stumbled upon the most important secret of my long life.

"It happened in Paris in 1883. Oscar was working on one of his more obscure plays, *The Duchess of Padua,* and I had been down to Marseilles with a delightful *matelot.* Oscar invited me to dine at a little restaurant on the Isle de St. Louis, not a smart establishment, but the proprietor kept a fine cellar. We were enjoying bouillabaisse and beef cutlets washed down with good champagne, when Oscar leaned across the table and touched the back of my hand. 'Bobbity,' he whispered, (that was my pet name, you know, I believe I mentioned it to you once before) 'Bobbity, the most ravishingly beautiful youth is sitting behind you. I can see his face, reflected in the mirror. How tragic that such a charming young man should have no companion.'

I turned my head and looked in the mirror. Oscar was right. The boy *was* beautiful. Naturally, Oscar called the waiter and ordered a bottle of champagne to be sent to the young man's table. The waiter carried out Oscar's request and all through dinner, through every clink of the ice bucket, we bided our time, taking surreptitious glances in the mirror, hoping the young man would turn to face us. It was like a game. Cat and mouse, perhaps, but who was the cat, who was the mouse? And then, I heard the sound of a chair being scraped back. 'Your coat sir,' I heard the waiter say, and then the young man walked up to our table. Except that he wasn't a young man.

"Oscar almost fainted with shock, and I admit I was deeply perplexed. Neither of us could understand what kind of conjuring trick had been played on us. For there was the man, and there was his reflection in the mirror, but the two images simply did not match. The man before us was not young, nor was he beautiful. He was old. He was very, very old. His teeth were brown, and long, like those of a rodent. His face was wrinkled. His long black hair was simply a wig.

"Oscar, being a gentleman, did his utmost to disguise his disappointment. The man bowed and handed us both his card. "I invite you both to my chateau in the Bois de Boulogne," the antique personage said. "I can offer you an experience that will be better than supping with panthers."

"To my surprise Oscar, who was usually adventurous, seemed alarmed. 'Come with me, Bobbity.' He clutched my sleeve. 'Let's make our excuses and go.' He had, however, made some use of our encounter; I'd already seen him jot down the phrase, 'supping with panthers' in his pocket book.

"Ah! If only Oscar and I had gone with Count Valkhov that night (for that was who we had just encountered), we could have drunk from the chalice of immortality. Still, Oscar *had* come upon the inspiration for one of his most celebrated stories, *The Picture of Dorian Gray*. He simply reversed the concept. Instead of a man growing old while his reflection in the mirror stayed young, he wrote of a man who remained young, while his portrait grew old and ravaged.

"After that time in Paris with Oscar, my life went on in much the same way. Then Oscar was disgraced, the twentieth century came and the Great War was terrible. But I did so enjoy the nineteen-twenties. And then, before I knew it, it was the thirties and I realised I was no longer young. I ricked my ankle very badly jitterbugging with a young transvestite from Vienna at a party at Cliveden. By 1937, I was down and out in Paris and London. And then, I chanced upon Count Valkhov's card in the pocket of an old evening suit

I was planning to pawn. I knew it was a sign. So I went to the Bois de Boulogne, and there was the chateau and there was the Count, looking very much the same as he had done all those years ago.

"I learned his history. He had been born in 1699 and left his native Russia during the peasant uprisings of 1775. Arriving in Paris, he met a young French aristocrat who helped him to cross over. The timing was unfortunate; it was the year they stormed the Bastille and started the Revolution. The poor Count had to hide in the wine cellars of the Chateau. The guillotine, as you must know, is fatal for both the living and the revenant alike. There were many unfortunate Night Wanderers on those tumbrils that clattered along the cobbled streets of old Paris to the roars of the sans-culottes baying for blood. Well, to cut the story short, the Count advised me to cross over as soon as possible. He gave me the address of a little club in Berlin and there I met young Klaus. I cannot say very much about Klaus. Particularly as the dear boy is no more."

"I'm sorry to hear that."

"*Requiescat in pace*." Ralphie dabbed his eye with a lace hanky.

I waited a moment. Clearly some tragic memory had been stirred and I needed to give him some space to grieve. Then I asked,

"And what happened to you then?"

"My transition was completed in 1944." Ralphie cleared his throat. "A false death certificate, bearing the phrase 'pernicious anaemia' was produced and my dear friends arranged for my interment in the crypt of St. Sebastian. I soon adjusted to my new existence. I have so many memories of that exhilarating new after-life. The joy of VE night, the sixties, Hyde Park in '68! (Poor, ill-fated

Mr Jones.) And then came the dreadful day that the Council chose to bulldoze St Sebastian's. The ignorance of those people. The prejudice! Those bureaucratic fools! And now, here I am, Dorian Gray in reverse." His eyes looked misty with recollection. "Wrinkled and gaunt as you see."

"Oh, but Ralphie," I felt obliged to reassure him, "You look superb for your age!"

"It is kind of you to say so," he said. "But look over there." He pointed with his death's head stick at the far wall. "Do you see that ornate gilt frame covered with a black cloth? What do you suppose that is?"

"Is it a portrait that's been covered up because someone has died?" I suggested.

"No. It's a mirror."

"A mirror like the one you and Oscar Wilde saw, all those years ago?"

"Exactly so." He took another sip of wine. "Has it never occurred to you how absurd it is, that old legend that the undead have no reflections? Imagine the bad hair days that would ensue from that! No, we do not cover mirrors for fear of not seeing ourselves at all but to avoid the pain of seeing ourselves as we once were." He stood up and walked over to the mirror. "This is a fine piece, rococo rather than baroque." He caressed the frame with his fingertips. "So ornate, all this gilt, those bunches of grapes. Genuine Louis Quatorze. And now, voila!" He whipped away the cloth. "Tell me what you see in the glass."

"Oh! Ralphie, is that you?" I stared at the reflection of a pretty, highly effete young man with auburn, shoulder length wavy hair, a full, curved mouth, silky-smooth skin and blue eyes like a playful kitten.

"It is. And in case you suspect a trick, observe this." Ralphie lifted his liver-spotted left hand to his face. With a simultaneous movement, the young man in the mirror lifted a smooth and unblemished hand to his. Then, as Ralphie patted his grey-white hair, the young man patted his auburn locks.

"Let this be a lesson to you," he said. "*Carpe diem*, seize the day. Grasp opportunity by the forelock, for she is bald behind. Never waste your youth, as I wasted mine. It isn't easy getting old. I deeply regret that I waited so long to cross over and it saddens me that I had to wait so long to find the companion of my heart, only to lose him again so soon. Be advised by me. Don't pass the chance of finding happiness with a significant other if it should come your way. Your guardian angel could still appear."

"My guardian angel?"

"Do you not believe in them?"

"I haven't ever thought about it."

"Then perhaps you should. Time is running out, dear lady, and although I will do my best to assist you, in the final reckoning, if you are really under a curse, only you can successfully lift the spell."

"And how do I do that?"

"Ah—that, remains to be seen, but perhaps an opportunity will present itself. In the meantime, I will continue with my research. I am expecting a consignment of books from my dear friend Count Valkhov and..."

"Oh! Yes! I nearly forgot to tell you. They've arrived. They're in the hall."

"Splendid! In that case, let us return to Arcadia Square. And allow me to escort you." He offered me his arm. "I don't wish to alarm you, dear lady, but I have a strong presentiment that the streets around here are no longer as safe as they were. The fog is rising, the spirits are angry, the veil between the living and the dead is growing thin, and it wouldn't surprise me at all if an apocalypse was imminent."

Twenty-Four

A Seat of Ancient Learning

Henbane is the herbe that exists on the cuspe of goode and evile; it smells like deathe, hence it often grows in graveyards or places where necromancy was practised in ancient tymes. You will knowe it by its leaves, sticky, hairy, sharp and poisonous. The flowers are leprous and eating them will resulte in hallucinations, palpitations and convulsions. All in all, the plant is suffused with much powere, ointment containing henbane is saide to helpe witches fly. Use it welle.

The Herbal Healings of Hieronmyous
Capellanus Vol 2.

Right, I thought, as I headed up to Hampstead carrying a canvas bag containing a pair of secateurs and some gardening gloves, I daresay I'll recognize the plant when I see it. My plan was to keep my appointment with Caspian's headmaster first, and then gather the henbane on our way home. I was glad that Becca had taken William out of school for a dental appointment this afternoon. I didn't want anyone else to witness this weirdness.

A light drizzle was falling as I got off the bus near Whitestone Pond and began making my way up Spaniards

Road. Netherwold School is not conspicuous to casual passers-by; the pedestrian route is to be found in a gap in the bushes on the heath, although cars can reach the site from the back through an unmarked entrance. I'd often wondered whether Mr Montague had been unable to get permission to put up notice boards or whether he was deliberately discouraging uninvited visitors. I suspected the latter.

I pushed an overhanging branch aside and went down the narrow, twisting path. The vegetation was thick on either side of me; beech trees with ivy-clad trunks, rhododendron and holly, and thickets of bramble made the gloom all the more intense. Twigs brushed against my shoulders like dead men's fingers and at one point I stumbled as my foot skidded in a muddy rut. I felt a considerable degree of relief when I finally emerged into the clearing and saw the school in front of me, standing proudly behind its semi-circle of lawn, with the Cedar of Lebanon on the right hand side.

Netherwold had been built as a gentleman's residence in the late eighteenth-century, and as a result of the alterations made by successive owners over two centuries, the place was now an eccentric mixture of conflicting styles. The balustrades were Neo-classical, the windows were Strawberry Hill Gothic, the red brick was Queen Anne, the portico was Palladian and the turret on the left-hand side was a mid-Victorian folly. The building had been semi-derelict when the school trustees acquired it; the roof had caved in, there were pigeons roosting everywhere and a tree was growing up through one of the chimneys. Even now, after all the money that had been invested in the restoration, the interior was somewhat shabby with uneven parquet flooring and several cracked, if original fireplaces. During last year's prize-giving ceremony, a huge quantity of ceiling plaster had fallen down in the middle of the Headmaster's report to the parents. Mr Montague's response to this cascade was to raise his hands high and cry out, "See, the joy of private education! No state school window dressing here! No rubber plants in the foyer and laminated signs saying 'Welcome' in fifty different languages. Instead, we have a genuine historic building, dripping with cultural resonances and academic endeavour!" I had to admire his spirit.

I went up the stone steps to the main entrance. The heavy oak front door, bearing the Netherwold shield of the Wyvern rampant appeared to be locked, so I seized the old-fashioned bell pull and gave it a couple of tugs. An impressive clanging echoed from within.

"Do come in." The school secretary, Mrs Walker, a plump, good-natured woman in her fifties, smiled at me as she opened the door. "Mr Montague will see you a minute, if you'll just take a seat."

"Thank you." I sat down on one of the benches outside the office.

The square entrance hall had a black and white tiled floor and wood panelled walls; a rickety chandelier was suspended from the centre of the ceiling, and as I looked up at the loose metal fixture at top, I hoped that no boy would ever be tempted to swing on it. There were a number of blackened, eighteenth century oil paintings hanging on the right-hand wall. Several of these showed scenes of the heath, and there was one of a race horse, depicted in that primitive, accidentally comic style with the front legs extended forwards and the back legs extended in the opposite direction, a stance that would have caused the poor animal to collapse on the turf on its belly. In pride of place, over the fireplace, there was a portrait of the original owner of the house: Ezra Stimsly 1756-1803.

It always seemed to me that Ezra Stimsly had a rather louche expression. There was something sinister about the curl of his lip and the way he seemed to be looking sideways out of the canvas, his painted eyes avoiding any frank engagement with an observer. He looked like the kind of man who would have joined a Hell Fire Club, gambled until dawn and ravished serving wenches before dying horribly of a venereal disease in a private madhouse. I could only hope that, contrary to appearances, his spirit was at rest.

"Ah! Mrs Deadlake!" Mr Montague's door swung open. "So glad you could come to see me at such short notice."

He was wearing a bright yellow waistcoat and a pair of black velvet knickerbockers under his gown, a refreshing change from the conventional, crumpled suit mode of so many male Head Teachers in the state sector. Mr Montague was a short, rotund man with a gleaming bald head fringed by a monkish semi-circle of thick, bushy hair and one of his many peculiarities was the way his eyebrows tended to move around in rapid fashion when he was speaking, as if they were a pair of dancing death's-head moth caterpillars.

"I see you are admiring the portrait of Ezra Stimsly." He extended his hand to me as I stood up to greet him. He gripped my hand warmly, holding on to it for too long, although whether through intent or in absent mindedness, it was difficult to tell. "It is the only picture of the man in existence," he continued. "Ezra Stimsly, minor poet, traveller and opium eater. Alas, if only his writings had survived!"

"His writings?" I managed to extricate my hand from his grasp.

"They may have extended to several volumes. Sadly, they were lost. Stimsley's entire *oeuvre* was burnt after his death by a puritanical niece to whom he had, rather unwisely, left Netherwold house, not knowing, I can only assume, that she

215

intended to use it as a correction house for the castigation of fallen women. As I believe I may have mentioned before, Netherwold House has a fascinating history and I am writing a small monograph on the subject. I shall be offering it to parents at a discount when it's published. But I digress. Do come through." He indicated his study with a sweep of his hand.

Mr Montague's study looked as though it belonged in an Edwardian school story. There was a worn Turkish carpet, several glass-fronted book cases and a collection of cricket bats propped up in one corner. The walls were covered with framed group photographs of the pupils standing in rows on the lawn; a pile of lost property, socks and cricket whites and trainers, spilled out from a cardboard box placed under the mullioned window. I was somewhat startled to see some new objects on Mr Montague's desk; a goat's skull, a pewter chalice and a black candle in a silver holder.

"Props for the school play!" Mr Montague exclaimed, gathering them up and moving them to a shelf. "We are staging *Dr Faustus* as no doubt your son has told you."

"Actually, Caspian hasn't mentioned it."

"Ah! He will soon enough, I daresay. I'm delighted to say that your son gave an excellent audition and will be playing one of the demonic imps who drag Faustus to hell at the end. He has a wonderful sense of the theatrical. Please, be seated. " He placed a chair with a balloon back and a red velvet seat in front of his desk. "Now," he continued, sitting down. "Of course, I want to talk about your son's progress as I stated in my letter, but there is another more sensitive issue I want to raise."

"Oh." I swallowed. "Is Caspian causing any concern?"

"Good heavens, no!" Mr Montague's eyebrows flew into a swift lambada. "Your son, Caspian Deadlake is quite possibly the most intelligent and talented boy in the school."

"That's good to know."

"I have all the interim reports from Caspian's teachers here." He reached into his drawer and pulled out some papers. "I'll give you a copy to take home with you to study at your leisure, but suffice it to say, he has achieved an A in Latin, his art work is very advanced and he is a whiz on the computer. His English is outstanding; he can read as well as any educated adult. He's *not* very keen on games, but as you know, here at Netherwold, we don't force the boys to do anything which is anathema to them. We have cricket of course, but we don't force the jolly hockey sticks ethos here."

"But perhaps Caspian should play games," I suggested. "He spends far too much time indoors, hunched over his computer."

"Goodness me, Mrs Deadlake, so did Leonardo da Vinci!" Mr Montague's eyebrows shot upwards like Nureyev in his prime. "Spent time indoors, studying, I mean. I do not refer to the computer, although there are suggestions that, given time, Leonardo could have invented such a device. At Netherwold, we are concerned with encouraging *actual* talents rather than forcing the growing child into a mould which doesn't fit."

"Yes, I do realise that. And I'm grateful for it. Only I worry about Caspian."

"You mustn't, Mrs Deadlake, you mustn't!"

How very different this was, I thought, to those painful conversations I'd had with Mrs Havergill, the Head Teacher of Blasted Oak. I didn't want to remember the way she used to 'share her concerns' with me, as she sat before me dressed in Scholl sandals, a peasant skirt, and a crisp linen blouse. And yet her concerns weren't unfounded, of course. Caspian had refused to speak to his teacher for weeks, he had drawn a self-portrait in which he'd depicted himself as a menacing black blob, he had devised a secret language with which to communicate with his friend William, and all this, of course, before the final incident that led to both boys being expelled.

"Mrs Deadlake?"

"Sorry." I realized I'd not been paying attention, lost as I had been in these ghastly recollections. "You were saying?"

"I was explaining that we don't, at the present time, want to put up the school fees. We are, however, short of funds for the restoration of the house and for the proposed new block for which, I'm glad to say, we do have planning permission. So, rather than increase the fees, we are seeking sponsorship." His eyebrows came to rest at last.

"I see. Well, I'd love to help, but my funds are limited."

"That's a pity. I was thinking that perhaps Mr Deadlake…?"

"You're welcome to write to him. But I'm afraid my ex-husband might not be amenable. He's rather…" I stopped. *A tight-fisted bastard.* Perhaps I couldn't say that here.

"Ah, well!" Mr Montague sighed. "It is as I thought. And now I come to the sensitive issue. Please stop me if I intrude but…I believe you are divorced from Mr Deadlake?"

"Yes, I am. And to be frank, it's for the best. To tell the truth, we're not on very good terms and…Peregrine is very much an absentee father. He pays these school fees, of course but his interest in Caspian is…limited."

"Oh dear, I feared as much. Did you know that Mr Deadlake was once a pupil here? Many decades ago, of course, and before my time?"

"No." I stared at him. "I certainly didn't. He never mentioned it to me."

"I imagine that he wouldn't have done. I've recently discovered some old school records that show he was asked to leave at the age of thirteen."

"Asked to leave? You mean expelled?"

"That is one way of putting it. I'm afraid I know no more than that. Well," he rubbed his hands together. "On to happier topics! The main reason I've asked you to come here this afternoon is that I wish to invite Caspian to join our Alpha Plus Elite programme."

"I'm not quite sure what that is."

"It's the Netherwold version of the state sector's Gifted and Talented initiative," Mr Montague told me, "And it is, I might add, far superior to anything those bureaucratic numbskulls can put into practice! Oh dear, there I go again, sniping at the opposition! But I expect you can guess my views. And I daresay you share them since you chose to take your son out of state education."

I decided not to correct him by pointing out that 'chose' wasn't exactly the word I'd have used to describe Caspian's exit from Blasted Oak or that my first son Seb had actually flourished in a very ordinary, rather chaotic, state comprehensive.

"What exactly will this programme involve?" I asked

"An extra class, after school on Wednesdays, and some out of school trips. But don't worry. At first, it won't cost you an extra penny. We expect great things from Caspian, very great things."

"And what would Caspian actually be learning?"

"That is something which we will negotiate with the pupils. The emphasis is upon a guided project of their choice. They might build a tree house, study the stars, create a time machine, (only joking), but in symbolic terms, the sky is the limit. Trust us, Mrs Deadlake, trust us." Mr Montague opened his palms and turned them upwards in the manner of a priest blessing the host. "At Netherwold, we like to feel we offer an alternative to the humdrum

219

options of the National Curriculum. You won't find any Government-generated claptrap here!"

"Well, that is actually rather a relief," I said, remembering 9X's lamentable Citizenship text book. "And what about Caspian's friend William? Will he be joining this group too?"

"In pure confidence, I can tell you that William has not displayed any of the burgeoning talent we have discerned in Caspian. But, since the two boys are such friends, we shall not be separating them. Now," he glanced up at the clock. "It's only an hour to the bell, so if you want to take your son home early, you have my blessing. You'll find him in the art room with Mrs Bartholomew. Good day, do call in again, any time."

He shook my hand again, his caterpillar eyebrows tangoing enthusiastically. I thanked him, and left.

There was an impressive if disturbing mural outside the art room. It depicted devils spiking cherubs on toasting forks and holding them over a fiery furnace, tormented figures being broken on wheels, and yawning graves filled with dancing skeletons. In one section, an elongated corpse-like figure was doing a kind of strip tease as it coyly undid its winding sheet in what appeared to be a sleazy Soho night club peopled by two headed freaks. Underneath, the caption read: 'Year 6 are studying the work of Hieronymus Bosch'.

I found Caspian sitting at a bench in the art room. He was sketching a human skull that was propped up on a black velvet cushion in front of him.

"Hi there," I said. "Have you had a good day?"

"Yes. Alas, poor Yorick." Caspian pointed solemnly at the skull. "Hamlet," he added helpfully.

"Excellent," I said. "Well, when you're ready, we can go home. How about a trip to Gelato Marina on the way?"

"That will be very acceptable," Caspian said gravely.

"Right, I'd better tell Mrs Bartholomew you're leaving. Where is she?"

"Tell Mrs Bartholomew?" Caspian frowned at me, "What would be the point of that?"

"It's a courtesy," I said. "And I wouldn't want her to think you'd been kidnapped."

"Mum." Caspian put down his pencil. "Who do you suppose Mrs Bartholomew is?"

"Isn't she your new art teacher? I know that Mr Prink left last term."

"Yes," Caspian agreed. "Mr Prink did leave. He's been replaced by Mr Martin. Mr Martin had to leave early this afternoon. And that's Mrs Bartholomew over there." He pointed to a glass case on the window sill.

"I don't quite…"

"You've fallen for one of Mr Montague's jokes," Caspian informed me, "He plays it on all the new boys. He says, 'Go to the art room and ask Mrs Bartholomew for one of her felt tips'. And then he comes in, points to Mrs Bartholomew's feet and says, 'Here are her felt tips!' Mrs Bartholomew is a Mexican red knee bird eating tarantula."

"Oh." My stomach flipped over.

"She wouldn't be much good as an art teacher," Caspian said. "She'd be useless at teaching perspective. Spiders have very poor eyesight! Why don't you come and say hello to her?"

"Okay." I felt slightly sick.

I approached the glass case cautiously and stopped about a foot away. A quick glance revealed that the creature was

221

positioned on top of a small log. It was very hairy indeed. I didn't want Caspian to know I was terrified. There's something so unsettling about the appearance of a spider. It's the look of readiness and the way the body is slung *beneath* the jointed legs. With ordinary English house spiders, there's the speed at which they move, and with tarantulas, there's that deceptive stillness. Suppose you saw one out of the corner of your eye and mistook it for a ball of fluff, went to flick it away and then...

"Shall I take her out?" Caspian asked. "I'm *allowed* to pick her up."

"Um, no, I don't think you should," I said.

"But I know how to be careful," he said. "I won't drop her. And I won't startle her. Do you know what would happen if I did? She could fire one of the hairs from her legs at me, and that would bring me out in a rash."

"Leave her in her case, Cas." I was making a huge effort not to retreat to the other side of the room, something all my instincts were screaming at me to do.

"Okay." He sounded reluctant. "But look, isn't she beautiful?" He pointed to the creature's bulbous body. "Her legs are divided into five parts, tarsus, metarsus, tibia, patella and femur, and those things that look like antlers are her pedipalps. I like Mrs Bartholomew. I'm really looking forward to it being my turn on the rota to look after her in the holidays."

"Your turn on the rota?" I swallowed. Now I really *was* breaking into a cold sweat.

"What's wrong, Mum?" Caspian gave me an inquisitorial stare.

"It wouldn't be convenient," I said. "I mean, suppose you were going to visit your father? You could hardly take Mrs Bartholomew on a plane."

"Oh, I don't know," Caspian shrugged. "They might not mind."

"They would, believe me," I said. "Right, let's go to Gelato Marina. Only," I held up the bag containing my gardening stuff, "There's something we need to do first. We need to collect some henbane. I think you'll enjoy that."

Twenty-Five

Further Instructions in Demonology

"Cool!" Caspian exclaimed as we stepped into the house. "Mega-cool!"

I was astonished by the joyous expression on his face. In normal circumstances, Caspian didn't reveal any emotion whatsoever. Barely an hour ago at Gelato Marina, he'd confronted his Vesuvius Sundae, complete with chocolate flakes, sprinkled nuts, lashings of raspberry sauce and lit sparklers with a dead-pan, blank, Buster Keaton look of indifference. But now, seeing the ghastly desecration of our hallway, Caspian was so ecstatic he'd forgotten to react like a Goth.

It had all happened since I'd left the house that morning, and it was as schlocky as a scene from a horror film. Rivulets of green slime were oozing down the walls, grotesque fungoid growths had sprouted along the skirting board and swathes of thick cobwebs were hanging from the ceiling. And as for that offensive smell...*oh good grief!*

"Ah!" Ralphie came down the stairs clutching a leather-bound tome. "There you are, dear lady. As you can see, the infection is spreading."

"*Infection?*"

"I speak metaphorically. Fortunately, as you can see, the problem is confined to the hall and the living room at present. Ah-hah! I see you have gathered some henbane. Excellent timing. We may yet defeat the demonic forces that are threatening to engulf us all."

"Cas." I gave Ralphie a warning glance. "Why don't you go up to your room and get started on your homework before supper?"

"You don't have to pretend with me, Mum." My son looked at me with a pitying expression. "I know we're living in a haunted house."

"We're not." I insisted. "This is just a little rising damp and…" I looked nervously up at the cobwebs. "Perhaps a few spiders. There are always a lot around in the autumn."

"But no English spider can spin a web that size," Caspian objected.

"I wish you hadn't said that, Cas."

"Are you not fond of arachnids?" Ralphie gazed at me with interest.

"Not particularly," I tried to sound casual and unconcerned.

"What a pity," he purred. "They are fascinating creatures, although they can be a by-product of paranormal activity. I'm afraid that unless decisive action is taken, we will have far worse creatures to contend with than spiders. Soon the streets of North London could be awash with zombies, and harpies will be seen flying over the Park."

"Homework, Cas," I propelled my son towards the stairs.

"You don't have to treat me like a child, Mum." Caspian frowned.

"Young man," Ralphie turned to him, "You have astonishing maturity. But I agree with your dear mother. This situation should not be tackled by a novice, whatever his potential. Now off you go to translate Pliny, or whatever it is you've been set to decipher at that advanced school of yours."

I dumped the henbane in the sink and reached into the fridge for a bottle of white wine. When this is all over, I'll cut down on my drinking, I told myself, sloshing chardonnay into a huge green goblet.

"Would you like to know what I have discovered?" Ralphie asked, following me into the room.

"Perhaps you'd better, " I said, "but I really hope it isn't anything too dreadful."

"It depends what you mean by dreadful." He put the book down on the kitchen table with a bang, sending up a cloud of dust from its pages. "I should explain that this book that Count Valkhov has sent me is a very rare volume indeed. *The Reliques of Lord Dalrymple of Suth.* It is believed there are only two copies left in existence. It would be extremely useful if we knew the whereabouts of that other copy."

"Why's that?" I took a gulp of wine.

"Because the person who is in possession of the other copy of this book is almost certainly the person who I believe, judging from the signs, is preparing to open the Maw of Mochelmoth."

"Someone is preparing to do *what*?"

"It's all in here." He tapped the ancient cover of *The Reliques* with his forefinger. "Have you heard of Lord Dalrymple?"

"No, I can't say that I have."

"Ah! If you had studied local history, you *would* have heard of him, although the darker side of his life has been kept out of the public record. Several centuries ago, Lord

Dalrymple owned an estate in this area when it was open country. Before these streets were built and the Park was laid out, there were marshes where a gentleman could go duck shooting. There were just a few rudimentary farm buildings and, most significantly, there was also Lord Dalrymple's lost mansion." He began to turn the pages of the book. "Come and look. Here is a plan of the house. As you can see, there were cellars and an intricate labyrinth of tunnels and here," he pointed to the middle of the page, "is the shrine Lord Dalrymple built underground for his satanic practices."

"Satanic practices?" I looked down at the diagram. I could make very little sense of the plan, all those brown, spidery lines, crossing and re-crossing on the stained yellow page.

"Indeed. Lord Dalrymple believed he had created a gateway to the underworld. The Maw of Mochelmoth."

"And where was it exactly, this mansion of Lord Dalrymple?"

"That is a matter of some dispute, but it was almost certainly very close to here. What we do know is that as Lord Dalrymple got older and more eccentric, his architectural ambitions increased. He built turrets and spires and Italianate towers. And then, on the night he attempted to open the Maw, the house collapsed in a maelstrom of terror. And Lord Dalrymple, aghast at the peril to which he had put his own soul, entered a monastery and left the bulk of his fortune to charitable causes in the hope of avoiding the fires of hell."

"So the 'Maw' was never opened?"

"Oh, I think it was, but it was sealed again when the mansion collapsed. Now someone is attempting to repeat the experiment." He turned the pages of the book. "Allow me to read you this extract:

'Through the summer, in the cellars of the Great House, Lord Dalrymple did commission the building of the shrine that was designed to receive the demon Mochelmoth, calling it the Maw. Tunnels were dug leading from the hunting lodge to the shrine, and much difficulty was experienced through the flooding caused by the heavy rains of August, causing the drowning of two servants and a dog. Still, such loss of life strengthened rather than weakened his resolve. As Lord Dalrymple said in his journals, 'The demon will take life, and it is better that it take that of underlings than our own.' As you can see," he looked at me with an ironic expression. "Lord Dalrymple had no real love for his fellow man."

"It doesn't sound like it."

"Quite. The account continues, *'As the leaves of autumn began to brown, Lord Dalrymple did recruit the necessary acolytes, five young people of particularly evil disposition. He tutored them in the necessary chants and the sounds. As time progressed, a heavy fog lay upon the land and many spirits were seen, as if risen from the dead. The ground grew swampy and miasmus-ridden and some did hear strange shrieking in the night. We ate the flesh of tortoises and drank the blood of bats, and hunted down the werewolf......'* I'm afraid that from this point, the writer becomes rather verbose. But there are other excellent accounts of the ritual that was attempted, notably in *Darnley's Demonologie*."

"But surely nothing like that can be happening right now?" I objected.

"I fear it can. Remember how, a few days ago, I mentioned how strange it was that there was so much fog in this area? That is an indication that someone is opening the Maw."

"Oh dear." I looked up at the cobweb around the light-fitting. No matter how many times I swept it away, it *would* keep returning. "So what can I do?"

"Secure the house. Distribute the henbane. Lay a few sprigs wherever there is a threshold or an entry, by which I mean doorways and window sills, electric sockets and phone lines. You will need plenty in the hall and you should unseal the living room door and put some in there too. The stalks must be placed in water in an earthenware vessel. I suggest you also place some in the sinks, basins, and the bath. Plug holes can be very problematic in these situations. You never know what may come up the pipes."

"Spiders?"

"Oh, no." He smiled slyly. "It is far more likely to be a paranormal manifestation. But take my advice and..." The *Dead March in Saul* chimed out.

"Ah!" Ralphie held up a finger. "You have a visitor."

Oh, good grief, who was that? I didn't want anyone to see my hallway, not even the person who wanted to read the meter. But on the other hand, it might be Seb, my sensible, elder son coming to put everything right. He might be home early for Hallowe'en, ringing the doorbell because he'd forgotten his key. With mounting hope, I went to the door. But it wasn't Seb. It was Josh and he was jumping around from foot to foot, looking more than a little manic.

"Blimey." Josh stared at the devastation as he stepped into the hall. "What's with all the slime?"

"Oh." I shrugged. "It's just a bit of condensation. You get it in newer houses."

"Do you?" Josh stretched out his hand to touch the wall, "But it's really wet! Have you tried getting an extractor fitted?"

Josh was in his cycle shorts and sleeveless vest, but he wasn't wearing the baseball cap, and his appearance seemed even more hirsute than when I'd seen him last.

229

"I'm not sure an extractor fan would be much use," I said.

"No? But look at all that fungus along the skirting board!"

"It's a bit of a problem, I admit. But come through to the kitchen, Josh. It's better in there."

"Good evening, young man. I don't believe we've met." Ralphie emerged from the kitchen, approaching Josh in an uncanny manner, as though his feet were hovering an inch off the ground. Which they were, I realized, as I looked down. Much to my relief, Josh hadn't noticed the party trick that was being demonstrated for his benefit.

"Pleased to meet you." Josh held out his hand.

Ralphie didn't shake his hand, but instead took hold of it, turned it over, scrutinized the palm with disturbing intensity. At last, he let go, frowning deeply.

"I must ask you a personal question." He gazed into Josh's eyes. "Have you been attacked recently?"

"I have, as it happened." Josh grinned cheerfully. "But I'm over it now."

"And what happened?"

"Well," Josh shrugged. "It was all rather random. A homeless man bit me."

"Bit you? *Hmm.* And where were you when this unfortunate incident occurred?"

"I was outside Chalk Farm Station."

"Chalk Farm Station." Ralphie repeated gravely. "At what time of night?"

"It was in the morning. Broad daylight...well, come to think of it was bit foggy."

"Foggy. I see. Well, my advice to you, young man, is to wear some silver about your neck. Give up eating meat for a month. And stay at home at night."

"Right." Josh nodded politely.

"And now I must take my leave," Ralphie said. "I have an appointment with my dear friend Georgia. She's going to take me for a spin in her new vehicle. We're going to visit Kensal Green, the route to Paradise, as G. K. Chesterton said. Good night to you both." He bowed and left.

"What an amazing old guy," Josh said. "Who is he? Some kind of New Age guru?"

"Not exactly," I said. "I shouldn't pay too much attention to the things he says. He can be very…imaginative. Would you like a drink?"

"Just a fruit juice please. I don't know why, but I've gone off alcohol."

"Right." I reached into the fridge. "Pineapple, orange or mixed tropical?"

"Mixed tropical. Thanks. Look, I hope you don't mind me calling in unexpectedly. I didn't see you at school today."

"I left at lunch-time. I had to go and see my son's head teacher."

"Oh. I see. It's just that I wanted to ask about those Chappaquiddick tapes."

"They're here." I picked up the box that was standing on the breakfast bar. "I was going to bring them into school. But they're just for your use, all right? No posting the material on YouTube or anything like that."

"Fine." He sniffed at his drink, and then bent over his glass, lapping up the juice in a weirdly animalistic manner. "Look, though, what about the rest of the band? Mad McArthur, Dingo, and Loon Tailor? Do you think they have any of the unreleased material?"

"They might, I suppose."

"Are you still in touch with any of them?"

"I used to visit Dingo sometimes. I haven't been for quite some time though."

231

"I see." Josh looked reflective. "Any chance I could have his address? I'd like to go and see him."

"I don't know that Dingo's up to receiving visitors, even now," I said. "He was very badly affected by what happened. Sometimes, he seems to have very little connection with reality."

"Don't you think it might cheer him up to meet a real Chappaquiddick fan?" Josh asked. "What harm would it do if you told me where he lives?"

I thought for a moment, remembering Dingo, the last time I'd visited, a few summers ago. He'd been sitting on the rusting garden swing at the bottom of the garden, dolefully squeaking an inflatable plastic hamburger over and over again, while his mother, Ella, had sat on a deckchair, shelling peas into a colander. I'd tried to get Dingo to talk, but it was one of his bad days, and then Ella had launched into a monologue, talking about Dingo as though he wasn't there: *'Derek never liked his step-Dad and that was when all the trouble started. Threw him out when he was fifteen. Then he started that group, and why he had to change his name to Dingo, after some nasty Australian dog, I'll never know. And he was such a good little boy, always on my knee, playing on his xylophone. I don't even like rock music, me, I like the James Last Orchestra. I wish Derek could have been the leader of a proper band.'*

"All right," I said, suddenly decisive. "It's number thirty-three, Sycamore Avenue, Leigh on Sea, Essex. There's a massive sculpture of Sid Vicious in the front garden. You can't miss it."

"Brilliant!" Josh beamed at me. "Thanks Dora. And don't worry, I'll be careful. But you know, I've got a gut feeling that I'm going to get on really well with Dingo."

"Yes," I said. "Perhaps you will."

Twenty-Six

Extra-Curricular Activities of an Undesirable Kind

Anarchy was reigning at Havelock Ellis High School. This was the third time the fire alarm had gone off today, set off by some disaffected kid or other, and now here we were, battling our way down staircase four to the muster station in the playground. There was so much pushing and shoving I was afraid there'd be a serious accident. I called out several times, appealing for calm, but my voice was lost in the hubbub. At least I've been released from supervising the class with Brian Belluga in it, I thought. A moment later, someone stabbed me from behind with what felt like the point of a pair of compasses, so all consolation fled.

"This is a bloody outrage," McTaggart fulminated as he elbowed his way through the melee. "Who's in charge? Where's that man Langford? Come back Mr Wheel, all is forgiven!"

Out in the playground, Paul Gogarty and Mr Randle were doing sterling stuff, yelling at the throng through loud-hailers, but even they were struggling to impose any order. At least three fights were in progress and a water bomb had been hurled from the roof.

"Line up! Line up at once! Treat this as a normal fire drill!" It sounded as though Gogarty was losing his Welsh tenor voice.

"Hello, Miss." The Honey Monster appeared in front of me. "I've got our work on *Lord of the Flies.*" He held up a Tesco carrier bag filled with tatty exercise books. "And I've brought some other stuff too. You know that lesson we had with you about the illegal immigrant?"

"I'm not sure that PSE lesson was supposed to be about illegal immigrants, Darren, but never mind, we'll talk about that later. Thank you for the books. You'd better get back to your class."

"They're still in the building, setting off the alarms, miss. But don't tell anyone I told you it's them, or they might do me over."

"Oh, Darren…"

"Dalston! Over here!" Paul Gogarty waved at him furiously. "Why aren't you in line?"

"I gotta go, Miss." The boy fled.

That poor kid, I thought. Something had to be done about his situation. Should I consult Aidan Langford? There was always the chance he could do something. He had such a way with 9X. But where was he at this moment? Now I came to think about it, I hadn't seen him all day.

"Looks like your friend Aidan Langford's deserted the sinking ship," Zelda told me as we sat recovering from the mayhem in Oddballs Corner.

"He's not my friend," I said. "But surely he hasn't given up already?"

"Must have done. He didn't turn up for a meeting with the Science department yesterday afternoon, and then Tracy in the office told me that he sent a fax in this morning, saying he'd gone to a conference and wouldn't be back until further notice. What's the betting this so-called 'conference' is in a posh hotel, with free lunches, free mineral water, free sweets, free ball-point pens and a voucher to visit the nearest lap-dancing club?"

"I can't imagine ARL at a lap dancing club." I giggled wickedly at the thought. "There's something so puritanical about him."

"And I can't imagine him staying at this school," Zelda added. "It's the same with all these ideological types; none of their ideas work in practice. Good riddance!"

When I returned from the shambles of Havelock Ellis High School to the dereliction of Arcadia Square, I found the hallway and the living room were still infested with slime and cobwebs. It didn't seem as though the henbane was having any effect at all. Once Caspian was settled upstairs, enjoying the hour between supper and bed when he was allowed to play a few computer games, I poured myself a large G. and T. and spread 9X's books and papers out on the kitchen table. Might as well get the job done.

I sighed deeply. As I feared, this so-called 'work' didn't look promising. I flicked through the exercise books, trying to decipher the hieroglyphics and doodles and desperately searching for something I could praise. Positive reinforcement was essential, I'd read in my *Practical Guide to Teaching*. Well, Bradley *had* managed to write the date legibly and not only had Chantelle written it, she'd underlined it twenty times using a variety of colours, slightly decreasing the length of the lines each time to create an upside-down pyramid. Unfortunately, that was all she'd done, unlike Nando, who had made his feelings on *Lord of the Flies* very clear:

That Piggy deserved all he got. I hate fat speccy people.

Oh dear. Where to start with that one? I turned to the Honey Monster's Citizenship book. No, *Darren Dalston's* book, I corrected myself quickly. Alas, this was no better:

The ill eagle immingrunts come here to use the NHS. They take our jobs and cough jerms in the doctors waiting room all uver us, my dad says, so we all get ill and dye of toober lossis.

'Toober lossis'? I was puzzled for a moment. I tried saying the word out loud.

Of course. *Tuberculosis.* 'My Dad says'… Oh no. I was going to have to challenge this piece, even if it did mean that Mr Dalston might storm into school and thrust his fist in my face.

"Ah, there you are." Ralphie appeared in the doorway. He was wearing a tailored overcoat with a velvet collar and was carrying an antique pigskin travelling case. "As you can see, I am about to set out on a journey."

"A journey? Where are you going?"

"I am going to Paris via the Eurotunnel. Georgia is driving me there to meet my old friend Count Valkhov whom I hope to persuade to come to London. The Count is highly skilled in alchemy and the occult and I have every confidence that he will know how to avert the threatened apocalypse."

"*Apocalypse?* Are you really serious about that? I thought you were joking the other night when you said…"

"No joke, I assure you. I'm afraid that if the Satanists who are planning to reopen the Maw of Mochelmoth succeed, there could be disastrous consequences."

"And what about the Count?" Domestic details pressed on me rather more than the prospect of this threatened apocalypse. "Is he coming here?"

"Oh, don't alarm yourself." He held up his hand. "I wouldn't dream of asking you to accommodate the Count. Besides which, he will need very *special* conditions. Georgia has prepared her cellar in readiness. I plan to be back by Thursday evening. I can only hope we will be in time."

"In time? In time for what?"

"In time to prevent the Maw being opened and the demon being raised."

"And when do you think this 'Maw' will be opened?"

"I have consulted the necessary astrological charts. All the conditions suggest it will take place this week. By now, the Arch-Priest must have instructed the acolytes to capture the sacrificial victim and he or she will be trapped behind the Gehenna gate."

"Sacrificial victim?" *Oh good grief, what if all this nonsense was actually real?* "Trapped behind the Gehenna gate?"

"I'm afraid I really don't have time to explain it all now. You can read about it in *Darnley's Demonologie.* I have marked the place in the book. Now, I advise you to stay in the house tonight. Secure all the windows, lock the front door from the inside, and batten down your proverbial hatches. And if you hear the sound of ravens pecking on the roof or the cries of ghouls in your cupboards, pay no attention. Don't alarm yourself."

"Listen, Ralphie..." I wasn't sure I believed in this demon, but perhaps someone else did, and if someone really had been kidnapped it was serious. "Shouldn't the police be informed? If there *is* a sacrificial victim..."

"The police wouldn't be unable to deal with this," Ralphie pulled on a pair of white evening gloves. "And besides, as yet, we have no concrete evidence concerning the identity of the High Priest or the Acolytes. But I must go.

You must be anxious to get back to perusing the intellectual endeavours of these young minds." He pointed to the papers and exercise books on the table with his death's head stick.

"Actually," I said, "I'm not anxious to get back to it at all. 9X's so-called work is doing my head in. It's barely literate."

"Really?" Ralphie picked up one of the exercise books, took an eye-glass out of his waistcoat pocket, and scrutinized a random page. "Well, all I can say is that English education has advanced considerably since my young day. It seems that even your least able students are familiar with Ancient Babylonian."

"Ancient Babylonian?"

"Most certainly." He held out the book. "See for yourself."

I stared at the book. It was Desmond O'Leary's, crumpled and stained, redolent with the smell of cheese and onion crisps.

"That's just graffiti," I said. "What kids call their 'tags'. They spray-paint them on walls to demonstrate their street cred."

"Ancient Babylonian," Ralphie insisted. "See here? My knowledge of the language is rather rusty, but I can translate these words, 'Oh great Mochelmoth, we salute you.' It would be reckless of me to read any more out loud, of course. Anything could happen. At the very least, a giant salamander with human arms could leap from your toilet cistern. Still, we have made progress. I think we may have identified the acolytes."

"The acolytes?" I stared at him in disbelief. "But how can 9X be the acolytes?"

"Very easily, if the High Priest has recruited them. Do you remember that account in the *Reliques?* The reference to five young people of particularly evil disposition?"

"Nando, Desmond O'Leary, Rizwan, Chantelle and Bradley. " I swallowed. "Oh my God!"

"Exactly." He nodded. "And have you ever heard them practicing the ritual? Humming in unison for example?"

"No, I…*oh!* That's exactly what I've heard them doing, in their Citizenship lesson. It's known as the death hum."

"Ha! Then I rest my case."

"But if it's 9X…" I was struggling to get my head round this. "I'll have to find them. I'll have to stop them!"

"Impossible, I'm afraid," Ralphie shook his head. "For one thing, you don't know where they will have taken their victim. And if you were foolish enough to enter the Maw of Mochelmoth, you would never be able to pass through the Gehenna Gate."

"Just what is this Gehenna Gate? You mentioned it before."

"The Gehenna Gate is a psychic security barrier, a dimension of dark energy that feeds upon the deepest of fears and phobias of the person attempting to breach it. Once the sacrificial victim has been placed in the Maw, the High Priest will have created one to prevent any potential rescue. No, you must leave this matter to the experts, to myself and Count Valkhov. However, I do have one question. In your opinion, who would 9X choose as a sacrificial victim?"

"I'm afraid that's obvious. There's this boy in the class they're always picking on. Darren Dalston."

"And when did you last see this boy?"

"This afternoon."

"Then, for various reasons too complicated to enumerate, including the unsuitability of his young age, he cannot have been chosen. And, as I said before, the sacrificial victim will have been in the Maw for at least twenty-four hours."

"But that's terrible!"

"Indeed. All the more reason for me to be on my way. Good night, dear lady and please don't ignore my advice. You do so at your peril."

I stared down at 9X's work, lying on the kitchen table in front of me. This just couldn't be happening, could it? 9X writing in Ancient Babylonian? No, they couldn't possibly...

But who knew, perhaps they could.

Twenty-Seven

Instructions in Demonology Part 3

A sacrificial victim, a High Priest, the Maw of Mochelmoth
... all of that sounded fantastical but, it occurred to me, even
if the story of Lord Dalrymple's activities was a fiction, the
plot of an eighteenth century Gothic novel, or a local legend,
that wouldn't stop 9X hearing about it. They might even
know the person who'd got the other copy of the *Reliques*.
My mind was racing. If they hadn't chosen Darren Dalston
as their victim, who would they choose and what would they
do to them? I wished Ralphie had stopped to explain more.
Ah! But hadn't he said there was a full account of the ritual
in *Darnley's Demonologie?* I raced upstairs and flung open
the door of Peregrine's office. There was the book, standing
on a lectern, with the pages held open by the grotesque,
mummified claw. Feeling more than a little apprehensive,
I bent over it and began to read:

*The Mochelmoth Ritual was first attempted by the
alchemist, Aladrad of Prague, in 1395. To open the Maw,
five acolytes of either sex and less than twenty years of age,
must be recruited by the High Priest. They must learne to
humme in unison at a level fit to split the eardrums of a
vampire bat. Then they must sprinkle the ground at the
entrance to the labyrinthe with the bloode of a werewolf and*

repeat the words of the incantation by moonlighte. After, they must bring he who is to be fedde to the demon to the shrine. He must come willingly but without knowing the true purpose. Choose one of integritie and intellect, one ye holde in high esteem.

Oh! Relief flooded through me! *Choose one of integritie and intellect, one ye holde in high esteem.* 9X couldn't possibly be involved in this farrago of satanic nonsense. They didn't hold anyone in high esteem. They were too filled with adolescent angst for that. They hated everyone, their teachers, their parents, the police, the social workers, even the person who served them in McDonalds. Still, I might as well finish reading this grim account:

Tie the victim hande and foote and to prevente further escape, breake ye the kneecaps with a lead implement that has been dipped in the urine of rats. But onlie resorte to full damage if he is not compliante and needeth the crushinge of all leg bones. Forme a circle around him and sustaine the humme of death for a full thirty minutes. Then the bodie must be purged with a serum of wormewoode dissolved in wine and no further foode to be administered. Then leave the victim alone to his fate.

When the thirty eighth hour is strucke, the demon will begin to rise, smelling the stench and agonie of the starvinge and dying manne. He will be eaten alive and....

This was horrible. But it wasn't real. It couldn't be.

"Mum?" Caspian appeared in the doorway. "I've just been talking to Seb on Skype. Do you want to have a word?"

"Oh…yes, yes, of course. And it's time you had a wash, brushed your teeth and got into your pyjamas."

Back to normality, or at least the reassurance of seeing my older son, his blond hair held back in a sports band, grinning into the webcam with a morass of beer cans, sports clothes, books and climbing gear behind him.

"Hi, Seb." I sat down at the computer. "Are you eating enough fruit?"

"Mum!" He laughed. "You always say that!"

"That's because I know you don't eat enough fruit."

"I'm fine, Mum." He moved closer, pointing to his face. "Look, no spots!"

"You never did have spots, Seb. I don't know why, but I still think you should…"

"Eat more fruit?" He took a swig from his can of Budweiser. "You're probably right. How are you Mum?"

"Oh, I'm fine." I hoped he believed me. Never, at any point in my life, had I burdened Seb with my problems.

"Good. Look, Mum, I am sorry about this, but I can't get home for the Hallowe'en weekend. Some of the guys here are getting a trip together to Snowdonia, last climb of the season. I've apologised to Cas. I know he likes me to take him trick or treating and help him put up the Hallowe'en decorations."

"Hallowe'en decorations?" I gave a hollow laugh. "We don't need to buy any of those this year!"

"What do you mean, Mum?" Seb looked puzzled.

"Nothing! Nothing at all. Forget I said it. There are a few autumn spiders in the house, that's all." *And ghosts and green slime and fungus and an elderly vampire.*

"I thought you'd got that worried look."

"Me?" I did my best to adjust my expression. "No. It's just…"

"You haven't been having any trouble from the wicked step-Dad, I hope?"

"I don't think we should call him that. Think of Cas. But I am sorry about how he was with you."

"It doesn't matter. I mean, it was just one of those typical step-family things. I can see the funny side. Remember those suppers Peregrine used to cook? All that spice. *Chilli con carne* with too much chilli. Those curries. Hot as hell! Absolutely diabolical!"

"*Diabolical?* Why did you use that word?"

"It's just an expression, Mum."

"Yes. Of course it is."

"Got to go, Mum, sorry." He glanced at his watch. "Squash court's booked. Sorry about Hallowe'en, but we'll make it up over Christmas, right?"

"Right. And you have a good time in Snowdonia, Seb. You will be careful on the mountains, won't you?"

"Of course. Bye Mum."

"Bye Seb."

I came out of Skype and was about to call to Caspian to hurry up in the bathroom, when I noticed an icon on his home screen that I didn't recognize, an image of a maze with what appeared to be a mythical creature at the centre. Another game he'd downloaded, I assumed; I hoped it wasn't anything that would be classified as an '18'. Better check.

As I clicked on the icon, the screen went black, and then an image of an inhuman, rotting face appeared. Worms were crawling out of its black, cavernous eye sockets; spiky bristles sprouting from its mouldering cheeks. *Grief,* Caspian must have disabled the parental controls that Seb had set up for me yet again!

"Cas?" I yelled. "Come here. There's something on your computer..." I broke off, as the rotting face rippled and disappeared.

A new image appeared; a sky lit up by the urban glow of street lights with a full moon floating out from behind a cloud. There was a canal, a derelict warehouse surrounded by high wire fencing, and a small arched bridge. It looked very much like a section of the canal that I knew. Then a shaggy animal, more wolf than dog, appeared on the left-hand side of the screen, sniffing and lurching along the canal. A message flashed up: *Kill the werewolf! Kill the werewolf!* The wolf-dog dodged through a gap in the wire fence into a yard and careered past the warehouse and around several dilapidated sheds heading for a small brick building with an open entrance.

Kapow! The word appeared on the screen as a stylized bullet hit the animal; there was an anguished howl as it keeled over, then lay on the ground, limbs twitching and blood spreading from its neck. A moment later, the creature transformed into an old, derelict-looking man with long straggling grey-brown hair. He was obviously dead.

"Hi, kids!" a voice announced in a cheerful Aussie accent. "You want to play this game for real? If you can get to level 7, you'll find the code and an email address. Send me that code and your details by the closing date and your names will be entered into the prize draw. Five lucky winners will get to open the Maw of Mochelmoth itself. Auditions will be held at a school near you. But remember, it's not for wimps! You'll recognize me; here I am!" A face filled the screen.

If I hadn't been shocked before, I certainly was now. There was no mistaking that pony-tail, that bronzed complexion and that cheery larrikin grin.

It was Tel.

Twenty-Eight

An Unexpected Act of Heroism

"Mum?" Caspian stood in front of me, dressed in his Jack Skellington pyjamas. "Why are you playing on my computer?"

"Cas," I tried to keep my voice steady. "Did you get to Level 7 on this game?"

"Of course I did."

"And," I continued, my heart beating rapidly, "did you email in your name?"

"Of course I didn't." There was just a hint of disdain in his voice and if I hadn't been feeling so alarmed, I might have reminded him not to speak to me like that.

"Are you sure, Cas?"

"Yes. I know all about being safe on the internet. Anyway, I don't think that's a very good game. I could have designed something much better myself. It was so easy to kill the werewolf and…"

"Cas," I interrupted. "Please promise you won't play this game anymore."

"Oh," he shrugged. "Why would I want to? The closing date for winning the competition was weeks ago. I'm going to delete it."

"Don't do that just yet," I said. "I may need to show it to someone. But shut the computer down now and get into bed.

You can read for half an hour, then it's lights out. What are you reading at the moment?"

"Ray Bradbury: *Something Wicked This Way Comes*."

How appropriate, I thought.

I poured myself a large drink and sat down at the kitchen table. I needed to think.

So Ralphie was right. 9X *were* involved. They'd played that computer game, then they'd been recruited by Tel and now they'd almost certainly kidnapped and tortured someone. *Oh no!* I had to ignore Ralphie's instructions and tell the police!

But what could I tell them that wouldn't sound completely deranged? '*Look, here's the evidence, it's in ancient Babylonian and here's this computer game and a book about an eighteenth-century nobleman, and a medieval text on demons...* 'No, no, they'd laugh at me, or worse still, get me sectioned. And now something else occurred to me. I was partly responsible, wasn't I? I was the person who'd left 9X alone with Tel. I couldn't just ignore this.

Even if I couldn't tell the police, I had to do *something*. It was all very well for Ralphie to tell me to wait until he got back from Paris with Count Valkhov, but if 9X really had imprisoned someone in that brick building down by the warehouses, then that person was in serious trouble. Stuck underground in a dark hole, starving, thirsty, tied up, suffering the pain of broken kneecaps, suffering from hypothermia, shock and probably pneumonia...oh good grief! And what about '*sprinkle the ground at the entrance to the labyrinthe with the bloode of a werewolf*'? Did that mean 9X had attacked an old homeless man like the one in the video game? Surely even they wouldn't go that far?

I mustn't panic. I must look for more evidence. I started rifling through the exercise books and papers again. There might be something here, something that wasn't in ancient Babylonian, but which would tell me more about what 9X had been doing. *Oh!* What was this sheet of paper that had just fallen out of Chantelle's book? Surely they couldn't have…but it seemed they had. The evidence couldn't be clearer

Not in school this week.

Gone to a confferance. Yours, Mr. A. Langford

Now I knew just who it was 9X had chosen and how they'd ensured their sacrificial victim wouldn't be missed. And there was no time to lose.

I rushed up to my bedroom and changed into some old jeans, a sweatshirt and my walking boots and then went to Seb's room and ransacked it for useful equipment; I stuffed a rope, a pen-knife, a heavy torch, a pair of waterproof trousers and a cagoule into his spare rucksack. He had so much stuff in here, even though he always took a lot of his climbing and pot-holing gear to uni with him. There would be other things I'd need; a first aid kit, water. Some iron rations, a blanket and…yes, here was Seb's spare caving helmet, that could be useful. I tried it on for size.

"Mum? What are you doing?" Caspian gazed at me from the doorway.

"Cas." I realized how breathless I was. "Get your overnight bag and your clothes for tomorrow. I'm going to take you up in a taxi to stay with Becca and William; I have to go out."

"But no-one will be there until late," Caspian said. "They've gone to the theatre."

"In the middle of the week?" I took a sharp intake of breath.

"Yes, don't you remember? They won the tickets in the school raffle."

I didn't remember but now I was completely dismayed. I wasn't prepared to leave my eight-year-old alone in the house, even if he *was* quite unlike any other eight-year-old known to man. According to Ralphie, ghouls were about to start screaming from the cupboards and ravens were going to peck at the roof. Cas would love that, but there were more commonplace hazards to consider such as a fire breaking out, or a local paedophile shinning up the drain pipe. Anything could happen and knowing my luck, it probably would.

"Go back to bed, Cas," I said. "I'm going to find someone to come here and stay with you."

"But Mum, I'm not a chil…"

"To bed, Cas! Now!"

I picked up my mobile, trying to think of a possible childsitter.

There was always Zelda. She might not be the obvious choice, but she only lived in Adelaide Road and if she jumped on her Vespa, she could be here very quickly. I rang her home number and waited for her to answer for what seemed an interminable time.

"Hi." Zelda whispered at last. She was there after all. What a relief.

"Zelda, it's Dora." My chest felt tight. "Listen, I know this is short notice but it's a bit of an emergency. I have to go out, and there's no-one here to keep an eye on Cas. Once he's asleep, he won't wake up or be any trouble, but if you could just…"

"Hey man! The eagle has landed!" Zelda yelled. This didn't bode well.

"Are you OK?" I asked.

I could hear music pounding in the background. It sounded like *One Step Beyond* by Madness.

"The eagle flies on Fri——day. Friday! Friday. Eagle... pie....eagle pie...." Zelda intoned the words like an insane monk attempting a Gregorian chant.

"Zelda, is everything all right?" My stomach twisted with anxiety.

"Got some friends here. Ska and skunk night, man, ska and skunk," Zelda slurred, "Whoo! Ow! Sorry, not quite focusing here."

"Zelda? Listen!" I gripped the phone tightly in my hand. "Have you taken something?"

"Smoked a few!"

"Then is there anyone else there with you? Anyone who could help? I wouldn't normally ask, but I really need to go out and…"

I stopped. I could imagine the kind of people Zelda was hanging out with at that moment. I doubted if I'd want any of them in my home, not even in an emergency like this. I'd have to think of something else.

"Do you have Josh's number?" I asked. "Might he be at home?"

"Josh is on his way to Leigh-on-Sea," Zelda said. "Don't ask me why. I expect he wanted some seaside rock."

"Okay," I suppressed a moan. "Never mind. Bye." I ended the call.

Now what? Could I take Cas with me? *No*. He'd absolutely love an adventure, of course, but what sort of mother would I be if I took him down into some filthy underground tunnel that was being used as a torture chamber? Besides, he had school tomorrow.

So who was going to keep an eye on my son, while I was risking life and limb in the Maw of Mochelmoth?

"There's always me, girl." A voice, soft as the dew on Hackney Marshes, had spoken.

"Davey?" I breathed his name. "Are you really here?"

"I'm really here, girl." It was his voice, there was no mistaking it. My heart was full; he'd come, heaven knew how, in this moment of need, selflessly and without question.

"But why can't I see you?"

"Dunno. But I'm here. Don't get in a flap. I ain't got long and you ain't got long. You've got things to do. I'll keep an eye on the kid for you. You get going. And don't forget the henbane."

"The henbane?"

"I told you that before. Look, girl, we'd better not waste time talking. Trust me. I can keep the kid safe. It'll be fine and I won't let him see me."

"O.K." I grabbed a handful of the plants from the earthenware basin by the sink. Then I ran back upstairs to say goodnight to Caspian.

"Cas, listen," I said. "You won't be on your own. There's someone here to keep an eye on things. He's downstairs. But I want you to stay in bed, all right?"

"Where exactly *are* you going, Mum?" He turned a page of his book.

"Oh, just out for a bit," I said.

"I think you should be more specific," he said. "Suppose you have an accident or don't come back and I have to tell the police where you went?"

"Cas, that's an awful thing to say!"

"I'm just being practical, Mum. It's what parents say all the time, isn't it? *I need to know where you're going?*"

"Yes. They do." There was, as always, a cool logic about Caspian's thinking. He was right, I did need to tell him more, although 'I am going to look for the Maw of Mochelmoth' just wouldn't do. I took a deep breath and chose my words carefully.

"Right," I said. "This is what it is. I'm going down to the canal. It's to do with some kids that I teach. They've seen that computer game you were playing. And I think they've taken it seriously and they mean to hurt someone."

"I don't see why you need to get involved, Mum." Caspian turned over another page.

"Cas, I do. You see the person they want to hurt is…" *An arrogant, annoying person who nevertheless doesn't deserve to die horribly because I stupidly told 9X that important teachers go to conferences.*

"Do you really think the canal is a safe place for you to go on your own at night?" I rather liked the way my son was admonishing me with a severity beyond his years.

"I'll be fine, Cas," I said. "I can look after myself."

"Well," Cas nodded. "If you're going into the labyrinth, you'd better take the map."

"*Map*?"

"Yes. It was part of the game. It was security protected but I soon hacked in and downloaded it. Look, it's over there, on the bookcase."

"Oh, Cas. That's brilliant." I picked up the piece of paper and unfolded it. The canal and the warehouses were clearly marked and with it, was a diagram of a complex maze of underground tunnels. "This is going to be a great help. Good night, then."

"Good-night Mum."

As I came down into the hall, I heard *Three Steps to Heaven* being strummed gently on a guitar.

"I'm going now, Davey," I said.

"You take care, then girl." I heard his soft whisper. "I won't let nothing bad happen here. Go now. You're going to be fine."

And it was with that ghostly assurance ringing in my ears that I opened my front door and went out into the night.

Twenty-Nine

Into the Tunnel

The fog was thick down by the canal; I certainly needed my torch. I kept to the side of the path closest to the bushes, walking as fast as I could. This isn't entirely my fault, I told myself, what about the naivety of the Havelock Ellis office staff? It wasn't difficult to work out how 9X had played this trick. One of them must have got into the old technology room where there was a fax machine, and had managed to send that message through to the school office. And Tracy, Kathy and Marie had taken it at face value. Why, for heaven's sake, hadn't they noticed the obvious forgery, the misspelling and the abrupt style? Even without that, did they really think Aidan would announce his absence in this off-hand way? And hadn't they stopped to wonder why he'd disappeared without warning the previous afternoon, missing a scheduled meeting with the Science Department?

But of course they hadn't. They were used to the behaviour of Mr Wheel.

The toe of my boot struck a discarded cider bottle. As it rolled away from me and fell with a splash in the water, I heard stifled laugher and a rustling in the bushes.

"Going somewhere special?" A figure stepped out in front of me, a slouching youth in a hooded top. His face was covered by a black balaclava, but I could just make out a pair of pale lips and two rather vacant eyes. The voice was faintly nasal; it sounded like Brian Belluga.

"I said, you going somewhere? I know you. You're that crap supply teacher."

So it *was* Brian Belluga, my tormentor again. He was standing far too close to me; I could smell the chewing gum on his breath and the stink of his fetid trainers. My fingers tightened on my heavy torch. If the worst happened, I could always use it in self-defence.

"Hello, lad," I said. "You're out late. Does your Mum know?"

Belluga gazed at me with contempt. Then, "Everybody out!" he shouted.

Several more youths emerged from the bushes. I was surrounded. There were seven of them, but I only recognized one of the others, a large, lumpy boy with studs in both ears who went under the nickname of Hard Boy. It seemed likely that the rest of them were also from Havelock Ellis, but as it was so dark and none of them were in uniform, I had no way of knowing. Perhaps it was best to treat this situation as a joke. A little light ridicule wouldn't come amiss, either.

"Do take that balaclava off, lad," I said. "It doesn't suit you. Or are you forced to wear it because your auntie knitted it for you for Christmas?"

"Shame!" Hard Boy leaned over and pulled the balaclava off Belluga's head. There was a mild scuffle but the other boys continued to block my path.

"You can't come through here," Belluga said in a sulky tone. "This is our manor."

"Don't be silly," I said, "Of course I can come past. This is a public footpath."

"Yeh? Well, maybe someone's paid us to guard it." Belluga folded his arms with an air of triumph.

"Don't tell her that, dickhead!" Hard Boy hit him in the stomach.

"Would that person be in 9X?" I asked, addressing the now doubled-up, coughing figure of Belluga.

"We ain't saying nothing," growled Hard Boy.

"We might go if you give us somefink." Belluga straightened up, eyes streaming. "You got anyfink we'd like?" He drew a bread knife from his pocket.

This situation was getting serious. Even if Belluga was bluffing with the knife, accidents could happen and I had a strong suspicion that a Belluga-bluff could turn into deliberate violence in a split second. And as for his companions, I knew Hard Boy was fond of putting people in head-locks. This called for a calm response and also a little creativity.

"I have got something with me," I said, "But I doubt if *you'd* be brave enough to try it."

"Yeah?" Belluga struck a defensive pose.

"You see, this stuff is really powerful," I reached into my rucksack and pulled out a handful of henbane.

"What's that?" Belluga demanded.

"Looks just like a weed to me," said Hard Boy.

"Exactly." I looked at him with what I hoped was a knowing expression. "That's what it is. *Weed.* Very, very special weed."

There was a chorus of disbelieving guffaws from the group but Belluga appeared to have taken the bait.

"You wait till we tell Mr Randle you've been dealing in drugs," he said. "You could get sacked for that, Miss."

"It's actually my dream to get sacked, lad," I said, "I don't really have time for teaching. It interferes with my kung-fu training."

"Yeh? Yeh?" Hard-One moved in closer. "Show us a few moves then."

This was going to present a problem. Apart from watching the high-kicks on *Buffy*, I didn't have any knowledge of kung-fu whatsoever. I didn't, in fact, know the difference between kung-fu, karate, tae-kwondo, ju-jutsu, judo, kendo, aikido or any other form of martial arts. All I knew was that where 'kick-ass' was concerned, I was the one who stood the best chance of being on the receiving end of it.

"How much do you actually know about henbane?" I said. "Do you even know what just one leaf can do? Are you ready to fly eight miles high?"

"Leave her. She's bonkers." Belluga's bravado seemed to be rapidly evaporating. "You don't want to mess with mad people."

Mad? Of course! That was how Zelda survived the worst classes at Havelock Ellis; she was unpredictable and scary, soft as butter one moment, and a furious hornet the next. Time for me to follow suit.

"*Haaaah!!!*" Holding the henbane in front me, I charged forward, narrowly avoiding Belluga, and kicking a rock into the canal with a decisive splash.

"Nutter." Belluga sounded unimpressed.

"Bugger!" A boy in an Adidas sweat shirt pointed towards the bridge. "Here comes the Fowl!"

Here she was, emerging out of the fog, Jen Fowler, dressed in a cut-away fluorescent top and tight cycle pants, pounding towards us, her bum bag bouncing up and down against her bony pelvis. So the kids called her the Fowl! Priceless! I couldn't wait to tell Zelda.

"These boys troubling you, Ms. Harker?" she stopped, panting, by my side.

"Not at all," I said.

"Miss," Brian Belluga pointed at the henbane in my hand, "she's dealing!"

"I think you'd better drop that knife, Brian," Jen Fowler said, ignoring his comment. "Or better still, hand it to me, and don't tell me I can't confiscate it because we're out of school because that makes no difference. Yes, thank you, glad you're being sensible. Now, cut along, lads, and leave Ms. Harker in peace."

"But Miss," Belluga persisted, "she's got a stash! Look, she's stuffing it in her bag!"

"I said, go!" Jen Fowler stood her ground. "You've all got coursework to finish and this isn't a good place for you to hang about. The penalty for threatening members of staff, on or off school premises, is expulsion. If I so much as see any of you around here again, expect to be dealt with extreme severity. Go!"

"Yes, Miss." With a reluctant shuffle, the boys moved off, making their way back towards the steps. As they reached them, I heard Belluga give a fake burp. Then they were gone.

"You have to be firm with kids like that," Jen Fowler told me, "Let them know who's the boss."

"Oh, we were just having a little chat," I said breezily. "Nice lads, those."

"They appeared to be intimidating you," she said.

"Oh, no," I said. "They were just being friendly."

"Friendly?" she frowned. "Are you quite sure? Brian Belluga stuck a metal spike into the last supply teacher's ear during a CDT lesson last term."

"He did?" I attempted to look surprised. "But he's such pleasant boy with me!"

"You don't know him," Jen Fowler snapped back. She was staring at me, her expression conveying a mixture of puzzlement and disapproval. I supposed I must look somewhat odd, particularly as I was wearing Seb's caving helmet. "Ms. Harker, those boys just made a very serious allegation about you," she added.

"Did they?" I shrugged. "Well, I'm afraid I can't stop. I'm on my way to the Somers Town Pot-Holers Ball. We all go in our gear, you see." I tapped my helmet.

Jen Fowler frowned, as if trying to summon up a cutting riposte, but it appeared she couldn't think of one. With a subdued snort, she headed off, flailing away past me, her limbs jerking like those of an arthritic giraffe. I continued on my way in the other direction.

I crossed the bridge and approached the wire fence by the old warehouses. There was a yellow police sign set up by the gates; I shone my torch towards it: *Serious Assault. Information Wanted.* I hoped the assault was nothing to do with 9X. *Kill the werewolf! Ka-pow!* There was also, by a gap in the fence, a metal sign with the caption, 'Guard Dog' and an image of a pugnacious animal that looked like the Hound of the Baskervilles on crack. This was an unwelcome development, as I hadn't got any doped food with me to fling into its slavering jaws. On the other hand, if there was a guard dog, why couldn't it have got out through this gap? I supposed it could be tethered on a long chain and still capable of charging around a corner and mauling an intruder.

I picked up a handful of gravel and flung it at the sign, then flung a larger stone at it, achieving a bull's eye, hitting the image of the dog right on the muzzle. Then I shook the fence and shouted, "Come and get me, then!" There was no response, not a single yelp or bark. It was as I'd hoped. Unless the owners of the property had been foolish enough to employ a deaf canine, there was no dog. I was going in.

I squeezed through the gap in the fence and started looking for the building I'd seen on the computer screen. About a year ago, it had been announced that this area had been acquired for redevelopment, but right now, there were no signs that any construction work was taking place. The warehouses, with their honeycomb of broken windows splattered with pigeon-shit,were the apotheosis of decay. It was difficult to imagine them ever being transformed into a block of luxury apartments.

I was only half a mile from the Lock, but I had entered an entirely different world from the one characterized by chic wine bars, boutiques and bistros. The ground was littered with lager cans, polystyrene cartons, old clothes, mattresses, defunct fridges and upturned supermarket trolleys. There were also the remains of a makeshift bonfire. Some rough sleepers must have been hanging out here. I began to feel apprehensive; what had possessed me to come in here on my own? I'd entered the twenty first century version of the City of Dreadful Night and the only person who knew about my mission was my eight-year-old son. How stupid was that? I took my mobile out of my rucksack, scrolled to the number of the *Lord Halifax* and pressed the green button. I didn't have Georgia's mobile number, I didn't even know if she had a mobile, but it did seem likely that the pub had an answerphone. I waited, then, to my relief, a recorded message cut in:

"*Hello,*" Georgia announced in her husky voice. "*'Don't assume I'm out just because I'm not answering the phone. If you're a burglar doing a recce, forget it love. But do please leave a message after the tone and I'll get back to you provided you're a friend. If you're a cold caller, sod off!'*"

"Georgia," I spoke quietly. "It's Dora Harker. Can you please give Ralphie this message? Tell him that I'm going to try and rescue the sacrificial victim. I know who it is and I have to do this. I'm at the old warehouses by the canal. I'm looking for a small brick building. I think the entrance to the labyrinth is down there. I'm going in." I switched off my mobile, and slipped it back into the pocket of my jeans.

I unfolded the map and held it under the torch-light. The sketch of the labyrinth was complicated, and I had yet to find the building it was under. I made my way along the side of the warehouse; still more litter on the ground, McDonalds cartons, sweet wrappers, a squashed plastic football. And there was something else. A trainer.

One trainer may look like any other trainer, but, as I'd discovered since taking up supply teaching, for teenagers, trainers are status symbols. Some of the trainers worn by the Havelock Ellis kids cost over a hundred pounds a pair, and were considered a mark of the coolest street cred. Other trainers, bought in the market or from one of the cheaper chain stores, were considered risible, an excuse for bullying and social class abuse. *'Your mum got your trainers at Tesco's'* was one of the insults that 9X were fond of hurling at the Honey Monster, and last week, according to Zelda, their fashion victim had hopped into her class, covered in shame and wearing only one trainer and with his right foot encased in a sock as full of holes as a slice of continental cheese. He'd told her that the class had stolen his other trainer to use in a game of catch and she'd had to provide him with another pair from lost property. And now this was almost certainly the Honey Monster's lost trainer, a cheap imitation of the latest Nike, with the words 'Action Boy' on the side, size ten and the initials 'D.D.' inscribed in ink on the inside. As I walked on, I found more evidence that 9X had been here; a school shirt and a ripped blazer with the name 'Darren Dalston' written inside in permanent ink, another mark of poverty, since all the better-off kids sported woven Cash's name tapes inside their uniforms. So this was 9X's dumping ground for stolen property and there, I realized, as I turned the corner, was the small brick building. This was the place I'd seen on Caspian's computer screen.

I went down the steps to the wooden door at the bottom, prodded it open and stepped into what appeared to be a storeroom, piled high with packing cases. The smell was disgusting, like a mixture of hard-boiled eggs and urine. How I wished I'd brought the face mask that Seb used to wear when he was cycling through the traffic at Euston on his way to his sixth form college. I hadn't factored in the possibility of bad odours when I was assembling my rescue kit.

I walked around slowly, shining my torch into the corners. Something brushed against my face. It felt like a cobweb; I uttered an involuntary shriek and jumped back, knocking into a . pile of crates that crashed down in front of me. And now I saw there was a trap door set into the floor.

I knelt down, and tried to lever it up. It took me a good five minutes to shift it, as it was stiff and there was no ring or handle but with the help of Seb's Swiss army knife, I eventually managed to raise it. I shone my torch down into the darkness and then consulted the map. Yes, there was a cellar with the entrance to a tunnel at the end. And oh, grief, here was a congealing puddle of red liquid.

Sprinkle the grounde with the bloode of a werewolf...

Those evil kids! What had they done?

"Mr Langford?" I called softly. "Are you down there? It's Dora Harker. Give me a shout if you can hear me!"

There was silence. I could see that the only way I was going to get down was to jump. That meant a descent of about ten feet, but if I was careful, I wouldn't injure myself. And if I dropped my rucksack in first, I could use it to break my fall.

It seemed an easy plan, but I still managed to graze my left hand and bang my knee as I landed. I crouched there for a moment, catching my breath. Then I took my torch out of my back pocket where I'd placed it for safety. It was still working, thank goodness.

I stood up, testing the ground with the toe of my boot. Oh, yuk, filth and mud. But I had to brave this. Ahead of me, there was an archway, and I just had to go through; it exactly matched the entrance to the labyrinth on the map. I stepped forward.

"Mr Langford?"

Again, silence. I made my way into the tunnel. I'd only gone a short distance, when the roof began to slope downwards. Could this be part of an old sewer system? It certainly smelled like it and the ground was getting increasingly squelchy underfoot. I tried not to think about the danger of being in an underground place where the roof might collapse, where anything might be lurking, and where flood waters might suddenly surge through.

"Mr Langford?" I called. "It's me, Dora Harker. Look, if you're here, make some kind of sound. And don't be dead down here or I'll never forgive you!"

There was no response. I stumbled forward. As I put out my hand out to steady myself, I touched something slimy and bulbous, something that felt like a dead toad. Ugh! How I wished I'd remembered to put on some gloves. I went on another ten paces. Now I had to stoop even lower. I could feel myself developing a crick in my neck. Worst still, I could hear sucking noises as if an entity with rubbery lips was making a mocking commentary on my progress. *Oh...* This was far worse than I could have imagined.

Now I'd reached a point where the roof dipped abruptly. I'd have to go on my hands and knees, crawling, pushing my rucksack in front of me, balancing my torch and the map on top. Thank goodness for Seb's caving helmet, but how uncomfortable it was and how I hated this experience. Pot-holing would never be my chosen hobby and whenever Seb told me he was going on an expedition of that kind, I felt cold with fear, thinking of the danger.

I slithered forward, trying not to hyperventilate, following the twists and turns on the map. The last thing I wanted was to find I'd gone down a dead end, and I could see there were some marked on the map. I tried to keep track of my movements; once to the left, twice to the right. I heard something behind me, an intermittent series of thuds as if small pieces of rock or mud were breaking away from the roof. I didn't want to focus on that. Suppose I got stuck down here? But now, thank goodness, here was another archway.

I shone my torch into the space. There was another tunnel ahead, not more than ten feet long, leading to a wider opening at the end. I could easily go through that and...*oh grief!* I breathed in so sharply that I felt a sensation under my ribs like a stab from a knife. How I wished I hadn't shone my torch upwards at that moment.

Judging from what I'd just seen, I'd just arrived at my own personal Gehenna gate.

In films that exploit arachnophobia for effect, there's usually at least one of the creatures that's preternaturally huge. In the old B movie, *The Incredible Shrinking Man*, the diminutive hero battles with a spider three times his size. But I don't need any exaggeration to induce serotonin-induced panic. Just one, fairly large but normal *Tegenaria gigantia*, the common house spider, would do. Like the eight-legged abomination that was inches from my face at that moment.

I took a deep breath, reminding myself of what Caspian said. Spiders have very poor eyesight. If that was the case, it probably didn't know I was here. All I had to do was duck down and ... the spider swung towards me.

I shrieked and dropped my torch.

Now I was in the dark; the moment it hit the ground, the torch must have gone out. Methodically, I began to explore the area around me with my hands, telling myself that accidentally touching a spider would be a minor thing compared to being trapped underground without hope of rescue. But of course I could be rescued; all I had to do was phone the emergency services. There'd be a signal down here, wouldn't there? And now I came to think of it, I could always use the light from my mobile to help me find the torch. I took it out of my pocket and held it up. No signal. Great. And, of course, only the dimmest of lights. The boys were always telling me I should get a new, state-of-the-art smart-phone, but I told them I loved my old faithful clam-shell. What did I want with wi-fi, apps, a camera, and all those bells and whistles? I only wanted to make a few calls. Now, I realised, my Luddite attitude had its drawbacks.

It took me a good three minutes to find the torch, but at last, it was back in my hand. I pressed the switch. Good, still working. Or perhaps not so good, not if it meant I was going to see that spider again. With a strong feeling of trepidation, I shone the light up at the archway.

The spider was still hanging there. *Perhaps it wasn't real.* If there really was such a thing as a Gehenna gate, the spider might be just a trick, a projection of my mind. All I had to do was duck under it.

But then the damn thing might drop down the back of my neck.

Surely it wasn't possible, but hadn't that *tegenaria* just got bigger? I was prepared to believe that it had. Now I could see its fangs, its abnormally well-developed fangs. And it didn't seem to be in the least afraid of me. No. Its manner was sentient and combative. I felt sweaty and sick. Every unpleasant spider experience of my life was coming back to me.

The henbane! Of course! I pulled a handful of the plants out of my rucksack and lashed out at the spider. There was a sucking sound, as if something was being vacuumed up a pipe. I couldn't see the spider now. I made my way forward, holding my torch in one hand and my rucksack in the other. Then I felt something brush against my wrist.

I just managed not to scream. I hadn't got rid of the spider at all. It had simply migrated to my sleeve.

"Damn you!" I smashed my arm against the wall, following it with a wild swish of the henbane. "That's enough!"

I heard a bloodcurdling mew, like that of a particularly vicious cat. This was ludicrous. Spiders did not, to my knowledge, make audible noises.

"I'm not afraid of you," I shouted. "There are far worse things to fear than spiders. So you can just get lost!"

There was a thud as something landed at my feet. I looked down; no spider, just a large stone that I must have dislodged when I hit the wall. This wasn't particularly reassuring; if the walls and roof of the tunnel were unstable, then I might risk being buried alive. I must go carefully, quietly...but I had to move forward.

"Mr Langford? Mr Langford, are you there?"

This time I thought I heard something; was it a subdued moan? Now the tunnel was getting narrower and the roof

266

was getting lower and lower; I'd have to crouch down and soon, I might have to go on my hand and knees. I took the map out of my pocket and examined it. It seemed I'd have to make a left turn, then a right, and then another left to reach the centre, but there was no way of judging the distances. And this was such a confined space...I hated confined spaces.

Don't panic, Dora, don't panic...don't give way ...

I felt as though I'd been crawling for hours, but perhaps it wasn't more than ten minutes. At last, the roof of the tunnel was getting higher and I was able to stand. I'd come to another archway. I stepped through it and found myself in a small, circular chamber with a high ceiling. There were six deep alcoves built into the wall, each one stacked with long, oblong boxes. And there, opposite me, was what looked like an altar, a long table draped with a cloth that must once have been black but was now speckled with green and grey mould. There was an upturned crucifix in the centre and the wall behind it was covered in carvings of mythical creatures, plumed snakes swallowing their tails, basilisks, gryphons and sphinxes. *Lord Dalrymple's shrine...* Could it be that I'd found it?

"Mr Langford? Are you here?" I almost choked on the stale air.

I wasn't sure, but I thought I heard breathing. So I wasn't alone in here. A terrible thought came into my mind; what if this whole thing was a trick? What if 9X hadn't kidnapped Aidan at all, but had set this up in order to get *me?*

I heard a crash; I spun round, the lid of one of the boxes, the topmost one in a stack of three, had fallen to the ground although I couldn't imagine what had dislodged it.

"Don't try anything, whoever you are!" I yelled.

267

"Here…"

The voice was hoarse and rasping, quite unrecognizable. And it was coming from under the altar.

"Who's that?" I demanded. "It had better not be one of *you*, you little 9X swines! Don't think I don't know what you're playing at, because I do! Right, I'm coming for you and I'm armed."

Bracing myself, I seized the cloth and pulled it away. A cloud of dust flew up; someone gasped and then broke into a paroxysm of coughing. I knelt down and shone my torch into the recess.

"Hello? Anyone there?"

"Water…really need…"

I only just managed to distinguish the words. If he hadn't spoken to me in that painful croak, I might never have recognized Aidan at all. I might not even have realised that what I'd found was a human being and not a bundle of old clothes. So much for the expensive suit; I doubted if he'd wear that again, it was so grimed with dirt. His face was filthy too, as was his hair and here he was, lying on his side, trussed up with ropes, so many ropes it seemed, around his legs, around his torso, around his wrists too…Oh, good grief! How long had he been here?

"Mr Langford, it's me, Dora Harker. Did they hurt you?" The sadistic words from Ralphie's book had just come vividly back into my mind: *breake ye the kneecaps with a lead implement that has been dipped in the urine of rats*….I touched his shoulder. "Oh, hell, you're so cold," I said. "Look, I've got a blanket, a spare jumper, some iron rations, water…"

"Dora…how did you…?"

"Don't try to talk. It's going to be all right. I've come to get you out of here."

"Oh, no," a smooth, insidious voice murmured in my ear. "You've got that *quite* wrong. I'm the one who's come to get *you* out of *here*."

Before I could even turn my head to see who was speaking two strong arms seized me from behind, gripping round the waist, squeezing the breath out of me. Then I was hurtled backwards with such sickening speed it felt as if my eyeballs had been dislodged from my skull. Then everything went dark.

Thirty

Blasts from The Past

I could hear music; Joy Division's '*Love will tear us apart*'. It didn't seem to be coming from the latest, digitally re-mastered CD since, alongside the tortured voice of Ian Curtis, there was a relentless clunking that suggested the turntable of an elderly vinyl record player was cranking itself round in a state of terminal anguish. What was going on?

More to the point, where on earth was I? Why was there such a foul taste in my mouth, and why was I bent over, my forehead almost touching my knees? I couldn't remember where I'd been, or what I'd been doing, but I did know that I was awash with nausea. It was the kind of sick feeling that seems to encompass your whole body from the toes upward, making any movement impossible. I'd only ever felt as bad as this once before in my entire life when I was a kid and some friends persuaded me to go with them on a frenetic fairground waltzer. While they'd shrieked with glee at the whirling movements, I'd felt increasingly ill, as my brain was hurled around my skull like a half-set jelly. When I finally got off the so-called attraction, I was a shaking, dizzy, pathetic wreck but at least, on that occasion, as I'd nearly thrown up on the concrete in the bright May sunshine in Margate, I'd known where I was. Right now, I was in some weird limbo.

I took a deep, gulping breath, trying to achieve some kind of equilibrium and nearly choked on the smell of stale booze, incense, orange peel and old carpet. I had a definite suspicion I was here against my will, and had a vague idea that I'd been interrupted in the middle of doing something important, but apart from that, my mind was blank.

I wished I could open my eyes but my eyelids felt so heavy. As I prised them apart with my finger-tips, the first things I saw, through my blurred, woozy vision, were my knees.

My knees? How could those be my knees, peeping through the rips in a pair of tie-bleached denim jeans? I hadn't worn ripped, tie-bleached jeans since my student days. And yet, now I came to think of it, I *did* recognize these jeans. They had once been mine. There was that little embroidered badge in the shape of a butterfly that I'd sewn on by the deliberate tear above the left knee. And now, as I raised my head slightly, I saw my feet, my bare feet. They were resting on a stained fawn cord-carpet and my toenails were painted alternately bright purple and black. Years ago, I'd thought it was very chic to paint my toenails in that way, not realizing it would make me look like a frostbite victim.

"Welcome back, Dora."

I didn't care for this unknown man's tone. He sounded far too smooth, triumphant and controlling. Who was he and how did he know my name?

"Welcome back? What's that supposed to mean?" My words emerged as a squeak.

"It means exactly what I said," he informed me.

"What the hell have you done to me?" I demanded.

271

"Me? Oh, I haven't done anything." There was a pause. "Yet," the man added, with insidious emphasis.

I sat up. I was in an untidy room, full of empty takeaway pizza boxes, crumpled newspapers and ashtrays. It was vaguely familiar. I'd seen that poster before, hadn't I? It was a parody of the MGM poster of *Gone with the Wind*, with Ronald Reagan and Margaret Thatcher posing as Rhett Butler and Scarlett O'Hara and with a mushroom cloud behind them in place of the usual backdrop of Atlanta burning. '*Gone with the wind*'. Very satirical although very outdated. Yes, I remembered, I'd bought it from a second-hand shop for my friend Leona, Leona, who I hadn't seen for twenty years, Leona, the passionate believer in unilateral disarmament, who used to say that as long as the UK got rid of its weapons, she didn't mind who blew us to bits, provided it wasn't the Americans. Leona, who along with Rosie and Kirsty, had shared student digs with me off the Holloway Road for a brief time during my first term at college

I stared down again at the fawn cord-carpet, at all the wine stains and the scattered orange peel. We used have quite a good system. Leona cleaned the bathroom, I used to buy the bread, milk and coffee from the common kitty, Kirsty used to put out the rubbish and it was Rosie's job to vacuum the floor, but the ancient hoover had broken after the first week, so she never could vacuum, although I tried to help by tidying the place up a bit. How could I possibly be back here?

"You might deign to look at me, Dora," the man said. "I'm over here."

Reluctantly, I turned my head. I didn't much care for what I saw, a young man with a straggly beard standing in the doorway, leaning lazily against the door frame and gazing at me in a manner that must have been intended to appear seductive. I didn't find his pose seductive at all. He was wearing jeans and desert boots, and a black T-shirt, and his black, crinkly hair was past his shoulders. I'd already decided he was a prize tosser.

"Don't you know who I am?" he said.

"No."

"What a pity. Because I know who *you* are. You're Dora Harker, later to become Dora Shuttlehanger, and then Dora Dellow. Two marriages and all before the age of twenty-one. What a messy life, don't you think?"

"A messy life? What right do you have to comment on my life?" I glared at him.

"Tell me, how old are you, Dora?" The man detached himself from the door frame and moved towards me.

"Don't come any closer!" I held up my hand in a warning gesture.

"Very well." He stood two feet away, but continued to gaze at me in a knowing, arrogant manner. "But do answer my question. It's important."

"My age is none of your business," I retorted. "But if you must know, I'm nearly forty."

"Really?" He looked quizzical. "Are you quite sure? Then how have you managed to get into those jeans that fitted you so neatly when you were eighteen? By the time you were thirty, you were a size fourteen, and then you put on at least a stone after Caspian was born. Oh, and I seem to remember that you have some liver spots. Two of them, on the back of your left hand. And yet look at your hands now. Are those the hands of a woman in her late thirties, do you think?"

I examined my hands. No liver spots. And no sign of my wedding ring, the one Dave bought me that I started wearing again after I divorced Peregrine. I stared at the room, at the rickety MFI bookcase collapsing under the weight of the books, at the old black and white TV, at the basket chairs, and the fold–up table and the Japanese paper lamp shade. It can't be, I thought, it just can't.

The young man sat down, cross-legged on the floor in front of me.

"Do you know what day it is?" he said. "It's the day before you meet Colin Shuttlehanger. Yes, tomorrow, despite the fact that you have an essay to finish, you will go to a Film Society screening of a silent classic, *The Flesh and the Devil*. Afterwards, you will meet Colin. You won't be very attracted to Colin at first, but he will lure back to his home with the promise of lending you a book. Kevin Brownlow's *The Parade's Gone By*. Does any of this sound familiar to you?"

"How do you know this?"

"Good question. But let's consider the significance of that day. Because the fact you met Colin sealed the fate of other people and of one person in particular. A person whom you believe died as a result of Gertie's curse."

"Who the hell are you?"

"Do you really not recognize me?"

"No, I….that is…"

A memory was stirring. A photograph that Cynthia had shown me with the caption 'Graduation Day' underneath it. There he'd been, in his cap and gown, with that ghastly student beard and that self-satisfied grimace, and now here he was, smirking at me in that same way. I couldn't see how it was possible, but…

"Oh, good grief! Peregrine!"

"Yes. It's me. Hello, she-who-will-become-Dora-Deadlake."

There was that awful grin again. It was intolerable.

"What do you want with me?" I asked coldly.

"An interesting question, Dora Harker." He edged closer. "Or should I say Dora Shuttlehanger? Or Dora Dellow? Rather too many surnames wouldn't you agree? Perhaps you should have exchanged your maiden name only once. That would have been more economical, don't you think?"

"Shut up!" I leapt to my feet. "Get out!"

"Get out?" Peregrine repeated. "But Dora, I've come to put everything right. I'm going to sort out your messy psyche."

"You can leave my messy psyche alone."

"But can I? Think about what's been happening. Your life has begun to unravel. Your past is haunting you. You are losing control! Now," he snapped his fingers, "how would you like to regain that control? How would you like to start all over again? This is your chance to prevent all the grief. I've brought you back in time, Dora. You're eighteen *again*. Don't go to the Film Soc. tomorrow night. Come out with *me* instead. Then you'll never marry Colin and his mother won't be able to curse you. And then Dave Dellow won't die. Wouldn't you like to save him, at least? Why not agree to my little bargain?"

"I can't. I just can't." My mouth felt dry.

"Why not?"

"Because, if you want the truth, I can't stand you!"

"Nonsense! Think of Dave Dellow! Suppose you could save Dave Dellow's life? Do you know how he died?"

"Of course I do. He was in a van that crashed."

"Yes, yes, yes." Peregrine shook his head impatiently, "I know that. But I'm talking about the *actual* injuries he sustained. He was in the front of the van. The force of the impact crushed all his internal organs, all his ribs were broken, a shard of glass went right through his neck, his left eye…"

"That isn't true. I spoke to Dingo. He told me exactly how it was, how he couldn't believe Dave was dead, because there wasn't a mark on him."

"You think I'd lie?"

"Of course you would. You were always jealous of Dave. I had to hide the photographs, take off my old wedding ring…"

"But naturally. Your duty was to your new husband."

I stared at his hirsute, smug face. What a bastard! '*Love will Tear Us Apart*' was still playing, as if on a continuous loop. I remembered, with a feeling of deep depression, just what had happened to Ian Curtis. All those doomed rock stars, Marc Bolan, Jimi Hendrix, Keith Moon, my Dave…

"I've just thought of something," I said. "If I hadn't met Dave, then Seb would never have been born."

"True enough."

"This is horrible!" I rocked forwards, biting my nails. "You want me to kill Seb."

"Not kill him, no. Just obliterate him. And you'll soon forget about him."

"Will I? I don't believe you!"

"You must have faith in the future I'm offering you."

"This is insane."

"No, Dora. You're the one who's losing it. But I can save you."

This couldn't be real. This place couldn't be real. But what if it was…ha! I'd just remembered something! My brain was getting into gear at last.

"OK," I said, slowly. "Let's get this straight. Am I really back in the flat that I shared with Kirsty, Leona and Rosie? The rest of my life hasn't happened yet?"

"That is correct."

"And the rest of the flat is just through that door? My bedroom…the kitchen?"

"Of course."

"And do you happen to know if Rosie's still going out with Sean Fehily?"

"*What?*"

"Sean Fehily," I said. "He was a nice bloke. Do you know if Rosie is seeing him? I seem to remember they broke up a few times, but…"

"Of course I bloody don't know anything about that!" Peregrine was losing patience. "I didn't do any research into the love lives of your flat mates!"

"Didn't you?" I edged towards the door. "Big mistake, Peregrine, big mistake."

It was an act of faith, going out of that room. For all I knew, the rest of the flat didn't exist at all and I might be about to be swallowed up by a black hole. But no, everything was just as I remembered it. Here was the hall, the stained drugget, the empty wine bottles lined up along the skirting board, Leona's red mac hanging on a hook. And then, as I went into the kitchen, I found the unhygienic sink piled with dirty dishes as usual, and I saw Rosie's trainers by the bin, covered in mud from her early morning jog in the park, and there, to my absolute joy, was the old chest freezer, the one that never worked properly and used to leak icy water all over the lino and inside, I hoped I'd find…

I lifted the lid and began rummaging through the packets of frozen peas, the bags of home-made chicken stock, the cheap ice-cream, and the raspberries I was saving for the trifle. Please let there be…*ah-hah!* My hands gripped the long parcel wrapped in silver foil. Success!

"O.K.," I walked back into the living room, the foil-wrapped object in my hand. "You've been warned, Peregrine. Get me out of here or I'll get you with this."

"What the hell is that?" He looked at me suspiciously.

"It's something you won't like, Peregrine." I advanced towards him. "You see, I've worked it all out. This is the Gehenna Gate, and I'm confronting my worst fears."

"What on earth are you talking about? What worst fears?"

"*You* are my worst fear, Peregrine. I thought it was that spider, but it's you. And you sold your soul to Asmodeus, didn't you? Asmodeus, the demon of marital unhappiness! The demon that Gertie brought down on me the day she cursed me. Asmodeus, the demon who specialises in killing bridegrooms. And I was safe at first, in that flat, with Mr Jowls smoking his fish, Mr Jowls, sending out a fishy fume just as the Archangel Raphael did. But then Mr Jowls went away, and the demon was let loose. And then you, a servant of the demon, tracked me down. The demon killed Dave, and now he's using you to persuade me to obliterate Seb. And if I don't get past this Gehenna gate, someone else will die too, a man with whom I have no intention of becoming romantically involved, but who doesn't deserve to die, trapped in the Maw of Mochelmoth!"

"I don't understand what you're talking about." Was it my imagination, or was he looking rather pale, suddenly?

"Don't you? Listen, Peregrine, I don't know how you come to be mixed up in all this, but I'm beginning to learn a lot about the darker regions and their denizens." As I spoke, I began to unwrap the object that I was holding in my hands, dropping some slivers of foil onto the carpet. "Maybe you knew all the time that Arcadia Square was haunted. Maybe that was why you bought the house. Perhaps you *wanted* to live on the San Andreas fault of the spirit world. And what about Cas, what have you been doing to him? Did you agree with Becca that he should be sent to Netherwold so that he could learn demonic skills? I've been terrified that he might take after you, but now I know he doesn't. He's going to keep piranhas. How do you like the sound of that?"

"He can't keep piranhas."

"Oh yes he can! And do you know what this is?"

"No, I bloody don't!"

"Then let me tell you. Sean Fehily brought it here for Rosie. He's a bit of oddball is Sean. Other guys bring roses. Sean Fehily loves fishing. So Sean Fehily brings *fish*."

"Put that thing back in the freezer, it's going to start dripping on the carpet." He was glaring at me, but his voice was wobbling. He put his hand to his mouth.

"Yes, it will drip," I agreed. "It's going to start defrosting soon. And you're going to smell it!" I pointed the fish, head first, at him. "This is a very fine trout!"

"I think you'll find, Dora that you can't....ooh!" he balled his right hand into a fist, and jabbed it into his guts.

"Something the matter?" I asked.

"Oh, fuck! *Aaaah....*" He bent double. "Oh, God, I... aaagh!" He clenched his fists, driving them into his stomach.

"You'll have more than a stomach ache before this is over!" I stepped forward, brandishing the frozen trout.

"Dora!" he gasped. "You evil bitch! Oh God—I'm going to be sick!"

"Too bad."

"Dora! You don't understand, I haven't..." He clapped his hand to his mouth, "Allergic....fish...."

"Exactly! Asmodeus of the fishy fume! Take this, you demon!"

"Dora! Dora!"

"You can't stop me now!" I lifted up the frozen trout. "You've asked for this! You bastard, you utter, utter, bastard!" I hit him hard across the shoulders.

"Dora!" He cried out in obvious pain.

279

I raised the fish up, and whacked him again. And again. And again.

"Dora! Dora!"

Who was that? It didn't sound like Peregrine. And now I couldn't see the room at all.

Thirty-One

The Perils of
Child-Centred Education

"Dora! Dora!"

Someone *was* calling my name with an urgency that verged on desperation, but it definitely wasn't Peregrine. Even when suffering from fish-imposed agony, his voice had never sounded so cracked and hoarse, as if in the throes of a bad case of laryngitis.

"Dora! Wake up!"

Why should I? I just wanted to drift back into oblivion. It would be such an effort to move, even if lying face down on the ground wasn't entirely the most comfortable position. I stretched out my hand and touched what appeared to be earth and gravel. This was seriously weird. Kirsty, Rosie, Leona and I might not possess a decent hoover, but I didn't remember our place being quite as dirty as this. In fact, it seemed the carpet had gone altogether. And what had happened to the familiar smell? The aroma of mingled incense, stale booze, old carpet and orange peel had evaporated and in its place, there was a filthy, rotting flesh-like stink as though something organic was steadily decomposing. Did this mean I wasn't in the flat anymore?

"Dora!"

Ah! I'd just realized why it was so dark; my eyes were closed. With an effort, I opened them. Oh dear. That hadn't made the slightest difference. Well, at least Peregrine had gone. But who the hell was this person calling my name? Was he a paramedic? They tended to use first names with complete strangers, as though familiarity was necessary when dealing with emergencies, although I'd never quite understood why. Had I been unconscious? Perhaps I had. The side of my head was throbbing. This didn't feel like a safe situation. I needed to protect myself. I felt around for the foil-wrapped trout.

"What have you done with it?" I demanded crossly.

"Done with what?" A voice croaked.

"With my fish!"

"Fish? What fish?"

"You know what fish!" I snapped.

"There was…no fish. It was a torch. You hit me with it…" I heard a fit of coughing. "Sorry…do you have… water…"

"Water! Oh grief, of course!" I struggled up into a sitting position. "I remember now. Mr Langford, is that you?"

"Yes," he rasped. More gasping and coughing. "You nearly knocked me out."

"Sorry. I thought you were my ex-husband."

"You thought I was…."

"I don't know what's happened."

"Nor do I. You were talking, then you just seem to black out. And then you came to, and hit me with…"

"The torch. Of course! And I must have dropped it. I have a bottle of water in my rucksack. If I can just find…" I crawled forward, stretching out my hands and scrabbling around on the ground. I touched stones and earth, and then my fingers closed around something hard and cylindrical. The torch. I pressed the switch. Nothing happened.

"Oh, damn!"

"What?"

"The torch isn't working," I said. "The batteries have fallen out. And now I can't find my mobile. I had it earlier."

"Cigarette lighter…in my pocket."

"Good. Pass it over then."

"Can't…hands tied. Literally."

"Oh. Oh, yes, of course. Which pocket?"

"Back pocket. Trousers."

"Right." I said. "I'm coming. Where are you? Oh." I'd touched something hard. Hell! "Is that you?"

"Yes, my knee…left knee."

"Right." I felt a certain sense of relief. At least he hadn't flinched with pain. That suggested those evil kids hadn't carried out all the instructions. *Breake ye the kneecaps,* had obviously been omitted.

I moved my hand upwards. Oh dear. Thighs, buttocks… yes, my hand was definitely on his…Best not to think about it. I reached into his pocket. I could feel something small and square. With a sense of relief, I took out the lighter and flicked it on.

The flame went out almost immediately and I only had a split second to look for my rucksack, but there it was just a few feet over to my right.

"This thing of yours is useless!" I said.

"Not mine. Confiscated…"

"I see. So I've no need to give you the smoking lecture. And I've got my rucksack. I know where it is now. I've brought a knife and…oh hell, wish I knew where those batteries were." I reached into the rucksack and brought out the bottle of water. "Right," I said, "First, you need a drink."

I unscrewed the cap. "Mr Langford, I apologise for this, but I'm going to have to feel for your face. Find your mouth, I mean. I don't want to shove the neck of this bottle into your eye."

"Dora..."

"What?"

"You don't have to keep..." Now he was gulping at the water. "Take it slowly!" I admonished him.

"Thanks," he gasped. "What I was trying to say," His voice sounded a little less hoarse, "is that you don't have to call me Mr Langford down here. Aidan will do fine."

"I can think of other things I'd like to call you," I said grimly. "But perhaps this isn't the moment. Right, Aidan, I've brought some glucose tablets, my son takes them on climbing expeditions, quick energy fix, just popping one into your mouth..."

"Thanks...Dora...what exactly did I do to make you hate me so much?"

"Who mentioned hate? Now, what about these ropes? Can you wiggle your fingers?"

"Yes. Just about."

"Good. Then it's unlikely that you've been tied up so tightly that your circulation's been cut off. And at least they didn't break your kneecaps."

"Of course they didn't," he sounded appalled by the suggestion. "They're not bad kids."

"Not bad kids? Is that what you think? After they left you tied up in the dark without any food or water?"

"There was some water, they rigged it up so that I could just reach it, you know, like in an animal cage, but it had a strange taste and made me feel sick."

"That would have been for the purge," I observed grimly.

"What purge?" He sounded bewildered.

"Never mind," I said. "This probably isn't the right time for all the gruesome details. Right," I flicked the cigarette lighter on again. "I need to cut these ropes If only I could find those torch batteries…"

"There are some candles in a box on the table above me. I saw them earlier."

"Brilliant!" I reached out for them. "So, this is the plan. I'm going to free your hands first and then you'll be able to have one of the cereal bars I've brought for you, while I cut through the rest of the ropes. And I'm going to have to go slowly, because I don't want to risk cutting you. How are feeling?"

"Absolutely humiliated."

"I meant, physically." I lit a candle, dribbled the wax on to an old dish I'd found, and set it upright. "I've no idea how long you've been down here but it's a miracle you haven't got hypothermia. Grief, there's a lot of rope here, and these are sophisticated knots. Who'd have thought anyone in 9X was in the scouts? Which one of them did this?" I reached for Seb's Swiss Army knife.

"I don't know. I was unconscious at the time."

"*What?* Mr Langford, I mean Aidan, I expect this will be embarrassing for you, but perhaps while I'm cutting through the rope, you could tell me what happened?"

"You mean you don't know?" He sounded bewildered. "You're not part of this?"

"Of course I'm not!"

"Oh, Dora, sorry, I didn't…look, I'm confused, I don't understand…"

"Just tell me the story," I said.

"It was lunch time," he began.

"Lunch time, yesterday?"

"No, today…that is…I was supposed to be meeting the Science department…"

"Then it *was* yesterday."

"Oh. Well, lunchtime yesterday then, there was a report that some of our kids were messing around by the canal, so I came down here and found Bradley, Rizwan and Chantelle down by the bridge. They ran towards me in a panic and said that Darren Dalston had hurt himself, he'd fallen down a deep hole near the warehouses, a kind of air shaft, and he was trapped. So I got out my mobile to phone the emergency services, and Rizwan crashed into me, knocking my mobile out of my hand. It fell into the canal. An accident, I thought at the time."

"No accident."

"No." He sounded rueful. "I can see that, in hindsight. Anyway, I told Chantelle to run back to school and get the office to phone for the fire brigade and an ambulance and then I went with the others. They showed me the air shaft, it's just over there behind that door of course…"

"Air shaft?" I interrupted. "Seriously? You got in here through an *air shaft*? I've just crawled for ages through the most vile, scary tunnels to get here, and all the time I could just have come down an air shaft?"

"Oh, Dora, you did that? For me?"

"I like to think I'd have done it for anyone," I continued to saw at the rope. "Although possibly not my ex-husband. But this is your story, not mine. Go on."

"Right. So I stood at the top, and I heard Darren calling out for help. He sounded terrified. I lowered myself down, and came through the metal door into here. And I found Desmond and Nando here, playing a recording of Darren's voice on their phones."

"One that they'd made earlier, while bullying him, I suppose?"

"I'm very much afraid that must have been the case. Then Chantelle, Rizwan and Bradley came in and Chantelle said 'Get him!' and Bradley produced the rope. I said if this was a charity kidnapping stunt, could we please do it my office at school, as I'd a lot of paperwork to complete."

"You said that!" Preoccupied as I was with sawing through the ropes, I couldn't help bursting into laughter. "You were down in this hole, about to be tied up and you started worrying about your *paperwork!*"

"Don't mock me, Dora," he said mildly.

"I'm not laughing *at* you," I assured him, stifling a giggle. "It's just that…"

"I really *did* have a lot of paper work. I have to produce a report every day and send it to Head Office."

"I see." I composed myself. "So then what happened?"

"Desmond picked up a brick and Chantelle said, 'Don't hit him with that, you div, use the chloroform.'"

"*Chloroform?* They had chloroform?"

"Yes. They all jumped on me and Bradley shoved a cloth in my face. I started to pass out. The last thing I heard was them all humming together."

"The death hum," I said.

"Death hum?"

"It's better if I don't explain that right now. Couldn't you have fought them off?"

"Of course I could. I could have knocked them all out flat. But then I'd have hurt them."

"You could have argued it was self-defence."

"Dora, do know what happens to anyone in the teaching profession who lays a single finger on a pupil these days, even one who does it for the best of reasons, like putting their arm round a distressed kid to comfort them?"

"Yes. They get accused of being Mr Pugh."

"Please don't remind me of Mr Pugh. The thought of him makes me sick."

"Me, too." Oh dear, I must remember not to be so flippant with this serious man. "There. That's the last rope. Can you get up?"

"I think so...oh..." He crawled out from under the altar, and got to his feet, staggering slightly.

"Careful..." I put a hand out to steady him.

"Thank you. Oh, Dora, I'm so grateful to you..."

"Thank me later. I just want to get out of here now." I could feel my phobia about confined spaces coming back with a vengeance. "So, can we get up through that airshaft? Where's the door?"

"It's here." He pulled back a curtain, revealing a metal door. "But...the handle won't move." He tried it again. "Could be jammed. Stand back, I'm going to take a run at it and..."

"I really don't think that's a..."

"Aaagh!"

"Good idea," I finished. "I'm surprised you didn't break your shoulder. Why didn't you just kick it? Mind you that would have been no use either. I expect it's been locked. Right, then it's the tunnel. And I'll warn you now, it's a hand and knees job in places. You'd better wear my caving helmet."

"I wouldn't dream of it. Dora, if you're not in on this, how did you know I was here?"

"Complicated story, no time now. Let's go."

Our progress was tortuous. This time, the tunnel seemed narrower, the space seemed tighter, the walls slimier, the ground wetter, and the air more stale and offensive. I called out instructions from behind, but I wasn't convinced they were the right ones. And then, after what seemed an interminable crawl, I was forced to admit I was struggling.

"There's something I need to tell you," I said. "This doesn't feel like the same tunnel as the one I came down."

"Since you mention it," he spoke with quiet deliberation. "It might not be. Please don't panic, but I've just…ah!" I heard a bang. "What was that?"

"My head getting up close and personal with a rock," he said ruefully. "We can't go any further. This is a dead end."

"A dead end?" I swallowed. "But we can't turn round here."

"No. But we just need to move backwards. Keep feeling along the wall in case there's a gap we missed. Ready?"

"Yes."

I edged back again, and reached out with my hands on either side. At last I felt the tunnel widening.

"I think I can stand up here…maybe this is the entrance… oh, no, it can't be, I can see the candles and…"

"What is it?"

"We're back where we started," I said.

"I don't understand." I stood by the altar. "We must have been crawling down that tunnel for at least twenty minutes before we reached the dead end. But now, after only a few minutes, we're back here." I heard a loud, cavernous rumbling. "Grief! What was that?"

"Just my stomach," he admitted. "Awful manners, I know."

"Oh, goodness, I forgot to give you a cereal bar. You must be starving and…"

"No time to worry about that," he said. "We've got to concentrate on getting out of here."

"But it's no good. We're never going to get out. This place is protected by magic, dark satanic magic." I knew I was losing it, saying far more than I ought to say, but now

I couldn't stop myself. "There's a Gehenna gate, and my ex-husband was there, and there was a spider, a huge spider, a spider from hell, and we're trapped down here, and we'll suffocate, and this is all *your* fault."

"My fault, Dora?"

"Yes! You were the one who was stupid enough to come down here with those evil kids and then let them tie you up! For someone who's supposed to be in charge of the school, you really are the most naïve man ever! And now, all because of you, I'm stuck here, underground, in the dark. And you don't understand, I've got responsibilities, there's my eight-year-old son and…"

"Dora, please keep calm. I'm going to look for… ah! Here they are. The torch batteries. Yes, this must be them. Can you hand me the torch? Right…." He paused as he slipped the batteries back in. "There! At least we can see better now."

"Yes, we can," I agreed. "But just look at where we are. See that altar? And those carvings? This is the shrine Lord Dalrymple built. This is the Maw of Mochelmoth."

"I've no idea what you're talking about." He laughed gently. "Listen, everything will be fine. Sooner or later someone at Havelock Ellis will believe 9X's story about the charity kidnapping and…"

"Oh for goodness sake!" The words burst out of me. "Don't you understand? 9X didn't do this for charity. They never told anyone about this. I'm the only person at the school who's worked out where you are. Everyone else thinks you're at a conference, 9X sent a fake fax saying that you'd gone to one and that you wouldn't be back until after half term. But you were never going to come back! That's why they left you here, tied up in the dark. You were supposed to die down here!"

"Die?" I could tell from his tone he didn't believe me.

"Yes, eaten by a demon! Why did I do this? Why didn't I just call the police? I've gone to so much trouble, just for you!"

"Dora…"

"What possessed you to trust those kids?"

"Well, I've always believed schools should adopt a child-centred approach to…"

"I don't want to hear about your philosophy of education right now!"

"Dora…"

"Stop saying 'Dora'!"

"You asked me to call you Dora, remember?"

"I withdraw my permission! Don't you see, time's running out? If you've been here since yesterday lunch time, then that's at least thirty-two hours, and it's in the book, *'When the thirty third eighth hour is struck, the demon will begin to rise, smelling the stench and agony of the starving and dying man. He will be eaten alive.'*"

"Dora, that can't possibly happen." I was appalled to hear him sounding quite amused. "Concerning the stench, I certainly do need a shower, and I admit I'm extremely hungry, but I don't think I'm actually dying, at least not yet. Of course we'll get out of here and…"

"Oh good grief! What's that?"

I grabbed his arm as a ferocious, primeval roaring broke out above our heads and a choking mass of debris crashed to the ground. I screamed as a chunk of rock narrowly missed my shoulder. There was a rush of air, a sputtering sound and then a grotesque, alien figure with outsize yellow hands and a single dazzling, bright eye in the centre of its head, leaned down towards us.

The demon had risen.

Thirty-Two

No flowers by request

I reached into my rucksack for the henbane. It was time for desperate measures.

"You can't take us!" I shouted, pulling out a handful of the foul vegetation. "Get away from here, Mochelmoth! Look what I've got! Henbane, this is henbane! Aroint thee, Demon!"

"Blimey!" The construction worker, whose miner's helmet, large gloves, and thick goggles I'd mistaken for the features of a primeval hell-beast, burst into a gale of mocking laughter. "Bloody junkies. I might have known it."

It was reassuring to see the night sky again with the nearby lights of Camden Lock creating an urban glow but on the other hand, this man in the fluorescent jacket sitting in his digger seemed more than a little hostile. It seemed we might have exchanged one type of jeopardy for another.

"So what are you doing in there?" The man looked down at us. "I'll tell you what you're doing. You're trespassing, that's what you're doing."

"I'm sorry," I said. "We didn't realize."

"Don't give me that." He spat out a lump of chewing gum. "You'd have to be blind not to see the signs. How the hell did you get there anyway? And who are you?"

"We're archaeologists," I said, improvising wildly.

"Archaeologists?" The man snorted. "That's a good one."

"Urban archaeologists," I said. "We're studying the history of underground London. I was looking for the remains of a tunnel system that was supposed to be around here and as you can see, we seem to have found something very exciting. I have reason to believe that this was a shrine built by an eighteenth-century nobleman and…"

"Don't talk soft." The man let out a mocking guffaw. "That's the store room of the Hell Fire Film Company; this used to be their warehouse back in the nineteen seventies, and that's an old film set. And you're on private property. I ought to report you."

"Please don't do that," I said. "Just help us get out of here and we'll go quietly."

"We'll see about that." The man removed his helmet and goggles. "Here," he stared at me, "Don't I know you?"

Oh good grief, Mr Jakes. This wasn't going well.

"I have a question for you," Aidan said, looking up at him. "I hope you won't mind me asking, but I'm just wondering why you're working on this site all on your own at night. I'm sure you have a legitimate reason, but it would be interesting to know who you are and…"

"I know who he is," I said. "His name's Mr Jakes, and he lives…"

"Sod off!" Mr Jakes came down from the digger. "This is what you're getting." For one awful moment, I thought he was to dump a load of earth on us, but then, to my relief, I saw he was lowering a metal ladder. "Right," he announced, "Let's be having you. And once you're up here, you've got two minutes to get off the site before I let the pit-bull out."

293

"There isn't a dog," I whispered, turning to Aidan. "He's bluffing. When I first came through the fence, I tested to see if there was a guard dog and…"

I was interrupted by a furious growling and barking coming the near distance. There was no doubt about it. We had to get out of here and fast.

We stumbled past the remains of the bonfire and the piles of old mattresses and half-fell through the gap in the fence onto the canal bank. We'd only gone a few more yards before Aidan collapsed on the ground.

"Give me a minute," he mumbled. "Sorry…" He rested his head on his knees.

"Hey." I knelt down beside him. "Don't apologise. Here, have some more water." I handed him the bottle. "And here's the cereal bar I promised you. Eat it slowly."

"Thank you…" He took it from me, his hand shaking. "Oh, God," he muttered. "The punishment of inhabiting a human body, never get used to it…the awful hunger, the pain…" He slumped forward.

"What did you say?" He must be delirious, I thought. Exhaustion, cold, hunger and shock, I supposed, that would do it. I saw that he was shivering, so I took Seb's thermal blanket out of the rucksack and put it round his shoulders. Then I stood up, and stepped back; my instincts telling me that here was a man who would want space and dignity, and who, foolish as it seemed, wouldn't relish being seen in at a moment of physical weakness.

"Sorry." He straightened up at last. "Talking gibberish," he said. "Not sure what came over me."

"Quite possibly a touch of concussion. You've grazed your forehead. Must have been when we were in the tunnel.

I think I've got some antiseptic wipes in here." I reached into Seb's rucksack.

"No need to make a fuss."

"There's every need. That wound could get infected. And I want to apologise too. For having that meltdown just before we were rescued."

"You don't have to apologise. But I didn't understand what you were saying back there. I thought it was a kidnapping stunt for charity. But then you said I was supposed to die. If it wasn't a charity kidnapping stunt, what was it?"

I considered my reply. Here was a man who inhabited the rational, everyday world and this was no time to explain about demons and satanic magic. A judiciously edited version of the truth would be best.

"It was all based on an online computer game," I told him. "My son showed it to me, and I think 9X must have been playing it and then decided to act it out. It's based on a legend about an eighteenth-century Satanist who attempted to raise a demon. He recruited some young disciples provide a human sacrifice, someone they held in high esteem. So, in a way, it was rather flattering that 9X chose you. I mean, I can see the logic of it. It wouldn't be a sacrifice if you killed someone you liked. Mind you, leaving you down there in that state wasn't exactly kind. But at least they didn't...." *Breake ye the kneecaps.* Oh dear, best not mention that.

"Those poor kids." He shook his head. "So little in their lives, just violent computer games, and failing at school and parents who don't listen to them. Is it any wonder they're drawn to things like that? They need our support so much. It's not their fault."

"I can't believe you're saying this! They've got all the makings of evil psychopaths!"

"I don't believe that. They're deprived and misunderstood. Sooner or later, one of them would have come back, or they'd have told a teacher they trusted, or even made an anonymous phone call to the police…"

No they wouldn't, I thought.

"But you could *still* have died!" I said. "Suppose they'd done this to a person with a weak heart, or a diabetic, or someone who needed regular medication or…And to tell the truth, you don't look at all well yourself right now."

"I'm fine. Appearances can be deceptive. And those kids need help. They need counselling of some kind."

They certainly need teaching a lesson. Hmm…I shall work on that.

"Dora," Aidan looked at me with a serious expression. "You've done so much already, but I've got to ask you for one more thing. Can you please not tell anyone at Havelock Ellis about this? If anyone were to know, I'd lose all credibility, and I wouldn't be able to complete the job I was sent there to do. I would be seen as a complete fool."

"I hate to break this to you," I said. "But there are plenty of people in the school who already think you're a complete fool."

"Thanks, Dora." He looked rueful.

"But," I continued. "In my opinion, you're the right kind of fool. You were convinced that Darren Dalston was down that hole, hurt and terrified. You went to save him, without any thought of your own safety. You were being a hero."

"I'm no hero, Dora."

"No hero? Then why did these people you work for, Sentinel Services, send you into Havelock Ellis as a trouble-shooter? It's not a job for a wimp. And they invested a lot of authority in you, promoting you to this post and…"

"It wasn't a promotion, Dora. It was a punishment."

"Now you've really lost me." I stared at him, utterly perplexed. "What on earth do you mean?"

"It's something I'm not supposed to explain."

"Oh." I gazed at him, more than a little perplexed. It seemed we were both keeping secrets from the other. Perhaps it was better not to probe too deeply. "We should move," I said. "It's cold and damp out here."

"Yes, I agree." He stood up slowly. "Do you have any idea of the time? I seem to have lost my watch." He patted his jacket pockets. "Although I do seem to have my wallet and my house keys."

"I can hardly believe it," I took my mobile out to check. "But it's only a quarter past eleven."

"Then I might still catch the last bus back to Crouch End. Of course, I'll see you home first and…" He staggered. His face looked alarmingly pale.

"Whoa!" I caught hold of his elbow. "You are *not* going back to Crouch End tonight. You're worn out, you're hungry and you're dehydrated. Come back to my place. You need a hot bath, a change of clothes, some food and a good night's sleep. "

"All of which are available at my flat. I wouldn't dream of imposing on you."

"But it's OK, my elder son's away at uni, so his room's free and…"

"Dora, no, really, I do need to go back to my flat. There are reasons…"

"Someone's there, waiting for you?"

"No. There's no-one. But I really would prefer…in fact, I insist."

297

"All right," I said. "To tell the truth my house is in a bit of state. I'd be ashamed for you to see the mess." *And Dave's there, isn't he? Oh, good grief, I was actually forgetting that!* "But," I continued. "At least let me call you a cab. Look, I seem to have run out of credit on my mobile, but there's a late-night grocers near my home and I can get a top up there. Shall we go then?"

"Yes." He nodded. "Let's do that. And Dora...Thank you so much. I can't believe what you've done for me tonight. And I thought you didn't like me."

"I'm not sure how much I *do* like you" I said. "But I might be warming to you just a little. But do watch your step, all the same."

"Davey?" I called softly. "Davey, are you there?"

I stood on the threshold, holding my front door ajar. From the street lighting behind me, I could see that the cracks, cobwebs and slime hadn't got any worse in my absence.

"Davey?"

I heard a faint sigh, then, something, little more than an invisible wisp, a remnant of what once had been, seemed to float past me. Then there was nothing, but I was remembering the sound of the sea, and the sand dunes and the marram grass, and the twang of a guitar being played in Dawlish, so many years ago.

Caspian was fast asleep, clutching Boris the bat to his chest, a look of gentle contentment on his face. A book from the Netherwold school library, *Caring for Piranhas,* was lying face-down on the duvet. I bent down, picked up the book and put it on the bedside table. How I loved the way my son looked when he was asleep; it was the only time he really appeared to be a child. I was just about to turn round and go out of the door, when he opened his eyes.

"Mum, you're covered in dirt," he remarked.

"Oh." I looked down at myself and saw he was right. "Yes…I'm about to have a shower. You should go back to sleep."

"I'm not sleepy." He sat up. "So," he continued in his unnervingly adult tone, "did you sort everything out?"

"Yes, I think so. You did do as I asked, didn't you? After I went out, you stayed in your room?"

"Actually, Mum, I did get up just once. I had to. I needed the toilet."

"Oh, well that's all right," I said. "Thank you for being honest."

"And I looked over the banisters and I saw Seb's Dad. I recognised him from the photograph."

"I think you've made a mistake, Cas," I said, trying to sound light and unconcerned. "Seb's Dad died long before you were born. The baby sitter was…"

"Seb's dad. A ghost." Caspian looked at me pityingly. "Let's be honest with each other, Mum. You know perfectly well I can see spirits. And so can you."

"Cas, I…"

"And while we're about it, I also know Ralphie's a vampire."

"Cas, Ralphie is just an old, aristocratic gentleman and…"

"He's a vampire, Mum. I'm really sorry to have to break it to you. But don't worry, most vampires are good. They keep the demons out."

"There are no such things as…"

"Mum! Don't try and protect me! I know about these things."

"All right, Cas. Perhaps we'll talk about this another time. It's late."

"Did you know Seb's not coming home for Hallowe'en?" He spoke in a matter of fact tone, but I sensed his disappointment hidden under this display of nonchalance.

"Yes, I was going to tell you. But instead of trick or treating with Seb you can come with me to the Hallowe'en disco at school on Friday. It's fancy dress."

"Cool!" He exclaimed, suddenly a little more child-like. "Then I'll come as Dracula. And I don't mean in a cheap black nylon cape and a pair of plastic fangs from Poundland. I want to do it properly. Which would you choose, Mum, the Christopher Lee version, or the Lugosi version, or Gary Oldman in the Francis Ford Coppola version, you know, the one where the Count gets rejuvenated and wears those little glasses and…"

"Cas, you're not supposed to have seen that film! It's an 18."

"Oh, Mum, get real. Of course I've seen it. I've seen it twenty times."

"Right." Here was a losing battle. "You should go to sleep, Cas. You've got a long day tomorrow."

"I know." He lay down again. "It's the start of the Alpha Elite Plus class at Netherwold. Oh, and can I go to a sleepover at William's afterwards? Becca did invite me, I meant to tell you. And then on Thursday, can we go to Dark Dreams to get our costumes for the disco? And then, at half term, can we buy the piranhas? There's a place on the North Circular where you can get the fish tanks, and all the equipment and…." He yawned. Then, quite suddenly, he was asleep.

I woke up with an appalling headache. As soon as I'd got Caspian off to school with Becca, I went back to bed, having phoned Havelock Ellis High School to say I wasn't coming in. It must have been nearly lunch-time when I was roused from a deep sleep by the door-bell. To my relief, the sound was the normal, brisk buzz. *The Dead March in Saul* was no more.

"Ms Dora Harker?" The woman on the doorstep held out a huge basket of white lilies, ferns and angel hair, everything white and green and dazzling and tied with a white satin bow. It looked beautiful but I was finding the scent of the lilies sickening.

"Yes, but who…?"

"Interflora." She pointed to the card. "That's all it says."

"Are you sure you've got the right house?"

"Yes. Nice arrangement, don't you think? I do hope the funeral goes well."

"Funeral?"

"Oh, sorry. I shouldn't have said that."

"Are you sure there's nothing else written on the card? Don't you know who sent these? Did someone phone in the order, did they mention…Chappaquiddick?"

"What?" She frowned. "No idea. I don't take the orders, I just do deliveries, sorry." She thrust the basket into my arms and without another word, she was gone.

I set the basket down on the kitchen floor. I had a very bad feeling about this. Lilies, gleaming white, that's what we'd had in abundance at Dave's funeral, even though I'd specifically said I didn't want floral tributes, just my own wreath of deep red roses. I'd said that anyone who wanted to send a tribute could donate to mental health charities or to spinal injuries charities. I'd been thinking of Loon and Dingo, and what Dave might have wanted, but instead, the flowers kept arriving, the wreaths and sprays of lilies with their sickening scent, all of them arriving anonymously and many of them to my flat, not to the funeral directors and I began to feel that someone was deliberately defying my wishes, even mocking me, although I couldn't think why anyone would want to do that. Later, Mad McArthur came, and tried to reassure me; there was a track on the band's album, he reminded me, a souped-up version of *Lily of Laguna*, and these flowers were coming from fans who meant well and I mustn't mind it. But I did, and I'd never wanted to see lilies again.

I'd always found immersing myself in dull but necessary domestic tasks an excellent distraction, so I launched into a full-scale house cleaning operation. I unsealed the living room door and ventured inside. I was delighted to see that the green, slimy lake had dried up, although the rug and the floor needed a thorough clean and the curtains looked musty and unloved. I flung open the windows, I steamed, I scrubbed, I shampooed, and then I moved on to the hall to repeat the process, and then systematically worked my way throughout the whole house. Cobwebs collapsed, cracks were filled, mildew and fungus disappeared under the onslaught. I hadn't felt so energetic for years. I am a practical woman, I told myself, and it will take more than a few demons to defeat me.

At five o'clock, I was just wiping down the surfaces in the kitchen, when my mobile rang. "Hello?"

"Dora, it's Georgia. Where are you?"

"I'm at home. I take it you're at the Lord Halifax? You must be if you've picked up my message."

"Yes, we're back from Paris. And Ralphie was concerned when he heard your message, he said it meant you'd gone on some dangerous mission, something he'd specifically told you not to do and that I was to phone you at once to check that you were all right."

"Well, as you can hear, I'm fine. And you can tell Ralphie, I succeeded. The sacrificial victim has been plucked from the Maw of Mochelmoth."

"Sounds intriguing! Can you come over? The Count is very keen to meet you."

"Yes, no problem. You wouldn't like a basket of lilies by the way, would you? Someone's sent some and I...well, the scent of them is just too much. I just don't want them. But they would look very well in the bar of the Lord Halifax."

"OK, then, bring them over. See you soon."

"See you."

I bent down to pick up the basket. I'd never seen such lush-looking lilies. Had they really been sent without a card? Perhaps it had been missed, perhaps it was at underneath the arrangement, and I could discover the identity of the sender after all. My stomach tightened, remembering that dream (had it been a dream?) I'd had at the Gehenna gate. There was one person, and one person only, who'd want to go out of his way to remind me of Dave's death. And if that dream had reflected any kind of reality, then there was one person, and one person only, who could have been behind that bombardment of funereal flowers all those years ago. Not a Chappaquiddick fan at all, far from it. *Peregrine.*

I lifted up the flowers, searching underneath. No card. But there was, however, something else, something that no-one would expect to find in a floral arrangement.

A single, black feather, larger than anything that could have come from a bird native to the UK. Now that *was* weird.

303

Thirty-Three

The Undead Pride-March

The bar was candle-lit and all the mirrors were draped in black. Georgia, dressed in a sequined silver gown and her feathered tiara, was standing at the bar, grooming the stuffed bear, Ursa Major, with a tortoiseshell-backed antique brush. Ralphie was in his usual chair, his death's head stick on the table in front of him and a glass of absinthe in his cupped hands. And there beside him, in another winged chair draped with a richly embroidered gold cloth, sat his Excellency, Count Valkhov of Paris.

The Count was decrepit but magnificent, his face wrinkled, his body shrunken, but his clothes elegant and antique. He was dressed in an embroidered brocade coat and breeches, a silk shirt, high, buckled shoes, and silk stockings, and he wore a powdered periwig that was arranged in neat little heaps above his forehead, with long extensions falling waist-length on either side. He wore a large, luminous, polished stone around his neck suspended from a gold chain and mounted in an ornate setting; there was a jug of thick, viscous, red liquid standing next to a pewter goblet on the table in front of him.

"So you are the woman who was unwise enough to go into the Maw of Mochelmoth alone," he croaked. "You have been foolhardy."

I tried not to wince at the sight of his brown, rodent-like teeth. They looked primed for attack; here was a Night Wanderer who inspired dread and awe in equal measure.

"I had to do it," I said. "It was a question of saving someone's life. Once I knew who the sacrificial victim was, I had no choice."

"Impressive," Ralphie purred.

"Forgive me if I do not stand to greet you." The Count extended his right hand, fanning the air with his long, crooked fingers. "My old legs no longer support my withered frame. Welcome, Miss Harker. It seems you have behaved with great courage, but your attempt to pluck the sacrificial victim from the Maw of Mochelmoth unaided could so easily have ended in tragedy."

"Indeed," Ralphie agreed. "Let us be grateful that such an eventuality was avoided. Now you must tell us the complete story. The first part, of course, I know; we identified the acolytes, the five young people of evil disposition, as Havelock Ellis pupils, but the rest of it puzzles me. What made you go out into the night so soon after my departure?"

"That's easily explained. I found the evidence that revealed the person they'd chosen as the sacrificial victim and I knew there was no time to lose. And Caspian had downloaded the evidence that told me where the Maw was, down by the canal, by those old warehouses. Those kids had been recruited through a computer game that had been put on the internet by a man named Tel. And I felt responsible because I'd been there when Tel came to the school, and I left him alone with them and…I'm not sure all the details matter. But now the victim is safe."

"Let us hope so." The Count said. "You took a great risk. You are a brave woman, Miss Harker."

"I'm not sure that I am."

"Oh, I think your ability to live unscathed in a haunted house speaks volumes." The Count inclined his head towards me. "My dear friend here has told me much of your history and there are certain subjects we must discuss. And in particular, this ex-husband of yours, Mr Deadlake."

"Must we talk about him?"

"I think," the Count's voice emerged from his withered lips like a creaking door, "That given this attempt to open the Maw of Mochelmoth, we must."

"You don't actually think that *Peregrine* is the High Priest? Oh no, the Gehenna gate..." My legs suddenly felt weak. "Then he did send...oh!" I dumped the lilies hastily on the bar.

"What lovely flowers, how kind of you to bring them!" Georgia put down the tortoise shell brush. "Now, let me get you a drink on the house. White wine?"

"You know, I feel like living dangerously," I said. "I'd rather like to try the absinthe."

"An excellent choice," Ralphie said. "Get your drink and then sit down with us and explain everything that happened in more detail."

*

"I must congratulate you, dear lady," Ralphie raised his glass. "Not only have you saved someone's life, you have averted an apocalypse. And let me assure you that the particular danger is past. According to the astrological charts that the Count and I have consulted, the conditions for the opening of the Maw of Mochelmoth will not occur again in the correct conjunction for another hundred and thirty years."

"Well, that's a relief!"

"Indeed it is," Ralphie agreed. "But there remains much unfinished business. First, we must track down the High Priest who engineered this foul endeavour."

"I assumed it was Tel."

"Unlikely. I suspect he was merely a pawn or a foot soldier. I would not discount the involvement of your ex-husband, Mr Deadlake."

"And you have been more than a little coy when it comes to telling us about the sacrificial victim," the Count added. "Can you not give us the name?"

"If I say it, you must keep it to yourselves," I said. "I made a promise…"

"You can trust us completely," Ralphie said.

"It's Aidan. Aidan Langford."

"Ah! I can guess what prompted you to attempt the rescue," the Count said. "*L'amour, n'est pas*? You have a particular fondness for the gentleman in question?"

"No, that wasn't it!"

"Are you sure?" He looked at me askance. "When you spoke his name, I thought I detected a certain…confusion in your manner."

"I think a girl's entitled to keep the secrets of her heart." Georgia gave the stuffed bear an affectionate pat on its mangy head. "Don't you agree, Ursa Major?"

"My concern here is not with sentimental attachment," the Count said. "But rather with your ex-husband and his association with the demon Asmodeus. I should explain that Asmodeus is not simply the demon of marital unhappiness. He is the bringer of death and misfortune to any man to whom a woman living under his curse becomes involved in the romantic sense. So, let us assume, Miss Harker, you had begun to feel a burgeoning attraction towards this man, this Aidan Langford...."

"No, no, that isn't what happened," I protested. "I didn't...I don't..."

"Please reflect on what I'm saying before you dismiss it out of hand." The Count frowned at me.

"Indeed, you should," Ralphie said. "Especially since I strongly suspect Mr Deadlake of being a dangerous person. Now although you have told us much, you have still been rather coy about the Gehenna gate? What did you see?"

"First there was a spider..."

"A spider? How mundane!" The Count flicked his long fingernails in the air dismissively.

"It wasn't mundane to me," I said. "I have an absolute horror of them. But then something else happened. I went into some kind of faint and then I found myself back in my past, in my student days, and Peregrine was there and he was trying to manipulate my destiny. Then I..." I couldn't say it, not *hit him with a frozen trout*. It sounded too surreal. "I got the better of him," I continued. "And then I was back in the tunnel. I expect the whole thing was a dream."

"It is far more likely you were drawn into another dimension," Ralphie suggested, "And that Mr Deadlake *was* behind the scheme to open the Maw of Mochelmoth."

"Peregrine is involved with two demons? Asmodeus *and* Mochelmoth?"

"Very likely. Demonology is a drug to some people," Ralphie said. "Well, the opening of the Maw has failed, but we can take no chances. There are other dangers abroad and thus the Count and I intend to take decisive action. We intend to reclaim the streets for the Night Wanderers. We will bring our people back, and find them a new home, gather them together and mount an Undead Pride March."

"An undead pride march?"

"Yes. We will bring back our old friends, Clarimonde Barnett, and the Varneys, Albert Karnstein, and the Mornington Crescent set. All the dark powers of the borough council, God damn their bureaucratic souls, will be powerless against the force we intend to rally. This area of London needs its Night Wanderers. We, the vigilantes, are returning to our rightful place."

"That sounds wonderful!" I couldn't fail to be impressed. "And will I be free of the curse of Asmodeus?"

"I'm afraid not." The Count sighed. "Lifting that curse is beyond our powers. You must do it for yourself."

"All on my own? Without help?"

"Yes, unless you can do the impossible, and enlist the help of an angel. In the Biblical account, as I'm sure you know, the angel Raphael routed the demon Asmodeus by burning fish on an altar, sending the demon away into Egypt, and thus the unfortunate Sarah was saved from the grief of losing any more bridegrooms. However, I don't believe Raphael is available to interfere in the lives of mortals today, if indeed he ever was." The Count chuckled to himself; it was a grim, rusty sound and not at all consoling.

"There's always the possibility of seeking the help of one of the Fallen," Ralphie suggested. "Although that's risky. They can be somewhat erratic."

"Ah! The Fallen Ones!" The Count's eyes glimmered. "I have not seen one for decades, no centuries. In my youth, I'd see them a great deal, flying with their great, dark feathered wings above the Bois de Boulogne in their sublime beauty. But today they remain well-hidden."

"Wait," I said. "I'm not following this. I don't understand what you mean by a Fallen One."

"Don't you know your Milton?" Ralphie looked at me reproachfully.

"Milton?"

"*Paradise Lost*. The fall of the rebel angels from heaven. Lucifer, the angel of light, who became known as Satan."

"Oh, yes, of course," I said. "But surely in *Paradise Lost*, all the fallen angels became devils?"

"No. Not all of them." The Count shook his head. "There were some who sought redemption for their sins, who wanted to return to the Light. And thus they were sent into the world, to suffer penance, forbidden to use their supernatural powers in all but a few circumstances. Their greatest punishment was to be trapped in the human form, enduring all the physical suffering that brings, so galling for those who once flew freely. And then, they would be sent out to bring healing to troubled places, prisons, mental hospitals, war zones and such like. And in that way, they hoped to win back their souls."

"However," Ralphie added. "These missions almost always ended in failure. The Fallen Ones tend to be too conflicted, too complex, and too prone to pride to succeed."

"I see." This was rather a lot to take in. "But, just as a matter of interest, how would I recognize a Fallen One, if I did meet one?"

"With considerable difficulty," Ralphie said. "There would be no dark feathered wings to alert you. But there might be certain attributes that gave the game away, certain unusual intellectual skills, surprising feats of memory, an overweening sense of self-belief. I would advise against relying too much on a Fallen One. They tend to be astonishingly attractive when it comes to looks, but they have a dark side and are liable to relapse into their old ways at any time."

"So, if I did want to lift my curse, the Fallen One might not be a lot of help?"

"You might choose to take the risk. I can't help suspecting that if it came to a duel between a Fallen One and a mortal who'd sold his soul to a demon, the Fallen One would be likely to win. "Well," he reached for his death's head stick. "We must bid you good-night. I shall not be returning to Arcadia Square tonight. Georgia has promised to take us for a drive in her superb vehicle to West Brompton. The Count has heard that there's a delightful dwelling to let there, overlooking the cemetery, and he is considering taking it for a season."

"And remember," the Count rasped. "If I can assist you in any way, please don't hesitate to ask."

"Well, since you mention it," I said. "Something has just occurred to me. Are you both able to meet me tomorrow morning at all?"

Thirty-Four

Citizenship for the Depraved

Whatever had happened to Havelock Ellis High School? Now that the fog had lifted, the' old building' looked more like a stately tower in the New Jerusalem than a place of doom. The brickwork was almost beautiful in the soft autumnal sun, those pleasing shades of warm ochre and soothing dove-grey. Even the filthy pigeons roosting above the caged windows suddenly appeared fluffy and benevolent. Children were playing innocent games with tennis balls and skipping ropes, and older pupils were walking together arm in arm, and talking in quiet, earnest, friendly voices. Had it not been for the word 'wanker' spray-painted over the 'Welcome to Havelock Ellis High School' banner on the railings, I might have thought I'd found myself in a different school altogether.

Zelda was sitting on a bench outside the Drama Studio, her hands wrapped around a thick red mug. She was wearing a black t-shirt under a pair of striped dungarees, and she looked deeply hung over.

"Hi." She sipped her tea. "Where were you yesterday?"

"I stayed home to clean my house."

"Sounds fun."

"Actually, it was very rewarding."

"Really? Well, I'm sorry about the other night. Did you find someone to babysit? Sorry I couldn't help."

"Oh, yes," I said. "It was fine." So much had happened since that night, I'd temporarily forgotten making that phone call. "It wasn't anything important."

"Good." She nodded. "Anyway, I've got a message for you from Josh. He's away, organizing something for the Hallowe'en disco, so he wondered if you could look after 9X, first lesson. Bad luck."

"Oh, that's all right," I said. "In fact, I was going to ask him if I could borrow them myself."

"You *want* to spend time with 9X?" Her eyes widened. "Are you OK?"

"Never better," I said. "The thing is, I've got some issues I want to take up with them."

"Who hasn't?" Zelda shrugged. "It's time those little horrors got what was coming to them. In fact, it's time this whole school was knocked into shape. But I'm not holding my breath. I *am* going to look for another job. No idea what though. I thought I could join a whaling ship. *Call me Ishmael*, you know. Sail to Newfoundland and do the whole Moby Dick thing, as long we don't actually have to kill any actual whales. Problem is, I feel sea-sick even on the Woolwich Ferry."

"Better stay here then."

"You're probably right. At least we've got half term coming up and…*Effing hell*! What's that coming across the playground?"

I turned my head and saw a group of kids standing stock still and staring at the big, black vehicle as it progressed steadily across the asphalt. Purple curtains were drawn over the windows at the back, obscuring the occupants from view. A hand, resplendent in a black diamante glove, waved majestically out of the driver's window.

"That," I told Zelda proudly, "is an American Cathedral hearse, a 1928 Charrington, complete with a vaulted roof and Gothic pillars. Excuse me; it's a friend of mine."

"Greetings." Georgia leant out of the window. She was wearing a black Edwardian mourning dress with a laced up bodice, and a wide-brimmed black hat bobbing with purple ostrich feathers. "Is everything ready for us? I do hope the room you've chosen is dark enough?"

"Oh, it's dark all right," I said. "The darkest room in the school. Follow me to the Drama Studio."

"Stand behind your chairs!" I barked. "No, 9X, I do *not* want you to put them into a circle so that you can play all those fun drama games you enjoy in here with Mr Majendie! You can forget all that. This is serious. Chantelle, spit out that bubble gum. Stand up straight, Nando. Bradley, put that game away in your bag or I'll put it in the bin. Rizwan, close your mouth. Desmond, you are not going to eat crisps! Chairs in a straight line, in front of the stage, and now, sit down in silence."

"Please Miss," the Honey Monster raised his hand. "Can I go to the loo?"

"Yes, Darren." I smiled at him. "You can. And you don't have to come back. You may go to the library until next lesson. And here's a ten pound note. Buy yourself a really good lunch."

"Miss, that ain't fair!" Desmond protested. "Why should he get all that dosh?"

"It's to make up for the sandwiches that you stamped on," I said. "Unfortunately, I can't afford to replace the trainer you stole from Darren, it was a top quality designer one, but I will be sending your mum the bill."

"Shame!" Chantelle stuck her tongue out at Desmond. "Yer mum! Teacher cussed you, dickhead!"

"Miss, tell her!" Desmond wailed.

"You are all about to be 'told'," I said. "Although not by me. Darren, please close the door on your way out. Now," I gazed at 9X. "Today, you have some visitors. The people who have come here today to speak to you are very special. It's very inconvenient for them to be here. They don't usually consent to give talks in schools. They're very different from the speakers you usually have, the ones who want you to like them. These people don't want to be liked. And they don't like you. They prefer the dark. So there will be no funny business with the black-out blinds or it'll be detention every week for a whole term. Right, 9X. Sit! And now, I want you to welcome my good friend, Lord Ralph Dunglass de Marney."

There was a clap of thunder as Ralphie stepped out through the curtains. Dressed in a long black frock coat and carrying a funeral urn under one arm, he leant on his skull-headed walking stick and gazed at 9X. His eyes were as cold as those of a long-drowned corpse. I could tell what he was doing. He was mesmerizing them. Soon, they wouldn't be able to leave their chairs even if they wanted to do so.

"Good morning," he purred. "I have come to deliver a Citizenship lesson, or should I say, a Personal, Social Education lesson. *PSE*. I have heard of the way this deplorable subject is taught in today's schools. It seems that you enjoy 'sessions' about drugs, joy riding, smoking, street crime, racism and sexism, by youth workers who use modern methods. You are put into groups, aren't you, and asked to brainstorm ideas on sugar paper? You draw spider diagrams. You are allowed to speak freely, and express your prejudices, and draw posters. And very often, your teacher, no, your *facilitator,* never actually imparts any solid information. You might meet a man in dirty jeans for example, who spends so long collating all the slang terms you know for various illegal substances that he never gets around to *mentioning* that it might be a bad idea to take any of them. But it won't be like that today. We will cut straight to the chase. Prepare to meet his Excellency, Count Valkhov!"

He pulled open the curtains. There was a flash of green light.

'*Raaaaaas!*' Chantelle exclaimed. Nando's mouth fell open; a gob of chewing gum landed on his lower lip and stuck there. Rizwan and Desmond gasped. Bradley looked as though he had wet himself. Even I had to suppress a sharp intake of breath.

The Count looked terrifying.

Without his wig and his fine embroidered clothes, he was bone-chillingly gaunt and bald. Wearing only a tattered, stained shroud, he was death incarnate. He sat in his high-backed chair, his long, skeletal fingers crooked like the legs of a particularly poisonous arachnid, if a spider could have legs tipped with long, yellow talons. His red-rimmed eyes had a malevolent, hypnotic glare. His teeth were bared. And there was a choking, palpable smell of putrefaction in the air.

"Count Valkhov," Ralphie told 9X, "has been undead for centuries. And he is a mind-reader. He knows everything about you. He knows, for example, which one of you it was who stole a box of pens from the French department last Monday."

"That one!" the Count hissed, pointing at Bradley.

I could definitely smell something. Yes, Bradley *had* wet himself! Had it been any other student, I'd have shown compassion and sent him, without drawing attention to his plight, to the office for the loan of another pair of trousers, but as this was a boy who'd joined in a conspiracy to get a perfectly decent man eaten by a demon, I let him sit in the puddle of his own making.

"The Count knows which one of you wrote filthy words all over the toilet wall."

"That one!" The Count pointed at Desmond, who paled instantly.

"The Count knows which one of you kicked in the door in the Science lab."

"That one!"

Rizwan let out a squeal.

"I know which one of you stole the chloroform."

"That one!"

Chantelle screamed.

"I know which one of brought the rope."

"That one!"

"But Miss…"

"Be quiet, Nando."

"Be quiet indeed." Ralphie gazed at him. "I must tell you all, the Count is not here to deal with trivialities. He knows something far more serious. He knows just who it was who tried to feed an innocent man to a demon and bring about a hurricane of hellish power that would have destroyed the whole of London."

"All of you!"

"But sir…" Chantelle began.

"Silence!" As the Count pointed at her, she was transfixed, utterly motionless, her mouth open, her face like a wax mask. The effect of her unnatural stillness on the others was sobering, to say the least. "It is my turn to speak."

"Yes," Ralphie agreed. "Listen to the Count."

There was a long pause, then "You amateurs," the Count rasped, turning his head slowly to stare with withering contempt at each member of 9X in turn, "You raw, foolish amateurs. You unpleasant little worms of corruption. You vain-glorious, immature weasels. You parasites! Do not suppose you can hide anything from me. I can *see* the secrets of your souls. I can *hear*, through the walls of your chests, the way your living hearts pump with your fresh young blood! I could tap into your brains and eat them raw except that I would not choose to devour such worthless dross! I know about your pathetic, evil, ill-organised scheme! Your half-baked rituals! I *know* what you tried to do!" He grinned horribly. "I *know* what you did last Tuesday."

"I think you should also know," Ralphie purred, "there are painful punishments for those who dabble in the occult. The Count has much more to tell you on the subject of the consequences of trying to raise demons and you had better listen closely. Stay in your seats, do not interrupt and there is just a *very* slight chance you will not be harmed. It wasn't a good idea to try and kill Mr Langford."

"Sir," Nando raised his hand. "May I say something?"

"Very well."

"Sir, we didn't want to hurt Mr Langford. We like him."

"I see. It is true enough, as dear Oscar said, that each man kills the thing he loves, but if you had even the slightest regard for Mr Langford, you wouldn't have left him to die an unpleasant death."

"But sir," Nando protested, "We was told that he wouldn't die. That once the demon ate him, he'd go back where he came from. To a better place."

"Alas, my dear boy," Ralphie shook his head. "You were deceived. There is no better place. That, at any rate, is my experience. And you must all learn to be kind. Without kindness, there is no point at all. And now, please listen again to the Count. He has more to say, much more. Be patient. It may take some time."

It took two hours, by which time, 9X were all quivering wrecks.

I was free for the last lesson of the morning and so I took the opportunity to go out for an early lunch at a little sandwich bar near the Lock. On my way back into school, I was just crossing the playground, when I felt a tap on my shoulder. I turned to find Jen Fowler behind me.

"I need to have a word with you," she said.

"Is it important?" I asked.

"Yes," she said. "It's about 9X. I've had some complaints."

"I'm not surprised," I said. "9X are a bunch of hoodlums. Anyone would complain about them."

"I don't mean I've had complaints *about* 9X! I mean, I've had some complaints about *you*. From other members of staff, including Angie Hucknall. Five members of that class have been weeping uncontrollably in the sick room. And Chantelle says that a vampire threatened to eat her brain while she was still alive."

"*Would* you still be alive if someone was eating your brain?" I mused. "Surely you'd die quite quickly?"

Her eyes narrowed. "You don't seem to be taking this very seriously."

"Well, it can't be serious can it?" I beamed. "You and I know perfectly well there are no such things as vampires."

"That's not the point! Who *were* those people you invited into the Drama Studio?"

"They were a theatre-in-education company, that's all. And they were very good."

"And who gave you permission to bring this company into school? Did you fill in the right forms? Did you assess the Health and Safety aspects of the visit?"

"Health and Safety?" I repeated. "Was that necessary?"

"Of course it was. I'm going to have to take this to a higher level. I shall be reporting this to Mr Langford."

"Oh, be my guest!" I felt completely reckless now. "It really doesn't matter to me. Because I'm not coming back here after half- term. I quit."

I was surprised to hear myself saying this; I hadn't even considered the matter before. But now, as I turned on my heel and walked rapidly away, I felt such a rush of euphoria I almost broke into a dance. My work here was done.

"Are you really not coming back after half-term?" Zelda asked. "I know it's awful here, but Josh and I will miss you."

"But we can still meet up at the Kebab House," I said, "After all, I only live down the road. And I'll be at the Hallowe'en disco. I'm bringing my son."

"That's good." She paused, then asked, "And what about Langford? Have you told him?"

"I'm a supply teacher. I'm paid by the day. I don't have to tell him. And besides," I felt just a brief tug of regret as I said it. "I haven't exactly distinguished myself here. And it isn't Langford's business if I…"

"Uh-ah!" Zelda shot me a warning glance, "Talk of the devil! Here he comes."

He stood before me in Oddballs Corner, a contrasting figure to those who usually inhabited it, in a new, smartly tailored suit. *Scrubbed up well then*, I thought, but had the tact not to say. I thought for a moment that the look of displeasure on his face was directed at Zelda, in memory of her 'P*ss*ng in the Shower' t-shirt, but then, to my consternation, I realised that the glare was intended for me.

"Miss Harker? May I have a word?"

"I...yes, yes, of course. What is it?"

"Not here. My office. Five minutes." He turned and walked swiftly away.

"Bloody hell!" Zelda rolled her eyes. "What have you done to annoy A.R.L now? That was bloody rude and peremptory even for him."

"Yes," I said, "Wasn't it? And to think that I..."

"And to think that you what?" She looked at me with curiosity.

Saved him from being eaten by a demon.

"Nothing," I said. "Well, I suppose I'd better go."

"I'd give him a head-start if I were you. He said five minutes. Look, Dora, don't take this amiss, but this isn't what I think it is, is it? Nothing to do with...some kind of affair you've been having with him?"

"Absolutely not! That's the last thing I'd want!"

"Sorry. It's just that sometimes I thought I'd picked up on a kind of frisson between the two of you."

"You didn't," I snapped. "Right, I shall walk slowly up to the wretched man's office. I might not come back to the staff room, but I'll definitely see you at the disco tomorrow night. I just hope this 'word' doesn't go on for long. I'm taking Cas to collect his Hallowe'en costume after school, and there's no way I want to disappoint him."

This time, he wasn't sitting at his desk in his shirt sleeves working on his computer. He was standing behind the desk, waiting for me.

"Miss Harker? Please come in."

"Miss Harker? I thought I was Dora now?"

"We're on school premises and this is an official matter."

Good grief! What to make of this? Did he have no memory of the night before last? Did he not remember that if it wasn't for me, he'd still be stuck underground in a dark hole, dying of dehydration, shock, and hunger? Or possibly dead already?

"Right." I stepped inside. "This is Jen Fowler, isn't it? She's reported me?"

"She's made certain allegations, yes. About a lesson that took place this morning. You hired a very unsuitable theatre-in-education group, it seems, and they terrified a class of our most vulnerable children. I'm obliged to investigate. It's a matter of concern."

"Trust me, everything's fine," I said. "I wanted to ensure that those 'vulnerable' kids, who just happen to have been dabbling in a form of Satanism, never hurt anyone again, not the Honey…I mean not Darren Dalston, and not even you. 9X deserved to be terrified." I felt my indignation rising. "And I did it for you. Don't you understand? No, obviously, you don't. I risked my own life for you, a man I find deeply annoying, if you want the truth, and this is how you thank me, summoning me to your office, which by the way is far too high up in the building, presumably because you think you're superior to everyone else and…"

"Dora…"

"Don't 'Dora' me, you arrogant man!"

"It seems I can't win." I thought I detected a degree of bitterness in his tone.

"No, you can't," I ploughed on relentless. "But you might thank me properly for saving your life."

"I thought I had." He sounded puzzled. "I sent flowers. Didn't you like them?"

"*You* sent those lilies? No, I hated them!"

"You hated the lilies?"

"Yes. Lilies mean funerals. Lilies mean death!"

"But to me, they mean peace, consolation, purity and…"

"My husband died."

"*Oh.*" He looked crestfallen. "I didn't know...but the other night you said...you referred to your ex-husband..."

"My third husband, the complete and utter bastard, *is* still alive." I told him. "But I'm talking about my second husband. He's been gone twenty years but..." I felt a prickling behind my eyes. *I will not cry, I will not!* "Dave was the only man I ever loved, I ever will love and..."

"Dora..." He moved towards me. "I'm so sorry."

"Get away from me! Look what you're doing to me, making me say stuff..."

"I apologise." He stepped back. "I didn't know you'd ever been widowed. I didn't know you hated lilies. I ordered them from the most exclusive..."

"What does it matter where you got them?" I was trembling with anger. "I'm finished with you! I'm going. I'm leaving this school. I wish you every success in improving this ghastly sink of a place, but let me tell you, until you develop a touch of humility, and stop being so high-handed and arrogant, you don't stand a cat in hell's chance of succeeding!"

Thirty-Five

Trick or Treat

"Good afternoon, dear lady."

"Ralphie, you're back!" I was delighted to see him standing on the doorstep. "Come in. How did it go last night? Is the Count taking the house near Brompton Cemetery?"

"Indeed he is." He stepped over the threshold. "And I, too, am moving out from here and returning to the Lord Halifax in the interim. A charming young man called Spud will soon be entering—with your permission, of course—to collect my belongings from upstairs and load them into his van. I trust that will be all right?"

"Of course. Although you've been so helpful, I shall be sorry to see you go. And I loved the way you transformed Peregrine's office."

"Ah yes, Mr Deadlake. I have only one piece of advice to offer regarding him. Do not remove the Mandala of Raphael from the front door." He sniffed appreciatively. "My dear lady, your house is scented so perfectly, you must have scrubbed it from top to bottom with every modern cleaning device possible."

"I did."

"And yet I can still detect the perfume of lilies, despite the fact you took them to the Lord Halifax last night. I gather they didn't come from an admirer?"

"There was a slight misunderstanding." I swallowed. "But it doesn't matter now."

"Ah well! Now, it only remains for me to thank you for my delightful stay in your clean, well-lit home. That soap you have, I found it very refreshing. Where can one buy it, may I ask?"

"The one containing New Zealand Manuka honey? At the health food shop in Regents Park Road."

"I shall remember that." He nodded. "Ah! I almost forgot. There is just one more thing I wanted to mention. That friend of yours, the young man who came to the house a few days ago."

"Josh?"

"Ah yes, that was the name. Is he aware he's suffering from Lupus Nocturni?"

"Suffering from…"

"Lupus Nocturni. Wolf of the night."

"Wolf of the…" My stomach flipped over. "You surely don't mean…"

"I do. Werewolves, Georgia tells me, have returned to the area. She found one scrabbling around in the dustbins in human form near the Lord Halifax a while back and sent him on his way. Quite right. I don't like to be prejudiced but if they go around attacking innocent people they mustn't be encouraged. And the full moon is nearly due. I don't want to alarm you but your friend is in danger."

"Oh, my goodness, poor Josh."

"Do not despair. There is some hope. Lupus Nocturni is quite a manageable condition these days, provided the sufferer acknowledges the problem. There are even support groups. 'My name is X and I am a werewolf. I haven't bitten another human being for five years, three months, two weeks and three days and…'"

325

"Stop!" I protested. "This isn't funny."

"I wasn't implying it was, my dear lady. I'm merely advising you how to look out for your friend. And in that respect," he reached into his pocket and brought out a small box. "I suggest you give him this. It's a small chain and a charm. Well, I shall be on my way now, but don't forget, the door of the Lord Halifax is often open. I'm sure you and I have many interesting conversations ahead."

Dark Dreams, Caspian's favourite costume hire store, had done us proud. Caspian was looking rather fetching in a well-cut Victorian suit, complete with necktie, top hat and tie pin, and those little glasses with the blue lenses suited him perfectly. He had, he explained, spent a considerable amount of time researching his Dracula outfit; he liked the evening dress elegance of the Lugosi version, apparently, but thought the slicked-back, widow's peak hair unflattering, and while Christopher Lee's version of the role had been definitive, he didn't feel he could compete with the height. There had, of course, been others, notably Louis Jourdan, Gerald Butler and Jack Palance, but finally, in Caspian's considered opinion, only the Gary Oldman version would do.

I hadn't had any intention of dressing up, but the assistant at *Dark Dreams* had persuaded me to discover my inner Goth and I was now dressed in a black two- tier taffeta skirt, a laced bodice, a pair of spike-heeled shoes, some fishnet tights, a pair of long black lacy, fingerless evening gloves and a Victorian-style jet choker. I decided I rather liked this get-up; the next time I went to the Lord Halifax, perhaps I'd enter in style.

Bauhaus's *Bela Lugosi's Dead* was pounding out from the Drama Studio and the fence around the building had been decorated with pumpkins, bats and skulls. The skeleton from the Science Lab had been placed by the entrance, posed in a sitting position in Mr. Wheel's old chair, with a 'Do not Disturb' sign hanging around its neck and its bony hands placed over its brain-pan as if in despair.

"Hi!" Josh rushed out to greet us. "You're here at last! You've missed the first hour, but never mind. Now, you must have some of Zelda's killer punch." He handed me a plastic cup.

"Thanks." I took a sip. "I've been looking forward to this. And Cas just thrives on this kind of atmosphere."

"Who can blame him?" said Josh. "There's nothing quite like the dark side of life, is there? And have you seen the sky tonight? The moon, it's just on the cusp, tomorrow it will be full and...*ow! ow!*" He rolled his eyes upwards. I was beginning to feel more than a little alarmed.

"Now that you mention it, Josh," I reached into my bag. "I've got something for you."

"A prezzie? For me?" His eyes lit up.

"Yes." I handed him the box. "I want you to wear it. It's a solid silver chain and a medallion. Look on it as a thank you gift. You and Zelda have been such good friends, and I'd never have survived here without you both."

"Have you got another job?"

"No. But I'm certainly not doing any more supply teaching. Listen, Josh, I know this is none of my business, but I think that you should go back to the hospital. Have those injections."

"I'm not having any injections! *Ow! Ow! Ow!*" He took the chain out of the box and started whirling it around his head. "Wow, Dora, this is great, but I can't wear this. Silver brings me out in a rash. *Ow, ow, ow!*"

"Stop it Josh!" Panicking now, I grabbed his arm. "Listen, you're not well, I...you're not going to believe this, but that man who bit you, he was a..."

327

"Calm down, Dora." Josh grinned. "There's nothing the matter with me. It's Hallowe'en. I'm just winding you up."

"Are you?" I felt more than a little dubious.

"Yes. And I think it's a shame you're leaving. What did you do to 9X? They've been behaving like little angels after you did that lesson with them. Do you know, they were the ones who created that mess, complete with pig's head, in the Drama Studio? They came to me to apologise. And they said that you…"

I said the sparrow,

'Cos your eyes are too narrow!

The music drowned out his next words. There was no mistaking that sound, the pounding of Loon Tailor's drums, the tortured singing of Dingo, the weird, sink-plunger noises engineered by Mad McArthur. And now the music seemed to be morphing into less familiar, a new version, an experiment, something that could only have come from…

"Josh!" I gasped. "Those tapes, I gave them to you on condition that you wouldn't use them. And now you're playing them here."

"Dora," Josh said quietly. "It isn't a tape. Go in and you'll see."

The Drama Studio was thronged with people, mainly the younger members of staff, several of them in splendid zombie costume. Zelda was up on the stage. She was wearing a clown costume; I could only assume she was trying to look like Pennywise from Stephen King's *It*, but she'd made a blurry mess with the makeup. And as for the wig…well, I supposed she'd made a good effort.

"Good evening everyone," she grabbed the mike. "We've got something special tonight. And it's special for more than one reason. Not just because it's a reunion, but because there's someone here tonight, a member of staff…well, she may not want to identified, but I hope she likes surprises, so put your hands together and welcome the band! Making their comeback, all the way from Leigh- on-Sea, it's *Chappaquiddick!*"

The curtains parted, the stage lights flashed. And there they were, up on the rostrum, the three surviving members of the band, together again after all these years.

"Evening all." Teetering slightly, Dingo, an older, fatter Dingo, but still recognizably Dingo, took the mike from Zelda. "What you just heard was an extract from our classic, *Who Killed Cock Robin?* This is our first live gig for a long time; be kind to us, you crummy bastards. Joke." He attempted a grin. "And now for the one that you've all been waiting for: *Pussy's in the Well!* Take it away, guys!"

Pussy's in the well!
Pussy's in the well!
Oh, bloody hell!

I couldn't believe it, but while circumstances had been cruel, time had been kind to Chappaquiddick. What had once sounded to my ears like a cacophonous bedlam was now raw, exciting energy. The music of my youth. I could feel tears of pure joy filling my eyes. I was transfixed. Those loyal, lovely guys, Dingo, the mike cupped between his hands, his face a gargoyle of derangement, Loon Tailor, playing the drums from the wheelchair that he now had to use, Mad McArthur bashing his keyboard with one hand and *kerplunking* his sink plunger on his forehead with the other. The lights flashed green and blue around them. Caspian was staring at them; I could tell by his expression he was entranced.

"Josh!" I shouted over the din. "How did you manage this?"

"With great difficulty," he yelled back. "The other night, when I went to Leigh-on- Sea, I found the three of them in Dingo's mother's living room, having a jam session. So I said if they fancied doing a practice set, nothing too challenging, they could start here. They took quite a bit of persuading, I tell you. But then…well, then I told them *you* would be here and…."

"Oh Josh," I murmured. "Thank you. Thank you for this lovely surprise."

"Mum!" Caspian turned to me. "This is brilliant!"

"Isn't it?" I sighed. "I'm so pleased to see those three guys together again."

"Four, Mum," my son corrected me. "There are four of them. Can't you see?"

Oh good grief…

He was right. I could see him. There was Dave, my beautiful Dave, playing those perfect riffs that used to lift Chappaquiddick above their heavy metal insanity into the sublime. He was standing a little apart from the others, and they didn't seem to have noticed him, but I could see him clearly. My heart was racing; I had to grab hold of Caspian to keep steady, and oddly enough, he didn't seem to mind.

Ding, dong, bell!
Give the old cat hell!
He…ell! He..ell! He…ll!.

Kerplunk.

Mad McArthur stepped forward and took the mike from Dingo.

"Right," he growled. "We're going to take a break now, but don't go away, because we've got something special. We made some demo tapes, a long time ago, and one of them tapes was never released. A solo from our guitarist. Well, Dave Dellow can't be with us tonight for obvious reasons that we prefer to forget. But there's one good thing we do want to remember. We want to remember Dave. We'll never forget his genius and we want to pay tribute to him tonight. So we're just going to sit quiet and listen to this recording. He composed it himself; it's called 'Paving for Dora'."

"We think he meant 'Pavane'," Loon Tailor said. "Only he couldn't bloody spell it."

There was an outbreak of raucous but affectionate laughter from the band. I felt a lump in my throat. I must have had that tape in my possession all these years and yet I'd never even played it. And now here Dave was, ready to play the solo he'd composed for me, and it was all flooding back, the beach, the marram grass, the sound of the sea, the 'mad old beach donkey', that first kiss. Young love, too fragile to survive in the real world with all its random cruelty. And then Dave began to play.

"Mum?" To my surprise, Caspian squeezed my hand. "He's a good guitarist, isn't he? Seb's Dad?"

"He's perfect," I said.

"And we're the only two people in here who can see him, aren't we?"

"Yes, Cas." I swallowed. "I think we are."

"It was great to see you again, Dora," Mad McArthur leant out of the van and shook my hand. "But we need to be making tracks. It's taken it out of Dingo, doing this set."

"I can see that." I looked at Dingo, who was sprawled out in the back, apparently comatose.

"We mustn't leave it so long next time," Loon Tailor added.

"I agree," I said. "You take care of yourself, too, Loon."

"Len," he corrected me. "I've dropped the nickname. Hope you enjoyed tonight."

"I did. Seeing you all…" I hesitated. "Seeing the three of you together again was great."

"You didn't mind us using that old tape of Dave playing, did you?" Mad McArthur asked. "We thought it was a fitting tribute."

"It was wonderful."

"Although it was a funny thing," Loon said. "When we were all playing up there, it really felt as though your Dave was still with us. It was though he never really left. Well, we'll be off then. Take care, Dora. Keep in touch."

"I will."

I watched as the van moved across the playground and through the gates into the road. I looked up at the sky. Tomorrow, it would be a full moon. Now, there were tiny wisps of cloud floating over its cratered face, and everything was so silent it seemed time had frozen.

"*Wotcha, girl.*" Oh! That voice! It was just behind me.

"Davey?" I couldn't move.

"Yeh, it's me. But don't turn round or I'll be gawn. I've got something to tell you. This is the very last time I can come and see you."

"Oh, Davey, no!"

"Listen, girl," Dave spoke softly. "I belong to your past. And the past is the past. It was all about being young, but you have to move on. You know what? By the time I was sixty, I'd have got fat. I'd have turned into a big white slug. I might never have played the guitar no more. I might have sat slumped in me chair all day, watching crap on TV. And you'd have been bored with me."

"That would never have happened."

"It might have done."

"But don't you understand?" I protested. "Whatever happened to you, it wouldn't have mattered. To me, you'd always have been the most gorgeous guy on earth! Your eyes, that lovely little v-shaped scar...we'd have grown old together! Davey, I don't believe you would have *ever* stopped playing the guitar, but even if you had, so what? I'd still have loved you, whatever you looked like, whatever you became, fat, old, and *even looking like your mother*!"

"Oh, come on girl," he chuckled. "'Ow could you have stood that?"

"Easily," I said. "Because you wouldn't have *been* your mother. You'd have been *you.*"

"But girl, I'm no good for you. You're alive and I'm dead. I'm brown bread! And now you've met someone else."

"Oh, Davey, no. There isn't anyone else."

"Yes, there is. Or there will be."

"There can't be. I don't want anyone else. Davey, don't go!"

"I really can't stay. Look after yourself, gel!"

"Davey!"

I spun round, forgetting, like Orpheus, that I'd been told not to look. And then I saw that there was no-one there, just the empty playground and the moon and a moment later, the doors of the drama studio were flung open and people in Hallowe'en costumes streamed out, shouting and laughing, tipsy and de-mob happy, all ready for half-term.

"Hi, Mum!" Caspian appeared by my side, a huge carved pumpkin in his arms, "Josh says I can have this."

"That's nice," I blinked back my tears. "Come on then, Count Dracula. Let's go home."

Thirty-Six

Normality resumes...

"I'm so glad you've come for supper," Becca gave the bean stew another stir. "It seems ages since we've had a proper talk. And thank goodness you've given up that job. You're looking more relaxed already. So, any plans?"

"Not yet. I just need to take stock. I've been having rather an odd time lately, to be honest."

"I gathered that. Want to tell me about it?" She reached up to the wine rack and took down a bottle of Rioja.

"I wouldn't know how to start. But it was all connected with my past, with my three marriages, and even my ex-mothers-in-law, and lots of stuff I thought I'd put behind me. It came flooding back in a weird way...I've been thinking about what my Uncle Horace used to say about me."

"The uncle who brought you up?" Becca poured us both a glass of wine. "Along with your Auntie Pam? You must miss them both very much."

"Yes, I do, but they both lived to a good age. Cas doesn't remember them of course, but Seb does. Anyway, Uncle Horace was a very generous man, but he never minced his words. He had very definite views on my three marriages. He said that first I'd married a man with no balls, then I'd married a man with no brain, and finally, I'd married a man with no heart."

"Oh, what pants!" Becca spluttered into her wine. "What absolute pants!"

"On the other hand," I said. "I think Uncle Horace might have had a point. Dora,' he used to say to me, 'Will you never get it right?'"

"I don't see why he thought it was your fault. There's no such thing as a perfect man, although when it comes to a combination of balls, brain and heart, I'd say that I have found that in Robin. As for your ex…Well, I don't doubt your Uncle Horace was right about *him*. He does sound like a heartless bastard. Have you had any more thoughts about what I said, about getting a proper divorce settlement? I'm sorry to be blunt, but I don't think the solicitor you had when you split from Peregrine acted in your best interests."

"I never had a solicitor."

"No solicitor!" She looked astounded. "You never told me that! Dora, what were you thinking?"

"I'm not sure I was thinking at all. At the time, I just wanted things settled quickly, to stop all the arguments. I agreed that we'd live apart for two years and then divorce by mutual consent, that I wouldn't cite his adultery by naming Jennifer Sheringham, and in return, he'd let me stay in Arcadia Square. Peregrine drew up the financial agreement. He'd pay the monthly mortgage, and he'd support Caspian until he was eighteen. There was, of course, nothing for Seb, and nothing else for me, and, of course, once Caspian was eighteen, I'd have to leave Arcadia Square. It seemed quite a generous deal at the time."

"Generous?" Becca looked at me with an incredulous expression. "But Peregrine's rolling in money! He can afford to support all of you and that includes Seb. And what about the future, where are you going to live, and what if Caspian wants to go to university? Who pays the fees then? Neither of you have any security at all! And Peregrine was the guilty party!"

"But I didn't want to be a gold-digger. Nor did I want a big legal tussle involving going to court. And…well, I don't know, I felt *guilty* somehow. For getting involved with Peregrine in the first place. I should have had more sense."

"That's hardly the point! You were his legal wife and you're the mother of his son. Besides, what has sense have to do with it? You could hardly help it if you fell in love with him."

"But that's just it. I don't think I ever was really in love with him, at least not in the way I was with Dave."

"Clearly not, but this isn't about feelings. This is about the law and finance and alimony and child support. You should have screwed Peregrine for every penny you could get!"

"But that's not me."

"No, I can see that. But you *must* get this sorted. Right, let me help. I'll get in touch with my solicitor, as I offered to do before, and she'll put the wheels in motion for you. She'll send a preliminary letter, an email attachment if you like, to alert Peregrine to the fact she's working on your behalf. Agreed?"

"I'm not sure. The thing is…" I hesitated. "Peregrine's a dangerous person. He's…" *Sold his soul to the demon Asmodeus.* "A bit psycho," I finished, choosing an edited version of the truth.

"Are you scared of your ex?" Becca looked deeply concerned. "Could he be violent towards you? There are Women's Aid organisations you know, and…"

"Actually," I said. "I'm not scared of Peregrine at all, at least not if it comes to a face to face confrontation.

All I have to do is throw a fish paste sandwich at him and he'll collapse."

"Collapse?"

"He's very allergic to fish."

"Anaphylactic shock?" Becca frowned. "I thought that was peanuts."

"In Peregrine's case, it's fish." I took a gulp of wine. "But while I'm not afraid of meeting Peregrine face to face, there's no knowing what he might do behind my back. And then there's Caspian. You said, didn't you, that Peregrine wasn't much of a father to him, but the thing is, I'm not sure how much I want him to be. I don't like the idea of Peregrine having an influence over him."

"In that case, the sooner you let me contact my solicitor on your behalf, the better. And let me assure you Sally knows her stuff and won't take any nonsense. So, shall I do it?"

"Yes, thank you. That will be good."

"Great." Becca returned to the Aga, checking on the bean stew. "So, what do you say to watching a DVD tonight, after supper? What do you fancy? Action thriller, Rom-com, period drama or spooky horror? Take your pick."

"You choose," I said. "Only maybe not the spooky horror." *After all, I get enough of that home.*

337

Thirty-Seven

Or does it?

What a beautiful feather, so black, so lustrous, so large, such an amazing sheen, and so silky to the touch. It might have been sent with the lilies, but somehow, I didn't want to part with it. I'd stuck it into the neck of an empty wine bottle and stood it on the kitchen window sill. Such an unusual thing to find in a floral arrangement; I could only assume it was a new trend, like the sparkly stars on sticks and stems of artificial berries I'd seen in florist's windows.

"Mum? Where did you find that feather?" Caspian was gazing at it with solemn intensity.

"Oh." I shrugged. "It was just lying around."

"Can I borrow it? It's for a project I'm doing at school."

"Yes. All right. Be careful with it. I'd like it back."

"Why, Mum?"

"Oh, no particular reason." I smiled with a false display of nonchalance. "Anyway, I'd be interested to know what bird this feather came from. It must be a big one. A condor perhaps. And if you're doing any research on the internet, you will be careful, won't you?"

"Mum, I always know what I'm doing."

And that, my precocious second son, is just what I fear.

I pushed open the living room door and collapsed on to the sofa with a sigh of contentment. My clean, well-lit home was my clean, well-lit home again, free of the slime, the cobwebs and the cracks. Bliss! Was it really only two weeks ago that I'd walked in here and found the ghost of Nanny Barrel Hips ensconced, hamster-like, on my settee? Had I been too harsh towards her? *No,* I decided. I could have forgiven her many things if only she'd been a good mother to Dave, but she wasn't. She dumped him on foster parents for most of his childhood, she'd taken no interest in his career, and when he died, she'd been too busy enjoying herself in Gran Canaria to come back for his funeral. I didn't even meet her until Seb was three and that had felt like too soon.

I reflected on everything that had happened. The mothers-in-law had been an unwelcome incursion, but I'd enjoyed having Ralphie as a lodger, despite my original misgivings. I'd felt quite a pang when I'd seen the 'charming boy', Spud, carrying all those *fin de siècle* items down the stairs, the green velvet curtains, the potted ferns, the peacock feathers and all the rest, and piling them into his van. Still, there would be many evenings in the Lord Halifax to enjoy and how fascinating it would be if all those Night Wanderers *did* return to this part of London, Clarimonde Barnett, Albert Karnstein and the rest. An Undead Pride March. Superb!

Now, I'd have to start considering my future. I was determined not to return to Havelock Ellis, but I didn't want to think about finding a new job until after half term. For a few days, I was going to relax, forget about the surreal incidents that had engulfed me over recent weeks. I felt no regrets about leaving that school, although it was a pity my association with Aidan Langford had ended on a sour note. So much for getting a reference! And maybe he had a point;maybe I hadn't behaved responsibly with regard to 9X. Perhaps there *was* some obscure Health and Safety regulation that stated you weren't allowed to bring real vampires into schools in order to scare the pants off delinquent kids. Ah, well, what did I care? I didn't want a teaching career anyway.

I dimmed the lights and began rifling through my DVDs. The other night, Becca and I had watched a light-hearted rom. com. together, and that had been an escapist treat, but now I felt in the mood for something long, absorbing and art house. I picked up my Ingmar Bergman box set. What was it to be? *Fanny and Alexander*. That was a brilliant film, I hadn't seen it for years, but I wasn't sure I was ready to watch a drama featuring a draconian step-father right now. How about *The Seventh Seal*? There'd be no Nanny Barrel Hips to ruin it tonight, but did I really want to be reminded of...

Da, da, da-da...

Oh hell! Not the *Dead March in Saul* again! I'd thought the doorbell had been fixed. Should I see who it was? At this time of night, I preferred to open the door on the chain. Or perhaps I'd ignore this summons completely. Wait a bit and see if the person (please not Brian Belluga!) would go away. Ah, yes, good...

So, no, not *Fanny and Alexander* or *The Seventh Seal,* but how about *Wild Strawberries*? That was a good film, and...

Da, da, da-da...

Oh, not again! And now someone was hammering on the door too. I supposed I'd better answer it before the whole street was disturbed.

"What the fuck's going on, Dora?" My unwelcome visitor's face was a mask of fury. "Who gave you permission to change the locks? And why have you opened the door on a chain? And what the hell is that mess on the front door?"

"Peregrine." I kept the chain on. "That's rather a lot of questions all at once."

"And you'd better answer them." He was speaking in a somewhat slurred voice I noticed. "My flight's just got in, I'm tired and I can't wait any longer to get some sense out of you."

I gazed at him in considerable distaste. He was certainly not looking his best, in that crumpled safari suit with what appeared to be a curry stain down the front. He was also carrying a large hold-all, was unshaven and apparently seemed to be under the impression he could stay the night.

"I see." I said. "Well, I've got a question for you. Why aren't you in Minorca and how much did you have to drink on the plane?"

"I think…" he suppressed a hiccup. "You'll find that's two questions, Dora."

"Right." I nodded. "Well, you only need answer the first one because I can guess the answer to the second."

"Don't get sarcastic with me! I'm not in Minorca because it's intolerable there, the villa is full of plebs, mother's so-called guests. And now, to top it all, you've had some bitch of a woman solicitor send me a shitty email, demanding a formal divorce settlement, accusing me of all kinds of misdemeanours. If you think that I'm going to be intimidated and bullied…"

"You'd better come in." I took the chain off and stepped back. "I can't have you shouting about our personal business on the doorstep."

"I'm not coming in until you remove that mess all over the front door. Get the turps."

"I don't think I have any turps." I stared at him. "And if I had, I wouldn't use it. A very dear friend painted that for

341

me, it's a protection, and it's called a Mandala of Raphael. Does the name Raphael mean anything to you?"

"Don't talk hippie rubbish to me! What I want to know, is who put you up to contacting this solicitor? Was it Becca, that Guardian-reading cow?" He belched loudly, emitting a gaseous smell of whisky and then, gulping, put his hand over his mouth. *Oh no, please don't let him throw up on the step!* "And I'm not coming in until you remove that mess! Do it now!"

"Do you mean," I considered this demand thoughtfully, "That you're *not* coming in *until* I remove it, or that you *can't* come in *unless* I remove it?"

"I don't know what you're talking about."

"Don't you?" I gazed him. "Are you quite sure? Well, never mind. I don't think you *should* come in and make an exhibition of yourself in front of Caspian. I'll talk to you in the solicitor's office when you're sober."

"I'm not drunk." He belched again.

"You *are* drunk. I think you'd better leave."

"Leave? This is my house! And *you*…"

"The thing is," I continued. "This isn't a good time. In fact, it's very inconvenient. I've been looking forward to having a quiet night in, and I'm sure you can easily stay at a hotel or…"

"Hello, Dora."

It felt like a miracle. Aidan had appeared, as if out of nowhere. He was standing a few yards away, just on the edge of the pavement, looking gorgeous in a blue and white striped collarless shirt and neatly laundered, black cargo pants. He was carrying a bottle of champagne, a stiff waxed carrier bag bearing the logo of an exclusive Hampstead deli, and a bunch of red roses. And now I felt faint with an emotion I hadn't felt for a very long time. Something I hardly dared to name to myself. Desire.

"Oh," I said, stunned into understatement. "It's you."

"Yes, it's me." He smiled. "I hope you don't mind me turning up unexpectedly, but I wanted to thank you properly for everything and also to apologise. I didn't mean any offence with the lilies. I hope you like these better." He indicated the roses.

"They're lovely," I said. "Thank you."

"And I've brought us a light supper." Aidan held up the carrier bag. "I hope I haven't been too presumptuous but I wondered if you would consent to…"

"Who the fuck are you!" Peregrine, who seemed to have been momentarily paralysed, advanced towards him.

"I hope you like seafood, Dora," Aidan continued, ignoring him. "I've brought smoked salmon blinis with sour cream. There are also some oysters, and a prawn salad and…."

"For God's sake take that filthy food away!" Peregrine's face was wreathed with revulsion. "I don't know who are you are, but I'm going to thump you if you say another fucking word."

"I really advise you not to do that," Aidan said. "I could do you a considerable amount of damage if I was to retaliate."

"Are you threatening me?" Peregrine adopted a combative stance.

"Not at all. Just stating a fact. Salmon blini?" Aidan held out the bag towards him.

"You!" Peregrine's face had turned a peculiar grey-green, a colour that looked all the more unhealthy under the street lighting. "I know your type! You're…" He stopped abruptly, staggering towards the gutter. He bent over it, breathing deeply.

"Are you unwell?" Aidan sounded solicitous.

343

The Practical Woman's Guide to Living with the Undead

"He's completely plastered," I said. "He's my ex-husband and I want him to leave."

"I'm not surprised," Aidan nodded. "Well, let's call him a cab—I'll summon one. Ah, here's one now. I'd better give the driver a large tip." He stepped out into the road, holding up his hand as a black, squat vehicle beetled towards us. How odd, it didn't seem to be a London cab at all, it was more like a...

"I'm not leaving in that!" Peregrine glared at him.

"Oh, but you are," Aidan assured him. "Perhaps you don't know who I am. Perhaps you do. But I know exactly what *you* are and I've earned enough credits to use my full powers and reveal myself as I really am, and you would really regret...ah, yes, this quaint old Black Maria is just for you. Do get in." The back doors flew open and Peregrine was propelled forward, moving with a series of jerks as if he was being pushed from behind by invisible hands.

"Right, I'm going, Dora," Peregrine fell into the vehicle. "But don't think I won't be back, don't think that I..."

"Exeunt!" Aidan raised his hands, and the back doors slammed shut. A second later, with a clanging of bells, the Black Maria sped off, far exceeding the twenty mile speed limit of the residential area.

"Wow," I said. "How did you...that is, what were you saying to him about your full powers?"

"I'd like to explain," Aidan said. "I feel I can trust you with my secret. But first, you have to invite me in."

"Invite you in?" I must have been feeling light-hearted as I let out a nervous giggle. "You're not a vampire, are you?"

"No, assuredly not. I just wouldn't barge into your house." He smiled. "And there's something else. I want to persuade you to come back to the school next term. I don't want you to leave."

344

"Why not? I'm useless at teaching."

"You might improve. And the thing is, Dora, you're the only friend I've got in the whole place."

"You think I'm your friend?"

"I hoped you might be. I have very few friends. And... Will you please accept these roses?"

"Yes, I will." I took them from him, cradling them in my arms and sniffing the scent. "Thank you. And come in, Aidan. I never thought I'd say this, but the truth is, I'm rather pleased to see you."

"I hope I haven't interrupted your plans for the evening." Aidan looked down at the DVDs scattered across the floor.

"No, not at all," I said. "I was just going to watch some classic cinema. And then, as you saw, my obnoxious ex-husband turned up. Thank you for seeing him off."

"My pleasure."

"It was mine too. Well, first let me put these lovely roses in water and get some glasses for the champagne. This is just so sweet of you. And I'm really sorry about what I said the other day. I shouldn't have..."

"Don't worry about it." He smiled. "Whatever you said, I must have deserved it. Listen, Dora, the thing I have to tell you may come as rather a shock, and you must promise me to keep this entirely to yourself but I..."

He was interrupted by a rabid, plaintive, howling coming from outside, an unearthly sound fit to freeze the blood of anyone of a nervous disposition.

"Oh, good grief!" I felt as though I'd jumped a foot in the air.

"Hey, it's all right!" Aidan laughed. "That was just a dog. Or maybe a wolf, we are close to London Zoo, aren't we?"

345

"*Wolf?* Did you happen to notice if there's a full moon tonight? It could be Josh!"

"Josh?" He frowned. "Do you mean Josh Majendie?"

"Yes."

"But why would Josh Majendie start howling like a wolf?" He sounded genuinely puzzled.

"Because..." I swallowed. "Because..." How could I possibly explain this? "The thing is..."

"Mum!" The door flew open, and Caspian burst into the room, carrying the black feather. "Don't be angry, but I've just hacked into the dark web and I've found out what this is! The feather isn't from a bird at all. It's from the wing of a...." he stopped, staring at Aidan. "Hello," he said politely. "This must be yours." He held out the feather. "Can you transform for me? I'd be fascinated to see a real.."

"Cas. You need to get back to bed."

"But Mum!" Cas looked at me with a pitying expression. "Don't you understand? Few mortals get to see one, but there are certain beings, it's all in the Talmud and it's not just a legend and..."

"Cas, you really mustn't let your imagination run away with you."

"Oh, Mum," he looked at me pityingly. "When have I ever been wrong about anything?" He turned to Aidan. "Goodnight. I do hope you'll come again. It's time my mother had a boyfriend and an ordinary human one wouldn't be much use to her when she's fighting demons." He stuck the feather in a vase. "Night, Mum!" He left.

"Oh dear." I turned to Aidan. "You mustn't mind my son. He's said to be advanced for his age."

"He's not just advanced, Dora," Aidan said. "He's a rarity. He's an old soul."

"An old soul? That sounds scary."

"It isn't in the least. And now...Dora, I really do want to get to know you better and I don't want to lie to you, you have to know the truth about me. You see, I'm a..."

"Wait! Wait!" I held up my hands. "Before you say anything, you need to know the truth about *me*. My life is full of weird stuff. My first husband was the son of a witch, my third husband sold his soul to a demon, this house is haunted, my lodger who just moved out is a vampire and... there's more, much more, and I don't expect you to believe me, but I can't involve you in this. You're a nice, well, relatively nice, ordinary man and I..."

"But I'm not, Dora. I'm not an ordinary man. That's what I've been trying to tell you. Please don't be afraid of this. I wouldn't want to frighten you but..."

Oh, heavens, his eyes! I'd always thought they were a compelling dark brown, but now they seemed black, blacker than any human eyes could be. In fact they *were* black, and now I. *was* beginning to understand. Hadn't Ralphie and Count Valkhov told me all about it, that night, sitting in the bar of the Lord Halifax?

The Fallen Ones...Flying with their great, dark feathered wings above the Bois de Boulogne...trapped in the human form, enduring all the physical suffering that brings, so galling for those who once flew freely....sent out to bring healing to troubled places, prisons, mental hospitals, war zones and...

And to a failing comprehensive school in North London, possibly the very worst place in the country. Oh good grief!

"Dora?" He looked at me anxiously.

"I think I get it," I said. "I really do. You don't have to explain. Except...the 'R' in the middle of your name, it must stand for...."

"Raphael, yes. I adopted the name of The One I wished to emulate."

"I see." My mouth felt dry. "And have you done.... um... many wicked things before you decided to work your way back to redemption?"

"How would you feel if I said yes?"

"I might actually be rather excited," I admitted.

"In that case, Dora," he moved towards me. "I'll…"

Another wild howling rent the air; the sound was closer now.

"Oh, good grief!" I grabbed at his sleeve. "It is Josh! We have to help him!"

Aidan's eyes were now so dark and other-worldly I could barely meet his gaze.

"Before we think of that," he said. "You need to be certain. Do you really want to let me into your life?"

"I do." My heart was beating very fast. "I really do."

Good grief, what was I saying? What else had Ralphie said? *A dark side...liable to relapse into their old ways....too complex, too conflicted, too prone to pride…*

I could just imagine what Uncle Horace would say: 'A man with no balls, a man with no brain and a man with no heart. And now you pick one with no soul! Dora, Dora, can you never get it right?'

This was going to be a leap of faith, no question. I might be in for more trouble. But on the other hand, there was the possibility that the curse of Asmodeus was about to be lifted from my life at last.

THE END

Acknowledgements

Many thanks to everyone who has encouraged me to complete this book, including

My daughter Stephanie, always a source of insightful advice!

Writer and artist, Paul Magrs. Thank you for the cover illustration of Ralphie in the bar of the Lord Halifax, and for your 'Fiction Doctor' services.

Barbara and Christopher Roden of Ash Tree Press who published the origin of this novel, the short story 'Never Speak Ill of the Dead', in *All Hallows 38*.

And to all family and friends, and in particular, to my fellow members of The Dracula Society, A Ghostly Company and The Everlasting Club.

Sue Gedge

CPSIA information can be obtained
at www.ICGtesting.com
Printed in the USA
LVHW020704170622
721468LV00001B/1

9 781839 759871